THE LUNAM CEREMONY

BOOK ONE, THE LUNAM SERIES

NICOLE LOUFAS

This is a work of fiction. Names, characters, places, and incidents are either the product of the author's imagination or are used fictitiously. Any resemblance to actual events, organizations, or persons, whether living or dead is entirely coincidental.

THE LUNAM CEREMONY, BOOK 1
ISBN: 978-0-9964946-1-8
Copyright © 2016 by Nicole Loufas
www.nicoleloufas.com

Editing by Holly Kothe and KD Phillips with Indie Solutions,
www.murphyrae.net
Cover design by Murphy Rae, www.murphyrae.net
Interior Formatting by
Elaine York/Allusion Graphics, LLC/Publishing & Book
Formatting
www.allusiongraphics.com

FOR MY PACK

CHAPTER ONE:

DESTINY

I pull out the top drawer of my dresser and unceremoniously dump its contents into the empty suitcase on my bed. I shove the drawer back into the slot and move on to the next. I'm not concerned with how or what I pack. The only thing running through my mind is where I will unpack.

If it were up to me, my next home would be a dorm room at the University of Las Vegas, but my life isn't my own. I don't get to decide where I live. Hell, I don't even get to choose who I love. My life is in the hands of fate, Mother Nature, destiny, whatever you want to call it. If you ask me, which nobody ever does, my life isn't ruled by fate or the moon. It is ruled by my mother, Layla.

I empty the last drawer into my suitcase then move on to the closet. It's almost empty; there is only one thing in there I would take. I run my hand down the pink taffeta dress I wore to my senior prom. Layla only let me go because she chaperoned. I didn't get to go to the after party or even to dinner with my friends. Prom, my high school graduation, the letter I received from UNLV saying I was accepted into their class of 2019—all of those things, those human things, mean nothing to my mother. I was put on this earth for one purpose, to maintain my family's bloodline.

My friends, if you can call them that, left for college months ago. I told them I was taking a year off to find myself. I was never really close to any of the girls at school. Layla said making ties to this world would only make it harder to leave.

She was wrong.

"Mom, what do people wear to a Lunam ceremony?"

Lunam is like a quinceanera, a bar mitzvah, and spring break all rolled into one night. The girls become women, the boys become men, everyone gets laid, and nobody remembers a goddamned thing.

"It isn't a formal affair, Kalysia," Layla yells from across the hall.

She's packing too. In a few hours I'll be heading to a new life and she will return to her old one. She took a leave of absence from her job at the women's prison so she could escort me to Lunam. The job is perfect for her. She loves to be in control of other people's lives.

After Lunam she will no longer be the boss of me. I'll have my own pack. One I am supposed to lead. In less than a week I will be in charge of other people's lives and I can't even cook. I'm only eighteen, I should be worrying about midterms and homework assignments, not how long my pack will survive on frozen burritos.

I could've pulled student loans and applied for housing. I could've had the life I want, not the one I was born into.

I could have.

I should have.

I didn't.

I couldn't do that to my mom. She's given up so much for me. I owe it to her to go to Lunam.

"You ready?" Layla appears in my doorway. She looks stunning in a pair of old jeans and a light blue sweater set. She has wavy brown hair that goes on for days, and eyes so blue they look like gemstones have been jammed into her eye sockets.

As a human my mother is beautiful, but when I saw her as a wolf, I thought nature could not have created a more perfect being.

I was eight when she took me into the desert to show me what we are. Her fur was dark brown with small white tufts around her ears. It was the softest thing I'd ever felt. Her eyes were the same sapphire blue, the only marker of her human self.

While most little girls heard fairytales about castles and princesses, my mom told me stories about witches and wolves. We call ourselves Lunam because we were born from the moon. Not really born—we were turned by Gaia, the mother of our kind.

Finding out I am part wolf was the coolest thing that ever happened to me. After seeing my mom turn, I was obsessed. I kept calendars in my room, counting down the days until my eighteenth birthday when I would have my first phase. I begged to hear stories about my mother's Lunam and how she met my father. Lunam isn't just a coming of age ceremony where I will phase; it's also where I am supposed to meet my true love. I can't even think about that without rolling my eyes. Phasing from a human into a wolf is more realistic to me than love at first sight. I've seen my mom phase; I know it's real. I've never seen her in love.

When I turned thirteen I stopped keeping the calendars. I was more interested in makeup and boys. Layla's stories began to feel like nothing more than fairytales. By the time I was fifteen, I ran from the room whenever my mother said the word Lunam. This prehistoric ritual was the reason I couldn't go to school dances or have sleepovers with my friends. I wasn't allowed a social life because I was born into a bloodline that an entire species depended on. A species I had no ties to.

Layla left my father when I was four. She moved us to a small town in the middle of the Nevada desert. I have no contact with my father or Layla's family. Now she expects me to give up my dreams, my life, for a family she ran away from—all in the name of destiny.

There were so many nights I cried myself to sleep, vowing I would never go to Lunam. I wouldn't let Layla win. All of that changed last year when she told me I was the last living heir to her family's bloodline.

I tried to pretend the pain in her voice didn't cause a knot in my stomach. I didn't think anything would change my feelings about Lunam until Layla promised I'd still be able to go to college. Not this year or next, but someday. And with the promise of someday paired with the guilt of my mother's legacy resting comfortably on my shoulders, I quit resisting.

I may have my doubts; but I know Layla wouldn't send me to Lunam if it wasn't something she believed would benefit me and my future. I trust my mother has my best interest at heart.

I close my closet door, leaving the dress behind.

"I'm ready."

I zip my suitcase without much effort. My entire life fits into carry-on luggage.

Layla smiles at me but doesn't say a word. There have been a lot of silent moments lately. I will miss my mom, she's all I've ever had, but I'm not sure she's going to miss me.

Layla is going to the Lunam ceremony with me; after that, she's free. I won't be her responsibility anymore. It doesn't seem fair. I'm the young one; I should have the world at my feet, not her. But I guess she's paid her dues. Eighteen years ago she had me, and she hasn't made a single decision that wasn't in my best interest since.

My mother is overbearing at times, but she is also the most selfless person I know. I assume all mothers are to a certain degree. It comes with the title. You're a mom; you give up your life, your dreams, your body, to give life to another human. I may be destined to produce an heir to my bloodline, but I am in no way ready to give up on my happiness or dreams for that to happen.

I look around the room one last time. I won't miss the twin-size bed I grew out of five years ago. I won't miss the smell of mold in the closet or the warm desert air that creeps in through the torn weather stripping around my window.

I don't have posters on my walls or stuffed animals on my bed. Holding sentimental value in toys or obsessing over boy bands are human connections that Layla didn't want me to form. She tried, but I still love One Direction, and nothing will ever change that.

Layla allowed me toys when I was little, but every year before Christmas I would donate my old toys to Goodwill. Some years she let me keep one or two. I had a stuffed wolf for six years; he was the last to go.

After I started high school, clothes became my obsession. Like the toys, Layla only allowed the necessities. Luckily, she and I wear the same size, so I dipped into her closet whenever possible. Not that she had a lot of options either.

Layla always kept things minimal. We have four plates, four glasses, two spoons, two forks, a knife set, one pot, one pan. No serving utensils or trays—we never needed them since we never really had company.

We've lived in this apartment for fourteen years, but it has never been a home. The apartment came furnished and we never added anything personal to it. It was always just temporary.

Layla could've raised me in her pack and spared us both the agony and the fighting that ensued when I wanted to go to summer camp or join the Girl Scouts.

Instead she brought me here and dangled a life in front of me that I could never have. Whenever I asked her why we lived here and not in the pack, she always gave the same answer. So I would grow up to be a strong leader. She said growing up outside the pack would allow me to become my own person. To think for myself and see the bigger picture. I guess In a few days; we'll see if it was all worth it.

My entire life has been a countdown to the day we go back. I want to say I'm excited about Lunam, about finding my true love, but really I think I'm just happy to finally get out of this purgatory. The day has finally come when my life begins.

CHAPTER TWO:

FAMILY

The road to the Lunam ceremony consists of a sixty-mile drive from the small desert town where I was raised to McCarran Airport in Las Vegas. The shuttle cost my mother one hundred hard-earned dollars. The shuttle is also late, and we have to rush through the airport to make our flight to San Francisco. Layla lets me have the window seat since this is my first time on a plane.

She hands me a pack of gum and a magazine. "You'll need the gum when we take off or else your ears will pop." She folds a piece of gum into her mouth and shoves her purse under the seat in front her.

I have no clue what she means by my ears popping, but I chew the gum anyway. I learned a long time ago never to question my mother. There's no point; she's always right.

We land an hour and a half later, and I decide flying is my new favorite thing. I'm lightheaded as we walk towards baggage claim. I'm finally out of Pahrump, Nevada.

I take in everything. The smells, the people, the long line for the bathroom. I don't care. Nothing is bringing me down. I want to see it all, starting with San Francisco, but Layla is on a schedule. Sightseeing is not on the itinerary.

"We'll come back someday and ride the cable car." She pulls her bag from the carousel. "I promise, Kalysia." She places her hand on my shoulder and smiles. Even though I want to sulk a little longer, her assurance makes me smile. My mother never breaks a promise.

I wonder how long it will be until we can come back. In a week I will be matched with a boy I've never met. We'll be linked together for the rest of our lives. If I'm being honest, the one small perk about this whole Lunam thing would be the boys.

What girl wouldn't at least entertain the idea of love at first sight? Layla swears my match will blow all my book boyfriends out of the water. This is one fact I pray my mother isn't wrong about.

My mother's relationship did not end in happily-ever-after. The details of my parents' split are also a mystery to me. I don't know anything about my father other than he was a pureblood alpha and is the leader of our pack. Every time I mustered the courage to ask about him, Layla's eyes filled with so much sadness. I couldn't bear to see her suffer, so I stopped inquiring.

He isn't worth it. In fourteen years, he's never sent me a birthday card or even tried to see me. If there is one thing I'm not looking forward to in the next few days, it's meeting my father.

The last leg of our journey is a one-hundred-mile drive to Middleton. A pit-stop on our way to Clearlake where the Lunam Ceremony is held.

The man at the car rental counter gives Layla a convertible, even though she reserved an economy car. Typical. Layla is always getting special treatment because, well, she's beautiful. She's only nineteen years older than me, so people mistake us for sisters all the time, which is why I started calling her Layla in public. It stopped the crazy looks from old ladies in the grocery store.

The convertible is red and totally Layla. She insists on driving with the top down even though the sky is filled with low, menacing clouds. When I voice my weather concerns, Layla laughs. "It's fog, Kalysia, not clouds. My God, you've never seen fog," she howls as we drive over the Golden Gate Bridge.

"I don't care what it is. I'm freezing!" I yell from the cocoon I created with my hoodie. I was raised in the desert. I've never even seen snow and now I'm about to live in it. Layla says my

Lunam class will be settled somewhere in the Sierra Mountains. Which means snow, lots of snow.

This year is the Altum Lunam. That's when the last of the pureblood heirs, like me, turn eighteen and a new branch is formed. We are the future of our kind. The leaders. The shit.

Both of my parents are descendants of the first wolves turned by Gaia, which makes me some kind of super alpha. Every eighteen years for the last six hundred years, someone in my family has not only participated in Lunam, they also produced an heir for our bloodline. It's overwhelming and also incredible.

In six hundred years, nobody in my family tree has ever let our pack down. Now it's my turn to continue the legacy.

The pressure is very real. Especially since the only future I ever wanted consists of term papers and sororities. Maybe a few romances and a couple of walks of shame. I don't want to be a leader. Not like this. I want to go to business school, run a company that does some good in the world. I don't want an entire species riding on my shoulders.

"Can you at least turn on the heater?" I pull the strings on my hood until it tightens around my face and squeeze my knees to my chest.

The cold isn't really bothering me. I'm just complaining for the sake of complaining. I am giving up my dream for her bloodline, the least she can do is make sure I don't freeze to death.

"Don't worry, sweetie. On the other side of that mountain is blue sky, I guarantee it."

She points to the large mountain standing in front of us, its peak is hidden by the dank, ocean-scented fog. We drive into the tunnel, and I can see the exit on the other side. The highway is bathed in sunlight. Bright, hot, burning sunbeams hit my face and I flinch. As always, my mother is right. I stay hidden under my hoodie to avoid a sunburn until the world around me disappears.

"Kalysia, wake up." Layla strokes my ratted, windblown hair.

My eyes are barely open when I hear someone yell, "She's here!"

A steady stream of women comes out of the small ranch-style house. My mother greets each woman with a hug. I see a few of them swipe tears from their cheeks, my mother included. I've never seen Layla emotional about anything or anyone.

"Kalysia, come here." She waves me over. "This is my sister, Jessie."

Layla has told me a few stories about Jessie. I don't think they're actually sisters. Women in the same pack use the term as a sign of endearment. Sort of like sorority sisters. Layla introduces me to Bonnie next. They were also in the Lunam Ceremony together and became good friends.

Bonnie's daughters—Sophie Ann and Krystal, are fraternal twins a year younger than me. They will have their own Lunam next year.

Every Lunam class for the next eighteen years will join the new pack, until the next Altum Lunam, when the last of the next pureblood heirs come of age. That won't be for at least another nineteen years, when my child goes to Lunam.

Just thinking about that gives me chills. I haven't even met the father of my child, and its future is already set in stone. The cycle will never end. It will keep going as long as purebloods keep going to Lunam. Six hundred years of tradition can't be wrong, can it?

A tall brown-haired beauty queen walks out of the house with a camera in her hand. She snaps a picture while Jessie introduces her.

"This is my daughter, Tandy."

Layla leaves Jessie's side to give Tandy a huge hug.

"She came down for the weekend just to meet you. She has to go home tomorrow, back to her new baby boy." Jessie's face beams with pride as she gives Layla the baby's stats. Weight: 8 pounds. Length: 22 inches. Name: Warner. Current age: 2 weeks.

"You look amazing," I tell Tandy. Her body looks as fit as mine, and I work out, a lot.

"Thanks, but it's just nature. We are back to true form within a week." Tandy twirls and the ladies laugh.

"I don't get it." I feel like I'm being left out of a joke.

"Why don't you girls go chat while we get dinner started?" Jessie hasn't let go of Layla since we arrived. She pulls her away, and I feel like this is the beginning of the end.

Tandy loops her arm around mine and leads me into the house. Jessie and Bonnie live together with Bonnie's daughters. I walk into the house and directly into the living room. The first thing I notice are the pictures that cover the walls. There is a large framed photo of Bonnie and a handsome man in a military uniform.

"That's our dad," Krystal tells me. She walks up to the photo, kisses her fingers then taps the man's face. "He died in a helicopter accident in Afghanistan or Pakistan. I can never remember where exactly."

"It was Kabul," Sophie Ann says as she walks past me into the hall and disappears.

"I'm sorry," I say to Krystal.

"It's cool, it happened a long time ago." She shrugs and follows her sister out of the room.

I'm here two minutes and I'm already blown away. I thought our kind lived and died for the pack. I guess we can also live and die for our country.

Over the next hour I learn more about myself than I have in eighteen years with my mom. For starters, our bodies heal quickly after our fifteenth birthday, which is why Tandy looks like she stepped out of a Victoria's Secret catalog two weeks after giving birth. Our healing process is accelerated when it comes to natural injuries like childbirth, minor cuts, and bruises. A bullet to the head or a knife to the chest will kill us just like a human.

I think back over the last three years, and I can't recall having any injury worth remembering. Minor cuts and bruises never really bothered me. I run ten miles a day and never get sore. I always thought it was conditioning and training. I wonder why Layla never told me about this convenient trait? Maybe because she knew I'd test it. Slicing my hand to see how fast I heal is so something I would've done. Part of me wants to go to the kitchen and do it now.

In between her schooling me on how this whole wolf thing works, Tandy talks about her son, Warner. She has a gazillion pictures on her cell phone. Warner eating, Warner pooping, Warner burping, Warner puking.

"I know it seems crazy having a kid at our age, but I couldn't be happier." Tandy sneaks a shot of rum in her diet coke then sits on the sofa beside me. "Hopefully, you'll get knocked up your first try."

I am mid-sip when Tandy starts talking about me having a baby. I literally choke on my drink. It's some sort of beer that Jessie cooked up. She said the drinking age doesn't apply to something she brews in her backyard. The ale is dark and tastes sort of nutty. Even though I've only drunk half a glass, I already feel buzzed. I clear my throat and tell Tandy I don't want to think about that yet. She asks me what I'm afraid of.

"Please tell me you're not a virgin."

"If I find a mate at Lunam, and we have, you know..." I giggle like an immature school girl rather than say the word sex. "It won't be my first time." I cover my face with a throw pillow and wait for Tandy's reaction.

She pulls the pillow away from my face. "Let me guess. Football player your sophomore year?"

"It was my sophomore year," I say in amazement. "How did you know?"

"Lucky guess." She winks.

"He was a wrestler, not a football player. I jumped him one day after school in a janitor's closet."

I like the casualness of our conversation. Tandy is easy to talk to, or it could be the beer. It feels good to finally confide in someone about that day. I wouldn't dare tell any of my school friends. They'd think I was crazy, or worse, a slut.

"I freaked out after it was over and ran home. I took a long hot shower then cried myself to sleep. Layla came home around midnight and made a beeline straight to my room; it was like she smelled it on me."

"She did." Tandy shrugs. "After Lunam you can sense things, especially when it comes to your children." Tandy takes a sip of her drink to hide the frown on her face. "Go on."

"Mom said it was in my nature then put me on the pill and a strict exercise program."

I ran seven miles a day in the desert heat and I'd still wake up sweaty from dreams about that wrestler.

After the closet incident I was scared to go back to school. I was afraid he would tell his friends, or even worse, want to date me. But neither of those things happened. It turned out he had a girlfriend. They had been dating for nearly two years. We never really spoke to each other before the closet. We were in the same lab group a few times, but that's it. After the closet he never even glanced in my direction. The only time he ever acknowledged our encounter was during a fire drill four months later.

I was walking somewhere in the middle of the herd inching our way to the exit doors when someone grabbed my hand. I turned to see him smiling at me. He held it for a split second then let it go. My heart just about jumped out of my chest. If it wasn't for his girlfriend waiting at the end of the hall, I might have pulled him into the closet again. That was the day I increased my daily run to ten miles.

"Layla blamed it on being an alpha. She said it's a natural instinct to take what we want. Do you believe that? I mean, do you believe we have no control over our actions? That it's all biological?"

Tandy nods her head as if she understands completely. "We can't fight who we are or what we'll become. The sooner you embrace it, the happier you'll be."

"You really believe nature makes us sex-crazed sluts?" I never believed in it, even when I was tearing that poor guy's pants off. I always felt like I could stop; I just didn't want to. The feeling started in the arch of my feet and traveled up my legs, through my inner thighs, until it was just an uncontrollable burning. I don't know what drew me to him. Why he was the lucky one.

"When nature calls, we listen," Tandy says. "Having natural instincts doesn't make us sluts. Acting on them does. Being on the pill diminishes the urge, and exercising helps, but it takes strength to fight it. That's why most females don't make it to Lunam."

"What do you mean? What does sex have to do with phasing?"

Tandy sits on the coffee table in front of the sofa and faces me. "What do you know about Lunam?"

I reiterate what Layla told me. "It's where I will phase for the first time and meet my soulmate." I choke on the last part.

"That's it?" She looks at me in disbelief. "Layla didn't explain anything else to you?"

"She just said I would find a mate, phase, and become a strong she-wolf leader."

Tandy laughs and sets her glass down. "That just about sums it up, but what did she tell you about the rules?"

"The stories Layla told me were mostly about Gaia and how we came to be," I tell Tandy. "Layla focused more on our history. She wasn't really big on answering questions about the future."

"That's her." Tandy points to a picture on the wall. "That's Gaia."

The picture depicts a beautiful woman in a long gown perched on a cliff, watching a wolf howl at the full moon. The sky is painted black and white, the only color coming from the raven hair of Gaia and the soft pale glow of her gown. I stand and walk to the picture.

"I've never seen her before. I mean, I've never seen a photo or anything really. I know the story of how she lost her tribe to sickness and turned a pack of wolves into humans because she was lonely. But it feels like just a story. I've seen my mom phase, but Lunam, Gaia, it never felt real. Is that weird?"

"No, not at all, considering you've been gone all these years. You're disconnected from the pack."

I make a grunting sound and return to the couch. I've been an outcast my entire life. I thought coming here would be different. That I'd be accepted for who I am. I guess I was wrong.

"We're not all that different," I tell her. "Obviously you've gone rogue, having your son before Lunam. You're not following tradition."

"I didn't do this on purpose. I ruined my chance to go to Lunam. Some people will see me as a failure."

I don't want to ask why she can't go to Lunam. She's already looking at me like I'm an outsider.

"Do you even know why I'll miss Lunam?" She can tell I have no clue.

I shrug and shake my head.

"Whenever your body has to regenerate cells from major injury, blood loss, sickness, it diminishes your ability to phase. I still carry the gene, and I can pass it to my children, but I'll never be wolf."

"I thought it was something we were born with that couldn't be changed." I can't believe what I'm hearing.

"We aren't that lucky. Broken bones or serious illness like measles or chicken pox will affect your ability to turn." She picks up her glass and drinks the last of her rum and coke. "I'll never turn because I had a baby."

She doesn't deliver this news with a heavy heart or regret. Just fact.

"You didn't care that you would miss Lunam? That you won't be part of the new pack?"

Joining a pack is sort of like joining the army. The pack provides everything we need. Food, shelter, jobs. I wonder how Tandy will support herself, her child. I guess I know the answer to that. She'll do it on her own. The same way Layla raised me.

"I have a good job and someone that loves me regardless of whether I phase," Tandy says with a huge smile that looks painful.

I raise my eyebrow at her and she tosses the pillow at me.

"Ok, I admit it! It does suck that I won't go to Lunam. That we won't be pack sisters." She makes a pouty face then forces a smile. Tandy was raised in this life and now she's leaving it behind. We have more in common that I thought. I would trade places with her in a second. Minus the kid.

"You are going to have a great life, Tandy. I know you will."

She rolls her eyes and sips her drink. I don't know if Jessie is supportive of her situation. She didn't seem upset when she was bragging about her grandson earlier, but it could've been for our benefit.

I take Tandy by the shoulders.

"You are smart and beautiful. I know you'll be an amazing mother. You're not a failure." I smile into her big blue eyes, and she leans her head on my shoulder.

I hear her sniffle into my hair and realize she's putting up a really brave front. Missing Lunam is probably a bigger deal to her than she's willing to admit.

"You're going to be an awesome leader, Kalysia."

I want to scoff at her remark, and fight the urge say something degrading about myself. But I don't because I hope she's right. I have no tangible trait that makes me better than Tandy or any other female. I won the genetic lottery. It's luck. That's it.

The sun has set but the house is still warm. Tandy opens the front door to let the breeze in and fills her glass with another shot of rum. The air is scented with earthy fragrances that are foreign to me. Cactus and desert soil smell dry and lifeless, so unlike the pine and eucalyptus trees that fill Jessie's neighborhood.

I stand and feel the effects of the beer. I center my gravity and walk to the screen door. The almost full moon sits above the trees, illuminating the block. Through the screen I see a million stars in the sky. I can't imagine why Layla would leave this place. I think of the story she told me when I was young. She said we left so that I could grow up to be strong, stronger than she ever was. But what does that mean? Why did she have to leave her family, her pack, for that to happen?

I turn back to the room and see Tandy on the couch cupping her left breast.

"You ok?" I laugh.

"Yeah, it must be Warner's feeding time," she says sadly. "I miss him."

I cross the small room and sit beside Tandy. "I'm sorry. It must be hard being away from him."

I want to ask where he is, who is caring for him, why she didn't bring him with her, but I don't want to upset her any further.

"I'm tired, let's go to bed," she says and stands up to close the front door.

"Ok," I say. Then, remember something I've been dying to know but was too embarrassed to ask my mom. "Can I ask just one more question."

She smiles at me and locks the door.

"Just one."

"So, after I phase, let's say I find my mate. What happens next?"

"Nature takes over," Tandy says with a sly smile.

I feel vomit creep into my throat, and it has nothing to do with the beer.

"We have sex, on the first date?"

"Like you said, we're all sluts."

Sleep doesn't come easy. I'm in a strange bed, in a room without air conditioning, with a head full of questions.

Mom comes to bed an hour later; she tip-toes into the room and gets in the twin bed beside mine. These are our last days together. I feel like I've squandered all these years studying geometry and English when I should've been learning from her. I could've been learning more about who I am and what I will become. Layla thinks she helped me by taking me away, but I'm not sure that's true. I have so many reservations about why I'm here and what my role is supposed to be.

My conversation with Tandy helped, but she won't be at Lunam. I'll be totally on my own. The thought gives me butterflies, but not really the bad kind. Could I actually be excited? Am I really looking forward to meeting my new pack, the love of my life?

I've never done anything I didn't want to do. I don't even understand the concept of peer pressure. The fact that I'm here and not in a dorm room must be proof that this is where I want to be. Where I belong.

CHAPTER THREE:

PREP

Since Tandy left a few days ago, I've been bored out of my mind. My mom, Bonnie, and Jessie have spent the last three days prepping for Lunam.

Helping Bonnie make the canopy that will cover the ceremony area is out of the question since I can't sew. Jessie chased me out of the kitchen after I dropped a tray of fresh baked bread.

These are my last days of freedom, the last time I'll be me, and I'm wasting them watching old episodes of *Full House* and binge eating with the twins. They were homeschooled and earned their high school equivalency last year. They aren't allowed to work outside the pack and are too young to work in it.

Sophie Ann spends her time reading and watching the discovery channel, while Krystal spends all day working up various hairstyles and makeup ideas on her doll heads. For twins, they are completely opposite. Krystal wants to go to cosmetology school when she turns eighteen. I hope that is an option for her, since it is most definitely not an option for me.

After Lunam I have to live in the pack and work to build a new division of the pack business. Krystal said the new pack business is a huge mystery. Nobody knows what we'll be doing, which she assures me is not normal. Everyone is dying to know what the elders are planning. The wait is finally over, because today is Lunam.

Nobody has asked me to help load the car or to chop the mountain of fruit Jessie has been cutting up since last night. When I walked into the kitchen for a cup of coffee, Jessie and Bonnie glanced at each other tearfully, like they know something amazing is about to happen to me. Layla is pretending it's not a big deal, but I can tell she's nervous for me. Or maybe a little for herself. She is about to face her pack, her family, everyone she left behind. I've heard them whisper unfamiliar names over the last few days. People that missed her and others that resent her.

We'll be leaving soon to drive to the ceremony site, so I let Krystal experiment on me. Anything to keep my mind occupied.

She is perfecting her smoky eye techniques when I ask her about the packs. The twins hold a wealth of information on pack life. "So, I'm confused. I thought we were one pack?"

"We were at first. The pack split up in the early nineteen hundreds. They thought it would safeguard our kind from sickness or war sweeping through and killing us off. Half the pack moved north to Mt. Shasta."

Krystal steps back to take in her work. She has a small vanity stacked with beauty supplies set up in her bedroom. Doll heads line a shelf above the mirror. It's actually kind of creepy.

"The rest of the pack stayed in the Tahoe area."

Krystal has me facing away from the mirror so I can't see her progress. She wants it to be a surprise.

"So, we're Sierra and they are Shasta?" I ask as I watch her search through a tray for the right makeup brush.

Krystal's eyes glance towards Sophie Ann. "Well, yeah," she says with a shrug.

"Sierra and Shasta are the packs, but we're mainly categorized by branch," Sophie Ann says.

"Close your eyes," Krystal instructs, and I close them.

I ask how many branches there are and Krystal says six. Sierra and Shasta each have three. The main branch of Sierra is El

Dorado. They are the oldest and control the elders' council and pack bank. I was born into Tuluka; they are next in line to take control because they have the most pureblood alphas.

Krystal spritzes my face with something and dabs around my skin. "Sierra had another branch, Yosemite. It's gone now."

"Do I even want to know what that means?" I swallow and brace myself for how an entire branch would disappear.

Krystal laughs. "It's not that big of a deal. They just couldn't sustain their existence."

Sophie Ann must see the confusion on my face because she jumps in. "What she means is the females of their pack got knocked up by humans."

"Oh." I remember what Tandy said about children before Lunam. "So, they didn't make it to Lunam."

"Exactly. Sierra lost a lot of good bloodlines to that branch. The females were lost to humans, and most of the men to World War II. Alpha men have a thing about the military." Sophie Ann looks at her sister, and they share a sad smile at the loss of their father.

Krystal says the third Sierra branch is Pinehurst. They run a cattle ranch in Central California. Sophie Ann thinks it's ironic that a pack of wolves owns cattle.

"We used to be natural predators, to sell cows for money goes against our ancestors' ideals. It's like a shark selling sushi."

Krystal rolls her eyes. "Ever heard of evolution, Soph? I thought you were the smart one."

Sophie Ann is all about traditions and living the way nature intended. If it were up to her, we would stay in wolf form forever.

"We'll see what tune you're singing next year after our Lunam." Krystal picks up a can of hair spray and lets out a long, steady stream, covering my entire head. I close my eyes and hold my breath. When she stops spraying, I cough and exhale. Krystal just laughs.

"You mean next year when you become some alpha douchebags sex slave," Sophie Ann says as she opens the window and fans the air.

"Shut up! You're gonna scare Kalysia," Krystal yells then turns to me. "You're not going to be anyone's sex slave. Unless you want to be." She winks and winds my hair around a hot curling iron.

"Lunam wasn't always about power and sex." Sophie Ann sits on the bed. "It used to be about reconnecting with our true selves. I'm hoping new leaders like you will change things." She smiles hopefully at me.

"I don't really know the rules." I shrug. I don't know how I'll be able to change anything. I can't even decide if I want to be here.

"You will be the leader of the most influential branch in our history. You're the first to have money and power right from the start. Tuluka is going to set the tone for our future," Sophie Ann says with so much conviction I'm afraid to tell her she's wrong.

What if she isn't wrong? Will I really have that much power?

I don't even know what the pack does, other than bits and pieces about wine and now the mention of cattle. Layla purposely kept it from me. She didn't want me to research the pack online. Layla is all about finding out the truth on an as-needed basis.

"I know the new business is top secret, but what other businesses does the pack have?"

"The Sierras grow grapes for fancy wineries," Krystal says as she teases my hair with a comb. "It sounds sort of lame, but they make tons of money." She pauses to spray another ozone killing layer of hairspray around my head. "Nobody messes with the Sierras. Not even Shasta, and they have twice as many members."

Krystal says Sierras are steadily losing members to the outside world. "It's not just pregnancy that keeps girls from Lunam. Some just want to live their own lives." She looks into the hall then leans in towards my ear. "Like Tandy," she whispers. "She's a pureblood." She shakes her head in exasperation. "I'd kill to have her bloodline, and she just wasted it on some beta."

"What branch is he in?" The wheels in my head start to turn. Maybe I can get them jobs in the new pack.

"None," Krystal whispers loudly. "He works at a Wal-Mart." She delivers this news as if it's the most horrible thing in the world. "His parents are betas that left the pack before he was born."

I think about the pep talk I gave Tandy. She must have needed that more than I even thought. I'm a pureblood and I was ready to bail on this whole Lunam thing. I feel undeserving of it. I definitely don't appreciate it and I'm starting to think I should.

"It could be worse. He could be a half-breed," Sophie Ann adds with a shudder. "Human blood in your line diminishes all chances of phasing. Nobody wants a half-breed baby. They're basically just hook-ups gone wrong." Sophie Ann laughs like a mean girl.

"Shasta is full of them. Well, that's the rumor anyway," Krystal says as she unravels my hair from her curling iron and sets it down. "Shasta sluts," she sneers and falls onto the bed next to her sister.

"Shhh." Sophie Ann jumps up and closes the bedroom door. "If Mom hears us talking shit about Shasta girls, she'll blow a gasket. I'm not about to get my phone taken away again."

Krystal stands up and starts to examine my hair. She must see the confused look on my face, because she drops her hand on my shoulder and gives me a squeeze.

"Don't worry, you will match with a Sierra. And next year when I turn eighteen, I want to join your pack." Krystal winks at me. "We're going to have so much fun!"

"Sure," I tell her even though I have no idea where I'll be in a year. I try not to think about it. I just focus on what's in front of me. Baby steps.

Layla interrupts with a single knock as she opens the door. "You ready to hit the road?" She brings her hand to her mouth, trying to hide the shock so evident in her eyes. "You, uh, look different, Kalysia."

"I did her hair and makeup. Isn't it great?" Krystal's face beams with pride.

I pray my mother isn't her usual truthful-to-a-fault self. I don't want to crush Krystal's confidence.

"Isn't it great, Mom?"

She puts her hand on her hip and leans on the door frame. "It's very chic. I'm just not sure it's you, Kalysia."

"Maybe I don't want to be me today." I wink at Krystal as I stand and walk out of the room to get my bag. Fake eyelashes and teased hair still won't hide the fact that I'm scared out of my mind. I hide my shaky hand as I lift my bag onto my shoulder.

The only other time I felt this nervous was when I stood in line to ride the roller coaster at the top of Stratosphere. My knees buckled as I looked over the edge. That was the first time I felt real fear. In the nervous, pee-your-pants sort of way. What I feel now is more like I want to puke then run away while I'm puking.

I walk into the bathroom and stare at the overly mascaraed hair-bear I've been transformed into by Krystal. I start to laugh at how ridiculous I look. No boy in his right mind would ever pick me for a partner. I have nothing to worry about.

I meet my mom out front. Jessie and Bonnie are packing the last of the bins in the trunk of the convertible. Mom offers more kind words for Krystal and tells her she has a good eye for color. She hugs and kisses Sophie Ann.

"You two be good," she warns. "I'll be back after Lunam, so you'll have to deal with me and your mom if I hear you've been acting up." They pretend to be annoyed, like teenage girls do, and assure Layla they will be angels.

I decide to ride with Jessie and Bonnie in the SUV after Layla mentions making a pit stop at a shopping center nearby. The idea of spending time with my mom is tempting, but shopping sort of kills any chance of us actually speaking. And shopping with Layla is torture. She always tries on a million outfits and usually ends up buying the first one in the pile. When she's on a mission, nothing and nobody can get in her way.

I give her a hug and tell her to hurry. I know I'm about to become a woman, but I still want my mom there for support.

"I will, honey," she says and hands me a little travel bag. "You'll need this."

I settle into the back of the SUV and open the bag. I laugh as I look inside. God, I hate when she's right.

I pull out a container of makeup removing wipes and start wiping my eyes. I use a handheld mirror in the bag to check my progress. It takes six wipes before I look like me again. My hair is a lost cause. I put it in a messy bun and sit back to enjoy the beautiful scenery.

The drive to Clearlake is a series of twists and turns into the mountains. By the time we pull to a stop in the gravel parking lot, I can't tell if the knot in my stomach is from the drive or fear.

I hop out of the SUV and stretch. Sweat slides down the back of my knees. In the desert the heat is dry, but here it's like a wet blanket being draped over my body.

Layla must have beaten her personal record for her fastest shopping time ever, because she pulls up only ten minutes after us; she looks as if she just rolled out of a salon. She unties the black silk scarf from her head, and there isn't a hair out of place.

She steps out of the car and I notice she is wearing a dress. It's a retro Marilyn Monroe style black and white halter that looks amazing on a curvy woman like Layla.

Bonnie and Jessie whistle when they see her. She spins playfully and poses by the car.

"Who are you trying to impress?" I ask as Jessie loads my arms with grocery bags.

Layla adjusts her boobs and smiles at me. "Just worry about yourself tonight, sweetie."

I've seen Layla on the prowl. She's had a few male friends over the years. There was one guy, Miles. They dated for three years. He was rich and had a boat. He took us to fancy dinners in Las Vegas and even got me tickets to Cirque de Soleil for my birthday.

One night I heard them arguing because Miles wanted to take us on a ski trip and mom refused to go. Miles ran a string of casinos and had a business trip in Reno. The argument escalated from her not wanting to go on the trip to problems in their relationship. Miles stopped by one more time to pick up some clothes he had left at the apartment, and I never saw him again.

After Miles, her relationships, if you can call them that, were all casual. When I questioned her about finding my soulmate, she always said the same thing. I'm different, stronger than she is, and she had no doubt I would make a match that would last forever. How do you argue with that?

After a short walk into the woods, we arrive at the ceremony area. The clearing is about half the size of a football field. A few dozen picnic tables and an old farm house are the only signs of human life in the middle of the forest.

This farmhouse has been the location of the Lunam Ceremony for the last one hundred years. From the outside it looks like a rundown bed and breakfast. Jessie opens the double doors and Bonnie walks inside ahead of me. The foyer looks like a fancy prep school. Opposite the door is a large staircase leading to the second floor; it's made of dark wood, with metal ornate hand rails.

"Down the hall on the right is the girls' dressing room," Jessie says. Then she points out the sign on the wall. "Boys are on the left."

Jessie walks to one side of the foyer and opens a set of large double doors. They lead to a huge banquet room.

"This is where the ceremony is held when the weather is bad."

The wall on the opposite side of the room is a series of French doors providing a view of the forest.

"You won't have to worry; the weather is clear for tonight." The weather is the last thing I'm worried about.

I follow Jessie into the kitchen; it looks like the kitchen of a four-star restaurant, with industrial-size appliances and several workstations. As I unload the groceries, she fires up the stoves and starts cooking. I don't really know what to do, so I decide to play sous chef. I empty a bag of chopped onions into a bowl and carry them to Jessie. I trip, and the onions fly into the air and land all over the floor. Jessie takes the empty bowl from my hand and pushes me out the door. "Why don't you go help Bonnie?"

Layla giggles in the corner as she forms hamburger meat into burgers.

"Bonnie is outside." She motions with her head as I leave the kitchen.

Hopefully, cooking won't be one of the duties I need to fulfill because I suck at it. I don't really have any skills to bring to the pack, other than my bloodline. From what I've learned so far, I think that's enough.

I find Bonnie laying out pieces of white cloth on one of the picnic tables. She shakes out each one before placing it on top of the growing stack.

"Are those shorts?" I point to one of the piles.

"Yep, those are for the boys," she says. "These are for the girls." Bonnie holds up a plain cotton dress that barely reaches my knees. The fabric is cut like a long t-shirt, with capped sleeves and a wide neck.

"Kind of short, don't you think?"

Bonnie laughs and places it back on the pile. "They aren't a fashion statement, honey. When you phase, whatever clothes you're wearing will be ripped to shreds. You'll change into this right before the ceremony begins. We can't have you kids running around here naked like they did in the old days."

"Can't have that," I say quietly.

"All of this must be overwhelming for you. I told Layla she should have brought you back two years ago and given you time to adjust. You've never even met any of the boys." Bonnie shakes her head. "You know your mom, she's so damn stubborn."

I love the fact that she knows my mother in a way that I don't. Layla had boyfriends, but she never had any female friends. She said it was because women were intimidated by her.

"There's no way I would've let her bring me back while I was still in school." Not when I was told I had until eighteen before fulfilling my destiny. "Maybe if I was raised in the pack, like Krystal and Sophie Ann, I would feel differently."

"Krystal is boy crazy; she could care less about Lunam. She just wants to fall in love. Sophie Ann is a purest. She believes in all the old ideals, like being naked at Lunam and reverting back to old traditions."

I think of what Sophie Ann said about raising cattle, and it makes more sense now, although, I can't imagine her wanting to hunt cows. "How much have we moved away from tradition?"

Bonnie hesitates a bit before she answers. "Over the years there are certain things we had to adapt to. I think our core values have remained intact. Family and prosperity in the sense of living rich and fulfilling lives have always been our main focus. Nobody expected our businesses to be so successful. We have to make sure everyone is taken care of. It might seem like money is what drives us, but really it is the wellbeing of our kind." She reaches down and opens another bin. She pulls out another pile of dresses. I fold them while she talks.

"Some see the success as a curse. They think the elder council, the pack bank, the selection of leaders, is all about power. It isn't. We have to make sure our legacy is protected. In this world, it's through money. Three hundred years ago we hunted game; the one with the largest kill was revered. It's the same core value."

"Who is on the council? What do they do?"

"The elder council rotates members every eighteen years. This year, the parents of the Lunam children will join the council. The members that no longer have blood ties to the new Lunam leaders will retire."

"So, my mother will join this year," I clarify.

"Yes, and we will finally have a voice."

Bonnie goes to collect another bin from the SUV while I wait at the table, wondering if my mother is using me.

Layla doesn't give a shit about money, but power is another thing. She loves being in control. Mom says she brought me back so I can fulfill my destiny. I'm starting to think I'm here to fulfill hers. She wants on the council, and the only way to get there, is through me. I sigh at the thought and catch Bonnie's attention as she returns to the table.

"Are you sure you're ok?" She pulls a pair of shorts from my grip. "Why don't you go for a walk or something?"

I want to ask Bonnie what kind of power the council has. Do they control the pack leaders? Money? My destiny? I want to ask her if Layla is the kind of woman that would use her daughter to gain power.

I have to believe my mother wants the best for me. If I don't, then my entire life has been a lie.

"No, I'm fine. Just taking it all in." I grab a pair of shorts from the bin and lay them on the stack. I think about the boy that will wear these. Will he be my soulmate? The man I'll be with for the rest of my life? The father of my children? I think I'm going to vomit.

"Were you nervous the day of your Lunam?" I ask Bonnie.

"Oh God, yes, and I was prepared. I can't imagine what you're going through." Bonnie pats my hand. "But, you'll be fine," she adds quickly.

"Did you know the boy that became your mate, I mean before Lunam?"

"I did know him. But, he wasn't the boy I thought I would match with. There was another one that I sort of had a crush on. We grew up together and I always thought he would be the one, but nature had another plan for me." She looks across the clearing like she is seeing her Lunam played out before her. She finally looks back at me and says, "It all worked out for the better. Kyle was the love of my life. I wouldn't give up the four years we had together for the leader of the pack."

"We really have no control in who we match with?" I question. "I mean, what if he's shorter than me or has really bad teeth?"

"*We* don't have a choice." Bonnie emphasizes we in her statement.

"By we, you mean females?" I catch on. Bonnie nods. "So, the males choose us, and it has nothing to do with nature?"

Bonnie sort of shrugs and nods her head. I want to murder Layla for allowing me to believe I had a destiny, when really my destiny is in the hands of some horny alpha male.

I find Layla in the kitchen, peeling potatoes. When she sees the look on my face, she puts down the peeler and leads me out the back door. "What's up?"

"Bonnie said the males choose their mates." I get right to the point. "It has nothing to do with my destiny, my feelings. It's all about the males."

Layla puts her hands on my shoulders; they are cool and feel good on my warm skin. Without wanting to, I start to calm down.

"Kalysia, do you really think I would bring you back here if I thought you didn't have a choice?"

"I don't know, maybe." I don't know what to believe anymore.

"Bonnie is not a pureblood. She didn't have a choice in her match, but I did. I knew I wanted your father from the moment I saw him. When we phased, the pull was even stronger. For Bonnie, it was different. She told me she felt lost and confused after she phased. When she made the connection with her mate, it felt desperate. I told you, only purebloods have a destiny. Tonight you will match with a pureblood. You will be a leader, and so will your children."

I've never heard Layla sound surer of anything in my entire life. If all of that is true, then why didn't she lead? "Why did you leave your pack?"

Layla steps back, as if my question pushed her away.

"Where is my father? Will he be here tonight?"

"Yes, your father will be here," she says, as she strains to keep her cheeks from flaring up. It doesn't work.

"You want to see him?" I gesture to her outfit. "Do you still care about him?"

Layla fidgets with the string on her apron and looks away.

"How can you tell me to believe in my destiny when you turned your back on yours?" This is the last day I will share with my mother, and we're fighting.

In the distance I hear car horns honking. More people are arriving. Jessie said there will be close to two hundred people here tonight. Layla and I turn in the direction of the voices growing louder and closer.

"We can talk later," she says. "I promise I will explain everything." She pulls me in for a hug then hurries back to the kitchen.

I stay in the woods. I'm not ready to face anyone, especially a father I've never met. I close my eyes and listen to the birds rustling in the trees. Wind flows through my hair, tinted with the smell of frying oil from the kitchen. For the first time in my life, the smell of something human feels wrong.

I move deeper into the woods where the air is cooler and darker. I close my eyes and feel the world around me. The smell of eucalyptus and moss fills my nose. I'm not scared anymore. In fact, it feels peaceful, quiet. I walk deeper in, until I can't see the sky, only the hazy rays of light that halo the branches above me. I lean against a large tree, feel its bark scratch my back. Even from here, deep in the woods, I hear voices. There must be a lot more people arriving. I don't want to go back. Can't I just stay out here until midnight? I will phase, and if there is a mate for me, he will find me, right?

CHAPTER FOUR:

SOCIALIZING

By the time I walk back to the farmhouse, poles have been erected, the canopy is up, and lights are being strung throughout the clearing. It's past noon, and the sun has moved to the west. In a few hours it will set, and the ceremony area will be illuminated by the moon. A moon that will determine my fate.

Layla is surrounded by people; her old pack I assume. She is glowing in her black and white sundress. I look at the older men and wonder which one is my father. Will I know him when I see him? Will he know me?

"Kalysia?" says a voice from behind me. "Are you Layla's daughter?"

I turn around and find a girl in a blue strapless maxi dress. "Yes," I say and hold out my hand.

"I'm Cassie, from Dunsmuir, I mean, Shasta," she corrects and shakes my hand. "I think we're sort of cousins." She laughs shyly.

I wonder why she thinks we're cousins. I don't have time to ask because I am bombarded with faces I've never seen before. They all know my name. They give me hugs and say we're related in some way or another. I try to be polite to everyone, but it's so overwhelming.

"Kalysia, do you think you can help me in the bathroom really quick?" Cassie grabs my hand and pulls me through the crowd. "Girl stuff, you know." Her warm smile softens the hard looks she's getting as we ease out of the circle of strangers.

"Thank you," I say and loop my arm with hers. "I have no idea who any of those people are."

"They're mostly cousins and aunts on your mom's side." Cassie seems pretty knowledgeable of my family tree. I wonder if she knows my father?

A group of girls shoot dirty looks our way as we walk into the bathroom. It's really more like a locker room with a line of shower stalls and open cubbies in addition to the bathroom stalls and sinks. It's only slightly cooler in here, but at least we're out of the sun.

"Nice shorts. Is that what human girls are sporting these days?" one of them says, and the others fall over themselves laughing. I am slightly underdressed. Most of the girls are in sundresses while I'm in ripped jean shorts and a white tank. I practically lived in this outfit back home. I already feel out of place, I at least want to be comfortable in my own clothes.

Cassie says the girls are jealous because I was raised out of the pack.

"How do they know where I was raised?"

"Everyone knows who you are, Kalysia. You're famous."

I tell her my life wasn't as glamorous as they all think.

"Well, at least you got to go to school. Most of us were homeschooled, and the only socializing we get to do is with each other. Everyone is so freaked out we'll get knocked up by a human we barely leave our compound."

Hearing words like homeschool and compound make me wince. "Ever heard of birth control?"

"What do you mean?" Cassie asks while she splashes cold water on her arms and neck.

"You know, condoms, the pill? Layla put me on it after—"

"What!" Cassie shrieks. She pulls me into a shower stall for privacy. "You were on the pill?" She whispers like it's top secret information. Pack life must be a lot more sheltered than I even thought. No wonder Layla took me away. This is what she meant by me being stronger, smarter than she was.

"Cassie, chillax. A lot of girls take it."

"Human girls, not us," she says.

"Maybe if more of us took it, we could solve the teen pregnancy issue."

Cassie doesn't find my offhanded comment funny. "Kalysia, never tell anyone, not even your match, that you were on the pill."

"What difference does it make now? I stopped taking it last month." Apparently, I won't need it after Lunam since I can only get knocked up during mating season, and only by a pureblood.

"Some believe the pill makes us sterile. There have been instances where females that took it were unable to conceive, ever."

Cassie's tone is serious. She really believes this; even though modern science says otherwise. Even if modern science doesn't apply to us, I know Layla would never jeopardize my ability to have children. It's basically the reason for my existence.

"It doesn't always happen the first time," I tell her.

"It's likely, especially if you are a healthy pureblood." Cassie opens the stall door. "Just don't tell anyone about the pill, ok?"

I salute her the way I do Layla when I'm being a smart-ass, except Cassie laughs.

We step out of the shower and Cassie fights for a spot at the wall of mirrors. She pulls out a tube of red goo and dabs some on her lips. "Do you want some?"

"No, thanks," I tell her. "Let's get out of here. I'm melting." I've never missed air conditioning so much in my life.

I pull her away from the mirror and out the door. The humid air actually feels refreshing after being inside. Cassie has her hair twisted into a bun, and I notice a tattoo between her shoulder blades. It's a small paw print; Layla has the same one on her ankle.

"Nice, tat, is that a wolf thing?" I saw a bunch of the girls in the bathroom with the same tattoo.

"No, it's a Shasta thing," Cassie says. "All the females have them."

"A Shasta thing? But, my mom has one and she is from Sierra."

Cassie stops walking and takes my arm. "Your mother was born a Shasta, not Sierra."

"She was born what?"

Cassie looks worried, like she's just spilled an important secret. "I just assumed you would know your lineage since you're practically royalty."

"What are you talking about?" I'm starting to think Cassie is the one believing fairy tales now.

Cassie takes my hand and pulls me away from the clearing; there are too many people around now. "Don't you know anything about your family? Who you are?"

"I guess not."

"You carry the blood of two original lines. Layla was born an Orrin. Your father is a Tallac. When the pack split, the Orrins went to Shasta as their leader."

"How does that make me royalty? Aren't we all really the same pack?"

"We are the same pack in theory. But time, politics, and money have created a wedge between the two sides. Someone like you, with blood on both sides, could be the link that brings us back together. You have pureblood from both Sierra and Shasta. That means you and your children can lead either pack or both."

I feel like someone just dropped a ton of bricks on my shoulders. Is this why Layla brought me back? So I can lead both packs? One was bad enough, but two?

Another group of girls saunters by, eyeballing me and Cassie. It's obvious the girls stay in cliques from their packs, branches even. Cassie explains that the Dunsmuir branch controls Shasta. They have the most alphas and control their industry, beer.

"The Sierra pack is run by two families, one controls the business, and the other controls the pack and its branches. They think it keeps things fair, but my father says it will rip them apart."

I wonder what side my father comes from, what drives him—power or money. Where would I be if Layla raised me in the pack? Would I even be speaking to Cassie right now? My stomach turns at the thought. Although I've only known Cassie a few hours, we are connected. I can feel it.

"Why don't you hate me?"

"I told you, we're family." She smiles and pulls me in for a hug. "I may be small, but if any of those bitches try anything, I got your back." Cassie puts her fists up. I know she means it.

Cassie is a petite version of my mother. Her hair is wavy like Layla's, and she has the same sapphire blue eyes, only she's about four inches shorter.

"Now, let's go fall in love!" she says and pulls me back towards the clearing.

Cassie insists we sit on top of a table where everyone can see us. It's a power play, she says.

After our talk, I'm feeling stronger, bolder. I even put on some of Cassie's lip gloss. Jessie's beer is being consumed by the barrel. There are kegs of it in enormous ice bins on both sides of the makeshift dance floor. A few females are dancing. Cassie calls them low alphas.

I've learned that a "low alpha" is someone with a parent who has never phased, either by accident, illness, or childbirth. Cassie says most low alphas don't even go to Lunam. I don't blame them. Why be part of a community that looks down on you?

I think about Tandy and her son. Tandy was a pureblood and now she is a beta. Her son is a low alpha that probably won't go to Lunam either. For some reason I start to feel sad for Tandy and Warner. I don't know why. It's horrible to think of people in this way, but it's the way the pack operates. We can't all be leaders. I want to ask Cassie about her lineage, but it feels intrusive. I don't know if she is the daughter of purebloods. I suspect she is if she's making comments about a low alpha.

Cassie takes a loose piece of ratted hair from my face and tucks it behind my ear. Her smile is so genuine, so loving, I don't give a shit about her lineage. I like her, and that's all that matters.

Just before sundown, Layla asks me to help her get something from the car. I haven't seen her all day. When I went to the kitchen earlier to sneak some food with Cassie, she wasn't there. Bonnie told me she was in negotiations. Whatever that means.

"I really like Cassie," I tell my mom as we walk to the parking lot. It's filled with cars now, and people walk around in small groups. Everyone is having a great time, including me. I don't want to ruin it by fighting with my mom, but I really have to know more about who I am before I lose myself to destiny.

"I guess it's sort of inevitable, seeing how we're cousins and she's from Shasta." The three beers I've consumed are making me brave, or maybe it's because I'm on the verge of womanhood. "Why didn't you tell me you were Shasta? I feel like an idiot."

"Because some things you need to learn on your own, Kalysia."

I'm frustrated when she doesn't offer any more of an explanation. Layla lets me pout until we reach the convertible. She pops the trunk and pulls a tiny box out of her purse. "This is for you." She hands me a Tiffany Blue Box, complete with a white bow.

My anger subsides while I tear into the gift. I flip open the small blue box and find a paw pendant inside. "It's the Shasta paw, isn't it?"

"Yes. Here, let's put it on. Don't forget to take it off before tonight, ok?" She takes the necklace from me and puts it around my neck. The paw sits in the middle of my chest, over my heart. "There is so much I wanted to tell you, but I never had the courage. I didn't want to overwhelm you. So, I focused on what I knew was important, your destiny." Layla takes me by the shoulders and looks me in the eye. "You feel it; I know you do."

I nod my head once. She's right. I do feel comfortable here, more myself. I just have doubts about my role and who I am meant to be. I still can't imagine myself partnering with a male tonight and becoming his sidekick. There are so many questions I have for my mother, but there is only one I am brave enough to ask. "Why did you leave?"

"I left for you."

I roll my eyes. This is the answer she's given me my whole life. I want the truth now.

"You had a destiny. You had a pack, and a mate, and you walked away from it all. Now you want me to embrace this life, a life I know nothing about. A life you ran away from." Layla's eyes meet mine. "You got me to Lunam, Mom. I'm not going anywhere, so please tell me the truth."

She nods, and I actually feel scared for her. For what she's about to say.

"I'm assuming Cassie told you I'm from Shasta and that I matched with a Sierra. What she doesn't know, what nobody knows, is that I chose him. Everyone believes the male is the dominate one, but I felt in control. I had feelings for Conall, the son of the Shasta pack leader. I adored him my whole life, but when I saw Monte, I felt his strength, his power, and I wanted it."

"Did you love him?"

"I did, in my own way. I respected him," she admits. "He's a good man, but even purebloods have to answer to others." Layla pauses when a group of boys walks past us. I feel all of their eyes on me and Layla.

"Hello boys." Layla's sultry greeting causes a few of them to stumble. I can't help but laugh.

"When will I meet my father?" I never realized how much it meant to me until now. Just having Layla was enough, too much at times. I can't imagine how my life would have been if my father were around. "Do you think he wants to meet me?"

"I know he does. He thinks you're beautiful," she says and strokes my hair.

"You saw him?" I realize she's spoken to him by the wistful expression on her face.

"We had a chat about you." She can't hide the grin any longer. I've never seen my mother smile this way. She's practically blushing. "I wanted to make sure we were both on the same page when it comes to your match and your future."

"What do you mean my match? I thought it was up to the moon?" I ask sarcastically. "Or will I really have a choice?"

"You, my love, will have the pick of the litter," Layla jokes and slams the trunk closed.

Guitar riffs and bass from the enormous speakers echoes into the woods. Laughter and loud conversations fill the gaps in the music as Layla escorts me into the farmhouse. We go up the stairs and down a dark hallway and stop at a door at the end of the hall. She knocks softly and turns the knob. A burst of cool air hits me in the face. The familiar chill of air-conditioning is refreshing.

I see two men sitting on opposite sides of a desk. They are Layla's age, and one of them has my eyes.

"Kalysia." Monte, my father, rises from his seat and walks around the desk to greet me. He pulls me into his arms and hugs me. This is the first hug I've ever received from a man. Miles was more of a hi-fiver or a fist bump. In the three years I knew him, he never once gave me a hug.

"Thank you, Layla," Monte says from over my head.

"For what?" she scoffs.

"For doing such a wonderful job raising our daughter." He reaches for her hand. "And for bringing her back." We stand, the three of us, my family, together for the first time. The moment is interrupted by the other man in the room.

"I'll leave you three," he says and stands.

"No, Conall, you stay. I didn't want to disturb you." Layla pulls her hand back from Monte's. "You two continue your meeting. We'll go."

Conall is the pureblood from Shasta's pack. The male my mother should have matched with. Conall and Monte are strikingly handsome men for their age. Both stand over six feet tall, with broad shoulders and fit physiques. Monte's hair is jet black and his eyes are blue-gray, like mine. Conall and Layla both have sapphire blue eyes and wavy brown hair. I see these are traits of the packs. I wonder why nature would allow them to evolve into two separate species, or if they carried these traits before the split.

We leave the air-conditioned room, and Layla insists I change into the sundress she bought me. She follows me into the locker room to change. The dress is a black, flowy material with a large red hibiscus printed on the side. It sits just above my knee and feels so much better than the cutoff jeans and tank top I had on. I let Layla fuss with my hair and even add some makeup powder to my shiny face. The sun is almost set; I know this will be the last mother-daughter moment we share before Lunam. Even though I'll see her tomorrow, I won't be the same, and neither will she.

"Your father was right," Layla says as she pins loose strands of my hair into a bun. "You are beautiful." I blush, even though it's just us. We sit in silence a few minutes; I feel like I should say something. All the questions I have escape me. It's nice just being here with her. When we're done, Layla returns to the kitchen with the other adults, and I set out to find Cassie.

"There you are!" she yells when she sees me. I hear the alcohol in her voice. "All the boys are here, and I want you to get first pick before these bitches make their move."

I laugh and take the half-empty cup from her hand. We both know what happens before Lunam is irrelevant. I down the warm beer in one big gulp and toss it over my head. "Let's go fall in love!"

The sun has set and the twinkling lights have been turned on. After what feels like hours, Cassie and I take a break from dancing and sit on a table.

"So, anyone caught your eye yet?" she whispers.

There are definitely a lot of good-looking boys here, but none that make me want to do unspeakable things.

"No, what about you?"

"See the tall one with the red baseball cap?" Cassie points to a boy in ripped jeans and a white t-shirt. He looks like he just rolled out of bed.

He glances in our direction, and we look away quickly, laughing like school girls.

"Cas, you could do so much better." I scan the crowd, looking for a better choice.

Unlike the girls, the boys socialize more with each other. I even saw them playing a friendly game of football earlier.

Like the girls, you can still tell them apart. The Sierra boys are clean cut in stylish clothes. They all wear sunglasses, have perfectly coifed hair, and exude confidence in a way only city-raised kids do.

The Shasta pack is definitely more laid back. They're almost all in jeans and tight plaid shirts that show off muscles they earned from manual labor. Unlike the Sierras, they are goofy and pounce around like playful puppies. There are pros and cons in both packs.

Three girls from Sierra bring me and Cassie fresh cups of beer and ask if they can join us.

"Sure," Cassie says and scoots towards me to make room for them. "I'm Cassie, this is Kalysia," she introduces us, but I can tell the girls already know who I am.

"I'm Leah," the tallest one says. "This is Clio and Patsy." The girls have the same long dark hair as I do. I wouldn't be surprised if we were related.

I asked Cassie earlier why we all look alike. None of the girls have highlights or hair shorter than shoulder length. She said it's just a Lunam thing. We all come to the ceremony in our most natural state. After Lunam we are free to look however we want. She even joked about chopping her hair and dying it pink, as long as her mate doesn't mind.

A steady stream of males passes in front of our table, each eyeing us like we're shiny new cars on display. It doesn't take long for me to realize why the Sierra girls asked to sit with us. Cassie and I have been garnering attention all night. If being close to us will help these girls make better matches, then by all means, ogle.

The first few chords of a slow song begin, and the crowd grows excited. I see a group of boys approaching and I turn to Cassie.

"You should dance with the one in the black t-shirt."

"Which one? They're all wearing black," she laughs.

I nod my head at the stocky boy with plaid shorts. "The one in the middle. He's cute."

45

"You think all the Sierra boys are cute."

She's right; most of my attention has been focused on the Sierra pack. I wonder if this is a precursor to who I will be matched with. My natural instinct is Sierra, not Shasta.

"Do you want to dance?" the stocky Sierra boy stops in front of Cassie.

"Sure," she says and hops off the table.

A boy wearing a white t-shirt with the phrase, "What Happens at Lunam, stays at Lunam," takes Clio by the hand and leads her to the dance floor.

"Does she know him?" I ask Patsy.

"Yeah, that's Tripp. They've had a thing since we were kids," she tells me. "Lunam is just a technicality; nothing will tear them apart."

"But it isn't up to them, is it? I mean, you can fall in love before Lunam, but it doesn't mean you will match?" I think of what Layla said about her feelings for Conall. None of that mattered after she met Monte.

Patsy looks confused by my questions. "If it's meant to be, it will be."

If Lunam is about destiny and I don't feel anything for anyone, can I choose to be alone?

Patsy excuses herself, and it's just me and Leah. Leah moves into Cassie's spot beside me and smiles.

"So, have you met him yet?"

"No, I guess I'm just going to wing it and see what happens after I phase," I say.

"You're not even the slightest bit curious?" she asks incredulously.

I shrug and sip my beer. "Of course I'm curious; I just don't know who *he* is yet."

"Well, he's sitting right over there."

She points across the dance floor to a guy sitting on the table opposite from mine.

He doesn't blink when he sees Leah pointing him out. He lowers his cup and rests his elbows on his knees. He's wearing plaid board shorts, vans with no socks, and a sleeveless white shirt with a fading sunset silk-screened onto the front. He tilts his head to the side in a gesture that is both cute and sexy, and smiles.

"Who..." I start to say and forget my words.

"That is Dillan Dukes."

CHAPTER FIVE:

LUNAM

Cassie's face pops in front of me, breaking the link between me and Dillan. I look around her, at the spot where Dillan was sitting, but he's gone.

Shoot.

I feel Cassie's enthusiasm as she sits beside me.

"Was it love at first sight?" I joke and nudge her with my elbow as I scan the crowd for Dillan.

Leah makes a strange snorting noise. She is scowling at Cassie. Cassie sees it, too.

Her smile fades and she just shrugs.

"What?" I look at Leah then back to Cassie.

The next song is a country line dance that draws a large crowd to the dance floor.

"I'll catch you later, good luck tonight," Leah says and skips to the dance floor to join Patsy's line.

Something seems to have changed between the girls since Cassie danced with the Sierra boy.

"Are you ok, Cassie?"

Cassie smiles, and I see she is holding back tears. "I'm fine, really."

"Is it Leah? Was it the boy? I'm sorry I made you dance with him," I apologize.

"No, it's not that. Leah has every right to be pissed; Drake is Sierra, a pureblood. I shouldn't have danced with him."

The self-depreciating look on Cassie's face tells me she doesn't think highly of herself.

"That's bullshit and you know it. It doesn't matter if we are Shasta or Sierra." I put my arm around Cassie and squeeze. "If we weren't meant to be together, then I'm an abomination." This makes Cassie laugh. "If we weren't supposed to love each other then why do we celebrate Lunam together?"

"We don't always," Cassie suddenly says. "The packs have their own Lunam. We only celebrate the Altum Lunam together. Really it's just so the packs can divulge their numbers to each other. The pack with the most purebloods leads. Sierras have the most, but Shasta has three times the alphas."

Three times? The twins said it was double.

"The divide in the Sierra pack is huge. You're either pureblood or you're nothing. Shasta has a different way of looking at things. If you have a child during Altum Lunam, that child is considered an alpha. Not pureblood, but of the Lunam moon. My father said eventually purebloods will run their course and Lunam alphas will take over. It's simple evolution."

I don't have time to drill Cassie with questions, because the music stops and Monte takes the microphone. Everyone stops what they are doing to give my father their full attention.

"Thank you all for coming. I know it was a journey for some of you, and I personally appreciate the effort you have made to be here tonight. As you all know, the Altum Lunam Ceremony celebrates the birth of our species. The gift bestowed upon us by our mother, Gaia. Tonight we fulfill the promise made to her by our ancestors to choose the life we want to live when you trigger the gene in your bloodline that allows you to phase under the full moon."

The crowd cheers, and Monte waits for them to quiet down before continuing.

"The form you choose is up to you. As your pack, we support your decision. However," Monte holds up his finger like a true politician and smiles, "we all know the perks of being human." He laughs, and the sheep, I mean, the crowd, laughs with him. He plants a serious look on his face as he continues. "It is through the sacrifice of those before you, and the sacrifices you have made, that will keep our kind alive and thriving." More clapping and cheering.

I just learned something about my father. He is a great speaker. And may be full of shit.

"Tonight you will also make your match. You will form a bond that will last for all eternity. The children you bare this Lunam year will be the future leaders of our society." The crowd erupts in cheer. "Lunam is a privilege that you are born with and one that is up to you to preserve for the next generation. I applaud all the parents here tonight; you did an excellent job raising these fine young adults." There are cheers from the parents of all the Lunam participants. "This Lunam is very special for me because my children are also here."

I don't hear the rest of the speech; I'm stuck on the word children. As in plural. More than one. I have a brother or sister? How is this possible? I understand having other children after Layla left, but how can he have more than one child in this Lunam? Unless…oh no.

I back out of the crowd and walk towards the woods, away from the lights. I need to find Layla. This must be why she left. The one thing I counted on was that my mate, if I found him, would be mine for life. Cheating and lying weren't something I thought we had to deal with. I walk back to the main building; it's empty. Everyone is outside listening to my lying cheating father give a speech.

If I can just find Layla's keys, I can take the convertible and go. I'll hide until Lunam is over and then I'll be safe. I tear through the kitchen cabinets looking for Layla's purse. It's nowhere in sight. Then I remember the room upstairs. I bolt up the narrow staircase two at a time. I hear voices coming from the room at the end. I recognize Layla's voice instantly.

"Conall, I understand your frustration, but you know Monte and the others will never accept half-breeds. If they don't phase, they aren't one of us."

"And if they do?"

"What are you saying? You've seen a half-breed phase?" I can tell by my mother's tone that something isn't right.

"No, of course not." Conall backtracks quickly. "I just think we need to start looking at other possibilities. In a few more generations, the purebloods will be too close in blood relation to match. We have to explore other options."

"They already have doubts about your bloodline. Bringing up the idea of half-breeds attending Lunam will only feed their suspicion," she warns.

"Is that why you converted? Were you worried about my bloodline? You've known me all my life, Layla," Conall sounds desperate.

"I know you are pure. But your children, the others in the pack, they are tainted, aren't they?" Layla sounds like she is baiting him. I feel sorry for Conall. Layla is using their old relationship to pump him for information on his pack. "I've heard stories."

"Where do you get your information? You've been gone all these years," Conall says. When Layla doesn't reply, Conall asks if it was from Monte. Even I hear the disdain in his voice.

A loud boom rattles the windows in the building and I hit the floor. It sounds like a bomb has gone off, but I hear laughing and the music comes back on. It was just fireworks. I make my way back downstairs and out the back door. I'll hide in the woods.

By the time the ceremony starts and Layla notices I'm missing, it will be too late to find me.

I see Bonnie and Jessie carrying out the white garments. It's almost time. I move towards the woods and I spot Cassie looking for me. I flatten myself against the wall and slide across it until I reach the end of the building. I round the corner and take off in a full sprint towards the woods. I make it three steps and then I trip.

That hurt.

I spit dirt from my mouth as I push myself up to a sitting position. I look down at my knee and hear someone laughing. When I turn my head, I see Dillan Dukes.

"Slow down there, speedy," he quips.

In moments like this, there is nothing you can say. All you can do is laugh. I burst into an uncontrollable fit of laughter. Dillan joins me on the ground.

"Are you laughing with me or at me?" I finally ask.

"A little of both." His voice is deep and sexy. He smells like sage and cigarettes. "I'm Dillan, by the way." He holds his hand out to me and I shake it.

"I know who you are. I'm Kalysia."

"I know who you are." He smiles and turns my hand over. "Don't worry about this." He runs his fingers across the scrapes on my palm. "After Lunam, you'll be all healed."

"So I've heard," I say as Dillan springs off the ground and helps me up.

We stand face to face in silence. I feel his heart beating between us and suddenly something sparks inside of me. This time the burning begins in my chest. My breathing becomes erratic. I taste his breath on my tongue, and I want to kiss him. I edge forward until we are chest to chest. He steps back. I reach for his hand, and he pulls away.

"Kalysia, we can't," he whispers into the space between us. "Lunam is beginning." He brushes his lips across my hand and walks away.

"Are you kidding me?" I call after him, but he doesn't even turn around. "Nice way to ruin a moment!"

I make my way to the locker rooms and find all the girls have beaten me inside.

"Kalysia!" Cassie calls from across the crowded room. She waves a white dress in her arms. "What happened to you?" She gestures to the dirt covering my arms and face. My hair has fallen loose and my dress is a mess.

"I fell," I say quickly and pull the dress over my head.

"Do you want to wash up?" She pulls me towards a shower stall.

"What's the point; I'll be covered in fur in less than an hour anyway."

"Oh yeah." Cassie stops. "In that case, take off your bra, you don't need it."

"I didn't realize we're going commando." I unhook my bra and fling it on the floor.

"Just the bra. It restricts the upper torso when we phase. You can leave your underwear; those pretty much get shredded."

I take a few minutes to take my hair down and shake some of the dirt out. I look at my reflection; this is the last time I will be me. After tonight, I am claimed by nature. I will be a slave to her whims. I lift my hand to my nose and sniff it. I smell Dillan's scent lingering on my bloodied skin. I'd know that smell anywhere. I close my eyes and see him watching me from across the dance floor. I see him near the keg when I pumped a beer, and watching me and Layla in the parking lot. He's been there all night, but I didn't notice him until Leah pointed him out. Well, it won't be hard to find him now that I have his scent.

"You ready?"

I open my eyes and see Cassie waiting as the other girls file out of the room. I reach around my neck and take off the necklace Layla gave me. I stash it with my dress in an empty cubby. "I'm ready."

I follow Cassie outside and we fall in line with the other girls. The boys are walking around the other side of the building in a single-file line. We will enter the canopy on opposite sides. Cassie said it doesn't matter who we pass through the canopy with, it's who we find on the other side that matters.

My heart is in my throat. I shouldn't have drunk so much beer. I feel like I'm going to be sick. I sidestep out of line to catch my breath.

What am I doing? I don't want this. I don't want to be here.

"Kalysia," Layla calls from the porch of the farmhouse. There is a crowd of adults lined up, watching us. "You'll be fine. Trust yourself." She is as calm as I have ever seen her.

I trust her.

My hands stop shaking as I fall back into line. I'm near the end now. At least I'll have a little more time before my destiny is determined.

As we near the canopy, I see a hand wave me forward. It's Cassie. Being near her will make me feel better. I slip out of line and quickly step in front of her. She offers me a reassuring smile before we are called to attention.

I look through the thin white canopy; the moon looks closer to earth than I have ever seen it. It's a large white ball that's been bounced too high and stuck in a web of stars.

An old woman stands in front of the two lines, holding a branch of some kind. She lights one end from a fire pit and then blows it out. White smoke billows into her face and surrounds her body. She's chanting words in a language I've never heard. Some of the girls in my line sniffle; I don't know if they are tears of joy or sorrow. I wonder if anyone else feels as uncertain as I do.

I want to look back at Cassie, but I don't want to break ranks. Suddenly I feel her hand in mine. She squeezes my fingers and releases them quickly. The gesture puts me at ease. I'm so grateful to have her friendship. I'm so happy she is sharing this with me. I just hope we won't be separated after this is all over. She is Shasta, so if she matches with one of her pack members, she will live in her mate's branch. Maybe that's why I was encouraging her to be with a Sierra. I don't want to lose her.

The old woman stops chanting and begins the ritual. "When you pass through the smoke, you will inhale the spirit of your ancestors, and you will inherit the gift that was bestowed upon us by our mother, Gaia. When you step into the moonlight, you will become one with nature and a child of the moon. Gaia gave us the ability to choose the life we want to live. Choose the form that will give life to your pack, your family, your soul. Come forth and be blessed."

This is my destiny. My life. My choice.

I chant the words in my head as I edge towards the canopy. I don't see the first few phase, but I hear howling echo from the trees. When I'm fifth in line, I see Clio pass through the smoke. She walks swiftly down the path side by side with Tripp. It happens so quickly; I don't even think Clio feels it.

One moment she is walking on two legs, and a split second later, she's running on four in the moonlight. Tripp is hot on her tail.

When it's my turn, I look to see who is standing beside me and find Dillan staring back. He smiles, and my stomach burns with desire. I'm so focused on Dillan I don't remember passing through the smoke. I don't realize what I'm doing until I see moonlight splayed across the dirt in front of me. I feel Dillan's eyes on me; he's waiting for me to go first. I'm stuck, I can't move. I don't want to be claimed by nature. I don't want to be claimed by anything or anyone.

I think about Gaia. She turned a pack of wolves into humans to save her from loneliness. We are a species born from one woman's desire for companionship. You can call it a gift, but it can also be seen as a curse. The wolves had no choice, I do.

I lift my foot to step into the light, but instead I step back. I hear Cassie gasp behind me. A voice in my head is chanting. *Go. Go.* Only I don't know which direction it wants me to move in. I start to turn around when I feel his hand grip mine.

"We'll do it together," Dillan says. We lock eyes, and he gently pulls me forward.

We stand at the edge of the canopy. Our past behind us, our future before us, hand in hand.

We'll do it together. His words echo in my head. He is the one. He will be my partner. *We'll do it together.*

CHAPTER SIX:

HANGOVER

The morning sun is bright behind my eyes as I creep back into consciousness. I stretch my arms over my head and kick my legs free from the sleeping bag. I'm sort of surprised to find myself in a tent, dressed in the tank top and shorts I always sleep in. I'm even more surprised that I'm alone.

I try to remember what happened after I walked through the Lunam canopy. I remember holding hands with Dillan, his smiling eyes through the smoke, and the sting in the center of my palm from where I fell, then everything goes blank. I

turn my hand over. The scratches are gone, just like my memory. I don't know how I got here or where I am. I don't hear anyone rustling around outside.

I do smell something.

Bacon.

The smell of breakfast makes my stomach growl. I find the bag with my clothes and bathroom stuff strategically placed so I wouldn't miss it. I put on my Vans, sling my backpack over my shoulder, and head to find food. The air is cool and feels nice. My tent is a few hundred yards away from the picnic area where the Lunam Ceremony was held last night. The canopy has been taken down, and tents have been set up all around the edge of the clearing.

The Sierra boy that danced with Cassie passes by me with Leah on his arm.

"Morning," I say and wonder where Cassie is.

I need to find her.

Leah and the boy smile and mumble good morning as they walk into the woods.

I don't find Cassie in the clearing where we ate and danced last night, so I head to the locker room. The room is humid from the showers. There are ten or twelve girls waiting in line; none of them are Cassie. I should probably shower too. I check my cubby and find my dirty dress, along with the necklace Layla gave me. I put my backpack in the cubby and take my toiletry bag with me. I use the restroom and brush my teeth.

The line for the shower has grown by the time I'm done. I grab a towel from a bin and take my place at the back of the line. Clio is the next girl to come out of a stall; her towel is wrapped tightly around her head instead of her body.

"Morning, Clio. Have you seen Cassie?" I ask her as she parades past the line.

She stops abruptly and blushes. "Hi Kalysia, I didn't see you." She pulls the towel off her head and wraps it around her naked body.

I don't understand why she is suddenly embarrassed just because I'm in here. The other girls sneer behind her back.

Clio tells me she hasn't seen Cassie and asks how my night was. I tell her it was ok. My less than enthusiastic reply causes strange looks from the other females, but none of them comment.

"Are you waiting for the shower?" Clio asks. I hold up my towel and toiletry bag, stating the obvious. "Why don't you go next? Rachel won't mind."

She turns to the girl prepping to enter the stall she just used. Rachel looks less than thrilled, but nods in agreement and gets back in line.

"No, that's ok," I tell them. "I'll wait."

Now the entire line insists I go next. They don't just insist; they beg me to go ahead of them. Their pleading is so desperate that I finally agree, just to make them happy. I wash my hair and face quickly. I've never had to shave; we don't grow hair on our legs or under our arms. It's one wolf perk I always liked.

After my shower I dress quickly in a pair of chino shorts and a white quarter-sleeve button-down shirt. The material is thin, so I wear a blue bra with white and yellow daisies printed on the cups underneath it. Layla always hated this outfit, but now that I'm a woman, she can't say shit.

The picnic area is crowded with people when I leave the locker room. I spot Layla at the same time she sees me. A smile spreads across her face. We meet at the buffet table, and she hands me a plate filled with my favorite things—pancakes, sausage, and a banana. I pour myself a glass of orange juice, and we sit at one of the empty tables in the sun. I bite into a sausage link and pour syrup on my pancakes. I feel her eyes on me as I eat. Syrup drips down my chin and she whips out a napkin.

"That's classy," she smirks.

I take the napkin from her with a dramatic eye roll. I know she wants to talk about last night. Even if I could remember, hashing out the details with Layla is the last thing I want to do. I eat my entire stack of pancakes and another piece of sausage before I look at her again.

"Look, I don't remember what happened."

"I know. It will come back to you slowly, and after you phase a few times, your recall will be quicker." She pushes my juice towards me. "Drink, you need to hydrate."

I take a sip. "Why is it all so fuzzy?"

"Your mind needs time to adjust. We think differently when we phase; our actions are based on instinct. We do what comes naturally, without question or doubt. Unlike a human, who overthinks, plans, predicts."

"How did I get in the tent? Who dressed me?"

"I left your bag in the tent, do you remember finding it?" Layla's question jogs my memory.

I see the tent; I smell my clothes. The next thing I know I'm standing at my bag pulling out my t-shirt and shorts. I don't see myself do it; I just see what's in front of me, the door to the tent, my hands unzipping the bag. "I guess."

"Do you remember anything else?"

I concentrate harder this time, and I see Dillan. We're outside; the moon is behind his head. He smiles at me and we kiss. The memory is like a scene from an adult movie. He's sitting on a bed, I'm on his lap. I feel his hands on my bare back; my fingers tangled in his hair. "No."

Layla smiles like she knows I'm lying and stands. "I have to help Jessie in the kitchen. Make sure you eat and drink. Phasing takes a toll on your body when you're new to it."

I give her a fake salute and gulp down the rest of my orange juice. I wait around the picnic area a little while, hoping to see Cassie. I eat a banana and have two more glasses of orange juice before I spot her walking towards the parking lot.

I bolt from the table and call her name, but she doesn't turn around. I pass through a group of couples making their way to the food when his scent stops me in my tracks.

I turn and find Dillan standing behind me. He wraps me in his arms and lifts me off the ground. I bury my face in his neck and inhale. His smell is tainted with soap. I hate it.

"How did you sleep?" he asks as my feet land back on Earth.

I barely remember anything that happened after I passed through the Lunam canopy, but I feel connected to Dillan. Comfortable and connected.

"Good, I guess."

"Why didn't you stay with me?" He pushes the hair off my face and tucks it behind my ears. His movements are so natural;

like he's been doing it for years even though we've only known each other a few hours.

"I don't remember."

He accepts my excuse with a kiss on the lips. He tastes familiar.

"Well, that will be the last night I ever spend without you."

To think I will spend the rest of my life with someone is overwhelming. I thought I would fall into some wolfy love spell and become smitten with my mate. I like that I still feel like me, but it scares me, too.

I sit across from Dillan while he eats his breakfast. He mows through a dozen sausages and two stacks of pancakes in record time. When he goes back for thirds, I look around and realize that nobody is mingling with each other. Couples sit side by side, eating and speaking in private conversations. When I see Drake and Leah together, I remember what I was doing when Dillan found me.

"I'm going to look for Cassie," I tell Dillan when he returns with a fresh plate. "I saw her walking towards the parking lot earlier, and I want to check on her."

Dillan sits down and pours syrup on his pancakes.

"You're so sweet," he says. I'm offended by his somewhat condescending tone. "But she's probably in a tent with one of the Shasta."

"How do you know?" I challenge.

"Look around, Kalysia. Everyone is either here or in their tents." He smiles and takes a bite. "Which is where I'm taking you as soon as I'm done eating."

Does he really think I'm just sitting here waiting for him to ravish me? My body tingles at the thought. I look at the other females fawning over the males; they look like desperate little puppies waiting to be played with by their masters. That is so not me.

"We'll see about that." I smirk.

Dillan takes my statement as a challenge. He leans over and kisses me. Suddenly a memory flashes in my mind. Dillan is above me. I feel him everywhere. My body is consumed by him. He pulls back with a smile and my heart kicks into overdrive.

I do want him, more than air, but I'll be damned if he thinks I'm waiting around for him to finish eating. I stand and start walking away from his table, unbuttoning my shirt as I go.

"Hey," he shouts. "Where are you going?"

I spin around and my blouse swings open, exposing my bare stomach and the blue, daisy-covered bra.

"I'm done eating," I shout and keep walking backward so he can see what he's missing.

Dillan drops his fork and leaps over the table; he reaches me in two steps. The couples cheer as he lifts me over his shoulder.

Once we're out of the clearing, he whips me around and cradles me in his arms.

Who's the boss now?

Dillan's tent is deep in the woods, away from the others. It's cool back here under the cover of trees. He sets me down and unzips his tent. I step inside first and kick off my sneakers. His tent is bigger than mine and holds a large rollaway bed. I stare at the disheveled bed covers. Was I here last night?

"Don't worry, the wheels are locked," he jokes. He zips the tent closed and kicks his shoes off.

I didn't realize how nervous I am until now. This isn't my first time, not even my first time with Dillan, if the flashes in my mind are real.

Dillan moves behind me and pulls my blouse off my shoulders. He kisses behind my ear and makes his way down my collar bone to my shoulder; all the while he holds my arms inside my shirt. When I try to turn to face him, he wraps his arms around my body and holds me in place.

"I'm the luckiest man here."

I feel his thoughts in his arms, his lips, his moist skin. Dillan Dukes really cares about me. I don't know if I can say the same about him, but the sexual attraction is undeniable.

He lets me go to pull his shirt off, and I turn around and kiss his chest. I run my hands along the muscles in his back. My body is on fire. The burn, itch, whatever you want to call it, is raging inside me.

We fall onto the bed and stay tangled up in each other for hours. We sleep, wake, talk, and make love until it's so dark inside the tent we can barely see each other. Dillan tells me about his childhood. He was raised in Napa. When he turned fourteen, his father sent him to a prep school in Santa Cruz. That is where he realized he loved to surf.

"The first time I stood on a board, it was on an eight-foot wave. I ate shit at the end, but I was hooked. I was in the water every chance I got. My dad didn't like it, but it kept me out of trouble."

Dillan was sent to school with a guardian, Othello. He was a beta, super loyal to Dillan's family. After a couple of years, they bonded and Othello stopped reporting every detail of Dillan's life to his father. In return, Dillan didn't tell anyone Othello was dating a human girl. Even though Othello is a beta and will never phase, dating humans are considered a taboo. Othello still carries the gene. One that can be passed to his children.

"Two summers ago I was surfing, and this dude asked me if I ever thought about competing. I never had until that moment. The guy signed me up for a competition in Huntington Beach. Othello and I drove down; his girlfriend even came with us. We told them he was my guardian. He was my guardian, just not my legal guardian." Dillan smirks and my heart jumps out of my chest.

He is so damn sexy. It's difficult keeping my mind on his story when I'm lying naked in his arms.

"How did you do?" I ask as I nibble his chin.

He leans his face to mine and kisses me slow and deep. I moan, and he moves me on top of him. "Do you want to hear this story or not?" He holds me by my waist, threatening to take me.

I feel the control he has over me and I back down. "Finish your story," I say and slide off his stomach.

"I won the whole fucking thing and was offered a sponsorship." His face is beaming.

"Holy shit! That's amazing." I kiss him on the cheek.

"My dad didn't think so." Dillan's tone turns dark. "He freaked out on me, and I don't even know what happened to Othello. My mom said he was fired because of his girlfriend. But I know it was me."

He squeezes me close, like I'm going to be ripped from his arms. Dillan says his father wasn't angry at his accomplishment. But surfing wasn't part of his future. He had family obligations. Something I've heard my whole life, too.

"My dad said I would have to revoke the contract. Only he didn't want to get lawyers involved and draw any more attention to our family. So, he had me fake an injury."

"How did you do that?"

"A pack doctor put a cast on my leg and produced x-rays that showed a break in my ankle that would prevent me from surfing for at least a year. That was enough for them to drop me."

"We have our own doctors?"

"Yes, what do you think we do when we get injured? It isn't like we can stop by a clinic for treatment. We have our own doctors, lawyers, you name it. We can't all get by on our good looks." He kisses my forehead.

"So pack members go to college?" I perk up at the idea of having an actual career.

"Yes. Of course."

My heart does a happy dance and I snuggle up to Dillan. Is it possible that I can have this man for the rest of my life and still go to college? This means Krystal can go to cosmetology school. This Lunam thing isn't as bad as I thought.

"Do you still surf?"

"No," he answers quickly, like the thought pains him. "I wore the cast for six months. I had to play it out in case anyone came around, so I decided to leave school. My father got me a private tutor, and I used the extra time to learn about the business. It wasn't like I was going to go pro or anything. I always knew I would have to come home for this." Dillan waves his hand in the air. "And you." He kisses the top of my head.

"You didn't even know I existed until yesterday." I kiss his neck and work my way across his chest.

Dillan sits up and brings my mouth to his. Even though we've been kissing for hours, he still feels new. We break away, and he focuses on my eyes in the darkness.

"I've always known you were out there waiting for me, and that I would love you."

His words, those words, cause a lump in my throat. "Did you just say what I think you said?"

Dillan kisses me in reply. I can't get lost in the kiss the way I want to. Not with that four-letter word looming between us. Hearing Dillan Dukes tell me he loves me so quickly worries me.

CHAPTER SEVEN:

OUTCAST

I wake to hushed voices and feel Dillan's warm body missing from the bed. I open my eyes and see his silhouette outside the tent.

"Ok, give us a few minutes, we'll be right behind you," Dillan says. Then he unzips the tent and climbs back inside with a lantern.

"Who was that?" I sit up and look around for my bra. Dillan tosses it to me along with the rest of my clothes. "Thanks."

Dillan has on a pair of shorts. He slips on a tank top then sits down to put on his shoes.

"That was Drake. He brought us a light and said they're going to clean up dinner soon. So, if you want to eat, you better get up."

I need food. I feel like I can eat a cow.

Twinkling lights guide us back to the picnic area. Our arrival doesn't go unnoticed. I blush at the attention. We've been holed up in Dillan's tent all day. Everyone knows what we've been doing; they were all doing the same thing, I think.

Dillan releases my hand to grab a plate and I move to the other side of the buffet table. Dillan looks wounded, like I abandoned him or something. I smile, comforting him, and load my plate with food.

"Do you want me to heat that for you?" Layla's voice calls from the kitchen door. I appreciate her distance. Being mothered after spending all day in bed with Dillan feels weird.

"No, I'm fine," I tell her. When I look up from my plate, I find Dillan standing in front of me, clearly agitated. "What?"

"Maybe I don't want to eat cold food?" I don't know him well enough to know if he's joking.

I wait half a beat to see if he breaks into a smile. He doesn't. He just continues to load food onto this plate. *Wow, really?*

Dillan is probably the hottest and most powerful guy here, but I'm starting to think he's also a bit of a crybaby.

"Sorry," I say in a way that sounds like I'm not sorry at all.

Dillan doesn't seem to notice. He mistakes my sarcasm as a real apology.

"It's ok." He picks up a fork and napkin then heads to an empty bench.

I'm confused. I don't know if he really was upset or just messing with me. I grab a napkin and a diet soda from the cooler and offer one to Dillan. He declines and motions to the Sierra boy near the keg. The boy pumps him a fresh beer and brings it to our table. Dillan thanks him, and the boy retreats back to his table. I wonder if Dillan is accustomed to being waited on because his family is rich, or if this is an alpha thing.

Dillan digs into the BBQ ribs on his plate like he hasn't eaten in days. I guess it's because of the phase and all the sex. I eat a piece of chicken and a heaping scoop of potato salad.

When I pop open my soda, it fizzes all over the table. I look around and laugh, but nobody is paying attention to us. Tables are full of couples, but like this morning, none of them are socializing.

"Why is everyone so quiet?"

Dillan shrugs. "Do you want to hear some music?"

"Sure."

Dillan takes a gulp of beer, wipes his mouth with his napkin, and then scans the crowd.

"Hey Drake," he calls across the clearing. "Get that DJ booth going. Kalysia wants to hear some music."

"No, it's ok," I protest. I want to kill Dillan for putting me on the spot. "You don't have to do that."

Drake leaves Leah's side and crosses to the DJ table. "It's no big deal, Kalysia. You're right, it's too damn quiet." He smiles at me and flips on the speakers.

The music energizes the couples. Drake and Leah dance, as well as Clio and Tripp. They all look so happy, so smitten. I wonder if Dillan and I look like that. I feel happy, content. I'm not as love-sick as I thought I would be. The physical attraction I feel for Dillan is obvious, but my heart and mind haven't quite caught up.

"How are you two doing? Can I get you anything? We have cake." Layla approaches tentatively. So unlike her.

"No ma'am, I'm fine." Dillan reaches across the table for my hand and squeezes it. "Your daughter is taking great care of me."

I'm appalled at Dillan's statement to my mother. What does he mean I'm taking care of him? I pull my hand back, and Dillan's smile falters slightly. I stand and pick up our plates, pretending my withdrawal wasn't intentional.

"We're fine, Mom."

Instead of putting the plates in the trash near the picnic tables, I carry them around the back of the building to the dumpster. I hear Layla's footsteps behind me.

"What was that, Kalysia?"

"I don't know what you're talking about." I toss the plates with more force than necessary.

I start to walk away, and Layla grabs my arm. "Is everything ok? I mean between you and Dillan?"

"Of course, why wouldn't it be? He's my match," I say bitterly.

"You are getting along? I mean, um, everything is working out?"

Layla's flustered way of asking if our sex is good makes me laugh. "Yes, Mom, everything is great" I laugh and Layla joins me. "He loves me." I laugh even harder.

Layla stops laughing. "He told you he loved you?" Her brow furrows in disbelief.

I'm a little insulted that she would think I'm lying. "Why wouldn't he love me? We're meant to be." I don't hide the sarcasm in my tone.

A small grin creeps onto Layla's face.

"What?" Her reaction has me curious.

"He loves you, Kalysia," she says with tears in her eyes and throws her arms around me.

Jessie calls Layla back to the kitchen, and I stay hidden by the dumpster, wondering why she is so happy to hear that a boy I just met thinks he's in love with me. I don't see the positive in that. It's too soon. It can't be love. It's just Lunam.

It's so easy to get caught up in the moment. I mean, hell, it's encouraged. The fact that I can see that leads me to believe Layla was right, as usual. I do have control.

"Kalysia?"

I spin around and see Cassie walking out of the forest. I run over and wrap my arms around her.

"I was looking for you all day!" *Well not all day.* "I can't wait to meet your match! Did you see who I paired with?" I feel a surge of pride that I get to call Dillan mine. The slightly tense moment that happened at the buffet table doesn't seem all that important.

"Kalysia, stop!" she says loudly and pushes away from me.

Cassie's eyes are red; it looks as if she's been crying.

"Are you ok? Did something happen? Was it Leah?"

"No, it wasn't Leah," she says quietly and looks at the ground.

"Did something happen with your match?"

"No, that's just it. I didn't make a match." Cassie bursts into tears and falls into my arms.

She was standing right behind me. She walked through the smoke.

"I don't understand; didn't you phase?" I ask her.

She slows her sobs to answer. "Yes, but I didn't match with anyone. There is always a chance. I just didn't think it would happen to me!"

"Is everything ok?" Dillan is suddenly by my side. "Are you injured?" His concern for Cassie pulls at my heart.

"No, she didn't match," I tell him quietly, even though I know Cassie can hear me.

Dillan's face turns sad, and I want to kiss him for being so compassionate towards my friend.

"Are your parents here, Cassie?" I wonder if they were among the others at the ceremony last night.

"Her father is here," Dillan says. I'm surprised he knows who she is. "Should I get him?"

"NO!" Cassie straightens up. When she realizes Dillan watching, her face turns another shade of red. "Please, I don't want to see him right now. I suspect he knows, which is why he's staying away."

Tandy said parents can sense things about their children. Just like Layla knew to keep her distance earlier. Cassie's father must feel the same way, but for other reasons, sad ones.

Cassie didn't match at Lunam. What does this mean for her, her status in the pack? Two days ago, I would have loved to be in her shoes, but now, after being with Dillan, I'm not sure anymore. For someone like me, someone raised outside the pack, this would be a get-out-of-jail-free card, but for a girl like Cassie, it's hell on earth.

Cassie excuses herself to use the bathroom, leaving Dillan and me alone.

"I feel horrible." I rest my head on Dillan's chest. I've been in bed with the strongest male here, and my best friend has been outcast. "She's been alone all day while we…"

Dillan wraps his arms around me and kisses my head. "This isn't your fault. This happens in odd years; it's a risk we all take."

"Not for you, there were more than enough females to go around."

"It's not like that every time. There have been years when the odds were flipped," Dillan says. "The packs submit their numbers the week before Lunam, so we know going in if it's an odd year and whose favor it will be in, male or female. We're all too vain to believe we aren't strong enough to make a match."

I wonder if I was on Sierra's list. Maybe I tilted the odds. "Did you know I was coming?"

I search Dillan's eyes for any hint of a lie. His reply is steadfast.

"Yes, my father told me a pureblood female was going to be here. That's you." He kisses my forehead. "You were meant to be here, don't doubt yourself for a second. We belong together."

I breathe a bit easier, but I can't stop thinking that if I wasn't here, maybe Cassie would be matched. Then again, if I wasn't here, Dillan would be matched with someone else. Murderous thoughts flash through my mind. I can't imagine him with anyone but me.

"What will happen to Cassie?"

"It depends on how her pack handles it. Her father will be upset; he might offer her to a low alpha in the hopes her children will have some hope to lead one day. Her life doesn't have to be horrible, Kalysia. She comes from a strong family, she'll be ok."

Dillan's reassurance does little to soothe me. I was still secretly hoping that she matched with a Sierra. The idea of moving away and starting a new pack was almost bearable when I thought she would be with me.

"Isn't there something we can do?" I plead. "I mean, what good is being a pureblood if we can't throw a little weight around? Not just to get beer service."

Dillan smirks at my comment. "What do you want me to do?"

"I want her to come with us," I tell him. "Can't she join our pack?"

Dillan shakes his head. "No, Kalysia. If you think her status will be bad at Shasta, it's nothing compared to how she will be treated in a Sierra pack."

"I'll protect her." I stand up tall as if I'm starting already, maybe I am. "I know she'll always have my back. I need a friend like her right now. Please, Dillan, do this for me?" I tiptoe and kiss his neck.

He moans when I bite his earlobe. "I'm in trouble."

"Why?" I pull back to look at his face.

Dillan kisses me hard on the mouth and pushes me up against the building wall.

"Because I will never be able to say no to you, Kalysia. Because I'm madly in love with you."

No, it's too early.

CHAPTER EIGHT:

ÑAPA

I looked for Cassie last night to tell her the good news, but she had disappeared.

To be honest, I didn't look long, because Dillan pulled me back to his tent.

Dillan isn't the first guy I've slept with, but he is the first I enjoyed. We fit perfectly in so many ways. I can't imagine being with anyone besides him.

I might not be in love yet, but I know there isn't another man on earth that can make me feel the way he does.

When I woke this morning, Dillan was gone. He left a note saying he had to meet with the adults regarding our branch. The Sierra couples are headed to our new home in the Sierra Mountains. Dillan and I would normally go straight from Lunam to our new branch, but Dillan's father wasn't able to go to Lunam.

This time of year is busy for the business, so we are going to Napa. I'm nervous about meeting him. I hope I live up to his expectations, even though Layla says it's my bloodline that matters, not my manners.

Layla and Monte are also going to Napa. Monte and Lowell Dukes run the pack together. My father is the power and Dillan's father is the money.

I walk into the kitchen and find it empty. The pots have all been washed and sit on the counters ready to be packed. I look in the walk-in refrigerator for something to eat. I find several packs of yogurt. I take one and walk out at the same time Dillan and Cassie walk into the kitchen.

"Hey you," Dillan leaves Cassie's side and gives me a kiss on the cheek. "I found Cassie for you."

A twinge of jealousy stabs at my chest. *Quit being stupid.* "Did you tell her?" I try to hide any bitterness in my tone.

"Of course not. I knew you would want to." He kisses me and my anguish vanishes. "I'll leave you to it. I gotta go help Drake pack his van."

"I didn't know alpha leaders had to help pack?" I tease him.

He's wearing jeans and a black t-shirt that show off his perfect surfer body. He looks more handsome today than he did yesterday, if that's possible.

"They do, unless they want a mutiny on their first day!" he calls over his shoulder and disappears into the sunlight.

I miss him already.

"What did you want to tell me?" Cassie interrupts.

I take both of her hands and tell her my plan to bring her to Sierra.

"No, no way. I don't want to leave my family. They're all I have now."

This wasn't the reaction I hoped for.

"If you come with me, you can go to college or get a job. You can do whatever you want. Love whomever you want." I came up with the college idea last night. It's what I would do if I were her.

Cassie shakes her head; I can see she is searching for a way to let me down easy.

"I appreciate it, really. But I don't want to go to college."

"Only because you never thought you had the option," I reason.

Cassie's entire life has lead up to Lunam. I bet she's never even entertained the idea of living a life outside the pack.

Cassie shakes her head and closes her eyes as if to hold in her tears. "I was happy to be in Lunam. I wanted to match and have children."

"You can still have children," I tell her. "You can fall in love on your own terms. Don't you see, you have options now. You can do things you never thought possible."

Cassie contemplates my plan for a few seconds. "I used to play school when I was little. I would round up all the kids and pretend I was their teacher."

"You can be that teacher now." I pull her into my arms and give her a huge hug. "I will help you."

"I wanted my children to lead one day. My family depended on it," Cassie says softly. "My father will never let me leave." She pulls away. "He needs me." Her face is adamant, and I see that this isn't just about her. "I know you want to help, but I can't let him down any more than I already have."

Tears tickle the corners of my eyes. "You're the first real friend I've ever had, and now I'm losing you."

"You have a whole pack of females fighting to be your BFF," Cassie jokes. "We'll see each other often. I'll make sure of it."

"Promise?" A tear rolls down my cheek at the thought of losing her.

Cassie nods her head and wipes a tear of her own. "I promise."

Layla convinces Monte to ride to Napa in the convertible. He agreed but is giving her a hard time about her driving skills.

"Why are you so worried? You're the one who taught me to drive."

I'm shocked when I hear this. Layla taught me to drive when I was fourteen. I was tall enough to reach the brake, and that was good enough for her. She said she never wanted me to depend on anyone for anything, even a ride home.

Hearing that Monte taught Layla to drive changes my perspective on their relationship. Maybe they did care about each other in some way.

It's strange, but Layla looks happier than I've ever seen. All these years I thought she hated my father. Looking at them now, it looks like they just went through Lunam.

Monte kisses me on the cheek and tells Dillan to drive safely. Dillan shakes his hand, and they disappear to the back of Dillan's truck.

Layla gives me a long hug. "I'm so proud of you."

It feels good in her arms. I relish the moment and let her pull away first.

"I'll miss you, Mom."

"Call me, every day if you want. I'll be at Jessie's." She opens the door to the truck and I climb in.

"When are you going back to Nevada?"

"I took a leave of absence. I want to see how things work out here," she says as Monte reappears. I thought I knew all of my mother's smiles, but this one is new. Or old depending on how you look at it.

It peeves me to know she kept me hostage in that desert hellhole all these years and now she just leaves without looking back.

"You ready?" Monte slides up to her and takes her hand. Layla winks at me.

"We'll see you in Napa." Monte waves.

Dillan jumps into the driver's seat and starts the engine. I wave at my parents.

My parents!

Standing hand in hand seeing me off just like parents do when their child leaves for college. I quickly wipe the tears, but Dillan notices anyway.

"Ah babe, don't cry. You'll see them tonight," He pats my leg.

"I know, it's not that," I tell him.

I had so many doubts about coming to Lunam, about who I am. I still have reservations about my feelings for Dillan and how I will fit into the pack, but I'm not afraid anymore. Not after seeing how happy Layla is. She needed this, she needed to come back. Not just for me, for herself.

I look back one more time and see Cassie walking to a black SUV with Conall, the leader of the Shasta pack.

"Cassie is Conall's daughter?"

"Yeah, you didn't know?" Dillan turns out of the parking lot and heads towards the highway.

That would make Cassie a pureblood; she should have matched with someone strong, like Dillan. I swallow back tears and close my eyes. How horrible this must be for her and her family.

"How does her not matching affect her family? Will her bloodline end if she doesn't have children?"

Dillan shrugs and says the Shasta pack doesn't think preserving their bloodline is a priority.

"Some think their line is already tainted. Cassie not matching sort of proves that. A pureblood always finds a mate."

"Cassie also told me that purebloods usually match within their own pack, but Layla matched with Monte. Maybe things change, evolve," I reason. "Just because Cassie is sweet and kind, it doesn't make her any less alpha."

"You see her as sweet, others see her as passive," Dillan says. "You weren't raised around the packs, you don't understand."

How dare he throw that in my face? I'm glad I wasn't raised in a pack.

"Maybe I see things from a fresh perspective."

Dillan smiles at my challenge. "I love how fired up you get over nothing."

He rubs the top of my thigh, and my skin tingles where his palm touches me. Without wanting to, I calm down.

"I'm worried about my friend's future," I say softly. "I wouldn't call it nothing. I just want her to have a good life. If I can help her in any way, I will."

"You're right, I'm sorry. If Cassie's future is important to you, then it's important to me."

"She doesn't understand there is a big world out there that doesn't care about her bloodline. If I could just show her. I know she can be happy leading a normal life." The life I wanted to lead until the moment I met Dillan.

"If it means that much to you, I'll talk to my dad and see what he thinks about transferring Cassie to our branch, ok?"

I jump out of my seat and kiss Dillan on the cheek.

"Thank you, thank you, thank you. I love you!"

Whoa! Where the hell did that come from?

"Did you just say what I think you said?" Dillan grabs the back of my head and kisses me as if the words mean something.

I return to my seat, feeling guilty. I didn't mean it like that. It's like someone saying: I'll be your best friend if you...

I stay quiet for most of the drive. I'm afraid to start any conversation that may end with "I love you." Eventually Dillan turns on the radio and music drowns out my thoughts.

When a corny love song comes on, Dillan sings the chorus softly to himself. It's the most adorable thing I've ever seen. If my only problem in life is falling in love with this beautiful, sweet, boy, then so be it. My life could be a lot worse.

When we pull to a stop in front of the large ornate gates that lead to Dillan's family home, I get nervous. I pull down the visor and check my hair in the little mirror. I have it pulled into a ponytail since I didn't have time to blow dry it this morning.

"You look beautiful," Dillan says and flips the mirror up. "You don't need to impress anyone."

That's sweet of him to say, but I flip the mirror down and make sure I don't have any food in my teeth.

The gates open magically, and Dillan eases the gas slowly towards the house. Or should I say mansion. There are several cars parked in the circular driveway; Layla's convertible isn't among them. When Dillan hops out of the truck, I take another peek in the mirror before I get out.

Dillan tells me to relax just as a maid appears at the front door. She looks like she wants to hug Dillan but refrains.

She tells us his parents are waiting on the veranda. Whatever that is.

I walk around the perfectly placed furniture, making sure I don't touch anything. It feels cold and unlived in, like a museum or a really expensive furniture store. We walk through a set of French doors and I realize a veranda is another word for a fancy patio.

"Hey Mom." Dillan greets a tall blonde woman with a hug and a kiss on the cheek. "Mom, this is Kalysia."

I step forward and hold out my hand, but Dillan's mom pulls me into her arms.

"It's so wonderful to meet you." She squeezes me the way a child hugs a teddy bear. "Are you hungry?"

"Let her get a chance to settle in before force feeding her." Dillan takes my hand and pulls me into his arms. "Where's Dad?"

Before Dillan's mother can respond, I sense someone standing behind us. Dillan spins around quickly, and his grip tightens on my shoulders.

"Adel, why didn't you tell me they were here?" He crosses the veranda and stands beside his wife.

"We just walked in the door, Dad," Dillan tells him.

"You must be Kalysia. We've heard so much about you," he says, ignoring Dillan's lukewarm greeting. "I'm Lowell." He extends a hand to me. "I'm so happy to finally meet you."

"Nice to meet you," I say and shake his hand. I've known Dillan less than forty-eight hours; I wonder how he knows anything about me.

We stand awkwardly for a minute before Adel offers us drinks. Dillan asks for a beer, while I opt for a diet soda. We sit at the large round table on the veranda, and Adel places two platters in front of us filled with cheese and fruit. I pluck a strawberry from the tray and stare at the rows of grapes that stretch out for miles.

"I didn't know you literally lived on a vineyard," I say to Dillan.

He smirks as if it's no big deal. I can't imagine what it's like to wake up every morning and look out your window to this. My window faced the back of a Quickie Mart, and you didn't want to look out that window. "You're so lucky."

"Yeah, I know." He squeezes my leg under the table. I jump slightly at his touch then recover quickly. I place my napkin in my lap and allow his hand to remain.

"I remember my Lunam," Adel says wistfully. Her cheeks flush as she sips her red wine.

Dillan makes a gagging noise beside me and I slap his arm.

"It was all so exciting. I couldn't wait for my life to begin. This is a very special time for the two of you. Appreciate every moment of it." She looks at Lowell, who is staring at his phone.

"Thank you, we will." I smile at Dillan and he leans in for a kiss. I turn my head at the last minute so he kisses my cheek.

He smiles at the coy look on my face and moves his fingers higher up my inner thigh. I inadvertently squeak.

Dillan raises an eyebrow at me as if the noise I made is code for something.

"Mom, I promised Kalysia a tour of the grounds," he says as he stands, pulling me up with him.

Adel smiles and tells us dinner will be at six sharp. "Don't be late, Dillan."

He gives her a sly smile and we excuse ourselves. Lowell stands and tells Adel he'll be in his office. I feel like a really horrible guest as we leave Adel alone of the patio.

"She'll be fine," Dillan whispers and whisks me through his childhood home.

Dillan's idea of a tour consists of the stairs and hallway that lead to his bedroom.

"I thought you were going to show me the property?" I fold my hands over my chest and stand in the doorway.

Dillan plops down on his king-size bed. "You've seen one vineyard; you've seen them all." He holds his arms out to me. "Come here."

"I've never seen a vineyard." I glare at him and try to pretend I don't want to spend the entire day in bed with him.

Dillan pulls off his black t-shirt, exposing a six-pack only nature could mold.

"I promise to give you a tour later." He crosses his heart with his fingers. If he didn't look so damn sexy, I may have protested longer, but my animalistic urges take over.

I step in the room and lock the door. Dillan bites his lower lip as I pull the straps on my sundress down over my shoulders.

"Do you want me?" I say as my dress falls away.

He jumps off the bed and kneels in front of my naked body. He kisses me softly on my stomach, making circles with his tongue around my belly button. I moan when his hand slides up my inner thigh. When he doesn't stop, my knees buckle and I lean into him for support.

Dillan must sense my needs, because he moves me to the bed. I lie down, and he lowers himself on top of me.

"I've never wanted anything or anyone the way I want you. It scares me how much I need you already." His words are heavy with emotion. I feel everything he is saying.

I don't know how to reply. There are no words. I love the fact that he wants me. Needs me.

"You have me, Dillan."

He does. I am his and he is mine.

If this is what my forever looks like, feels like, then I am the luckiest girl in the world. I try to stay quiet, knowing Dillan's parents are nearby, but it's difficult not to get lost in him. We've spent the last two days in bed, yet everything still feels brand new. I don't think I'll ever get tired of him.

"Was everything ok? I mean, were you satisfied?" he asks when we finish.

"Of course, can't you tell?" I can sense his pleasure. I assumed he could do the same.

"Yes, but you were...quieter than before."

I roll onto my stomach and rest my head on his chest. "Your parents."

Dillan rolls his eyes. "We're post Lunam. They know what's up."

"I know, but it still feels weird." I kiss the space above his heart. "Don't worry, when we get to our own place, I'll be so loud the entire pack will need ear plugs."

Dillan pulls me into his arms and kisses me. "Look, I know you're confused about your feelings for me." I start to protest, but he stops me. "Don't say anything, ok. I'm not asking for reassurance; you will never have to say it to me. I can feel it, sense it." Dillan touches his forehead to mine and looks into my eyes. "Don't doubt my feelings for you, ever. Ok?"

All I can do is nod. There is nothing for me to say. I do feel Dillan's love for me. I feel it in his touch. I taste it in his kiss. I sense it in the way he loses himself in me when we make love.

My body, my heart, and my mind are telling me that Dillan Dukes loves me. He also knows I don't feel the same way. Not yet. I never thought he sensed my feelings the way I do his. He feels my apprehension, my doubt. I climb onto his lap and he moans. I want to love him the way he deserves to be loved. I let myself go and let out a little howl. *I will fall in love with Dillan Dukes or I will die trying.*

At five o'clock I force myself out of Dillan's bed. After a quick shower we head downstairs. Monte and Layla are already there.

We barely have time to say hello before Adel ushers us into the dining room for dinner. I sit between Dillan and his father. Monte and Layla sit across from us. Two more people sit at the end of the table near Adel. They are associates of Lowell's, human business partners. Todd and Elliot are partners in every sense of the word.

"I hear congratulations are in order." Elliot holds up his wine glass and points it towards me and Dillan.

I look back, confused.

"Oh," Adel giggles. "I told Elliot you two were honeymooning upstairs."

"Dillan's window was open," Layla whispers across the table, doing a poor job hiding a smile. "We had to move inside."

I feel my face turn ten shades of red.

"It's not what you, it was the tele—" I stammer. Dillan places his hand over mine and stops me from making a bigger fool of myself. He raises his glass to Elliot and the rest of the table follows.

"Thank you, Elliot. We couldn't be happier." Dillan clinks his glass with my mine and gulps down his wine.

"Lucky girl." Elliot winks at me.

I blush at the attention and take a sip from my water to hide the ridiculous smile on my face.

"Your father tells me you are leaving tomorrow," Todd interjects, and the conversation turns to business just as our dinner arrives. "Have you seen the camp yet?"

"Camp?" I whisper to Dillan.

A maid places a plate in front of me with a small round piece of meat sitting in the center. It's surrounded by roasted vegetables. I want to devour it, but I know I have to wait until the rest of the table has been served. Table manners and etiquette I picked up when Mom was with Miles.

Dining in five-star restaurants was the thing I missed most about Miles. Once Layla dumped him, it was back to crappy chains and fast food.

"Yes, the new branch will take residence near Meyers. The camp is rustic, but quite nice," Lowell tells me.

I look at Dillan; he doesn't look the least bit surprised. He must know about the camp already.

"We're taking it back to, how do you say it, old school, right Lowell?" Monte laughs and sips his wine.

"I wouldn't call it old school. They have heat and running water," Adel chimes in.

"They better, or we won't have a new branch for long," Layla interjects and the table laughs.

I wonder if Todd and Elliot are following the conversation better than I am.

From the look on their faces, I'd say they know more about pack life than I do.

"Everyone, please eat," Adel says from the end of the table.

You don't have to tell me twice. I dive in and try to keep up with the table conversation. Dillan tells Todd he hasn't seen the camp, but he's excited to get up there and start making money for the pack.

I thought our existence was secret. I wonder if they are beta or somehow connected to the pack. Lowell and Monte chime in with details about distribution and sales analysis. Their words are foreign to me so I focus on my dinner.

"What will you do, Kalysia?" Elliot asks as I'm forking the last piece of meat into my mouth.

I try to chew quickly, but the bite was huge. Elliot smiles at me from the other end of the table and I shrug.

"She'll be learning the business as well. Kalysia has a great aptitude for numbers. She'll do well handling financials," Layla says to Elliot. Her words catch the attention of the entire table. Monte smiles sheepishly beside her.

Lowell looks at Layla like he wants to rip her head off then his face suddenly goes blank. It happens so fast I don't think anyone noticed, except me.

He slices into his meat and glares in Adel's direction. She offers a nervous smile as she pours herself another glass of wine.

Dillan remains silent. I want to strangle Layla and then hug her. I hate the attention she's drawn to me, but I also understand why she did it.

I am smart and strong. I can do more for the pack than shoot babies out of my uterus. The fact that her comment has caused this much tension tells me that having Cassie move to our pack is a better idea than I even thought. A woman's worth should have nothing to do with her ability to breed. I can only imagine what is happening to her right now.

Are people whispering behind her back? Calling her a failure. That won't happen in our branch. With my protection, she can live however she chooses. She can go to college, fall in love, and have children on her own terms.

The chatter turns to Lowell's main business, grapes. I find out that the Sierra pack made their living as field hands for a winery in Napa. In the early seventies, Lowell Duke Sr. convinced his branch to pool their money together and buy a small vineyard. The business evolved from one vineyard to ten. Now they broker grapes for wineries all over the country. At some point Lowell senior bought out his partners and took over the business.

The Duke family has a lot of power over the Sierras because it was their business that started the Sierra pack's success. The Duke family has the controlling interest in Sierra-Duke Brokerage, LLC. The pack and the elder's council each get a percentage of the business, and the Duke's keeps the rest. From the look of this house, I'd say the rest is a lot.

All the money in the world couldn't buy the Dukes' leadership. Monte's family, the Taillac's, are still the Sierra pack leaders. As one of Monte's children, I am heir to the pack.

Monte lifts his nearly empty wine glass and the table follows his lead.

"To Dillan and Kalysia. The two of you will finally make this partnership a true family."

"To family," Layla adds.

The table repeats her, and I smile at my mother, feeling so grateful that she brought me here, to this life, and gave me the family I've always wanted.

Adel rings a small bell, and three women rush in to remove our plates. It's like a scene from a movie. They return just as quickly with dessert.

Adel says it is chocolate cake with a raspberry merlot sauce. My plate is set in front of me and I dig right in. Layla catches my eye and points to her chin. I know she's alerting me to the fact that I probably have raspberry sauce dribbling down my face. I dab my mouth with the napkin in my lap and peek at Dillan.

He hasn't touched his cake. I really want to eat his, but I'm afraid Layla will stab my hand with a fork if I make a move for it.

After dessert the table disperses into pockets of conversation in the sitting room.

They actually call it that.

My mother and Adel discuss the impressive art collection the Dukes have amassed over the years. Adel points out a small painting from a French artist and tells Layla that Dillan sent it to her for her birthday last summer.

Apparently, Dillan was in Europe touring wineries in Paris and Italy, before spending a few months with a brewmaster in Germany.

Dillan and I are standing in front of the oak bar that stretches along the wall. Elliot is on the other side pouring drinks for everyone. He tells me he worked as a bartender to pay his way through college. Now he owns six restaurants in the bay area and is partnering with Lowell to open three more.

"You sound very busy," I say.

He places a soda in front of me and drops a cherry inside with a wink.

"Lowell is a very passionate man when it comes to business," Elliot says as he pours Dillan a beer from the tap. He hands it to Dillan then starts on another drink.

Dillan looks like something is bothering him. He's been quiet since we left the dinner table. I try to strike up a conversation.

"I didn't know you traveled," I say and sip my soda.

"I didn't know you had an aptitude for numbers," Dillan spits back.

I'm startled by the edge in his voice and a little bit pissed. I can't tell if it's the alcohol, he had three glasses of wine during dinner, or if Layla's comment really upset him.

I glance at Elliot, who is pretending not to listen. "That was just Layla being Layla."

Dillan leans against the bar and looks me in the eye. "So, you don't want to learn the business?"

I start to say no then think otherwise. I don't need to lie to Dillan. If he loves me the way he says he does, he'll accept me as I am. No apologies.

"Of course I want to learn the business, but that's just how I am. I'm naturally curious. It doesn't mean I want to run the company one day."

That's the truth. I don't know what I want or where my life is heading.

Dillan's shoulders relax. He even smiles a little. "Ok," he says. "I don't see any problems with you learning the industry. Let's start with this." He hands me his beer.

"You gotta learn your product."

I take a swig. "We're selling Aunt Jessie's beer?"

"It isn't just hers, it's a pack recipe."

Dillan starts to tell me a little about how we will be in charge of brewing and distribution.

"So, we won't be part of the grape business?" I'm a little disappointed that I won't get to travel around the world visiting wineries.

"Nope, we will run a new division of Sierra-Duke," Dillan says with a huge smile. "We're going to make our own mark in this world." His eyes glance towards his father across the room. His disdain for Lowell is apparent.

"Can I get a whiskey sour." Monte knocks on the bar and prompts Elliot to make his drink.

He does it in a way that isn't pretentious at all. Monte has sort of an Alec Baldwin thing going on. He's authoritative in a down-to-earth sort of way. People, like Elliot, are happy to oblige him.

Dillan excuses himself to use the restroom and leaves me alone with my father. Elliot hands Monte his drink then joins Todd and Lowell on the veranda for a cigar.

"So, how are you adjusting?" Monte asks. He taps his pinky finger on the side of the glass in a nervous tick sort of way.

"I'm fine," I say and sip Dillan's beer. I look around as we stand in an awkward silence. I can only think of one thing to say to my father and I'm not sure it's going to come out right. I take a big gulp from the glass before I speak. "I didn't know you had another kid."

Monte looks taken aback. "Yes, I do."

"Is that why my mother left you?" I feel my skin grow warm, and I don't know if it's the alcohol or anger.

"No, you have it all wrong, Kalysia." Monte puts his hand on my shoulder. "Layla knew—"

"Is everything ok?" Dillan appears out of nowhere and pulls me into his arms.

Monte jerks his hand back, as if Dillan is going to bite it off.

"Everything is fine." I flash a fake smile at Monte. "Excuse me." I hand Dillan the now empty glass and walk out of the room. I follow Dillan's scent to find his bedroom. I fall onto his bed and scream into his pillows.

When Dillan strokes my back to wake me, it's dark outside. I turn over and clear tangled hair out of my face.

"What time is it?" My voice is hoarse from sleep.

"A little past midnight." Dillan hands me a bottle of water. It's a fancy square glass bottle. "Are you feeling better?"

Layla must have made up some excuse for why I left. She's always one step ahead. I nod and drain half the bottle.

"Did everyone leave?"

"Layla and Monte are in the guesthouse. What did he say that upset you?"

I don't really want to talk about it, but I don't want Dillan to think I'm shutting him out.

"I asked him about his other child."

"Oh." Dillan takes the bottle from me. "What did he tell you?" He seems very curious for some reason. Dillan snooping into every aspect of my life is something else I'll have to get used to.

"I asked him if Layla knew he cheated and if that was why she left. He tried to say she knew about the other kid and then you interrupted us." I stroke his arm.

I'm glad Layla left him. I just don't get why she's with him now. Maybe enough time has passed and she forgives him. Maybe I should too, but it feels new to me.

If he hadn't cheated, Layla wouldn't have left, and I would have been raised with both of my parents.

"I would've liked to know who my sibling was. I always wanted a sister." I think of Cassie.

"I can tell you who they are," Dillan says cheerfully.

"There was more than one?"

"He has two other kids, but you only met one of them, Leah," Dillan says.

Holy crap, Leah is my sister.

"Does she know? Why didn't she say anything?"

Dillan shrugs. "I don't know, maybe Monte told her not to."

That makes sense. He wouldn't want me to cause a scene at Lunam.

"Who is the other one?"

Dillan says the other one is a male, Rusty. "He's twenty-one. You'll meet him at camp."

I feel my dinner creep into my throat.

"You're telling me Monte had a child before Lunam?" I do the math in my head.

"When he was fifteen?"

"Yes, sometimes things happen before Lunam. It didn't make him ineligible."

"Yeah, but the poor girl that had his bastard child was!" I yell.

I don't know why I'm yelling. I don't even know this girl. But I do know another girl in her shoes. Tandy. My mother had to have known. Why would she choose someone like him? I need to know. I have to know.

CHAPTER NINE:

DUTY

I pound on the guesthouse door. It's late, but I know she's awake. She opens the door in a blue silk robe I've never seen before. She steps to the side and lets me in without a word.

I launch right in.

"Did you know he had a baby before Lunam? Did you know about Leah? Is that why you left him?"

Layla sits on the loveseat and covers her legs with her robe.

"Kalysia, sit." I cross my arms over my chest and remain standing. She sighs and says, "I knew about his son. He didn't keep it a secret. But the life you have before Lunam is irrelevant to the person you become after."

"So, you're telling me he isn't a womanizing pig with a gang of bastard children running loose in the pack?"

Layla looks towards the hall. "Keep your voice down. It wasn't like that. Your father is one of the last pureblood Sierra males. There is a lot of pressure put on males to breed. It's the only way to ensure bloodlines. Not all of his choices were his own. He did what was right for the pack."

I sit down with a thud. I imagine my father at fifteen being forced to impregnate some poor girl. "Who was the girl?"

"She was an older unmatched female."

I have to get Cassie out of her pack before something like this happens to her.

"Do things like this happen a lot?"

"Yes. But we can change all of that. You can." She stumbles on the word tradition. "With you leading Sierra and me on the council, we can pull the pack into the twenty-first century. Change it for the better." She places her hand on mine.

"Why didn't you tell me about the council?"

Layla rubs my back.

"If I told you, it would have swayed your decision. I wanted you to work off of instinct, to use your gut. If you didn't want to go to Lunam, we wouldn't have gone. But you never fought me on it, Kalysia. Think about it."

For all the bitching I did about Lunam, I never stopped her. If she had told me about my father, I would have used my head and not my instincts. I hear rustling in the bedroom and remember Monte is here.

"You forgive him?" I nod my head towards the bedroom.

"It's complicated and it's late." Layla stands. "We can have this conversation another time, when it's just us." She offers me her hand. "I love you, Kalysia."

I hug my mom and tell her I love her, too.

"Will you be here in the morning when I leave?" I ask her as I reach the door.

"Of course, we'll see you off then head back to Jessie's."

We, she says, meaning her and Monte. They are a "we" now.

I wrap my arms around myself and hurry back to the main house. The air is moist and freezing cold. Fog fills the night sky; I can't even see the moon. Something catches my eye on the second floor. Dillan is watching me on the balcony. His protective manner is something I have to get used to.

First Layla and now Dillan. I guess I should be happy to have two people who care about me. I could be in Cassie's shoes right now. Alone.

I open the door to his room. He's moved from the balcony and is sprawled across the bed, wearing only a pair of boxers. I kick off my shoes and slide under the covers to warm my feet.

"Is everything ok?" He rubs my arm. I tell him I'm fine. "I have news. Do you want to hear it now or tomorrow morning?" He slides under the covers with me and turns off the lamp beside the bed.

I don't want to talk anymore. I cozy up in his arms and feel my eyes beginning to shut.

"It's good news, you'll want to hear this."

"Ok, but I can't take any more drama tonight."

"My father said he will talk to Conall and request Cassie's transfer."

Dillan doesn't finish whatever he is about to say next because I pounce on him.

"Thank you! You have no idea how much this means to me, Dillan." I kiss his cheeks, his eyes, and then his mouth.

He grabs my hips and flips me onto my back. "My life goal is to make you happy, Kalysia. I'm going to give you everything you've ever wanted, and I'm going to love you more than any woman has ever been loved."

"Promise?" I whisper.

Dillan presses his lips softly to mine then pulls back with a wicked smile. "You bet your ass."

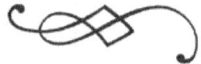

The morning sun fights to make an appearance through the lingering patches of fog as we stand outside saying our goodbyes. Dillan's truck is packed and ready to go. Layla hands me a cell phone and tells me it's programmed with her new cell number. I promise to call her when we get there, wherever *there* is.

I let Monte give me a hug and I apologize for acting like a brat. He tells me to forget it and shoves a bulky envelope in my hand.

"What's this?" I open the flap and see a stack of money inside.

Monte takes the envelope and shoves it in my backpack.

"It's an emergency fund. It's from both of us." He motions to Layla.

She smiles and points at Monte behind his back.

The pack will provide my food, housing, even clothes, but I gladly take Monte's money. I don't need it, but someone else I know might.

Dillan's father is in a meeting and doesn't see us off. Adel relays his goodbye as she hands me a cooler with sandwiches and snacks. It's only a two-hour drive northeast, but we have enough food to last two days.

A half hour into the drive, Dillan asks for a sandwich. I pull one from the cooler and unwrap it. A delicious smell fills the truck. It's the same luscious meat we had for dinner.

"Did your mother make this?" I hand Dillan the sandwich and then unwrap one for myself.

"Yeah, she's sort of a foodie." Dillan takes a huge bite while maneuvering around a delivery truck. "Food is really important to her," he says hesitantly.

"How so?" I bite into the soft roll and juice from the meat slides down the side of my face. I wipe it with my arm and search for a napkin in the cooler.

"My mother's family were purist. They believed in living off the land, no contact with the outside world. Food was scarce when she was growing up."

"So, she wasn't part of the Tuluka branch?"

"She was, but her parents chose wolf as their dominant form. When she was born they were forced to live as human, but refused to live in the pack. They lived off the grid until she was seven. When the elders found her she was severely malnourished and barely spoke. Othello said it was the worst case of neglect the elders had ever seen. Othello's mother worked as a nanny, he was there the day she was brought in. Othello and my mother were raised together, of course he didn't go to Lunam being a beta, but I think he really cared about my mom. That's why he worked for my father."

Dillan says both packs live as human and rarely ever spend time in wolf form.

"Lunam was the first time I'd ever seen anyone phase."

"You've never seen your parents as wolf?" I ask him.

"No. No way, my father would never phase in front of me." Dillan shivers at the idea. Like he's picturing his father naked or something. "If pack members are phasing, it's something they do in private." His eyebrow raises and he turns to look at me.

"Have you seen Layla?"

I always thought phasing was the best thing about our kind. It's disheartening to hear that others don't see it the same way.

"Yes. And she was beautiful."

Dillan turns his eyes back to the road.

"You were beautiful. I couldn't take my eyes off of you."

"You remember what I look like?" I'm jealous, because I can't recall my time as wolf.

"I phased back before you and I watched you explore the forest. You were so graceful, so at peace. Then you saw me and I thought for a second you might rip my throat out. Lucky for me you phased and jumped into my arms. I knew in that moment that I would love you forever."

I don't say anything. Nothing I say will compare to the words Dillan just gifted to me. I kiss his hand and offer him a bottle of water.

He smiles at my attentiveness.

"Thanks, babe." He sucks down the entire bottle and tosses the empty container on the floor of the truck.

"Sorry if my mom forced food down your throat. She's gotten better over the years, but she's still scarred."

"I just thought she loved to cook." I take another bite of my sandwich then wrap it back up. "Are there many purists left?" I think about Sophie Ann and wonder if she would be willing to starve for her ideals.

Dillan says most of the packs have acclimated to normal society, but there are a few he's heard of up north, near the California-Oregon border.

"My father is the closest thing to a purist you'll find now. He's fixated on restoring the bloodlines. Pureblood numbers are so low that in a few years we'll all be too close in relation to breed. As crazy as our traditions are, we draw the line at brothers and sisters reproducing."

"Good to know." I shudder at the thought. I think about my mother and what she said about us changing pack traditions.

"Maybe this is the natural evolution of our kind. This was bound to happen sooner or later, right?"

"Not if my father can help it. We all have some pureblood in us. We all came from the same wolves, it's just that the line gets diluted. For instance, a pureblood has a child with a beta. That child goes to Lunam and matches with another pureblood. Their child is just alpha because of the diluted beta blood. My father wants to change that. He says after three generations; the line should be considered pure."

"As long as the alpha keeps matching with purebloods?"

"Yes, exactly. You catch on fast." Dillan pats my leg. I feel like socking him in the side of the head.

"How do they know if a line has been diluted? Who keeps track?"

"When a child is born it should have the characteristics of the father."

I look at Dillan's profile. His strong jawline, blue-gray eyes, dark hair, and tan skin. We look a lot alike. Who is to say the baby won't look like me?

"Children born with diluted bloodlines don't look like us?"

"They have small imperfections. Lighter hair, darker eyes, paler skin. It depends on the father. Purebloods have a mark on the back of the neck, at the base of the hairline."

My hand goes to the back of my head.

"It's there. Your hair covers it. You can see mine." Dillan turns slightly so I can see the back of his head. A small, perfectly round mark sits at the base of his skull. I run my fingers over it as he turns back to face the road. It's completely flush to his skin, like a freckle.

"Gaia marked her original pack. She was afraid she wouldn't recognize them among the other wolves. Anyone who carries the blood of the first fifteen has the mark and is considered pure."

"Our child..." I trail off, unable to finish the thought. I can't even imagine having a baby.

Dillan turns to me and smiles.

"Yes," he says and gently runs his hand down the side of my face. "Our kid is going to be the best leader this pack has ever seen."

I hate that his or her future is already decided. I sigh and look out the window. I don't want to bring a child into a pack that forces boys to breed with women. One that places value on who your partner is or whether you have a mark on your neck. Any child of mine is going to have a choice in life.

Dillan continues talking about blood tests and how it will prove that the Shasta pack is tainted.

"There are rumors that Shasta has been experimenting with half-breeds for years."

I recall the conversation I overheard between Layla and Conall. He wanted to invite half-breeds to Lunam.

"Everyone knows the entire Shasta pack is tainted. Conall told my father that after two generations, the human blood is expelled from the bloodline. He and my father argue about it all the time."

Dillan recalls a time when Conall, Monte, and Lowell were arguing over bloodlines and Conall wanted to prove that a half-breed was just as strong as a pureblood. They were camping somewhere near Shasta territory; it was an annual father-son trip.

"Conall called this boy over to our table. He was taller than me by a few inches. He had this scar across his eyebrow, so I knew he was human. Conall told the boy he had to arm wrestle me. The kid looked like he was going to shit his pants. My father and Monte started cracking up. When they realized Conall was serious, they pulled me to the side and basically told me I would let the entire pack down if I lost. We walked back to the table and I sat across from the boy. My heart was beating out of my chest as they counted us down. I got the first jump on him. I was winning, but the boy was strong. Just when I thought I had him pinned, my arm started to give out. I lost my balance. That little waiver gave him the upper hand. Sweat was pouring down our faces; it was the longest arm wrestle I've ever been in. I remember looking into his eyes and seeing a bead of sweat drip off the end of his nose. I watched it land on top of my hand as he forced my arm down. Then I heard my father's voice. He said, 'Don't let us down; don't let your pack down!' Then all of a sudden my arm started moving in the opposite direction. The boy was pulling my hand on top of his. Before I knew what was happening, I was pinning him. My father and Monte lifted me on their shoulders and danced around the table. The boy shook my hand and just walked away. He didn't care that he lost."

"What does arm wrestling have to do with bloodlines?"

"Nothing I guess. Conall was trying to prove that half-breeds are just as strong as purebloods, and he was right. Only the boy debunked his theory in another way. If that boy were strong, in heart and mind, he wouldn't have let me win."

"You're wrong, he was strong in heart and that's why he let you win," I tell him.

"So, you're saying I have a weak heart?"

Jesus, he so temperamental.

"No, I'm saying he had a strong heart, too. Sacrificing your happiness for someone you barely know, that takes courage and strength. Let me ask you something? How did Monte and Lowell treat that kid after he lost?"

Dillan reflects for a moment then says, "Not very nice."

"Imagine what would have happened if you lost?" Dillan flinches at the thought.

"It takes a strong person to lose with dignity."

"See, this is why I love you. You can twist something like losing into a good thing!" Dillan grabs my hand and brings it to his lips.

I'm not sure if his remark is sweet or condescending. I decide not to dwell on it.

"So, why is everyone so afraid of half-breeds? Aren't we all technically half-breeds?"

"No, we are not. We are wolves in human form with a gene that allows us to shift back to true form. Half breeds are humans with a gene that allows them to shift to wolf form."

"Sounds like the same thing to me."

"Well, it isn't." Dillan is getting agitated. "And soon we'll have a blood test to prove purity, and the Shastas will have no place to hide."

"Why does it matter?"

"For the merge. We have been trying to merge the packs for decades. We're finally at a point where that can happen. You being here will make it happen, because you have the blood of both packs. Our children will have the blood of both packs."

I blush when he mentions *our* children.

"The pack with the most pureblood alphas leads. Right now Shasta is claiming to have the numbers. But we don't believe their numbers are accurate. The blood test will show purity, and my father estimates more than sixty percent of the Shastas documented as pureblood will be invalidated, giving the Sierras control of the pack."

"What does it matter if I have blood on both sides?"

"It's about council votes. It works like the US government. Republicans and Democrats in the senate. The majority rules."

Did he really just reference political parties? The idea that we were one big happy pack is starting to dissipate. We're a species that determines worth on an arm wrestling game. Layla is right, changes need to be made. We are just the women to make them.

CHAPTER TEN:

CAMP

We arrive at the campsite, and I find that it is just that. An old abandoned summer camp for kids. The camp sits on the edge of Ice Lake. The name worries me.

I hate the cold.

We are greeted at the entrance by Drake and Tripp. They open the huge metal gate that surrounds the camp, and we pull in. After they close and lock us inside, the guys jump in the back of Dillan's truck. A dozen or so trucks are parked in a makeshift lot, but Dillan drives past them to the center of the camp, where everyone is waiting.

Leah, Clio, Patsy, and her mate, Ray, are standing in front of the group. All of the high-ranking Sierra Lunam couples are here. There are ten other adults, and I see a few kids in various stages of childhood. This is my branch of the pack. My new family.

They gather around Dillan and me like we're rock stars. I look in the crowd for Cassie's friendly face and remember she isn't here. I wonder what kind of reception she received in Dunsmuir.

"Hey sis," Leah greets me, and I put thoughts of Cassie out of my head for now.

"I hope you aren't pissed at me for not telling you at Lunam, but well, you know."

I tell her it's ok and that I look forward to getting to know her. She seems happy to hear this.

Clio and Patsy offer to help me unpack, while the guys drag Dillan off to tour the compound. One thing Lowell mentioned at dinner last night was that Dillan and I are the leaders of this pack. The older, more experienced members are only here as advisors. We are in charge.

After the welcome we received and the doting that's already begun, I am starting to feel the pressure of being a leader.

I look around and see dilapidated buildings encircling us. Lowell said the camp was rustic, this is barely inhabitable. Even our apartment in Nevada was better than this.

"Where am I sleeping? Please tell me it isn't a tent."

The girls giggle as they lead me to my cabin, which they tell me is in the back of the campsite, the last cabin before a clearing. About one hundred yards behind the cabins sits a tall tower that overlooks the entire camp.

"What's that?"

"It's the fort." Leah laughs. "You know how boys are."

I ask if people are really up there on lookout and she says yes.

"We are in the middle of nowhere. We need our own security from animals and thieves."

I guess that makes sense. I shouldn't look at it as being locked in the compound. The gate is actually here to protect us. I have to stop being so negative.

We arrive at my cabin and the girls start to giggle.

"Welcome to your new home," Leah announces and produces a key from her pocket.

A weathered piece of wood is nailed above the door. It says Iroquois. Clio sees me reading it and tells me all the buildings have names.

"I have Mt. Diablo," she says. "Patsy has Mt. Rainer, and Leah is in Blackfoot." She points to the cabin we just passed. Looks like Leah and I are neighbors.

Leah opens the door and a rush of warm air smacks us in the face.

"Sorry!" She runs to the thermostat to turn it down. "I must have left it on when I was straightening up last night."

"By straightening up she means christening every empty cabin in the camp!" Patsy laughs and Leah pretends she is joking.

"Don't listen to her, Kalysia. Her family are all known liars." Leah sticks her tongue out at Patsy.

From the outside you would never guess that the cabin has been transformed into a posh bungalow.

"This is amazing." I run my hand along the plush wine-colored sofa. The art on the walls and the perfectly placed vases on the table have Adel written all over them.

Leah shows me the small but completely updated kitchen, and then leads me into the bedroom. The bed sits in the center of a square room. It's not as big as Dillan's bed, but it will do just fine. The duvet is made of some sort of luxurious velvet, and there are about twenty pillows laid out in perfect order.

I ask Leah if all the cabins look like this. She says no, but they have been updated with basic amenities. It makes me feel a little bit better.

There is just one more room, the bathroom. The last door in the hall is a large closet.

"There's just one bedroom?" I wonder aloud.

"What were you expecting?" Clio asks.

"I just thought, you know, there would be an extra room for..." I can't even say it out loud.

"For children?" Leah guesses. I nod. "Our children will be in the nursery with the nannies."

I guess I should be relieved that someone more qualified than me would take care of my child, but on the other hand, it's so callous. I can't imagine a stranger raising me better than Layla did.

"It's the way the pack works. The children are all kept together. It's a safety issue," Leah explains.

I hear a knock on the back door, followed by stomping. I leave the girls fussing over the jetted bathtub to see who is making all the noise. I find Dillan and Drake on the back porch, kicking mud off their shoes. Dillan looks up with a smile.

"Do you love it?"

I step into his arms and kiss him.

"You know I do."

He gives me a good hard squeeze then sets me down. "I should actually call Adel and thank her."

Dillan smiles and kisses my cheek.

"She'd like that."

The fridge is stocked with food and beer. I pull out a six-pack and hand them out. We settle in the living room, and I realize for the first time in my life, I have a place that feels like home.

I stand in the middle of the room and raise my beer.

"To family," I toast. Leah puts her hand over her heart and looks as if she may cry.

Dillan stands beside me and raises his beer.

"To family," he repeats, and everyone raises their bottles in unison.

Over the next few weeks, we fall into a comfortable routine. Dillan wakes at the crack of dawn and goes for a run. After he leaves, I get up and shower. I'm still not totally comfortable with him seeing me in my morning state. By the time he returns, sweaty and exhilarated, I am presentable.

Dillan usually kicks his running shoes off and pads quietly through the cabin, hoping to find me in bed. One of these days I will oblige him, but for now, I get up to start my day.

Leaving our bed is a difficult task. We aren't the only ones; Leah and Drake spent three days in their cabin our first week here. Dillan had to pound on their door to get Drake out.

I set up a schedule for everyone to follow; this makes everyone accountable for their time, even me.

Leah and Patsy are in charge of meals, Clio works in the nursery, and I keep everything in order. We have inventory to maintain, supplies that need ordering, and a large group of betas that need supervising.

I know it sounds cold, but betas are a pain in the ass. They literally sit around and do nothing until given a task. But once they have something to do, they get it done.

My problem is coming up with ways they can help. I didn't believe Leah when she told me betas are like a pack of wild dogs, but she was right. When you leave them to their own vices, they will eat, drink, and fight all day long.

I don't think it has anything to do with their breeding, it's just that nobody has ever made them accountable. They're followers, they don't know how to govern themselves. I totally understand, sometimes it's easier being told what to do.

Responsibility is overrated.

Layla worked three jobs at times, so making sure we had things like milk and toothpaste fell to me. Learning those things early really helped me get organized. I find myself silently thanking my mother a lot lately.

Our camp is growing very popular in the pack. We have a long list of betas and low alphas that want to transfer in. The betas in our pack are not chosen at random.

Monte and Lowell handpicked each one. We have males that specialize in carpentry, electrical, computers, and even some ex-soldiers, Carrick and Sid. They're from Drake's family, cousins I think. They stroll around in camo pants and tight army-green t-shirts.

Sid is a bit of a flirt. He brings flowers to all the single females, and they follow him around like he's Elvis.

Rusty and Carrick butt heads a lot. Whether it's about what kind of light bulbs burn longer or which truck gets better gas mileage, they will always be on opposing sides.

Dillan says I shouldn't worry; they will eventually fight it out. I don't like the idea of anyone in camp fighting, but Dillan says it's how the males determine their rank. Rusty shouldn't have to rank, since he's my brother, Monte's son.

Rusty is a great catch for someone like Cassie. He is the son of a leader, he has pure blood, and he's a really nice guy.

He's also a workaholic.

It's a shame, because Rusty has a really good heart. The only time I've ever seen him without a smile on his face is when Carrick is around.

I leave the lodge, the large building in the center of camp, and head out to do food inventory. It's late November, and the air has turned a bitter cold. I tighten the scarf around my neck and pull my beanie down to cover my ears.

Leah said we're getting low on milk and eggs. The food is kept in the Hopi cabin; it's the closest cabin to the lodge where we eat. There is a large outdoor dining area, but it is way too cold to have meals outside.

Some of the cabins have kitchens, but we prepare all the meals in the lodge. That was one of my rules. I didn't think it was fair for those with kitchens to take food back to their cabins. Dillan wasn't too thrilled when I pulled the food and beer from our refrigerator and placed it with the rest of the camp food. I let him keep a case of wine Adel had hidden in a cabinet behind a set of pots that I've never used.

If we ever do open a bottle, we'll share it with whoever wants a glass. That's the way it should be. The food is for all of us, not just the council members. If we want steak, everyone gets steak. Drake and Leah had different views on the food distribution. They felt we should have first dibs. Even Dillan sided with them, although he told me later that he didn't want to create any kind of animosity between us and them. It's good to be on opposite sides every now and then just to show we're fair.

I never realized there was such a divide between alphas and betas. It's strange to have my peers, and members of my pack, look at me differently. I don't feel more powerful, but I am, and I have to know my role, my place, in order to keep the balance.

Twigs and leaves crunch under my boots as I walk to Hopi. The playground outside the lodge is empty. Some mornings the children play on the swings after breakfast, but it's too cold now.

The infirmary building doubles as the nursery. It's decked out with cribs and playpens. There's even a bedroom for the nannies. Most of them have children of their own, so they don't mind sleeping close to the smelly, crying, little monsters.

I reach the cabin and pull my keys out. Locking up the food was another issue for me, but Dillan adamantly agreed with Drake and Leah on keeping the food safe. Their argument about keeping animals and small children from pillaging our food supply seemed reasonable. I still felt shitty for having to lock the others out. I suggested we leave the key accessible to the adults, but I was shot down.

"What the others need is balance; they can live without a midnight snack," Dillan had said.

I guess he was right about that too. Other than Clio asking for extra juice boxes for the children, no one has ever bothered me for extra food.

Besides Dillan and me, the other council members have keys—Rusty, Leah, Drake, Ray, Patsy, Tripp and Clio. We had to install the same type of governing system in camp that the pack uses. Someday we might have actual power over the pack, but for now we just run our little piece of it. It feels very elitist, but we need the structure. People need to know who is in charge.

Who to go to when something is wrong. Who to turn to when they need a favor. I try to keep things fair. Like food. We sign our name beside the item that has been taken and mark the quantity. This keeps us honest and accountable. We all do it, except Dillan. He never comes here. He doesn't even have his key on him. It's hanging on a hook in our kitchen.

Hopi is climate controlled. The pantry is set to sixty-five degrees, which felt cool when we arrived in late fall. Now it feels warm inside. I pull my beanie off and unravel my scarf. I grab the clipboard off the wall beside the walk-in fridge and see Leah's name beside the items she took for breakfast this morning. Clio also stopped by for yogurt and granola for the kids.

We are down to fourteen dozen eggs and the milk is close to expiration. Looks like we need to make another food run. The closest grocery store is forty miles away in Folsom. The highway is a narrow two-lane road that winds through the mountains. I get car sick every time I go on a run. Since we need to go shopping, I might as well inventory the dry goods. The less time I spend on that road the better.

I'm halfway done when I hear someone pull into camp central. I look out the window and see Dillan's truck.

I didn't even know he left the camp.

He's never left without telling me before. I hope everything is ok. I run outside to see what's going on, leaving my jacket in Hopi.

The cold air hits me like a brick wall. I stop to go back and get my coat, then I see her. She hops out of the passenger door and looks around. I forget the cold and sprint towards her.

CHAPTER ELEVEN:

SHASTA CLAUSE

Cassie spins around just as I crash into her. The warmth of the truck and Dillan's scent surrounds her. It feels odd smelling Dillan on another female. Something pinches the inside of my stomach. Cassie is crushed in my embrace, unable to move or speak. I feel her arms squeeze back and hear her sniffle.

"Are you surprised?" Dillan leans on the side of the truck.

I leave Cassie and run into his arms. I kiss him hard, forgetting Cassie is there.

Dillan drops Cassie's bags on the ground, then twists his fingers in my loose hair, and pulls my hips to him. The movement makes me shiver.

"Where's your jacket?" He starts to pull his coat off, but I stop him.

"I left it in Hopi. I'm fine." My body disagrees. I shudder in the cold breeze, and Dillan wraps me in his coat.

"I'll go get it," Cassie offers and steps away. "Just point me in the right direction."

Dillan's radio hums and he fumbles in his pocket to pull out the handheld radio.

Cell reception is horrible up here, so the guys use the handheld. Sid calls them walkies.

"What's up, Drake?" Dillan speaks into the walkie.

"We'll go together," I whisper to Cassie and step out of Dillan's arms.

He pulls me back for a goodbye kiss then jumps back in the truck and drives slowly past camp central towards Genny.

Genny is the building with all the camp controls, like power and Wi-Fi, if we can ever get it working. We're lucky to have electricity and running water, for that I'm grateful.

I help Cassie with her bags. There are only two of them, and we head to the cabin I reserved for her. I never gave up hope that she would come. Even after Dillan told me his father was having no luck convincing Conall to let his only daughter leave his pack for ours. Cassie is the last of his bloodline. Asking him to let her leave and join another pack with no hope of producing an heir was a long shot. But I had faith and now she's here and I couldn't be happier.

"Mt. Shasta." Cassie reads the name above the door while I fish for my master key.

"Yes." I smile as the lock clicks open.

The cabin is a large open room with a small kitchen and decent-sized bathroom. It was filled with old board games and a pool table. Ray and Tripp wanted to set it up as a man cave, but I pulled rank and told them to find another cabin. Mt. Shasta is four buildings away from mine and sits on the edge of the woods, so Cassie can have some privacy.

Patsy helped me clean it out, and we moved furniture from one of the empty remodeled cabins into this one.

"It's cozy," Cassie says as she sets her bag on the sofa.

"It converts to a bed, see." I pull up a cushion to show her the bed underneath. "We can get you a real bed if this one isn't comfortable. I just figured the space is small, and this way, you can fold it up in the daytime in case you have guests over."

"Yeah, right," Cassie says bitterly. "Like Sierras really want to socialize with me."

Her tone surprises me. "I'm a Sierra." It hurts me to think of us as enemies.

"The females here will see me as a threat." She picks at a loose thread on her scarf.

I take her hand and pull her onto the couch.

"Everyone here knows how important you are to me. I have your back."

Cassie looks up and smiles. I can see there is something she wants to say, but she holds back. Then I recall our last conversation. She said she didn't want to leave her family, and now here she is with me, because I wanted her.

"Cassie, if you don't want to be here, I will tell Dillan to take you home." The thought of her and Dillan driving back to Shasta together causes a pain in my chest. Maybe I'll have Rusty take her home.

"No, I agreed to come. I wanted to see you. I'm just feeling out of place and I miss my family already." Her eyes are glossy with tears.

I pull her in for a hug. Dillan's scent has faded, thankfully. "Don't feel out of place, this is your home now. I will make sure everyone knows it."

I leave Cassie to get settled in and head back to Hopi to finish the inventory and let Dillan know we need to make a food run. The sun feels warm on my face; I lift my chin and inhale. I'll never be able to live in the desert again. I'll miss the smell of the trees and grass too much.

Suddenly, this place doesn't feel so bad. I have Dillan and Cassie. My life is complete. Once Cassie gets enrolled in classes and maybe even meets people outside the pack, she'll see this was the best option for her.

I finish the inventory and lock up. The children are finally outside playing; I hear their laughter and screaming before I even reach the playground.

I wave at Clio. She's sitting on the bench with one of the older kids, reading a book.

"Kalysia," she calls to me. "Wait up." I stop and let her fall in step with me.

"I heard about Cassie," she says cautiously. "Are you ok?"

"Why wouldn't I be ok? I asked her to come, she's my friend. Actually, she's family."

Cassie called us cousins, but I know now that is what pack members call each other whether they have actual blood ties or not.

"Look, I don't believe in this Shasta-Sierra pack rivalry. My mother was Shasta and my father is Sierra, I feel connected to both sides. I expect all of you, especially my closest friends, to respect my wishes and accept Cassie as part of our family now."

I watch Clio shrink down a bit. Her head bows and she walks half a step behind me. "Do you understand?" I stop and look down at her.

"Yes," she says quietly. "I understand, she's family." Clio nods and steps back even further.

"Maybe you should get back to the kids," I suggest and she shuffles away.

My office, if you want to call it that, is next to the lodge. It's a small building, about ten feet by ten feet in size. It's just one large open room with a small storage closet off to the side. Leah and I each have a desk and computers that Leah deems useless without an internet connection.

I use mine to track inventory, and I started files on everyone in camp. Just to keep records of births and matches, that sort of thing. This way there is no question as to our bloodline or lineage.

I also have spreadsheets for job assignments, so we know where everyone is supposed to be at all times. I keep track of all of our food runs, and soon I'll track our beer deliveries.

The brewing is going great. I only visited the brewhouse once since I've been here. It's a trek up the hill by foot. The only vehicles that can make it through brush and trees are reserved for the people that work out there. So, unless you hitch a ride in the morning with one of the workers, the brew house is cut off from camp.

Dillan said we need to start distribution soon, but we are still waiting on licensing. Technically, we are brewing illegally. Not only by human law, but we are also breaking a pack rule.

When Dillan's grandfather bought the winery that started Sierra-Duke, he created a set of rules. These rules were put in place so other branches couldn't start similar businesses and compete with Tuluka. Dillan called it a non-compete clause. The irony of it is that nobody ever had enough power or money to compete, and now the rule is biting them in the ass.

In the mid-eighties, Shasta found a niche of their own. They started brewing beer. Every branch has their own variation of the same recipe. Shasta was the first to bottle and sell it. They opened a brewery in Dunsmuir, where Cassie is from, and their business took off. Soon they were distributing beer all over the country. The Tuluka branch is now breaking its own rule by jumping into the beer industry.

All of the branches are required to give the elders a percentage of their business. Thirty-seven percent to be exact. The Dunsmuir branch used money from the pack bank to start their brewery, so they have to give a higher percentage to the elders. Conall has to give more than fifty percent of his profit to the pack bank.

Dillan says Conall has been looking for a way to buy the elders out. To do that, he needs a lot of money. The Sierras offered to help, but he refused. So, Lowell and Monte decided to start a beer business of their own. Thanks to the non-compete clause, they have to get permission from Conall before we can sell a drop.

Dillan thinks Conall is dragging out his approval because once the Sierras start to brew, he will lose even more power. The pack with the most money and pureblood alphas will eventually run the elder council and bank. I just hope Conall makes his decision soon, because according to Dillan we are at max capacity. We need to sell the beer we've made before we run out of places to store it.

Cassie being here may be an indication that Conall has decided to let us brew, and he's just making Monte and Lowell sweat it out. It isn't like he can actually say no, the elders would overrule him if he did. Asking Conall for permission is mostly done out of respect.

I'm going through the latest stack of mail when Leah walks in. "Hey," I say. "I have the list we need for the food run. Do you want to radio Drake and let him know?" I look out the window at the ominous clouds looming overhead. "We should go before it snows."

"Yeah, ok." Leah sits at her desk and fiddles with the knobs on her radio.

"What?" I say when I catch her watching me.

"I just heard Cassie is here."

I can't tell if she's just stating a fact or if she's upset. She can't still be angry about Lunam. It was one dance.

I raise an eyebrow to her. "Seriously? You're going to give me crap now?"

Leah shakes her head and holds her hands up. "No, no. I just wanted to make sure you're cool with this?" She says hesitantly. "You understand the position she is in, right?"

Cassie is in no position whatsoever.

"She doesn't want any trouble; she's here because I asked her to come. And, we need her father to agree to let us brew."

Leah nods like she is considering what I've said to be true. But I can tell by the look on her face that she doesn't believe me. I drop the mail on my desk and look at her.

"What is it?"

"A girl like Cassie, an unmatched pureblood." Leah rolls her eyes as she says this. Cassie's lineage is under debate. "A female like her is a wild card."

I stifle a laugh and ask her what she means.

"Have you ever heard of rule seventy-five?"

"No." I shrug.

"This allows pureblood males to mate with multiple partners. This way we will get the maximum amount of pureblood births. It was put in place in eighteen seventy-five. It's been used every Lunam since."

"What does that have to do with Cassie?" I ask, but I already know where she's going with this.

"Rule seventy-five is how Monte ended up with two kids at Lunam. It means any one of the males in this pack can mate with Cassie this season, and there is nothing we can do about it."

"I get it; you're worried about Drake."

I'm only partially joking. I know what she is getting at, but she's wrong.

"No!" Leah exclaims. "Drake would never be with a Shasta."

The look of disgust on Leah's face angers me.

"Then get to your point? We have work to do," I spit back.

Leah stands and slams her hand on the desk; this small act of defiance causes my skin to grow warm. I lean on my desk and glare at her until she backs down.

"I guess I don't have a point, sis," Leah finally says. "I just want you to watch your back."

"Isn't that what I have you for?" I crack a smile, but Leah just walks out of the office.

Integrating Cassie into the pack is going to be harder than I thought. I have to show everyone she isn't a threat and that I trust her.

CHAPTER TWELVE:

SNOW

The last four weeks have been hell on earth, hell on a frozen earth. I never knew how cold snow really was. When you see it on TV or atop the peak of a faraway mountain, you think, *ah snow, how beautiful and soft you look.*

You see kids in commercials making snow angels and tossing snowballs that disintegrate upon landing. I don't know what kind of snow they have on TV, but it is nothing like the hard-packed, wet, sticky crap we have here. The snowballs Dillan and the rest of the men hurl at each other have broken several windows. I've fallen twice on something called black ice. The kids all have runny noses, and my hands are in a perpetual state of cold.

Having Cassie here has been comforting. She still doesn't mingle with others as much as I'd like, but we spend a lot of time gossiping in my cabin. I think I finally convinced her to register for school.

There's a college in Folsom where she can take classes a few times a week once the weather is clear. I've wished, on more than one occasion, that we could switch places—in theory of course.

My feelings for Dillan are growing stronger every day. Having his child is starting to feel less like a duty I need to fulfill, and more like an honor.

I've stopped complaining about it to Cassie, since her only chance to keep her bloodline from diminishing is to conceive during this mating season. Her choices are slim. All the high alphas are paired up. The only alpha I would even consider matching her with is Rusty. But he is hell-bent on staying single and childless.

He jokes about child support and dirty diapers, even though he knows those are human issues. Our children are raised together, their food, clothes, and education are paid for out of pack funds. Each branch gets an allowance for education. Dillan said all the Sierra branches allotted money for college. Cassie tells me it's different in Shasta.

The Dunsmuir branch controls the education funds for all branches. Almost all the kids are homeschooled because they're afraid of commingling. Each branch has females that act as teachers. They use the education money to buy computers and workbooks. Any leftover money is redistributed to other areas, like housing.

Shasta members live mostly in trailer parks owned by the pack. She moved into a house with Conall once the brewery and pub started to make money. According to Cassie, Shasta is just now coming into its own. They are working on building more housing, and they sent two boys to college last year.

Now Sierra wants to compete for business. She says she doesn't have any animosity towards the Sierras, but her facial expressions tell a different story.

If Cassie matched with a pureblood alpha from Shasta, that would've solidified her pack's future. Without a clear heir to the Shasta pack, the Sierra's will gain full control in a merge. The future of their pack was riding on Cassie and she failed. Cassie knew there were only two pureblood Shasta males in Lunam; she took a chance and lost.

I feel bad for her, and that's why I'm trying like hell to make sure her future isn't one of servitude. She doesn't need a partner or mate to determine her worth. I tell her that every day. Hopefully, she starts to believe me.

"Can you please remind me why they chose this camp for us?" I call to Leah, who is running beside me towards Hopi. Snow flurries pick up the fresh-laid powder, making visibility very poor. The children's play structure has frozen over, as well as the water pipes to half the camp.

"Because they want us to stay indoors and screw like animals to produce heirs," she yells loudly so I can hear her through my ear muffs. "And to torture us," she adds as she loses her balance.

I grip her arm and hold her up, but it's difficult with the wet snow and our hysterical laughing. We make it to Hopi in one piece and begin to strip off our top layer of clothing. I take off my snow-covered beanie and gloves then unzip my snow jacket, and hang them all on the wall. Leah does the same.

I pull the inventory list from the wall and notice a strange entry from the night before. This can't be right. Dillan's name is listed beside a bottle of red wine from and a package of dark chocolates.

"Looks like someone had fun last night." Leah reads the list from over my shoulder. "If you let me and Drake have a bottle of wine, I won't rat you out to the others."

Alcohol taken from Hopi can only be consumed in the lodge. We don't allow anyone to sit around drinking alone, not even couples. Alcohol is for social occasions only.

Last night, Dillan didn't come home with a bottle of wine, and I helped Patsy close up the lodge. Dillan wasn't there. In fact, he didn't come in until late. I assumed he was with Tripp and Ray, working on the water pipes and the electrical issues.

"Well, can we have a bottle?" Leah asks from the pantry. "It is New Year's Eve."

"Yeah, sure," I tell her, and she squeals with excitement.

"I gotta go. I think I left the lights on in my cabin." I grab my hat and coat from the wall and leave.

My breathing is labored as I drudge through the snow. We got six inches last night, so the path from Hopi to my cabin on the opposite side of the camp is thick and hard to walk in.

I should radio Rusty and ask him to get someone out here to clear the path. It's dangerous, and one of the children may fall and get stuck. But I don't want to talk to anyone right now. Not until I figure out what is going on and where Dillan was last night with a bottle of wine.

Why would Dillan pull wine from Hopi when we have a secret stash in our cabin? If he wanted a bottle, all he had to do was come to the cabin and get one. Unless he didn't want me to know about it.

My heart is in my throat as I burst into our cabin and head straight to the kitchen, tracking mud and snow all over the floor. Dillan's key, the one he never uses, is gone. I begin to cry.

I don't know how much time has passed when Clio finds me on the floor.

"Kalysia, are you hurt?" She searches my hands and face for injuries. The rest of my body is hidden by my snow jacket.

Her radio buzzes, and she hurries to reply, "I found her! She's in—"

I pull Clio's radio from her hand and switch it off. She staggers back onto her knees like she's afraid of me.

I take a deep breath to calm myself and try to think of a reasonable excuse for why I'm crying on my kitchen floor. I can't tell her the truth; I don't even know what that is. Clio stays silent beside me. The only sound in the house is my radio beeping in my pocket.

Clio finally stirs; she pulls her feet from under her and sits on the floor. She clears her throat to speak, but I stop her.

"Tell them you found me sleeping in my cabin and that I must have caught a cold from one of the children. Make sure they know I don't want to be bothered."

"Ok," Clio says quietly and starts to stand. "Can I get you anything? Tea?"

"No, thank you," I say and give her walkie back. Clio steps over me to head out the back door and I grab her hand. "If Dillan asks..."

She shakes her head. "Don't worry, he's not here. They went on a run this morning to get some supplies for the brew house. They aren't due back until this evening."

I should feel shocked that I'm only hearing about this now, but I feel nothing, as if my body is in energy-saving mode.

"Who went on the run?"

Clio looks confused. "What do you mean?"

"You said *they* went on a run. Who went with Dillan?" I brace for her reply, knowing the answer could expose the person who has betrayed me.

Clio stares at the knobs on her walkie.

"Um, you know, the usual." She won't meet my ice cold glare.

The next thing I know, I'm on my feet and in Clio's face.

"Who is it? Who is with him?" I hiss.

Clio cowers and looks at the floor as she speaks. "It's just, you said she was family."

I'm in a full sprint to Cassie's cabin. I leap up the stairs and turn the handle. It's locked. I bang once on the door and it rattles the windows.

We never lock our cabins. The betas don't have master keys; they need access to the cabins so they can clean or drop off laundry.

The idea of someone stealing never even crossed my mind. Especially with Sid and Carrick's hi-tech security system. There are cameras with facial recognition all over camp. Besides, nobody here has any reason to steal. Everyone has everything they need.

Except Cassie.

I fish around my pocket for the master key and fumble with the lock, but it's hard to get the key in with my trembling hands.

"Here," Clio says, "let me do it."

I step aside and allow Clio to open the door. She walks into the warm room ahead of me. The sofa bed is unmade, the blankets askew. My mind plays dirty tricks on me as visions of Dillan and Cassie flood my brain.

I start to see the things that Clio and Leah were warning me about.

Cassie sitting next to Dillan in the lodge, Dillan and Cassie walking back from the tower together, and Cassie sitting in the snowmobile with Ray and Dillan, coming back from the brew house.

I thought he was showing her around for the benefit of her father, to convince Conall to lift the non-compete clause.

"I thought you knew," Clio says quietly.

"What are you talking about?" I yell.

"I noticed her shadowing Dillan, but you said you knew why she was here, so I kept my opinions to myself. I told Patsy to do the same. I don't think Leah noticed. Cassie never stays around her too long."

"Dillan was just showing her the camp so she would convince her father to let us brew." Even as I say this, I don't believe it, not anymore. "Cassie is my friend; she came here to be with me." *I was going to live vicariously through her and her through me.*

Clio shakes her head. "She didn't come here for you, Kalysia. She came for Dillan."

CHAPTER THIRTEEN:

GAME CHANGER

It's dark by the time Dillan returns.

Clio radios me, as soon as Tripp drives out to meet his truck at the gate. Clio is the only one who knows about my meltdown today, and I plan to keep it that way.

After she left, I went back to Cassie's. I looked for the empty bottle of wine, but it wasn't there. Dillan isn't that stupid, he must have tossed it in one of the dumpsters. I didn't find the chocolates either.

I found no trace that Dillan was in her cabin, except his scent. It was all over the cushions of her sofa bed. Not the mattress, just the cushions. Which means they didn't even have time to open the bed. The thought is like fire in my veins.

I've had all day to think about what to say, what I would do. I even considered leaving. That doesn't accomplish anything. Leaving Dillan would mean abandoning my family, and I would be no different than Layla. At least she had me; if I left I'd be outcast and alone.

I'm bound by my duty as a pureblood and leader of this pack to stay. When it comes down to it, for all my whining about college and having my own life, I can't leave. I don't want to. I also don't want to be part of some polygamist love triangle.

I wish my phone worked. Layla would know what to do, how to handle Cassie. Actually, she would say I'm an idiot for bringing her here.

Nobody can help me now. I need to figure this out on my own.

I hear Drake call to Dillan from their cabin. He'll be here any minute, and I still haven't decided if I should confront him about Cassie. I pick up the half-empty wine bottle and take it to the kitchen sink. I place it next to the empty one on the counter.

"I'm home, babe." Dillan's voice is like nails on a chalkboard. "You awake?"

I hear him kick his boots off and hang his coat on the hook by the front door. I place my empty wine glass in the sink and then head to the bathroom.

"There you are," he says when I walk out of the kitchen.

I keep my eyes on the floor until I enter the bathroom. I turn on the sink and begin to brush my teeth. Dillan slides up behind me and wraps his arms around my waist. I smell her on him. This isn't the first time, but now I know why.

Dillan senses my frigidness and pulls back. "Are you ok?"

NO! I scream in my head. *I'm not ok, you lying cheating bastard! How could you do this to me? We were supposed to be partners, for life. You and me. Now you've ruined everything.*

I spit out a mouthful of toothpaste and toss my toothbrush into the cup on the sink then turn off the water.

"I'm fine," I say through gritted teeth.

I spin out of Dillan's arms and walk to the bedroom. I gain nothing from accusations; I need actual proof before I can confront him. In the meantime, I will swallow my pride and smile like some helpless, lovesick beta.

"Have I done something?" Dillan stands hesitantly in the doorway to our bedroom.

Deep breath, Kalysia. You can pull this off; you're stronger and smarter than he is.

"I'm just tired, I guess." I unzip the fleece hoodie I've had on all day and sit on the bed.

Dillan crosses the room and kneels in front of me. "Are you sure you're ok? Leah said you've been cooped up all day with a cold." He presses his hand to my cheek. "Do you need the doctor?"

"No," I snap. *Deep breath.* "I'm fine."

Dillan doesn't seem to notice I'm seething as he stares at me with his lying eyes. His ignorance irritates me.

Doesn't he know me at all?

"Lie down and I'll bring you some water." He runs his hand along the side of my face. His eyes are full of concern, or maybe it's guilt. I can't tell anymore.

Maybe I don't know him either. I force a smile and scoot onto the bed. Dillan pulls the throw blanket from the bottom of the bed over my legs. It's amazing how attentive cheaters become when they know they're on the verge of being outed.

Dillan leaves, and I look around the room. My room. I don't want to leave this room, this cabin, or the camp. This is my home. Dillan returns with a glass of water and a strange look on his face. His eyes narrow when he looks at me.

"Here." He shoves the water in my hand and walks out.

I throw the blanket off my legs and charge after him. I slam the glass on the kitchen table and water splashes onto the floor.

"What the hell is your problem?" My voice bounces off the walls.

I see Dillan's arms tense through his tight-fitting thermal shirt. He spins around with a wine bottle in each hand.

"Who was here!" He drops the bottles and they crash onto the floor then leaps across the shattered glass and grabs my arm.

"Let me go!" I try to yank free, but he is too strong, much stronger than me. "How dare you accuse *me* of being with someone else, when you're running around behind my back with Cassie!"

His grip loosens, but he doesn't let go. "I know what's going on, Dillan. How could you do this to me? To us?" My voice cracks. "I trusted you." A traitorous tear runs down my cheek.

Dillan's eyes fill with fear.

"It's not what you think." He clears his throat. "I didn't want any of this to happen." His voice cracks as he struggles to maintain his composure. "I love you, Kalysia."

I yank my arm, and this time he lets go. "How dare you say that." I stand taller and try to meet his eyes. "You don't know the meaning of the words."

"And you do?" Dillan spits back. "You've never even told me you loved me."

His words feel like a knife in my chest.

"All I have ever tried to do was make you happy, and all I wanted in return was for you to love me."

He's right. He has been the perfect boyfriend, partner, mate—until now. But he's wrong about my feelings for him. I don't express myself as easily as he can. He said I didn't have to say the words; he could feel them.

Dillan sees the anguish in my eyes and softens his tone.

"I know you care for me. But if you had a choice, would you choose me or would you choose another life?"

My eyes dart to the floor. The question isn't fair. He knows my answer, because he would choose the same way.

"You wouldn't be here if it wasn't for your father," I start to say, but Dillan holds his hands up to stop me.

"You're right, I wouldn't be here if I didn't have a duty to my family. Neither one of us would be *here*." He looks relieved in a way, like he's been holding this truth in for a long time. We stand only a few feet away from each other, but we are miles apart. "I know you would rather be in a dorm writing boring English lit papers and going to frat parties." He tries to joke, but I'm too tired to smile. "I have an idea where I would be."

His eyes drift above my head as he imagines the life he would live if we were free.

"You want to leave," I say. The thought of him not wanting me crushes my chest.

The one thing I've been holding on to this entire time is the fact that Dillan and I belong together. If that isn't true, then my whole life is a lie. A juvenile fantasy that I've created in my head. I choke back tears and try not to crumble to the floor.

Dillan feels my body give out and snaps back to reality.

"If I had a chance to leave, one that wouldn't disrupt the lives of people I care about, I would take it." He looks at me with a sad expression. "But I can't imagine any kind of life without you." He takes both of my hands and holds them between us. "I love you, Kalysia. I know in my heart that it's real." His foots slips on a piece of glass and he lifts me into his arms and carries me to the living room.

He sets me down and we look towards the unlit fireplace.

"What do we do now?" I pluck the threads on top of the sofa. I want to ask him if he loves Cassie, but the words are like razor cuts on my tongue. "I mean, what happens to us?"

Dillan shrugs and slowly shakes his head. "I don't want to hurt you. I never wanted to hurt you. You have to know that." Dillan hesitantly steps towards me. When I don't back away, he steps closer. He takes my hand in his and I turn to face him.

"Things would be so much easier if I didn't have feelings for you."

His words are like a kick to the chest. He doesn't want to care for me. He doesn't want to love me. Because he wants her.

He's right, things would be so much easier if we didn't care about each other. Then maybe I could walk away. We could walk away and not look back. But I do care. About the pack, and about Dillan. I wish this was easier.

If I let him take me in his arms and kiss me. I can forget about the betrayal and the epic failure that is my life. For now.

And that is what I do. I place my hand on the side of Dillan's face, he leans into my palm and closes his eyes. I guide his mouth towards mine. The kiss full of longing and heartache. I lead Dillan to the bedroom and we make love with more emotion, more love than ever before. It isn't even about pleasure, although feeling Dillan inside me is like perfection. I don't want this with anyone else. I only wish Dillan felt the same.

After we've finished, I lie in his arms and wonder if he held Cassie this way. Did he kiss her head and tell her she was amazing?

Stop it, Kalysia.

Thoughts like that will drive me crazy. I just want to enjoy this before I'm forced to deal with what to do next.

Dillan rubs my shoulder and kisses my head. "It's ten-thirty," he says.

I look at the clock. "So?"

"It's New Year's Eve; we should go to the lodge with the others. They're expecting us."

He's right, but I don't want to leave our bed. I don't want to face the reality of our lives. I don't want to see Cassie. Seeing Cassie will make it real, again. Right now, I'm happy pretending Dillan and I are the same two people we were in his tent at Lunam.

"Come on." He sits up and I fall face first into the bed. His scent lingers in the sheets, mixed with the fabric softener the betas use. I sniff deeply; the smell is strong, much stronger than the faint smell I detected on Cassie's sofa.

"Let's go, beautiful," Dillan says as he pulls on his boxers. He opens the dresser and takes out a clean t-shirt, pulling it on with a huge smile on his face.

Is it arrogance or ignorance that allows him to pretend he isn't breaking my heart. Doesn't he have any remorse at all? I can't leave this room until I know exactly what happened between them.

"Before we go, I need to know if you were with her last night." I pull the covers over my naked body.

Dillan reaches for the thermal pants we all wear under our clothing. "Was I with who last night?" He pulls them on along with his snow pants and zips them up.

"Cassie."

Dillan sits on the edge of the bed with a confused expression. "Why do you think I was with Cassie?"

His attempt to play dumb is beginning to piss me off.

"You pulled wine and chocolate from Hopi last night," I say. I look at his hands. I wonder if Cassie's hands fit in them as perfectly as mine. If her body tingles at his touch.

Dillan stands quickly and looks down at me. "You think I took wine for me and Cassie?"

"And chocolate," I say quietly.

Dillan lets out a loud laugh. "The wine was for Rusty. I was trying to butter him up."

"Rusty? Why?"

"Because I was hoping he would agree to mate with Cassie, so I wouldn't have to."

Dillan looks at his feet, embarrassed.

I sit up to make sure I'm hearing him correctly. "Are you saying you haven't slept with her?"

"Of course not!" He throws his hands in the air. "I would never *cheat* on you, Kalysia. The deal my father made with Conall was that I would give him an heir to their bloodline. I never planned to go through with it. I don't want her, I want you."

This is the first I've heard about any deals. "Lowell and Conall made a deal? Does this mean they have agreed to let us brew?"

Dillan stands, his face twisted in anger. "If Cassie and I have a child, Conall agreed to merge the packs."

Holy shit. That is huge. If Dillan and Cassie have a child, it will carry both bloodlines, and be able to lead both packs. That means I'm off the hook. But where does that leave my parents?

"Does Monte know about this?"

"I don't think so. My father told me not to tell anyone. Not even you."

"Oh," I say quietly. "I'm glad you did."

"Look, Kalysia, I never planned to go through with it. I only agreed so they would let Cassie come here, for you. I figured I would get one of the other alphas to take my place. Conall doesn't care about my bloodline; he just wants an heir for his family." Dillan pulls me in his arms. "Lowell is the one trying to vie for power. He wants to push Monte out. If I have a child with Cassie, our baby will be the link to merge the packs. Only it will be his heir, not Monte's."

I don't know Monte that well, but I know he is a good leader and he has a good heart. That is why he won the power to lead over Lowell. Being a shrewd businessman doesn't make you a great leader. It also doesn't make you a great father. Lowell is a money-hungry mongrel and now he is trying to overthrow Monte. If I never pushed for Cassie to come here, this would have never happened.

"So, this is all my fault?"

"Don't say that. If you want to blame anyone, blame me. I should have opted out of Lunam. I thought about running, you know. Then I saw you. You looked as scared as I was. I thought you might be running away too. Then you fell and, well, you looked as unsure of it all as I did. I thought, if I match with her, it won't be all that bad."

I remember the moment he's taking about. I was running, until I saw him. He was the reason I went back. He was the reason I went to Lunam in the first place. He is my soulmate.

"We were meant to be together, Dillan. In some way, it was our destiny. We can help each other. We will do it together." I repeat the words he said to me at Lunam.

Dillan kisses my cheek and squeezes me to him. "I'd like that. I just wish your brother was as understanding."

"Did you expect him to just jump at the opportunity to sleep with Cassie?" I'm proud of Rusty for having some self-respect.

"Well, yeah," Dillan laughs. "Most males in his situation would. But he's, uh, *different*." Dillan raises an eyebrow when he says this.

"What do you mean, *different*?"

Dillan smiles and runs his hand over his head. "Um, Cassie isn't his type."

"I don't believe that. Cassie is gorgeous." A sting of jealousy stabs my chest when I think of her now.

Dillan paces the room. "I mean, Rusty doesn't find Cassie sexually attractive."

"Maybe he prefers blondes or something." I don't see why Dillan is so worked up.

"No, he prefers men."

CHAPTER FOURTEEN:

SECRETS

Being raised in the human world, you learn sexual orientation isn't a personal preference, it's something a human is born with. I'm not so sure how it works in wolf packs when our entire being is based on breeding.

"Will he be ok?" I worry about the others and how they will react if they find out.

"I'm ok with it, so they have no choice. But it isn't something that is normally accepted. If he were in another pack, they could do something drastic."

Dillan doesn't have to elaborate. I know the kinds of things homophobes do.

"Well, we have to protect him." I stand up, ready to take on the world. Dillan's eyes glide over my naked body. I pluck his dirty shirt from the floor and pull it on.

"I'm serious; we have to keep his secret."

"I'm not sure Rusty wants to keep it a secret. He's happy with who he is and he doesn't really care what others think. But his partner does."

"He has a partner?"

"Yeah, but he won't tell me who he is or if he's even in our pack. I suspect he is, which is why he wouldn't agree to mate with Cassie."

Dillan's walkie beeps from the living room and we both jump. It isn't like they can hear us, but you never know.

It's Drake asking if we are on our way to the party. Dillan looks at me for final approval.

"Fine, let's go party," I stay and stomp into the bathroom.

We arrive at the lodge forty-five minutes before midnight. Clio's eyes grow wide when she sees us hand in hand.

Everyone is here, even most of the betas, except for the few that are with the children. Most of the females are dressed in snow pants and fleece—it's too cold for formal attire. Leah and Patsy are in jeans with high-heeled boots. Leah is wearing a low-cut blouse that crisscrosses in the front, complimenting her already tiny waistline, while Patsy is in a red cashmere sweater that looks one size too small. I spot Rusty in the corner with Tripp and Ray, doing shots.

I look around the crowd and wonder if his partner is here tonight. Sid and Carrick join the guys for a shot and Rusty moves away. I wonder if Carrick knows about him, and that's why they don't get along. It's possible, but I don't think Carrick is the kind of guy that would keep it a secret. Carrick wouldn't pass up an excuse to tease or bully my brother. He is the reason I need to protect him. Without me, who knows what will happen under someone else's rules. As long as I'm in charge, he will never have to worry about who he loves.

"Have you had enough wine for the night or should I get you a glass?" Dillan whispers with a smile.

"More, please." I kiss his cheek and take off my coat. I hang it on a hook as he heads to the makeshift bar the guys have set up.

As soon as Dillan is out of earshot, Clio rushes to my side. "Is everything, are you—" she stammers.

"It's fine. It was a misunderstanding." I glance around, looking for Cassie. "Is she here?" Clio tells me she left about thirty minutes ago. "Good."

Dillan returns with my wine and says hello to Clio. She lowers her eyes and mumbles happy New Year to him before walking away. "What's her problem?"

I shrug and take a sip of my wine. It doesn't go down as smoothly as it did earlier. "I'm going to get a snack, are you hungry?" Dillan kisses me and says he's fine.

Leah has a fancy spread of cheese, salami, olives, and crackers on the table. She also unwrapped some snack cakes we give the kids for dessert and placed them on a plate.

The last New Year's party I went to was with Layla and Miles. His company threw a big party at one of the Vegas hotels. I snuck too much champagne, and as the crowd counted down the last thirty seconds until midnight, I was puking in a potted plant in the back of the room.

To me, New Year's Eve marked one year closer to my inevitable destiny. I guess it was the same for everyone here. It's finally up to me, to us, to make the best of the lives we've chosen. We may have been born into this life, but we went to Lunam willingly. We all want to be here. Even me.

"Two minutes!" Drake announces. He checks his watch with the large clock on the wall.

I scan the room for Dillan. I'll be damned if I miss my first New Year's kiss. I see everyone moving in the direction of their mates. Suddenly, the door opens and a gust of cold air invades the room. Everyone turns to see who it is.

Cassie looks apologetically at the group and quickly closes the door. I used to feel bad when she walked into a room full of condescending eyes, but tonight, for the first time, I feel nothing. The urge to protect her is gone. She knows why she came here, and she let me believe it was for my benefit. She's on her own now.

Dillan appears quickly by my side, with Clio not far behind him.

"You ok?" he whispers in my ear then looks back at Clio. "Do you need something?"

"Uh..." She locks eyes with me. "Um, no," she tells him then walks back to Tripp and the others.

"She's acting weird, right?"

I tell Dillan she was worried about me earlier because of my cold. He lets it go as the countdown begins.

"Ten, nine, eight..."

Even I join in.

"Seven, six, five..."

I see Cassie cross the room to join us.

"Four, three, two, one!"

The room explodes with joy. Dillan pulls me into his arms and kisses me softly on the lips.

"Happy New Year, Kalysia." He pulls me into his arms and muffles the sound of the room. "I love you," he whispers into my hair.

I pull back and say the first words that come to mind. "I love you."

Dillan's eyes sparkle as he leans in and kisses me again.

This is going to be our year. The year we decide our fate, our future.

The pack is hooting and whistling. Drake shoves a glass of champagne in my hand and we toast.

"To family," Drake says and clinks Dillan's glass.

"To family," the room echoes.

I turn to clink glasses with Leah and then Patsy. When I turn to my right, Cassie is waiting to greet me.

"Happy New Year." She offers me a one-armed hug. I don't hug her back.

Clio stands behind Cassie, watching my reaction. She looks ready to pounce on my command. It's nice to know she has my back. All I have to do is say the word and Cassie is gone. But I won't. Not yet.

"Happy New Year," I tell her, and then turn to see Dillan watching our exchange.

The anger I felt earlier has diminished. Watching Cassie give Dillan a hug causes something different altogether. Something worse than anger. Pain.

Dillan is polite, but quick to move away. I'm grateful for his tact. I can't be in the same room as her right now. I leave Cassie in the middle of Leah and Clio to get my coat. Dillan sees me and nods. He is saying goodnight to the others when Rusty taps my shoulder.

"Happy New Year, sis." He hugs me and kisses my cheek. I pull him into my arms and squeeze him tight.

"Happy New Year. I hope you spend it with someone you care about." Rusty looks at me strangely. I want to tell him I know and that I don't care, but this isn't the time.

"Hey Rusty," Dillan interrupts. They shake hands and say goodnight.

Dillan helps me with my coat while Rusty opens the door. "I'll walk you out. It's pretty brutal out there."

Dillan tells him we'll be fine. "No, you stay, enjoy yourself. Make sure these guys don't drink too much, they have work tomorrow."

Rusty promises to wind the party down in an hour. "Have a good night you two."

The door is almost closed when I yell, "I hope you enjoyed the wine!" I see a flash of fear cross Rusty's face as he disappears behind the door.

CHAPTER FIFTEEN:

VISITORS

Dillan and I hurry back to our cabin but neither of us are ready for sleep, so we do what we do best.

In between the insatiable bouts of sex, we have our first honest conversation.

"I'm trying to get this business up and running so we can leave. My parents left after two years because my father had money. I can do the same thing. I know I can."

I figured we would be here at least five years. We are supposed to establish the business and solidify the pack before we leave. That is why we are so secluded. It's not just to torture us, like Leah said. We're supposed to form an unbreakable bond. I think about how close we are and it's only been a few months. We are becoming stronger as a group, it's the camp I'm not so sure about. It's already falling apart.

"Once we get the brand established and start making money, we should have enough to leave and make it on our own. I want to do this without help from my father, not that he would offer any." Dillan is so bitter when it comes to Lowell.

"We don't need a lot of money." I snuggle up to him.

"You say that now." He kisses my forehead.

"I don't need verandas or sitting rooms to be happy. You should have seen our apartment in Nevada."

We kiss, and I think he will flip me on my back and take me again, but he stops.

"I want to give you the life you never had. I want to see the world with you, and then settle down somewhere so you can go to school. We need money for that. The pack stipend for new members won't be enough for us to live on, especially with a baby."

I feel all the air in my lungs deflate. I forgot about that. More like I try not to think about it. The stipend is something I never really gave any thought to. I know the amount you get depends on your job and how much time you've spent in the pack. It's paid like a paycheck. We're all employees of Sierra-Duke, LLC. Once our license comes through, our branch will be employed by Howlin' Ale.

Since we're years away from making a profit, Dillan's plan to leave isn't very realistic. What do I know about reality? Most of the time I'm faking it, pretending to know the answers to things I am completely clueless about. Like being a mother.

I sit up to give myself some space. If we are being honest, then I need to tell Dillan how I feel about motherhood.

"I know I wouldn't have the role of a normal mother if we stayed in the camp. Nannies would take care of our baby." I swallow hard. "It just doesn't feel right bringing a child into a world that I would gladly run away from. It's so hypocritical."

Dillan processes what I'm telling him, but doesn't say a word.

"If we leave, that means all responsibility falls to me, and I don't think I'm ready for that. Going to college is my dream. I just don't see it happening with a baby on my hip."

To my surprise, Dillan feels the same way. "I know. I think about that all the time. My father had so much riding on me. He invested a lot of money on my education, to make sure I would be capable of taking over for him one day. The pressure to succeed was too much."

Dillan tells me he kind of cracked when he was thirteen. He started acting out, fighting with the other boys in the pack. That's when Lowell sent him away to school.

"Boarding school and surfing kept me busy. I didn't have time to think about Lunam, what it meant. Males look at it from another perspective." Dillan nuzzles my neck. I know exactly what he's talking about.

"You were just thinking about the sex." I slap him playfully on the arm. "So, you weren't looking for your true love at Lunam?" I don't hide the sarcasm in my tone.

"Hell no," Dillan boasts. "I was just trying to get laid." He braces for another slap, but I don't punish his honesty.

"So everything you told me was bullshit?" It stings a little to think he was feeding me a line of crap the morning after Lunam when he said he loved me.

Dillan throws his leg over mine and holds me between his arms. "No, I really did fall in love with you. I just didn't go in believing I would."

I want to tell him I didn't believe in it either. I didn't fall in love at Lunam. I didn't know I loved Dillan, not one hundred percent sure, until tonight.

Dillan's shoulders slump a bit. "You're just going to leave me hanging?" He allows me a little breathing room and leans back to examine my face. He knows I didn't fall in love with him at Lunam, but I think he's finally confident enough in my feelings for him to ask the question.

"I did go to Lunam thinking I would find my true love," I say.

"And?"

I run my hand through his hair and pull his forehead to mine. "And, I found it."

The idea of losing him to Cassie kicked my ass into gear. Whatever was holding me back has disappeared. For the first time in my life, I know what it is to be in love. And it scares the shit out of me.

Dillan pulls me to him and wraps me in his arms. "I want our child to be born out of love, not obligation. I would never use it as a weapon or to gain power." He's thinking of himself when he says this.

Lowell is counting on Dillan's success to help him rise in power. He won't let us go, not unless he gets what he wants.

School, leaving, traveling. It's all a fantasy, and we both know it. "We don't have a choice. We were born into this life, and now we have to bring another life into it." Dillan pulls me into his arms and holds me tight. "We'll figure something out."

For once, I wake before Dillan. I take a quick shower, replaying highlights from the night in my head. He still makes my insides burn when I think of him, but now I feel just as strongly in my heart.

I turn off the water, grab a towel, and step out of the shower. I'm drying my hair when I hear someone pounding on the door. It must be important if they aren't using the walkie.

I grab my sweats and a fleece jacket from the chair in our room and slip them on. Looking at the clock beside the bed, I see it's almost noon. I hurry to the door and peek through the front window to see who is on the porch. My heart stops.

Lowell Dukes is at the door with Drake, Ray, and Sid.

I run back to our room and see the shattered wine bottles glistening on the kitchen floor. Double shit.

I don't know if I should clean the mess, wake Dillan, or get the door. The pounding gets harder, more impatient.

"Kalysia?" Dillan's groggy voice calls out from the bedroom. "Is someone here..." his voice trails off then. "Fuck, I overslept!"

I appear at the door as Dillan jumps into his pants. He throws on a shirt and bolts past me to the bathroom. "What are you doing? Get the door."

I don't want to get the door. I don't want to see Lowell, not like this. I stop at the mirror in the hall—my hair is a tangled mess. Dillan flushes the toilet and opens the bathroom door with his toothbrush stuck in his mouth. His hair is wet, like he dunked his head in the sink.

"Guh da dore," he mumbles.

"No, it's your father!" I whisper loudly.

Dillan's eyes bulge and he violently spits toothpaste from his mouth. "What!"

I nod, mocking his shocked face in the mirror. He drops his toothbrush, wipes his face on a towel, and spins to face me.

"What the fuck is he doing here?"

I shrug. "I don't know. He's probably here to check on us, check on the camp."

I hope that's all he wants. I don't need him here trying to brainwash Dillan into screwing Cassie during mating season, which begins in two weeks.

All children born this year will be Altum Lunam alphas, future leaders. If Cassie doesn't have a child her family loses control of the Shasta pack.

Dillan walks to the front door on his toes and looks out the window.

"Fuck," he says quietly and pulls his boots from their spot beside the door. He moves to the sofa and puts them on while I freak out in the hall near the kitchen.

"Are you going to let him inside?" I whisper.

Dillan lifts his finger to his mouth to shush me.

"I just need to know if I should clean this." I motion to the mess in the kitchen.

Dillan ties his boots and joins me at the kitchen door.

"No, I'll tell him you're still sleeping. Wait until we're gone then call one of the betas. I don't want you to cut yourself." He strokes my back and kisses the top of my head. "I'm sorry I lost my temper last night. I'm sorry I doubted you." He takes me in his arms for a quick hug, then lets me go and takes a deep breath, preparing himself for his father's wrath.

I accept his apology with a nod. I remember the way he grabbed me. If we didn't heal so quickly, I would have a pretty nasty bruise on my arm.

Dillan's radio beeps from the kitchen counter. "Shit." He runs and grabs it; the battery is almost dead. "I'll come find you when he's gone." He kisses me then heads to the door. He pauses with his hand on the knob before he opens it.

I duck into our room and close the door just in case Lowell demands to come inside. I hear Dillan greet him as if he hasn't been pounding on the door for the last fifteen minutes. After the door closes, I run to the window and move the curtain to the side.

Lowell is storming down the path towards camp central with Drake by his side. I see Dillan stop Ray and gesture to the cabin.

Great, he's probably telling him to radio Rusty to have someone clean the mess. I better get dressed.

A few minutes later, there is a knock on the door. I yell for the beta to come inside as I finish drying my hair.

"It's in the kitchen, I think there's a broom in the closet," I babble as I leave the bathroom. I look in the kitchen, it's empty. I turn and see Rusty standing in the living room.

"Oh. Sorry, I thought you were someone coming to clean the glass."

"Ray called it in, so I knew you were alone." Rusty shifts his weight and stares at the floor. "I wanted to uh, talk to you about..." He trails off like someone turned down the volume on his voice.

143

He clears his throat. "I'm assuming Dillan told you why I won't match with Cassie."

I nod, embarrassed for him, for me.

"He did, and I'm totally fine, with, you know." I wave my hands around. "I love you no matter who you love."

Rusty lets out a loud sigh. "Phew." He pretends to wipe his brow. "I was worried you wouldn't take it so great." He wrings the beanie in his hands. "You know, since now Dillan is sort of stuck with Cassie."

"No, it's totally fine." He doesn't know that Dillan is going to tell his father to piss off. "He isn't going to do it. Cassie will have to find another sperm donor."

I pluck my boots from their shelf. Rusty continues to wring his beanie.

"Are you sending someone to clean the mess?" I ask as I put my boots on.

I want to go find Leah and see what's going on with Lowell. I lace my boots and reach for my jacket. Even though the sun is out, the air is still freezing.

"Kalysia." Rusty watches me move around the room like he's rooted in place. "Are you sure about Dillan and Cassie?"

"Yes. Dillan told me he wouldn't go through with it. He wouldn't do that to me."

I pat Rusty's hand and smile at his concern. It warms my heart to know he cares about me.

"That's good news. I really thought he was going to do it, especially after the deal Lowell offered him." Rusty releases the death grip on this beanie. "I'll send someone right away." He puts his beanie on his head and opens the door.

"Wait." I stop him. "What deal?"

The color in Rusty's face drains.

"Lowell told Dillan that if he mated with Cassie this season, he would release him from the pack."

"What does that mean, release him? He would be kicked out of the pack?"

"No, being released is like a get-out-of-jail-free card. Dillan would still be Sierra and would get benefits, full benefits, for the rest of his life. He just wouldn't have to live in the pack; he could have his own life. How amazing would that be? Reaping the rewards of the pack, but leading your life, by your own rules?"

I sit on the sofa, feeling like someone just pulled my happy card.

Dillan is giving up a life out of the pack, a life that we could have together, anywhere in the world, for my ego? All the plans we made last night, they could become reality if Dillan gets Cassie pregnant. We wouldn't have to wait until the business made money, we wouldn't have to worry about money at all. And I wouldn't have to have a baby.

I find Cassie in her cabin. She lets me in without a word. I notice she's cleaned up. Her bed has been folded back into the sofa, like she's expecting company. I wonder if Lowell came to see her, to plot against me.

"Kalysia, is something wrong?" She stays near the door in case she needs to make a quick getaway.

I need to keep my cool. She will never agree if I lose it.

"I know why you're here. Dillan told me." I wait for her to say something, apologize, but she just stares at her feet. "I thought we were friends?" I struggle to get the words out without breaking into tears.

"I am your friend," she says quietly.

"Bullshit!" I slam my hand on the back of her sofa. So much for staying calm.

Her eyes dart up, and she steps back into the doorway.

"I care about you." She holds her hands up defensively, as if I may strike. I let her speak. I want to hear what she has to say. "I didn't want to come here; my father was going to match me with a male from our pack. He didn't go to Lunam because he's a half-breed. I was fine with that. I didn't want any trouble."

Dillan was right; Conall doesn't care about his bloodline if he was going to match his daughter to a half-breed that has no chance of ever leading. All the rumors about Shasta are real—they are tainted. That isn't my problem. Not anymore.

"My father is so set on merging the packs, on gaining power over Monte, that he'll do anything to get him out."

I make a noise of disgust. I can't believe he would whore out his only daughter to hurt my father.

"And you just go along with it? You don't even try to put up a fight?"

"I would never second-guess my father." Cassie stands straighter. I feel her energy return to her. She is a pureblood, but she has no idea what that means.

Layla was right, taking me away made me stronger. I think for myself, not the pack.

"I was happy to match with whomever he chose for me. Then Lowell showed up with a proposition. They said they would match me with an alpha from Sierra. I didn't know it was Dillan, I swear. Lowell told us the day I came here."

I think back to the day Cassie arrived. Dillan played it so cool, like nothing was wrong. Anger chokes me.

"We were in shock, and after Lowell left, we vowed never to tell anyone. Dillan said he would find another alpha for me, but I guess it didn't work out."

Dillan must have thought Rusty would be the perfect solution. He is a much better choice than the half-breed Conall would have matched her with.

"Did he tell you who the alpha was?" I pray she doesn't know. The fewer people that know Rusty's secret, the safer he is.

"No." She shakes her head. "He just told me it fell through. That's when I decided to leave. I tried to call my father from the phone in the brew house but it wasn't working. That's why I went on the run with Dillan. I called him from a payphone in town while Dillan picked up a new phone for the brew house. My father must have called Lowell and told him I was leaving, that's why he's here today."

Dillan must be in hell right now. Lowell will never accept Dillan's defiance. He will see him as weak, just because he loves me too much to hurt me.

"Kalysia, you know the last thing I want to do is hurt you or Dillan. I love you like a sister and it killed me to keep this from you. I'm going back to Dunsmuir today."

"No!" I stand and walk to the door.

Cassie jumps at my sudden movement. She cowers when I stand before her. The power feels good and insidious. I take her hand to show her I won't hurt her.

"You can't leave. You have to go through with it. You have to sleep with Dillan. Do it for me."

CHAPTER SIXTEEN:

MIND LOST

"You've lost your mind." Cassie paces around my living room in disbelief. "You want me to have Dillan's baby?"

The more I try to convince Cassie that having Dillan's baby is in everyone's best interest, the stronger I feel about the situation.

"Yes, it's the best solution for everyone. You will get a strong heir; a leader in both packs. Lowell and Conall will get what they want, and Dillan and I can leave."

It's a win-win all around. I just have to stay strong and keep telling myself that one night, one child, will not change what Dillan and I have. We will still be us, nothing can change that.

"And Dillan is on board with this?" Cassie takes a large gulp from her wine glass while I clean the broken glass from my kitchen floor.

I guess Rusty forgot to send the beta. He's probably running around with everyone else trying to appease Lowell. I hate to think about what will happen to him after we leave. He's Leah's brother too, she must know about him. If Drake is put in charge, he will protect him.

We finish off a bottle of wine, and I'm considering opening another when my radio beeps. It's Leah, dinner is ready. I ask her if Lowell is staying, and she grumbles yes.

Cassie and I walk into the lodge together; Clio and Dillan are the only ones who look shocked.

Lowell makes a big show of putting his plate down to greet me. "Kalysia, how wonderful to see you again," he says with a forced smile.

If I didn't know what he was plotting behind my back, the sudden show of affection would have freaked me out.

"It's nice to see you too. How is Adel?"

Lowell says she's fine and escorts me to his table.

"I missed you today on the tour of the camp. Dillan said you weren't feeling well."

I look up and see Dillan at the buffet. He is trying to hurry to the table, but one of the beta males is pestering him with questions.

"I'm fine, just too much wine last night." I feign a hangover. "I'm lucky Cassie was here to take care of me. You know Cassie, don't you?" Cassie hasn't moved from the door; I wave her over.

"Yes, Conall's daughter. I orchestrated her transfer to your branch. Dillan told me how much it meant to you." Lowell's sinister smile almost sends me over the edge.

"I made you a plate, Kalysia." Dillan shoves a plate in my hand and ushers me to the opposite side of the table.

Dillan must have been watching us while he made my plate, because he has lasagna piled on a bed of lettuce, topped off with ranch dressing and croutons. I sit at the opposite end of the table and pretend to eat while Dillan sits beside his father with a beer.

Turns out Lowell didn't just come here to ruin my life, he has good news—our license came through, so we can start distribution, and he already has buyers.

I'm too wound up to listen to Lowell lecture the guys on quality and building the brand. I dump my plate and I retreat to the corner of the lodge where we have a few sofas set up, and a television that doesn't get cable. Cassie finishes her dinner and joins me.

The lodge empties quickly nobody wants to hang out with Lowell here, so it's easy to hear their conversation. Dillan tells Lowell we have enough product to fill his orders, they just need more drivers. Drake suggests they hire outside help, but Lowell says absolutely not. Everything stays within the pack. Lowell thinks we should reach out to Shasta for help. It would show our enthusiasm to join forces.

They decide to make a run to Mt. Shasta this week to enlist drivers. I see the longing in Cassie's face when they mention heading up to Shasta. I know she wants to see her family, but I can't let her go. Not now. If she leaves, she may never come back.

By some miracle it doesn't snow, and Lowell is able to leave around eight. Dillan doesn't even walk him to the gate.

"Are we telling him tonight?" Cassie whispers from behind the magazine she is pretending to read. I give her a look that is part "I don't know" and part "shut the hell up."

I'm waiting for Dillan and Drake to finish talking so we can walk back together. I want to break the news to him as soon as possible.

Leah finally emerges from the kitchen. Her face lights up when she sees Drake waiting for her. She drapes her arms around his neck and kisses his cheek. Drake seems happier at the sight of her. I envy them.

"Ok, let's go." We stand up, and Cassie walks to the door to retrieve our coats. Dillan watches Cassie and me closely. He's trying to figure out what is going on. When Cassie hands me my jacket and gloves, Dillan finally stands.

"Dillan, can you walk us back, please?" I have Cassie ask him this. I know it's cruel, but I want to see his reaction.

Dillan narrows his eyes at me. "Sure." He walks to the door and puts on his jacket and beanie.

We walk in silence until we reach Cassie's cabin.

"Kalysia, are you going to tell me what you're doing?" Dillan says from behind me. Cassie stops and turns to him, but I grab her arm.

"Let's get inside," I call over my shoulder, dragging Cassie alongside me to her front door.

Dillan kicks the snow off his shoes for what seems like forever while Cassie and I wait inside near the fireplace. Dillan finally enters the cabin and closes the door. He walks to the tiny dining table across from the sofa and leans against it, crossing his arms over his chest.

"What's going on?"

"I know why Lowell was here." I stand beside Cassie, a unified front. She promised she would back me up no matter what.

"We need to discuss this in private." Dillan gives me a cautionary look.

"No, this involves Cassie too. She should be here."

"Ok," Dillan nods and makes a huge effort not to look at her.

"Rusty told me about the deal your father offered you."

Dillan uncrosses his arms and steps towards the sofa. He grips the cushions and looks down at his white-knuckled hands.

"I know what you're thinking, and I wasn't going to take the deal. I would never hurt you like that."

Seeing him so distraught makes what I'm about to say a bit easier. Giving my approval for him and Cassie to have a child feels like a gift. It also makes the pain I feel in my chest a little more bearable.

"I know you wouldn't hurt me. Which is why I spoke to Cassie this afternoon and we decided—"

"Kalysia, let me finish." Dillan stands up straight, towering over the sofa. "Lowell isn't going to let this go. I tried to reason with him, but he won't back down. I have to give him what he wants, or he will disown me." Dillan squeezes his fists to control his anger.

"You don't have to worry about that." I try to interrupt him, but he is too angry to listen.

"He said I will be outcast, and that you," he closes his eyes in disgust, "he said he would make sure you were given to another alpha. Like you're some piece of meat!" Dillan punches at the sofa, and we hear wood crack. "He doesn't care that I love you. He doesn't care about anyone but himself!"

Dillan is on the verge of a complete meltdown. I could have spared him this anguish. I should have found him earlier and told him about my plan. If I had, he wouldn't have angered Lowell. Dillan moves quickly around the sofa. Cassie and I jump backward.

"I love you, Kalysia, but I don't have a choice." My heart is in my throat. "I have to do as my father says." His eyes drift to Cassie, and she looks away.

He's telling me he will take Cassie this season with or without my blessing. My head is spinning. I move to the sofa and sit down. I thought I would have to convince him to be with her. I was going to persuade him to do it out of his love for me and mine for him, so we could live happily ever after on our terms. But all that is out the window now. Lowell made this about him. Dillan is obeying his father's wishes regardless of my feelings.

"I never should have gone to Lunam." Dillan paces from the fireplace to the door. "I'm sorry." He looks from me to Cassie. She holds his gaze a few seconds before looking away.

This isn't about me, it never was. I can tell myself it was my idea, convince myself that this is what's best for me and Dillan. At the end of the day, it's what's best for Lowell.

Dillan stands in front of the fire with his head in his hands. Cassie floats somewhere between us. She will always be a wedge in our relationship. In nine months there will a new piece to this puzzle.

Cassie clears her throat and I look towards her. She is staring at Dillan. "Um, Dillan, I think Kal—"

"Don't," I demand and Cassie stops. I don't want to hear her voice right now. This night has gone horribly wrong. Telling Dillan that I want him to sleep with Cassie for me seems like a joke.

"Kalysia, come here." Dillan reaches for my hand and I jerk away.

I don't want to be touched by him, by anyone. I run out of the cabin, into the snow. I run past our cabin, into the woods, and phase.

I phase back almost immediately, and I find myself lying face up in the snow. I pull something from under my back, it's my boot. Half of boot. Snow begins to burn my bare back.

"Kalysia!" Cassie yells, and the next thing I know she is helping me up.

"Hurry, I don't want anyone to see you like this." She ushers me to my cabin. I don't protest. I don't do or say anything. My mind is a jumbled mess of words and feelings.

Cassie disappears then returns a few minutes later with a towel to cover my half-naked body. "Take off your pants, I'm running you a bath." My pants are held together by shreds of cloth. I pull them off, then follow her to the bathroom.

My feet burn when I step into the bathtub. I submerge my frozen limbs and wait for my muscles to relax. My mind catches up to itself and my chest starts to ache.

Cassie walks into the bathroom with a bottle of water and sits in on the edge of the tub. "I can't believe you phased like that."

"You saw me phase at Lunam," I snap.

"Other than women phasing after mating season and the occasional male phasing on a dare, it isn't something I've seen very often."

"Isn't the whole point of our species the fact that we can phase to wolf form?"

"I mean, yeah. But we don't actually do it. We choose human form over wolf. This is the body we live in. Being wolf is part of who we are, not what we are."

Her philosophy is completely screwed up. Dillan said we are wolf living in human form. Wolf is what we are.

"Is that what Shasta believes?" I don't hide the sarcasm in my voice.

She just shrugs and nods her head. "I don't make the rules. It's just the way it is." Cassie stands and turns on the faucet to wash her hands.

"And you never question the rules?" I sit up and pull my knees to my chest. "You just do whatever your daddy tells you to do, even if that means whoring you out to my boyfriend?"

Cassie doesn't look at me; she keeps washing her hands. "I'm sorry. I never wanted any of this."

"I know," I say softly. "I shouldn't blame you. Hell, two hours ago I was begging you to go through with it. Now, I'm just being a baby."

"I understand. You wanted this to be on your terms, and now it's on Lowell's. Believe me, I get it." Cassie turns off the water and dries her hands on a towel. "I've been told what's best for me my entire life. Nobody ever asks me what I want."

Her words start to sink in. Even I tried to tell her how to live her life.

"Cassie, do you want to have a baby?"

"Yes, of course," she says.

I bolt out of the water and grab her by the arms. Her entire body stiffens as I stand naked in front of her.

"No, I mean do *you* want to be a mother? Not for your father or the pack. Is this something you want?"

Her bottom lip quivers, and she blinks back tears. "Yes, more than anything."

"Ok." I let her go and pull a towel from the rack. "Then the plan is on."

Cassie tries to protest but I stop her.

This isn't what I want or even Dillan, but we will benefit from it. I can set my ego, my heart, aside for one night. Knowing that Cassie will get her dream makes it easier to swallow. We can all get out of this with what we want.

I tell Cassie I'm tired and send her back to her cabin. I ask her not to tell Dillan about my phase. She promises to keep it our secret. If there is one thing I know for certain, it is that I can trust Cassie with my secrets.

Twenty minutes after Cassie leaves, Dillan shows up with a bottle of whiskey. He sits on the sofa in front of the fireplace, and I join him. He offers me the bottle, and I decline.

"I forgot you drown your worries in wine," he smirks. "I'm leaving." His voice is absolute. "I never wanted this anyway." He takes a pull on the bottle and stares into the fire. He's in pain. I can help relieve him. If I tell him the plan I concocted today, before Lowell threatened him, maybe he'll see the positive in all this.

"We can both leave." I rest my hand on his leg. "If you take his deal, we can leave together."

Dillan shakes his head. "No, I won't put you through that. And I won't ask you to leave with me when I have nothing to offer you. No way to care for you."

"What is this, the nineteen-fifties?" I stand up and stare Dillan down. "I don't need you to take care of me. If we're together, it's because we love each other, not because I need someone to pay my rent."

Dillan takes another pull on the bottle. "And the baby?" He chokes on the last part.

"It's one night, one child, and we will be free. We can move far away from here and live a normal life. You can surf."

He raises his eyebrows a bit when I mention surfing.

"I've never even seen the ocean." I drop to my knees in front of him. "You can show me everything I've missed."

I kneel between his legs and kiss his whiskey tainted lips. "Nothing will change between us."

Dillan looks at me skeptically. "You can walk away from your duty to your parents?"

I think about Layla. What she sacrificed for me and wonder if she meant it when she said my happiness is all that matters. I have to believe she wants what is best for me. If that's a lie, then there is no reason for me to be here anyway. "Yes, I can."

Over the next two weeks, things start to feel normal again. We talk openly about when the consummation will take place. I said the first night would be best, better to get it over with. But Cassie believes they should wait until the third or fourth night.

The mating season starts on the first full moon in January and lasts about five days. All children conceived during this time will be born under the harvest moon, between September and October.

Dillan and Cassie's baby, as well as Leah and Drake's, will be pureblood alphas. They will be leaders one day, just like their parents and grandparents. Monte still has Leah to carry his line. Layla's bloodline will end with me. Sometimes I catch myself feeling guilty about that. She'll get over it. She's with Monte now, she doesn't need me. Nobody stopped her from leaving to do what she wanted, and nobody is going to stop me.

Dillan comes in just as I finish getting dressed.

"One of these days, I'm going to walk in here and you're going to be waiting for me, naked." Dillan lifts me into his arms and kisses my neck.

"Today is not that day." I kiss the top of his head. He smells like the brew house.

"How is it going?"

Dillan is training Ray and Tripp so they can take over as brewmaster after we leave.

"We had to toss out an entire batch today because Ray forgot to turn the heat down." Dillan sets me down and runs his hand over his face. "I just hope one of them catch on soon. We only have ten months."

We decided to leave right after the baby is born. Once Cassie produces the heir, Dillan is released from his duty. Since I am not giving the pack an heir, I'll relinquish my place in the pack. I can leave with Dillan's permission, which I have, but I won't get a dime from the pack. I don't want to live off of Dillan, but I don't have a choice right now. I just want to enjoy being free.

I have a list of places we're going to visit. Dillan wants to find Othello; he thinks he may be living in Santa Cruz. So that is our first stop. After that, he wants to take me to Australia. He's never been, so it'll be a first for us both.

I unzip Dillan's pants and pull him on top of me. He jerks at my force and laughs.

"Have you been working out?"

My new muscles have been from running on all fours, but I don't dare tell him that. As far as Dillan knows, I haven't phased since Lunam. We aren't the only animals out here; Dillan wouldn't approve of me running in the woods alone.

After we leave here I hope I can convince Dillan to phase with me. I dream about running through deserts and along beaches in wolf form. I know he'll love it, too.

I squirm underneath him and flip onto my stomach. Dillan lets out a low growl as he tears at his clothes and yanks my jeans down. When he takes me from behind, I scream out in pleasure. Dillan doesn't slow down when he nears climax, he charges forward and explodes louder and harder than I've ever felt. Sometimes the quick ones are the best.

I pull up my jeans and turn over. Dillan collapses on the bed with his pants still down around his ankles.

"That was fucking awesome."

He reaches out for me, and I offer him my hand. He pulls me to him.

"I love you." His words cause little jolts of pain in my chest. I know he loves me and I love him, but knowing that he will share this same experience with Cassie in a few days taints them a little. Dillan senses my despair.

"You're still ok with this, right?"

"Of course." I scoot off the bed and pull my hair into a ponytail. "It's just one night." I twist the band around my fingers. It snaps and shoots across the room.

"Whoa!" Dillan covers himself. "You trying to maim me?"

"I don't want to hurt your junk. Then you can't knock up my best friend."

I turn and leave the room to get another hair tie. Dillan doesn't like when I tease him. He is treating it like a business transaction. Just a quickie and he's out. Not a good quickie.

I'm looking at it from a different perspective. It's like Dillan is helping her build a bookshelf. He shows up, bangs some nails, and leaves. A friend doing a friend a favor. He's worried about how he will feel after. He isn't sure he can live with the guilt. I've told him a hundred times; he will have the rest of our lives to make it up to me.

At dinner, I feel the anxiety in the room. Clio has been keeping a close watch on the moon cycle. She says it isn't an exact science, and since we still have no internet access, she can't confirm it. If her calculations are correct, we are twenty-four hours away from the full moon. The fact that Cassie wants to wait a few days seems like a better idea.

I decided not to keep the arrangement a secret. The more people that know, the less doubt Conall and Lowell will have about who fathered Cassie's baby.

Leah was livid when she heard my plan. She thought Dillan was pulling a rule seventy-five and would have Cassie and me, the way Monte did with our mothers. When I told her I wasn't having a child, her head almost exploded. Until she realized that her child would carry on our bloodline and be Monte's heir. She suddenly became a lot more understanding, but still shoots daggers at Cassie whenever they cross paths.

Dillan and I have chosen not to tell anyone we are leaving the pack. Only Cassie and Rusty know about the deal Dillan has with Lowell. It's going to break my heart to leave everyone; I really do consider them family. But there is no way I can stay after the baby is born.

"We just don't have enough drivers to make the deliveries." Drake looks tired. He's been trying to coordinate all the deliveries Lowell set up for us.

"If Ray and Tripp split their routes and pull all-nighters, we are only one driver short for the Tahoe-Truckee run. It's the easiest run as far as distance, but the weather is unpredictable, and none of the guys want to be stuck out there. If we don't come up with a solution soon, I'll have to go. Leah's going to kill me."

None of the men want to be gone during the full moon. Unlike me and Dillan, the rest of the camp is looking forward to mating season. Dillan doesn't want to force anyone to go and miss their chance to conceive, but he can't leave camp until Ray or Tripp learn how to brew.

"I'll go," I tell the table. "It's an easy run, I can do it in one day."

Dillan huffs and takes a drink from his beer bottle.

"It's not a terrible idea," Drake starts to agree, but Dillan slams his bottle on the table and he shuts up.

"There is no way you're going out on your own." Dillan stands with his plate and heads back for seconds.

All of the men have been eating like horses. It's a full moon thing. Their bodies crave nourishment. Watching Dillan blindly prepare to be with Cassie hurts, a lot.

I shake my head at Drake to drop it. This isn't an argument he needs to be part of. This is between Dillan and me.

Clio bursts into the room with a smile worthy of a gum commercial.

"I was wrong!" she announces. "I got my mother's almanac in the mail today. It confirms, the season started this morning."

She waves the yellow book in the air. The couples in the room spring from their seats in celebration.

I look to Dillan and find his sad eyes looking back. This is killing him. I have to keep a positive face. I need to stay strong for him. I force a smile and bring my plate to the kitchen. Leah follows me in, barely able to contain herself.

"You know our deal? I don't pester you about Cassie and you give me Drake." Leah places a stack of dishes into the sink.

Tonight is her night to clean up. She turns on the water and hastily pulls the rubber gloves from the shelf.

"Go, I got this." I take the gloves from her and put them on.

She squeals and kisses my cheek.

"You're the best!"

I hear Drake whoop a few seconds later, and soon the hall is quiet except for the clinking of the dishes as I wash and rinse.

I bite the inside of my lip. The pain is nothing compared to the ache in my chest at the thought of Dillan and Cassie. Suddenly, I feel his hands on my shoulders and I close my eyes. He's still here. He's still just mine.

I lean into him and fight to hold in my tears. *It is one night that will grant us the rest of our lives.*

I shake off my grief and pull a pot into the sink. Leah has been making a lot of chili lately; this is the third night this week. She says it's the easiest meal to make and goes a long way. I guess that's true, but the pot is a bitch to clean.

"Here, let me help you." Dillan moves me to the side and takes the scrub brush from my hand.

I move the loose hair from my face using my forearm. This is probably the first time Dillan has ever done dishes. I take the gloves off and offer them to him, not that they will fit his hands.

He shakes his head no, never taking his eyes off the stubborn stains on the bottom of the pot. I pull a towel from the rack and start to dry. We wash and dry every dish in the lodge in silence.

CHAPTER SEVENTEEN:

NOT IN THE PLAN

I wake in Dillan's arms, knowing this may be the last morning we share before he goes to Cassie. This is the second day of the full moon.

The fact that I'm not having a child means my mother's line, the Orrin line, will end with me. If I choose to have a child later, it won't hold the same power as a first Lunam child. I just hope Layla understands why I'm doing this. I don't think her bloodline is important to her. I mean, she is the one that crossed over to Sierra. If maintaining a Shasta line mattered, then she would have chosen Conall, not Monte.

I hate these early morning internal debates. I might as well get up since I can't sleep. When I try to sit up, Dillan tightens his grip. I feel him aroused on my leg. It kills me to abstain from sex with him, but we can't risk it. I don't want to conceive. I can't bring a child into this world. When Dillan and I do have a baby, which is not something I have ruled out, it will be *our* child, not the packs.

"I better get up, before nature takes its course." I whip the blanket back and let the cold morning air cool him off.

He grabs my arm and pulls me back down. He tosses the covers over our heads and holds me tight.

"Let's pretend we're someplace else. Where do you want to be?"

I giggle and play along. "Um, how about a beach house in..."

"Cancun," he finishes my sentence. "I stayed in this amazing villa one summer with my parents. My father let Othello take me to see the ruins; instead we went zip-lining in the jungle. It was awesome."

I love the way Dillan's eyes light up when he talks about Othello. He really meant a lot to him.

"And what will we do today?" I want to keep the game going. "Will you take me zip-lining?"

"No, I want to see the ruins with you."

He kisses my head and squeezes me to his chest. I relax in his arms and imagine the life we will have once this is all over. These moments make everything worth it.

"I've always thought it would be cool to have sex in one of those ancient temples."

I squirm in his arms and pretend his comment offended me, when actually it doesn't sound all that bad. My squirming arouses him further, and for a second we lose ourselves in a kiss. Dillan breaks away first.

"You better get up now, before I can't stop."

He slides off of me and I have to remind myself it isn't rejection. Even if my heart feels like it's being ripped from my chest.

The camp is deserted; most of the couples have resigned to their rooms. This mating season isn't just special for purebloods. Any child born this year will be an Altum alpha no matter who their parents are. This is a chance for betas to contribute to the pack with an alpha. Altum alphas are future leaders, which means better rank for their parents and siblings.

Ray is the son of a beta and an alpha, but he was born during Altum Lunam, and that is all that matters. If something were to happen to the purebloods, the next in line to lead would be an Altum alpha.

We agreed to keep the key to Hopi under the mat so people won't starve while Leah and Patsy are off kitchen duty for the next week. I'm even covering for Clio in the nursery.

Mara runs the nursery. She is an unmatched alpha in her mid-fifties and has no children. Clio said since she's a low alpha, her family never pressured her to breed. Prejudice is a real problem in the packs.

"Good morning, Mara." I place the box of supplies she requested from Hopi on the counter.

She thanks me as she scoops up one of the babies and carries him to the changing table. My duties are mainly to keep order. I make sure the kids don't eat crayons or hurt each other, while Mara takes care of the smelly things.

"Can you grab Taylor from her crib? She's been yelping all morning."

I look at the line of beds in the room. There are three with babies in them. They all stare back at me with large round eyes. She said 'her', but I can't tell them apart.

"Which one is Taylor?"

"The girl," Mara huffs as she tosses a dirty diaper into the pail.

I roll my eyes at the back of Mara's head.

"They all look the same," I say then notice small pink bunnies covering the pajamas of the one on the end.

I approach Taylor's crib slowly, like any minute she will morph into a wild animal and bite my hand off.

"Hey there, Taylor. I'm just going to pick you up, ok?"

Taylor looks at me, utterly confused when I reach down and place my hands under her arms.

"There we go." I hold her over the crib, unsure what to do next. "Where does she go now?"

Mara is still occupied with diapering the baby on the table; she just waves her hand in the vicinity of the playpens. I walk with

Taylor at arm's length, hoping she doesn't spew something on me. When I move her over the top of the playpen, she lets out a blood-curdling scream.

"Holy shit!" I pull her back and look in the playpen to make sure there isn't a snake or something inside. I pull Taylor close to my body and rest her on my hip. She instantly stops screaming.

"Did I do something?"

Mara finally finishes dressing the baby on the table and watches me from the other side of the room.

"Look at that."

I look down at Taylor, who is smiling up at me. Her big blue-gray eyes sparkle in the morning sunlight.

"She doesn't act like that with anyone." Mara sets down the baby in her arms and goes back for another.

Her remark warms me. I'm glad to hear I'm not as inadequate as I thought. Not that I'll need these skills anytime soon.

Taylor and I share a moment. I bounce her on my hip and she giggles. She's not that bad, and she doesn't smell like a sour rag, like some of the others.

"Who's her mother?" I ask while I bounce around the room, making Taylor and the other kids laugh. Their smiles are infectious.

"Taylor's mother is not with us anymore. She died in a car accident last summer." Mara says this quietly, like Taylor might actually understand what we're talking about.

I cradle Taylor's head to my shoulder, blocking her ears. "And her father? Is he here?"

"Of course, we came together." Mara passes out sippy cups full of milk. The older kids suck them down the way the males drink their beer then run out of the room.

"Who is her father?" I try to see if I can guess, but they all have the same Sierra blue-gray eyes and black hair.

"Carrick," she calls from the kitchen.

I'm stunned. I had no idea Carrick was a father. I hold Taylor in front of me, but I don't see any of his brutish traits in her sweet face. Taylor giggles when I hold her up. I make a game out of it and spin her around.

"I wouldn't do that," Mara warns. "She's already had her breakfast; you don't want it all over you."

"Oh." I stop and put Taylor down next to the other babies. "I feel like I should know more about these children. I mean, I don't even know their names."

Mara doesn't miss a beat. "That one there is Mack." She points to the baby next to Taylor. "The two in their beds are Lars and Gavin. The older kids are Romi, Madeline, Jake, and Roger."

The older ones are glued to the television in the other room. We don't get cable, but there is a wall of DVDs.

"How often do their parents come and visit?" Mara looks confused. "I mean; do they ever see them?"

"This place is more like a daycare for some. The older ones sleep in their parents' cabins every night." Mara winds a diaper in a plastic bag then stuffs it into the trash.

Now that the camp is full, most of the betas share cabins. There is an all-male and all female cabin for the single betas. Some cabins house two or three couples. The cabins have been split into private areas with partitions, the kind you see in an office building. When I voiced my concerns to Dillan he said it's all temporary. Once we start to make money we will build more cabins or even get trailers.

Everything is riding on the success of the business. I won't be here to see how things play out. I hope Leah and Drake have the same vision for this place that Dillan and I do.

"Where do the children sleep in the cabins?"

"Madeline sleeps on an air mattress and Jake's parents have bunk beds in their cabin. The others are still small enough to sleep with their parents"

I'm horrified by the sleeping arrangements these families have to endure to be together. It's wrong and I should do something about it. I could, if I were staying.

"Your children will have a special place in here." She points to a room off the kitchen. "All pureblood children get the best care. We can't have them getting sick." She winks at me. Mara's comment doesn't sit right with me. Children shouldn't get better care than others based on their bloodline.

"Pureblood children need around-the-clock care and protection." Mara washes her hands then plucks two apples from a bowl on the counter and starts chopping. "Unlike these little monsters. They come and go as they please." She hands Romi a piece of apple.

I watch Romi run back to the television. She's probably five or six years old and she has to share a bed with her parents. It's wrong. She deserves better than this.

"When I get here in the morning the kids are already here. What time do you open?"

"This is my cabin. My room is back there." She points to a door down the hall. "Depending on work schedules. I usually have at least two or three overnight. The rest are dropped off pretty early in the morning so their parents can get to work."

Taylor pulls on my pant leg and holds her arms up to me, while Mack crawls to Mara.

"Well look at that." Mara shakes her head. "She likes you."

My heart swells at the sight of Taylor's smile. I reach down and pick her up.

"You know kids are contagious." Mara says as she wipes Mack's nose.

"Eww."

"I don't mean this." Mara holds up the dirty tissue. "I told Clio not to worry; she should be the first one to turn up pregnant with all the time she spends in here."

"I gotta go." I place Taylor on the floor. She whines a little then crawls over to a pile of blocks and starts to chew one.

"Come back for lunch if you can, we can always use the help." Mara waves as Lars or Gavin start to cry.

I tell Mara I'll send someone if I can't make it. The last thing I want is to catch the baby bug. Not when I'm so close to having everything I've ever wanted.

I run into Clio on the way to my office. Her eyes are red.

"Late night?" I tease.

Clio shakes her head and wipes her nose.

"What's going on? Are you and Tripp fighting?" I wrap my arm around her shoulders.

"No, it's not that. We're fine. It's my stupid body." She throws her hands in the air.

I have no clue what she means.

"I'm not ovulating," she blurts out.

When I ask her how she knows, she goes into an elaborate explanation that involves mucus and her body temperature.

"My optimal day for conception is tomorrow, but Tripp has to leave for the Truckee run in the morning. He'll be gone all day." She sniffles and wipes her wet eyes. "If I don't get pregnant, we'll have to wait an entire year to try again."

She doesn't mention the fact that their child won't be Altum alpha; she's just upset about not having a baby. Clio wants to be a mother. Something that felt so foreign to me a few days ago. After spending a little time in the nursery. I can see how one of those little monsters might seem like a good idea for some people.

"Isn't there anyone else that can go instead? Why can't Rusty make the run?" Clio grips my arm. "Please Kalysia, talk to Dillan and get someone else to take his place."

All of the drivers we hired from Shasta left this morning to make their runs.

I leave Clio and radio Dillan. It's close to eleven; he is most likely in the brew house. To my surprise, Dillan replies that he is in our cabin. When I arrive, he's sitting in the kitchen with a glass of wine. It isn't normal for him to drink this early.

"What's going on? Why aren't you at the brew house?" I take my coat off and toss it on the table.

Dillan kicks out the empty chair and pours me a glass of wine. I sit down slowly and take the glass from his hand. He doesn't need to say a word; I can see it in his eyes.

"Cassie called."

He nods and pours himself what's left of the bottle.

I don't want to drink; if I drink I'll puke. I stare at the wine in my glass and think about the vineyard outside Dillan's bedroom. Cassie has never seen the sunrise from Dillan's bed. She will never have what we have. She may share her bed with Dillan Dukes, but she will never have his heart.

I reach for Dillan's hand. He doesn't move when I squeeze his fingers. He stares into his glass, his eyes amassed with pain.

"It's ok, Dillan." I force a smile that is so painful, I want to scream. But breaking down now won't help. I need this to happen so we can leave here. I need to be strong for him.

"What am I supposed to do, run to her cabin and..." He stops before saying something horrible. "I don't know if I can go through with it. Just thinking about you sitting here waiting for me. It kills me to think of you alone."

He's right; I can't just sit around here. I'll go crazy.

"I'll go on the run with Tripp." He grips my hand so tight I hear my knuckles crack. "It will be best for both of us if I'm not here."

Dillan's jaw tenses, but he doesn't say no.

"I'll leave in the morning and be back by dark. It'll be like it never happened." I shrug like it's no big deal.

"Ok." He drains his glass and kisses me gently. The moment is full of so much love, yet I feel like a fraud. I say this is for both of us, but really it's for me. I'm being selfish. I have to be. When he pulls away, I can't meet his eyes.

"I need to get to the brew house. Cassie will have to wait one more day." He finishes the wine in my glass, tilts my pain-stricken face to his, and says, "I love you."

It takes everything in my power not to break down and cry.

After he leaves, I think about my conversation with Clio and wonder if Cassie has been monitoring her temperature. I wonder if today is her day.

I knock on Cassie's door and wait for her to answer. I know she's here, she rarely leaves her cabin these days. She opens the door like she's surprised to find me on her porch.

"Can I come in?" I ask when she doesn't move from the doorway.

She steps to the side and I see her bed is out. The sheets smell freshly washed. Bitch.

I don't know why I'm so angry. This is what I want. I planned it. I have no right to take this out on Cassie.

"Dillan isn't coming." I try to soften my tone. "You'll have to wait one more day. Will that work?"

I glance around the room and see a bottle of wine on the table. I agreed to let all the couples take a bottle in celebration of the mating season. That was before I knew Dillan would be with

Cassie. It takes all my strength not to pick it up and slam it against the wall.

"Uh, I guess so." She wrings her fingers together. She's nervous, I can smell it on her. I want to apologize, but my ego won't let me.

"Are you monitoring your cycle?" I use Clio's words to sound like I know what I'm talking about.

"Oh, yeah, it looks like today or tomorrow." She looks everywhere but at me. She can't look me in the eyes.

If this really were the business proposition we said it was, then why is she so nervous? So guilty? Why am I so angry? I need to get out of here. I move towards the door and she opens it. I don't say goodbye when I brush past her. I'm a few steps from her porch when she calls to me. I turn around and the morning sun bounces off the window, blinding me.

"He's still...I mean, everything is still going as planned?" she stammers.

"Yes," I shoot at her and walk away.

The one day in my life I want to never end flies by like Mother Nature is on fast forward. I spend most of the day alone in my office. I update my work distribution spreadsheets, make a new list for the next food run, and try like hell to get on the internet.

When I bother June and Sam about it, they say once the storm clears they will put up more antennas. June has a small radio that gets the local road updates. She tells me there are back-to-back storms coming in, so the likelihood that we will get internet is nil.

Dillan radios me around three to say he's pulling a late shift; he has to get this next batch done tonight since there won't be anyone around to monitor it tomorrow. I tell him I understand.

"Will you come see me before I leave in the morning?"

The radio is silent for a few seconds before his static-filled voice comes through.

"Even if I'm not finished, I will come say goodbye."

Oh God, don't tell me that. Don't say you'll come to say goodbye. Like you're the one leaving me. Leaving me for her.

I squeeze my eyes closed to fight back the tears. I'm so glad he can't see me, see how much his words hurt.

"I gotta go, I love you." A loud beep echoes behind his words, it's the timer.

I click my radio to tell him I love him, but it's just dead air.

"I love you, Dillan," I say, even if he can't hear me.

I drop my radio on the desk and rest my face in my hands. I don't know how I'm going to get through the next twenty-four hours. I need a distraction, something to keep my mind off Dillan and Cassie.

"Sorry," Mara says from the door. "I didn't mean to interrupt."

"No, come in." I sit up and smile like my life isn't in total chaos. "What's up?"

Mara is holding Taylor. "The kids are getting tired of cold sandwiches. I was hoping there would be a hot meal tonight."

Oh shit. Leah and Patsy are still locked in their cabins. I grew up two blocks from a Whole Foods. Their deli doubled as our kitchen. I'm great at warming things up.

"I'm not asking you to cook." Mara senses my distress. "I just need someone to keep an eye on the kids while I whip something up."

Taylor giggles in Mara's arms and reaches for me. This is just the distraction I need.

Mara gets to work in the kitchen making something called Hungarian Goulash. She cubes what is left of the steak, adds a bag of chopped potatoes, tomatoes, an entire jar of paprika, then tells me it will be done in an hour. While Mara cooks, the kids and I share some quality time. I play peek-a-boo with Taylor, and lose three games of Candy Land to Roger and Madeline. This is the first time the lodge has been filled with kids since we arrived. Somehow the kids make the lodge feel even more like a home.

Before the timer buzzes, the lodge smells amazing. When Mara deems the meal complete, she tops it with sour cream, and serves it with the almost stale bread from the pantry. It's a step up from Leah's chili, that's for sure.

Mara radios the children's parents and tells them dinner is ready. They start to trickle in a few minutes later.

Gavin's parents are older betas. Pete works in Genny with June and Sam. He's an electrical genius. His partner, Elle, is part of the group of females that run the laundry and clean cabins.

It doesn't take long to see why the children usually eat in the nursery; the kids are loud and messy. Madeline and Roger, literally, haven't sat still since their parents arrived. They run around the tables, knocking over chairs while screaming at the top of their lungs. Mara and the others scold them for my benefit, but I really don't mind. The joy on their little faces lifts my spirits. You can't help but smile and laugh with them.

"Who wants ice cream?" I yell, and the kids stop in their tracks. They raise their hands and yell, "ME! ME!" Even Taylor, who is sitting in Mara's lap, raises her hand.

I wonder where Carrick is. It isn't like he's with anyone tonight, and he's always in the lodge around dinner time. It would be nice to see him with Taylor. I'm sure she misses her father.

I grab my coat and head over to Hopi to get the ice cream. I'm halfway there when I see Clio walking towards the lodge. I wave her over. Her eyes are even more swollen than they were today. I forgot to radio her earlier and tell her my plan. I pull her into Hopi with me.

"Dillan agreed to let me go on the Truckee run," I tell her as I lift the top of the freezer and pull out a tub of ice cream.

"How does that help me?" Clio's bitter tone is unlike her. "Sorry, Kalysia, I'm just edgy tonight. I know my window will be closing soon, and there is nothing I can do. I don't see how you going with Tripp tomorrow will make it easier. He will still be gone all day." Clio takes the ice cream from me and heads towards the door.

"No, that's just it. I'm going to Truckee tomorrow, and Tripp is staying here, with you."

Clio turns around with a horrified look on her face. "You're insane." She closes the door to Hopi and pulls me farther into the pantry. "You will never get away with it. If Dillan finds out..." She shudders at the thought.

"Dillan will be occupied." I clench my jaw. Clio's eyes dart to the floor. She's embarrassed for me.

"All you have to do is keep Tripp in bed all day. By the time they realize I went alone, I'll be back."

"Who is going to tell Tripp he doesn't have to go? He will want to confirm it with Dillan."

She's right, he will. I need to enlist one more person to help me pull this off. I send Clio back to the lodge with the ice cream and head to Rusty's cabin.

It takes him a few minutes to answer the door. When he does, his hair is disheveled, and he's dressed in a loose pair of sweats with no shirt.

"I'm sorry to bother you, but I need your help."

Rusty listens to my crazy plan and adamantly refuses. "No way." He paces on his porch. The fact that he didn't invite me in leads me to believe he has someone inside. "I can't lie to Dillan."

"You won't be lying to Dillan; you'll be lying to Tripp. All I need you to do is radio him and say you found someone else to go on the run. Coming from you, he won't question who it is." I take his bare hand in my gloved one. "Please, I need to get out of here."

Rusty's stance falters when he sees the pain in my eyes. "What do I tell Dillan when he finds out? Because he will find out."

He's right. Dillan will know that I went alone, but what can he say? He will be so guilt-stricken that he can't be mad at me. Especially when I return safe and sound.

"Tell him I told you it was ok." Rusty shakes his head; he knows that won't be good enough. "Ok, then tell him I told you he agreed because I didn't want to stay in camp while he was fucking Cassie."

"That's even worse, Kalysia." Rusty runs his hand over his head. "I'll deal with his wrath when the time comes." He pulls me into his arms. As cold as it is outside, he feels warm.

I may have only met Rusty a few months ago, but we have a bond. We're family, true family.

"Thank you." I bite my lip to keep from tearing up. "Now get back inside and tell whoever is in there that I'm sorry for keeping you."

Rusty doesn't deny my accusation; he smiles mischievously and closes the door.

I return to the lodge and help Mara clean up the dinner dishes. When we're done, I find Taylor asleep in her highchair. I kiss her sweaty forehead and hand her to Mara to take back to the nursery.

The lodge is eerily quiet. Every movement I make echoes, and I feel how alone I am. I can't wait to get out of here tomorrow. Other than a couple of food runs, I haven't left camp. It'll be nice to be out on the road, on my own. I've never been alone before. The idea makes my stomach tingle, in a good way.

I turn off the lights and close the door. I check my watch—it's past midnight. I round Leah's cabin and hear her laughing. They must be enjoying every second of their seclusion. I wish. I wish nothing. I don't want to get knocked up, which is the whole point of all of this. They aren't just having sex; they are trying to

175

make a baby. A baby that will grow up in this life and have no say over their own happiness. No thank you.

I open the door to my cabin, and Dillan's scent smacks me in the face. I wish he were home now, although I think I know why he's staying away. He doesn't want to test our resolve. If we spend the night together, we won't be able to control ourselves.

The thought soothes my conscious. I thought it was just me not wanting Dillan's baby, but he stopped this morning. He doesn't want me to get pregnant either. We have plans. We want to travel and see the world. Having a baby, even if it is for the pack, will bog us down. I don't think I could leave my baby behind, not anymore. Not after spending time with Taylor. She isn't even mine and I know I will miss her when we leave.

I think about Leah and Cassie, how blindly they follow the ideals of the pack with no regard for right or wrong. This is a result of being raised as a pack child. One that is cared for by people like Mara and taught that their worth is measured by their bloodline.

Whatever becomes of Cassie's baby, I know she will always be there to care for it and love it, even if Dillan isn't. I just hope that leaving after the baby is born, doesn't cause Dillan any pain.

There is too much going on in my head to sleep. I open the back door and look around. It's quiet, the way it gets before it snows. I walk to the woods, undress, and stash my clothes. I leave two sticks crossed over each other as a marker, in case it snows and my clothes are buried. I phase quickly, before my human feet turn numb. I run along the edge of the perimeter gate, behind the tower, to a small opening I discovered in the far east corner. It's blocked by a large shipping container, but I am small enough to slip underneath.

I make no sound as I trot up the hill, towards the brew house. It only takes me a few minutes in wolf form. I don't like being this close to the building; I don't want to be spotted. I stay close to the wall, edging along until I reach the back stairs. I just want to see him. I put one paw on the step to go up, when I notice a snowmobile is gone. I sniff the air and catch Sid's scent. We only have three snowmobiles in camp. There are two here now, which means someone is using the other. I sprint back to the perimeter gate and slide through. If Dillan is on his way home, I need to beat him there. I decide to take my chances and run through camp rather than skim around it.

I can hear Leah and Drake talking. Ray is singing to Patsy, and then I hear him. I hear Dillan.

I skid to a stop and sniff the air. He's close by. I slink to the last building, the one with no back door. His scent grows stronger. I hear his laughter, followed by her voice. A low growl builds in my throat. I have to see him; I need to see him. It's a risk, but I stand on my hind legs, my front paws steadying me on Cassie's back window. He is standing at her door. The bed is open, but untouched. I concentrate on my hearing.

Dillan's voice is like an echo in my head.

"I just wanted to stop by and make sure you were still ok with this?" I detect something in his tone– fear, anxiety, anticipation.

She tells him she is fine and asks him to come inside. She is nervous, excited.

"No, I can't stay. I have to get back to the brew house. I just wanted to, I don't know. See you."

I hop down and run, I can't hear anymore. I don't want to feel the tension between them. The sexual tension. I run to our cabin and phase back to human. I run up the steps and slam the door shut just as I hear Dillan's snowmobile pass by. The hum of the engine fades as he heads back to the brew house. He didn't even stop to see me.

He drove back to camp for her. He's probably counting the minutes until I leave.

Another great idea, Kalysia. Leave camp so he can screw Cassie in peace. He'll probably make love to her in our cabin. He'll probably feed her chocolates and lick wine from her skin, in my bed. He'll ruin the sheets. Ruin everything.

She can have him, those two deserve each other. Following their parent's orders like sheep. They may be brainwashed morons, but I'm the fool that didn't see they were setting me up all along.

I thought Dillan was doing this for *our* future. I was wrong. And now I can't stop him. If he doesn't do it, his father will disown him. I definitely can't condone it. Not now that I know he wants her. He's probably wanted her for years. Long before either one of them knew my name. She is probably his real match, his true soulmate. I don't belong here. I never did. All I can do now is leave.

CHAPTER EIGHTEEN:

LOST AND BROKEN

I don't wait for Dillan to come say goodbye. As soon as the sky is light, I radio Rusty and tell him I'm ready to go. To my surprise, he is up and says the truck is loaded and waiting at the front gate. I dress quickly and head out to meet him. I don't want to see Dillan. I don't think I can hold my tongue about last night. I just need to get out of here.

Rusty and Carrick are having one of their never ending debates when I arrive.

"He can't take this truck." Carrick points at the back tire.

"We don't have time to unload and reload the other truck. Besides, this one has a full tank of gas." Rusty walks to the driver's side and sees me listening. "Hey, there. You're all set; I even warmed up the cab for you."

Carrick looks at me, then back at Rusty. "What the fuck?"

Rusty ignores Carrick's surprise. "You got your cell?" Rusty grips my shoulders and looks me in the eye.

I hold up the worthless cell phone Layla gave me. It's never caught a signal; I have no idea if it actually works.

"When you clear the mountains, you should get good reception. Here is Monte's number just in case." He hands me a business card and kisses my cheek. "Piece of cake."

I'm grateful for Rusty's hurried demeanor. The sooner I leave, the less likely it is I'll be caught.

"I'll be fine." I force a small smile, but I can't hide the hurt from my brother.

"Are you ok? You look...tired." He studies my red eyes.

I like his choice of words. "I'm ok. I need to go."

Rusty nods and steps aside so I can climb into the truck. "Your packing slips are clipped to the board on the passenger seat. You shouldn't have any problems finding the drop-offs. If you do..."

"I got it, Rusty." I close the door and roll down the window. "I doubt anyone will know I'm even gone."

I try to make light of the situation, but I keep hearing the longing in Dillan's voice when he stood in Cassie's door. I can't get it out of my head.

"Does Dillan know about this?" Carrick asks as I roll my window up.

Rusty waves goodbye as I pull out of the gate, then closes it behind me. I can't help but feel I'm leaving for more than just a delivery run, like I will return a whole new person. I know one thing for certain, when I do come back, things between Dillan and me won't be the same.

I find all the drop-offs without issue. When I get to my last stop, Gallup Saloon in Truckee, it starts to snow. The parking lot is nearly empty, aside from a beat-up camper parked alongside the worn down building. I put the truck in park and look at the address to make sure this is the correct place.

Snow quickly piles on the windshield, but I make out a blur in the doorway. I push down on the windshield wipers to clear my view. A short, stout man in a cowboy hat is waving me inside. I guess this is it. I get out of the truck and run to the door.

"Can I help you?" the man says in a southern drawl.

The snow is slick with oil and mud. The old guy offers me a hand and pulls me under the awning.

"I'm from Howlin' Ale. I have your delivery." I realize I left the clipboard in the truck and start to walk back into the snow.

"Hold on there, darlin', you get inside. I'll get my ranch hands to grab the kegs." He ushers me in before I have a chance to object.

The inside of Gallup Saloon is lit up with neon signs. It looks like Las Vegas threw up in here.

"I'm Bud." He offers me his hand.

I start to say my name when all of a sudden music blasts into the bar.

"Goddamn!" Bud covers his ears and yells something in Spanish. I have no idea what he says, but the music evaporates as quickly as it started. "Sorry about that, we're workin' out some kinks in the sound system." He sticks his finger in his ear and jiggles it around. "Kali, was it?"

"Uh, yeah." Sure.

"So, how many of them kegs did I order from that slick-talkin' sales rep of yours?" Bud moves around to the back of the bar and fishes around for something.

"I left my paperwork in the truck, but I think its two kegs." Since that's all I have left, aside from a couple of cases I have in the cab. Rusty left a note saying I should drop off some samples to a list of bars in Tahoe City if I have time and the weather holds up.

"Ah hah." Bud holds up a slip of paper and confirms it was two kegs. "He tried to sell me four, but I told him folks around here like plain ole beer. It's hard to sell that fancy shit." He smiles. "No offense." He tips his hat and bows his head.

"None taken." I smile and check my watch. It's 2:30. I'll be back at camp around four, six if it snows the whole way. I just hope Dillan and Cassie are done by then. Who am I kidding, I hope they're done now. It isn't like they need to do it more than once. Do they? I should know these things. I wish there was someone I could talk to. There is one person that would know.

"Do you have a bathroom I can use?"

Bud points me to a small hallway that leads to the unisex bathroom. I pull my phone from the pocket of my coat and check for a signal. It's full strength. I push Layla's picture and wait for her to pick up.

"Kalysia? Are you ok? Where are you?" She knows there is no signal at camp, so she must assume I left, and she's right. She's always right.

"Chill mom, I'm fine. I'm in a bathroom stall in Truckee," I say just to freak her out.

"What! Why? Where is Dillan?" I hear the TV in the background go silent.

"I went on a delivery. Dillan is back at camp." I stop there. I don't want to tell her what he's doing. I've effectively blocked it from my mind until now.

"Why are you on the run? Where are the others?" She asks irrelevant questions that I don't bother to answer. "Why aren't you with Dillan?"

I know exactly what she means by *with*. She knows that the season has started and I'm out gallivanting in the snow wasting precious mating time. I bite on my cheek and debate on how I should tell her that I'm not going to have a Lunam baby. "Things got complicated."

Layla suddenly gets quiet. She knows something is up. Just like when I was a kid, she knew I was going to do something stupid before I did. The longer she says nothing, the more worried I get.

"Mom?" I finally say, hoping I lost signal.

"I need to know exactly what is going on," she says in a slow, controlled tone.

I sigh into the phone and look at my reflection. I don't know why I'm so scared of her now. She isn't here; she's off living her own life, making her own choices, just the way she always has. This is my choice, my decision, my life.

I launch into the story quickly, glossing over the minor details and sticking only to the ones that matter, like Dillan getting disowned and me being passed around the pack if he didn't produce an heir. When I get to the part about Dillan and Cassie, she explodes.

"You did what!" I hear something break, a glass maybe. "You have a duty, to me, to your father. Does that mean anything to you?" I haven't heard her this angry since the night I snuck out to go to a party my freshmen year in high school. "I commend you on being selfless. I know how much pressure is on Cassie, believe me, I know. But we have a bloodline that you need to protect. Not to mention Monte will lose control of the pack to Lowell."

Monte, Layla, and Lowell care only about themselves. "I don't understand why you, of all people, can't understand why I'm doing this. You left your pack..."

"I left to protect you!" I hear the desperation in her tone. "I left so you would be the strong alpha female I couldn't be. So you would learn to make decisions with your head and not your heart."

I feel like I think too much with my head and not enough with my heart.

"I am thinking with my head, mom. The baby will mean nothing to Dillan."

"You're wrong, Kalysia. The baby will be everything to him."

Layla's words send a shiver down my spine.

"You alright in there?" Bud clears his throat from the hall. "I got some lunch waitin' for ya."

I cover the receiver with my hand.

"Yeah, I'll be out in a sec."

I hear Bud shuffle away from the door and put the phone back to my ear. I missed whatever Layla was saying.

"I gotta go, Mom. I'll call you again soon. I love you." I click the phone off and shove it in my pocket.

I play back Dillan's words from last night. *I guess I wanted to see you.* He doesn't mean it. He can't mean it. If he did, then what does that say about our relationship?

At least Monte's other conquests were results of rule seventy-five, a rule that was set up to protect the pack, not to secure power for one man. Now that Layla knows what Lowell is up to, I'm sure there will be consequences. At least I know one thing—she will have my back. She will protect me, even if she wants to kill me right now.

"There you are," Bud says as he stands behind the bar, tending to a couple of patrons at the other end.

"My wife, Sissy, insisted we feed you before sending you into the snow. This is her famous pulled pork sandwich." He gestures to the plate in front me. "She won't take no for an answer."

Luckily, I'm famished. I pick up the sandwich and take a bite. The barbecue sauce is sweet and smoky, just the way I like it.

"Whadya think?" He leans on the bar with a confident grin.

I give him a thumbs-up. "It's perfect."

"It's an old family recipe," Bud says and places a bottle on the bar in front of me. It reads *Willis's West Coast BBQ Sauce.*

"You can take that bottle home with ya." He winks. "Tell all your friends," he says and tips his hat like a cowboy in an old western movie.

I laugh with my mouth full of food and start to choke.

Bud sets a tall glass of water on the bar in front me. "I would offer you a beer, but the snows comin' down good now. You'll need all your wits about ya when you get back on the road. How many more stops you got?" Bud wipes the bar down with a rag then tosses it over his shoulder.

I gulp down the water and wipe my mouth with a napkin. "You were my last delivery for the day."

"Saved the best for last, huh?"

"I guess so." I drink the last of my water and stand up. "I should get going. Thank your wife for the sandwich."

Bud meets me at the end of the bar and walks me to the door. "You tell that rep of yours if this stuff sells like he thinks it will, you can add us to your regular route on one condition." He opens the door and a blast of cold knocks me back. "I get to see your pretty face come delivery day?"

I tap Bud on the arm. "You're a married man."

"Happily married," a female voice calls from the back.

"She's going to get me tonight for that one!" he whoops and slaps his hands together.

I zip up my coat and step outside. My boots crunch in the fresh snow. "It was nice to meet you, Bud. I look forward to next time."

"Likewise." He tilts his hat. "Now, you drive safe. The highway is just up past the light; you'll see the sign for eighty-nine south on the left."

"Got it!" I high knee it back to the truck. The windshield is blanketed in snow. I hop in and crank the heater. Even the cold air blowing from the vents is warmer than the air outside. I pull my phone from my pocket and plug it into the charger dangling from the dash. The wipers swipe the windshield, and I see Bud standing in the doorway. I don't like having an audience; just knowing he's watching makes me nervous. I put the truck in reverse and push softly on the gas, moving straight back. When I put the truck in drive and push the gas, the back end sways to the side.

"Whoa!" Bud comes running out, with no coat, his arms flailing in the snow. "Feather it," he calls out.

I give him a thumbs-up. I forgot the bed is empty now and much lighter. I downshift the four-wheel drive and try the gas again. All four tires spin and I move forward. I got this.

I wave to Bud one last time before I turn out of the parking lot. I've never driven in snow; the flurries fly at the windshield in

3D. I'm disoriented for a few blocks. It takes some concentration to look beyond the mesmerizing vortex of white flakes swirling in my face. The blue and white highway marker is half covered in snow. I make out the number eight and half of a nine. This must be the left Bud told me to take. I veer onto the highway and point the truck towards home.

As soon as I gain my bearings I remember what I'm going home to. Will he be back in our cabin waiting for me? What do I say? Part of me hopes he's angry about my leaving the camp alone; this will distract us from what is really on our minds. What we're really upset about.

I check the trip counter on the dash. I've only gone fifteen miles in half an hour. At this rate it will take me three hours to get home, and that's if highway fifty is clear.

The turn-off should be coming up any minute now. I look at the road markers and none of them look familiar. In fact, I haven't seen a single sign for Tahoe City or highway fifty. The snow is coming down even harder now. The wipers can't move fast enough. I see a blurred sign up ahead. I slow to a stop to read it.

"Highway forty-nine?"

I flip my hazard lights on and pull to the side. I grab the map from the floor and open it up. I trace my finger from Truckee to Tahoe, no highway forty-nine. My eyes drift above Truckee; I find the fork where forty-nine meets eighty-nine north. Shit. I've just driven half an hour in the wrong direction.

I put my blinker on and look around, the road is empty. I crank the wheel to the left and push the gas slowly. I don't want to get stuck in the snow.

"Come on, baby," I chant to the truck as it eases forward. Then suddenly the back tire lifts and comes crashing down. What the hell was that?

I jump out of the truck and run around the back. A piece of rebar protrudes out of the snow, and my tire is quickly deflating.

"NO!" My voice doesn't even echo because the snow is falling in sheets, insulating the air. Even if I could change a tire, I wouldn't be able to in this weather.

I run back to the truck and pick up my phone. Who am I going to call?

Layla will freak out if I tell her I am broken down on the highway. Calling Monte almost guarantees he will tell Layla and possibly even Dillan. The only working phone is at the brew house, and Dillan probably isn't there to answer it.

I'm on my own and I'm more than capable of calling a tow truck. I tap four-one-one into my phone and wait for an operator to pick up. The line clicks and dies.

The snow must be distorting my cell service. Great. I know I saw some buildings a half-mile or so back. Maybe I can use a phone there. I look out the back window and see a pair of headlights heading my way. I can flag the driver down and ask for help.

Layla's voice rings in my ears. *Never get in a car with strangers.*

It's good advice for a ten-year-old. I'm eighteen now, and I'm an alpha wolf. I can handle myself. I think.

The headlights slow as they approach the back of the truck, and I slink down in my seat. Some alpha.

I grab a bottle of beer from one of the cases and place it beside me. It's not the best weapon, but it's better than nothing.

The headlights belong to a truck. It pauses behind me, then slowly pulls away.

Oh no.

I sit up and roll the window down.

"Wait!"

I wave my arm out the window. The truck stops in front of me, and I see the empty flatbed. It's a tow truck.

CHAPTER NINETEEN:

JASE

The driver jumps out in his yellow snowsuit and jogs to my window. He looks like Kenny from *South Park* in his goggles.

"Looks like I found you just in time," he yells over the snow. "You headed to Quincy?" He points north.

"No, I'm sort of lost."

"You can't really be sort of lost. Either you know where you're going or you don't."

"I was looking for highway eight-nine south." I hold up the map.

"Well, you found it, its right's there." He points to the other side of the street.

He's got jokes.

"I mean, I made a wrong turn back in Truckee. I'm headed towards Tahoe."

"Yeah, you're totally lost then." He is all teeth and goggles when he smiles. "You also have a flat tire."

"Thank you for stating the obvious." I lift an eyebrow at him. "Can you fix it?"

"Not out here, but I can tow you back to town and get it fixed. The only problem is they just closed eighty-nine between here and Truckee. I'm headed home, to Quincy, before they decide to close the whole damn thing."

"I need to get to Tahoe today." I look at the clock on the dash, it's already fifteen past four. "Do you know if they'll open it back up soon?"

Goggles shakes his head. "It's not likely. It's pointless to get trucks out here to clear the road when it's coming down like this. They would rather keep people like you off the road."

I don't know what to do. I look around the cab of the truck. I can't just stay here. Dillan is going to kill me, if this crazy tow truck driver doesn't do it for him.

"What's it going to be?" He shivers and claps his hands together. "I need to stay ahead of Caltrans or else we're both stuck."

"Ok, I guess I'm going north." I roll the window up and put the beer in my pocket.

I pull on my gloves and jump out of the truck. My boots slide on the icy pavement and I start to fall.

"Careful." Goggles wraps his arm around my waist and sets me straight again. "My truck is unlocked and warm. Go get in. This will just take me a sec."

"Thanks," I say and walk to his truck. I open the door and jump in. The heater is on full blast. I turn the vent to my feet and pull my gloves off. The radio on the dash crackles and a male voice calls out a series of numbers. Then he calls a name. "Jase, you there?"

I hear Goggles reply on his handheld. "Jase here, what's up, Luck?"

The voice asks for Jase's location. He confirms the roads are closing and suggests he hurry back. "Lacy will strangle you if you miss her birthday."

"Yeah, yeah. I'm picking up a stray and heading back now." I hear a low hum and see the back of the truck tilting like a draw bridge.

"Oh yeah," the voice says. "Male or female?"

I grip the bottle in my pocket and look out the back window to see how Goggles answers.

"Quit being a douche," he reprimands the asshole on the other end of the line.

"Aw, she must be hot. You always get protective when they're hot."

The humming starts again and I see the truck being lifted onto the flatbed. I'm annoyed that the guys are having this conversation about me. But at least Goggles/Jase didn't reply. Hopefully that means he's a nice guy.

"All loaded, heading in." The radio clicks off. I sit back and release the death grip on my beer bottle. Just when I start to relax, the radio crackles.

"She's hot, Jase out." The door flies open and Jase hops in the driver's seat.

"You ready?"

I give him a nod and look straight ahead. So much for being a nice guy.

"I knew it!" The voice laughs over the radio.

Jase jumps in to turn it down. "Sorry about that," he apologizes.

I shrug and keep my eyes straight ahead with my hand wrapped around the bottle in my pocket.

Jase pulls onto the road and we head north, away from camp, away from Dillan and Cassie.

I must have dozed up off, because when I open my eyes, we're in a town. I check my watch; it's five thirty. Dillan must know I'm gone by now.

"Are we almost there? I need to make a phone call."

I yawn and look at Jase. I let out a small gasp when I see the man staring back.

He's taken off his beanie and goggles. His dark hair is a mass of waves that fall in perfect little swells on the crown of his head. His bluish-gray eyes sparkle under thick eyebrows.

"You ok?" Jase distorts his face, and if I wasn't already drooling, I definitely am now. He's hot. Like fireman calendar hot.

"I'm fine." I look away, but as soon as I do, I sneak a look at this profile. His parents must be supermodels.

"You look familiar," he says as we pull into a driveway. The sign above the building reads Jase's Tow and Repair. He puts the truck in park and turns in his seat to look at me.

I know I've never met Jase, because there is no way I would ever forget that face. "I just moved to California from Nevada so I doubt we've met."

"Really, when?" Jase gathers his gloves and hat from the seat.

"Last fall." I pull my beanie over my head and pick my gloves up off the floor.

"Well then you must look like someone I should know." Jase looks me over one more time before opening his door.

Someone he *should* know? Was he flirting with me? Something inside me feels warm and tingly. This is bad, really bad.

I get out of the truck and Jase points me towards the office where he tells me that Lucky will take care of me.

Lucky, the voice on the radio, looks to be around my age. He's a smaller, less good-looking version of Jase. He has me fill out some forms while Jase unloads my truck. I skip the home address and just give him my cell phone number.

"Is this good?" I hand back the clipboard, and he says it's fine without ever looking at the paper.

Jase appears in the doorway and says, "I have good news and bad news."

I sigh and put my head in my hands. "Give it to me quick."

"That's what she said," Lucky cackles.

Jase punches his arm and sends him to close the shop.

"The good news is, the truck had a spare. I put it on. Bad news is, they closed eighty-nine."

He pulls out a laptop and shows me an alternate route that will take me east, through Sacramento.

"You might have a better shot that way. The storm is moving north, so the roads here and here are clear." He points to spots on the screen. "You'll be in Tahoe at about nine or ten." I try to focus on the map, but all I see is the way the light of the computer screen dances off Jase's eyes. "So what do you think?" Jase spins the laptop away and leans on the counter.

"Uh, I don't know. What do you think?"

Jase looks at me strange and shrugs.

"I don't know; I mean; I guess it depends on how badly you want to get home."

"I don't want to go home." I'm shocked at how the truth just fell from my lips.

Jase breaks into a huge grin and I find myself smiling back. "Ok, then. Do you want to go to a party?"

Lucky pops his head in the door and interrupts me before I can answer.

"All closed up, boss. I'll see you at Joe's." He looks at me with a sly smile. "It was a pleasure, Kali."

I didn't realize I gave him the name Bud used. It seems fitting. I don't want to be Kalysia right now. I don't want the responsibilities, the pain, the anger.

Tonight, I want to be Kali—the Howlin' Ale delivery girl.

"So, where's this party?" I lean on the counter and lift my eyebrows to Lucky, the flirty way I've seen Layla do.

"Seriously?" Lucky looks from me to Jase. "I knew today was going to be a good day."

After a lengthy debate, Jase thinks it's best that I ride to the party with him in his Bronco rather than on the back of

Lucky's bike. The Bronco is an older model, tricked out with enormous tires and a roll bar. Lucky follows us on his motorcycle. The roads in town are wet, but Lucky races by doing a wheelie like it's nothing.

I cringe when he slices through a couple of big rigs. "Should he be doing that?"

"He's a fast healer," Jase jokes.

After a short drive, we arrive at a motel called Main Street Lodge. It's a horseshoe-shaped property with rooms that form a u-shape around the parking lot.

During the drive, I find out the party is for Jase's cousin, Lacy. I have to admit I was relieved Lacy was a relative and not a girlfriend.

The lot is already full when we arrive. Smoke from a barbecue billows from the small patch of grass that wishes it was a lawn. We pull into an empty space and Jase jumps out.

He rushes around the truck and opens my door. It feels like a scene from a Nicholas Sparks movie. I take his hand as I step out of the truck. I look at our hands clasped together like two pieces of the same puzzle. He squeezes tighter and blushes.

"Sorry, it just feels right," he says.

I think of Dillan and Cassie. Even though they are doing more than holding hands, I know it's wrong. I slowly slide my fingers free, and the moment I do, I regret it.

Jase looks slightly disappointed, but he doesn't show it for long. We are bombarded by a group of people. Jase introduces me to everyone as if we're at this party together. Like I was invited and not just some stray he picked up in the middle of a snow storm.

Jase's cousin Lacy is serious and reserved. She is the total opposite of Jase's younger sister, Delilah.

Delilah is a ball of energy. She dances when nobody else does and sings like nobody is listening. I love her.

The motel is owned by Jase's uncle Joe and his aunt Martha. They are a couple of retired flower children that moved from San Francisco to escape the capitalism that now encompasses the city.

After Jase introduces me to half the party, I finally settle down with Joe as he barbecues on the lawn.

"Yeah, we don't care much about equity or property value. If we did, we wouldn't have bought this place." Joe laughs as he flips burgers on the grill. "I still can't wrap my head around someone paying six bucks for a cup of coffee." He shakes his head and takes a drag on his hand-rolled cigarette. "What do you make of that, Kali?"

"I don't know. I was raised in a little city in the middle of the desert." I take a sip from the red solo cup Delilah handed me. It smells like orange juice spiked with pineapple flavored vodka.

"Now see!" Joe points his spatula at me. "Your parents had the right idea."

I nod and take a bigger sip from the cup. I like this, anonymity. It's so much easier than real life. Lacy stops in front of me to get a burger from Joe, and I ask her how old she is.

"I'm eighteen." She shrugs like it's no big deal. "How old are you?"

"Wait, let me guess." Joe taps the dirty spatula to his temple. "Twenty-one."

I'm flattered he thinks I'm older. I consider lying to him, but I change my mind at the last minute.

"No, I'm eighteen. I'll be nineteen in October."

"Oh. My. God. I'm turning eighteen next month! You have to come to my party! We're having it at the Elks lodge; it's going to be amazing." Delilah spins in a circle, and then hugs her cousin. "No offense."

Lacy rolls her eyes and walks away with her burger.

"Darn, I thought you had to be older, since you're wearing that Howlin' Ale jacket." Joe adds another stack of burgers to the grill.

I forgot I had on a Howlin' Ale fleece under my snow coat.

"Yeah, we're Shasta Brew people."

My heart is in my throat when Joe says Shasta. I look around the group; these people can't be Shasta. They're human. I can sense it. I think. I look at the blue eyes and wavy brown hair that some of the older people have. They could be Shasta, except for the small imperfections they carry. Most of them are overweight; wolves don't even get winter weight.

Jase places a chair beside mine and sits down. He has a beanie on, but it sits far back on his head, exposing his forehead. He is the only one here aside from Lucky that has the poise of a young wolf. If not for the small scar above his left eyebrow, Jase could pass for one of us.

Lucky is Joe and Martha's son, and they are without a doubt human, so that rules him out. He's just your typical cocky teenage boy.

"Don't look so worried. We aren't going to roast you over a fire just because you work for Howlin' Ale," Joe teases. He takes a long drag on his cigarette. "You got any of that swill on you?"

I tell him I have a few cases in my truck, and he sends Lucky to the garage to retrieve them.

Joe heads into the house for more meat, leaving Jase and me alone.

I sip from my cup and try to avoid eye contact. Something about his blue-gray eyes makes me feel a way I shouldn't.

Jase shifts next to me and clears his throat. He's waiting for me to look at him. Now I'm really not turning around.

The legs of his chair scrape the ground, and I feel that he's moved closer to me. I angle my body away from him even further. Jase lets out a soft laugh. It's a game now. I wait for his next move.

195

Twenty seconds pass. Then thirty. I don't feel him behind me anymore. I turn around and find the spot where he was sitting empty. Even his chair is gone.

I stand and scan the crowd. I can't believe he bailed that fast. I shouldn't care. I shouldn't feel rejected. I shouldn't feel anything for him. I sit down with a huff then freeze when I feel someone beneath me. I jump up and find Jase sitting casually in my chair. He takes a pull on his beer and smiles. He slouches like he doesn't have a care in the world. His swag is off the charts.

"I was sitting there." I pretend to be annoyed, but I'm sure it comes across as flirting. Layla flirts all the time to get her way. As long as I stay in control, I have nothing to feel bad about. I'm just having fun. Innocent fun. Unlike Dillan and Cassie.

"I know." He smiles and pats his thigh. "Have a seat." Thoughts race through my head. Bad thoughts, good thoughts.

"I can't," I say. I should tell him why, but I don't. I'm not Kalysia tonight. I'm Kali. Kali doesn't have to explain a damn thing.

"How about a tour then?" Jase stands and offers me his hand.

I stare at his warm, inviting palm.

"Ok," I say. I put down my red solo cup and shove my hands in my pockets.

Jase takes the small form of rejection with a mischievous grin.

He leads me through the crowded parking lot, pointing out an ice machine that looks like it's been around since the turn of the century, and a vending machine that only works if you kick the right side three times. We make a quick turn past a utility closet and come out at the back of the motel. There's something that resembles a pool and a Jacuzzi.

"In the summer the water is blue, I swear."

I laugh and continue to follow Jase around the motel. We move next to each other easily. Every now and then he places his hand on the small of my back to guide me in another direction. It feels so nice, so right.

"And over there is the trailer I sleep in." He points to a small camper-like thing that hooks onto the back of a pick-up.

"Good to know," I say sarcastically. The ego on this guy. Ok, maybe I would sleep with him if I really was just a delivery girl. But I'm not.

"Hey, just thought you'd like to know. In case you have a bad dream or you need a cup of warm milk." Jase bumps my arm with his like he's just teasing. I roll my eyes like it's the most ridiculous thing I've ever heard and not something I will most likely dream about tonight.

"What's that?" I point to the wooded area behind the motel.

"It's part of the Plumas National Forest." He steps closer to me and says, "Don't worry, I'm the most dangerous animal in these woods and I would never hurt a creature as beautiful as you."

He brings my hand to his face and kisses my knuckles. My heart thumps in my chest and a familiar burn rises in my belly. I suck in the cold night air and step away.

Jase holds my hand a second longer then lets me go. "Sorry if I overstepped."

"It's not you." I look at my feet and debate on how to tell him that I'm not free. I have no right being here, pretending like my life is my own. "My life is complicated."

Jase takes a step back. "Ooh, that's a problem," he winces. "See, I don't do complicated." Jase steps back further like I have germs or something.

"Really?" I challenge him and step forward even though I should run in the other direction.

"Yeah. I do casual. On very rare occasions I'll do complex. But never complicated. Complicated always turns into messy. And there is no way in hell I'm doing messy again." Jase starts to walk away, and even though he's rejecting me, it puts a smile on my face.

I walk back to the party and see my truck pull in and park next to Jase's.

"I thought I would save you a trip to the garage tomorrow and personally deliver your vehicle, ma'am." Lucky hands me the keys. "And, I couldn't carry all that beer back on my bike." He winks and closes the door.

Lucky hands Joe a beer and pops one open for himself.

Joe takes a long pull from the bottle. "Oh, this is not good, my friend." He points his bottle to me. "See, I have friends at Shasta Brewing, and when they find out about this, they won't be too happy to know they have competition."

I know Joe is just joking, but the accuracy of his statement causes a knot in my stomach.

"How did you get this gig?" Lucky asks as he pops open his second bottle. "Pretty sweet company truck to boot."

Delilah slides up beside me and hands me a fresh red solo cup then prances off. I shrug and take a big gulp. "I have friends in high places." I wink at Lucky.

"Sweet." Lucky nods. He seems like really a cool guy, someone that would've been perfect for Cassie.

I can't believe I'm still trying to match someone with her. She doesn't need a match now. She has mine. I shudder at the thought and down half of my cup.

I don't want to think about her or home. I look around for the one thing I should stay away from. As I'm scanning the crowd, Martha walks outside, carrying a cake. The party pauses to sing "Happy Birthday" to Lacy. She blushes and blows out her candles.

Afterward, Lucky plugs his iPod into the truck's stereo system and cranks the volume. Delilah pulls me over to dance, and I don't fight her. Tonight I am Kali, the Howlin' Ale delivery girl, and I want to dance. I dance with Delilah for two or three songs. I lose count. The one thing I don't lose sight of is Jase. I'm aware of his presence, where he is in the crowd. Whenever I look for him, he's always staring back. When a slow song comes on, Delilah ditches me to dance with a cute blonde boy.

I'm walking towards the barbecue when I feel someone tap my shoulder. I turn around and see Jase.

"Can I have this dance?" He holds out his hand, and I take it without a second thought.

He walks me to the bed of the truck, near the rest of the couples, and spins me around before pulling me into his arms.

I think of Dillan. Being in Jase's arms is a betrayal to him, to what we share. Then I think of him in Cassie's bed, and the sick feeling of guilt dissipates. My head is foggy from the alcohol. It doesn't feel the same as the buzz I get from wine or beer. This is stronger, sloppier. It makes what I'm feeling a little easier to bare.

"Do you believe in fate?" Jase whispers into my ear.

I shrug. "I don't know. I thought I did, now I'm not so sure."

"I think I was meant to meet you today."

"It was a coincidence. I wasn't even supposed to be on that road."

I wouldn't be if Dillan wasn't with Cassie.

"That's exactly what I mean. Something forced you onto the wrong highway. If you would have pulled off the road a few inches farther north or south, your tire wouldn't have popped. You would have turned around and gone home." His grip tightens around my waist. "It was fate that I found you."

It wasn't fate that brought me here. It was me playing God with other people's lives. If I would have just accepted my destiny,

I would be home in Dillan's arms right now. I would want to have his child, not offer my best friend as a proxy.

"I don't want to think about fate right now. Can we just live in this moment?"

"Absolutely." Jase pulls me close and gently rocks me back and forth to the music.

I feel Jase press his lips to the top of my head, and my body melts into him. He is something I can't have. I will never have. He is what I gave up for Lunam.

I am bound to Dillan in a way that I can never be with Jase. Even though I feel his warm breath on my face and his strong hands wrapped around my waist, Jase is a fantasy. None of this is real.

When the song is over, I break away. This is as far as I go. I don't know what will happen when I return home. But I know that I love Dillan. On the off-chance that I'm wrong about what I saw, what I heard between him and Cassie; I won't jeopardize my relationship for a drunken mistake. I step out of Jase's arms and try to smile. He has a longing in his eyes that makes it hard to walk away. I don't want to leave the warmth of his body. Not yet. I can stay in this fantasy a little longer. One more song.

I'm about to give in to the voice when someone calls his name.

"Hey Jase, gimme a hand with these heaters, will ya," Joe calls.

Thank you, Joe.

Jase nods to Joe then looks down at me. "Thanks for the dance, Kali."

He called me Kali. He doesn't even know my name. When I leave here, we'll never see each other again. He will be a fantasy in my head. Something I will never speak of to anyone. Ever.

Jase walks away to help Joe, and I go on a search to find my red cup. I end up getting a fresh one from Delilah, then I head back to the parking lot and pretend I'm not watching Jase as he hauls heaters from the supply closet.

Joe calls Lucky's name as he crosses the parking lot with a cute redhead on his arm.

"Luck, would it kill you to give us a hand?"

"My hands are full right now," he drapes his arm over the girl's shoulders and lifts the beer in his other hand.

Lucky spots me sitting on the tailgate of my truck and winks. Then let's go of the girl and walks towards me.

"I forgot to tell you." He disappears into the cab of the truck, then returns with my cell phone in his hand. "You have like a million missed calls from someone named Layla."

Oh shit.

I run inside Joe and Martha's apartment and lock myself in the bathroom. I click the voicemail app and brace myself. The messages are various stages of Layla demanding to know where I am, pleading for me to call her back. I think she even sounded scared in one, like I'd been kidnapped or worse, ran away. The last one is calm, too calm.

"I won't bother you anymore tonight. Just take this time to reflect on what's important. It's not too late to fix this. I know you'll do the right thing. Trust your instincts, Kalysia. They will never steer you wrong."

I doubt she would say that if she knew what my instincts were thinking right now.

There's no way I'm calling her back, but I do need to check in with Rusty. He must be freaking out. Not to mention Dillan. As I dial the brew house, I feel like I may puke. I lean on the sink and stare at my reflection in disgust.

"Hello?" a tired voice answers.

"Drake?"

"Kalysia! I didn't believe it at first, but when I saw Clio bringing food back to her cabin, I knew something was up. Then

Tripp told me Rusty called him and, well, I figured it out. What were you thinking?" Drake is hyperventilating.

"How's Dillan?" He's the only one Drake didn't mention.

"Uh, what do you mean?" He clears his throat.

"Where's Dillan? Does he know?"

"Well, uh. Yes, and no," Drake stammers. "Rusty told him you were snowed in. The weather got pretty bad here too."

"Well, it's not really a lie. I am snowed in. I also got a flat tire." I hear someone in the hall outside the door, and I turn on the water.

"Where are you?" Drake sounds like he's trying to deflect my questions.

"I'm in Quin... Where is Dillan?" The fact that Dillan isn't at the brew house tells me what I need to know.

"He's still with her?" My throat cracks and I fight to keep the tears at bay. It's difficult with all the alcohol in my system. "Tell me the truth, Drake."

"Yes, but it isn't what you think," he adds quickly. "After Rusty told him you were ok, Cassie called, and I don't know what she said, but he went back. He didn't want to, Kalysia. He really didn't."

"But he did," I say louder than I should. "So, he thinks I'm stuck in some hotel alone and he just rushes back?" I yell into the receiver. I start to unravel as thoughts of them tangled together on her sofa bed fill my head.

"He thinks Tripp is with you." If he doesn't know Tripp is at camp, he must really be preoccupied. "Rusty said you were stuck. Dillan still assumes he went with you." Drake sighs loudly. "When he finds out what really went down, we're all fucking dead."

"No, you're not; this is between him and me. I'll make sure he knows that." I pound the wall with my fist and feel it give slightly. "How's my sister?" I ask to calm my nerves.

"She's unquenchable." I like the way Drake's voice lightens when he thinks of her.

"Ewww. TMI, bro." I tell him not to keep her waiting long and that I will be home as soon as the roads open. He says he will relay my message to Rusty, not Dillan, and we hang up.

When I leave the bathroom, Martha is waiting on the other side of the door.

"Is everything ok, Kalysia?"

"It's great." I smile and move past her so she can use the restroom.

Wait. What did she just call me? I spin around, and she escorts me into the bedroom.

"Your mother called." She closes the door and sits on the end of the bed. "She said she traced your phone here with a GPS thingamajig."

Of course she did. "What did you tell her?"

"I told her you broke down and that my nephew towed you to his shop. She seemed relieved to know you were here with us."

Why would she think Layla is relieved that I'm here? She doesn't even know where here is.

"Does Jase know who you are?" Martha fixes the corner of the bedspread and avoids eye contact with me. "I recognized your mother's name from her caller ID. I know her family. I know who you are, what you are."

I step back towards the door, ready to bolt. Martha stands and moves towards me.

"Don't." I warn her and step back.

"I don't mean you any harm. I'm a friend." Her voice is calm and even. "I have a half-sister, Gale, who is Shasta. She's Jase's mother."

I relax my stance and process what she's saying. "Jase's mother is part wolf?"

Martha tells me her father had an affair with a female from Shasta, and they had a baby girl.

"My mother took her in because the pack wouldn't allow the baby to stay with them. When Gale turned eighteen, her real mother came to take her to Lunam."

"Half-breeds aren't allowed at Lunam," I tell her.

"Shasta has their own ceremony." She says this like it is something insidious, dirty. "An older alpha, a pureblood, chose Gale. She didn't want him, but she couldn't refuse. You can't refuse. That is how Jase was conceived."

"I don't understand. Lunam is about matching with your soulmate. Your life partner—it's a mutual thing."

Martha doesn't know as much as she thinks.

"At the official Lunam, maybe. Shasta has their own rules." Someone yells for Martha, and she tells them to hold onto their britches.

I can't get over the fact that Jase is the product of some poor girls' stolen innocence.

"Does Jase know all of this?"

"Of course. There are no secrets in our family." Her words sound like a warning. "Gale ran away with Jase. She left him here with us then left the state."

"What about Delilah?"

"She was born a few years later to another female. A friend of mine in the Dunsmuir pack reached out to me and asked if I would take her. When I found out she was Jase's half-sister, I couldn't say no. His father is a powerful man. He's also an egomaniac that thinks he can take what he wants from whomever he wants. I wouldn't be surprised if he has a dozen more children." She stands and moves to my side. "We've gone through a lot of trouble to keep the kids safe. Jase is special. You being here puts him in danger. If you leave and never return, I won't tell him who you are. But if you stay, he has a right to know who he is dealing with." Martha's message is firm, but her angelic smile at the end softens the blow. She thinks I'm someone that will bring harm to Jase, but she's wrong. I would never cause any problems for Jase, for any of them.

"We keep clear of the pack, both packs. We don't want to draw any attention our way."

I nod my head to let her know I understand. I don't belong here. Yet, something inside of me is happy to learn Jase is like me. At least part of him anyway.

I return to the party smiling. Knowing Jase is a Shasta wolf means our connection is real. He's as much a Shasta as I am. It makes sense now.

I scan the rowdy partiers and find him smiling at me from across the parking lot. I stomp through the crowd, my eyes never leaving his.

Lucky crosses my path, and I swipe the beer from his hand. I take a swig and keep walking.

Jase throws his head back and laughs. From my peripheral vision, I see others watching me, watching us. I stop in front of Jase; we are face to face, chest to chest, lip to lip.

"We need to talk," I breathe into his mouth. His lips part, and I pull away before he can even exhale.

Jase takes me to his trailer. It's a small space, the size of the living room in my cabin. I walk past the small table and sit on Jase's bed. He raises an eyebrow and clicks the lock on the door. "Just for privacy."

I nod in approval, and he closes the curtains above the table. He busies himself with minor house cleaning. He shoves a couple of water bottles into an empty Taco Bell bag and places it in the sink. I feel his nervous energy. I like that I make him nervous. It will make for a great story later.

I'm the last of my mother's line, so I know there is no chance he's an Orrin.

"Jase," I say as he moves towards a small radio on the counter. He stops and looks at me. "I spoke to Martha. She told me about your parents." I don't want to upset him by bringing up his conception.

He twists his face like he has no clue what I'm talking about. This must be something he does out of habit when people question him. "Martha's drunk."

I stand and cross my arms. "Really, so you aren't Shasta?" I hold back the smile that is fighting to escape my lips.

Jase is wolf, this means my attraction to him is a natural reaction. He could've been my match.

"Martha did a lot of acid in the sixties," he tries to joke.

He needs to know I'm friendly, not someone who will hurt him or tell his secret.

"It's ok." I reach for his hand, and he steps back.

"I don't know what you think I am, but you're wrong." The air in the trailer grows warm.

"Jase, it's ok. You don't have to lie to me..." I want to tell him we're alike, that it's ok, but the hatred and fear in his eyes tell me none of that will matter.

"Maybe you should go." He pushes open the door, and cold air fills the trailer.

I can't believe he's kicking me out. I brush past him and bury my shoulder into his chest. Jase grabs my forearm. I spin around, ready to punch him. I stop when I see the pain in his eyes.

We stand almost touching; I smell beer on his breath. He swallows back whatever he was about to say and lets me go. I walk back to the motel without turning around.

After I left Jase in his trailer, I didn't feel like returning to the party. I asked Joe for a room, he gave me the key to room three.

It's in the back corner of the property. From the window I can see Jase's trailer. He never returned to the party.

When the last of the humans go inside, I decide to go for a run. I creep past Jase's trailer and undress just inside the woods. I'm not familiar with this area, so I keep my things close to the road. It's late, nobody will find them.

I phase and take off at a full sprint into the forest. I smell rabbits and hear squirrels in the trees. I pick up speed, and I slice through the cold night air. I smell water, a lot of water. I skid to a stop, causing rocks and dirt to fly out over a cliff. I walk to the edge and look at the reservoir down below. That was close.

I turn around to head back to the road when I hear something behind me. I look into the darkness and see a pair of eyes staring back. He takes three cautious steps towards me, and I feel my hind legs crest the edge of the cliff. I growl a warning. Whoever it is doesn't know who I am. I'm an alpha. I will tear his neck out.

Jase suddenly materializing in front of me.

"Wait!"

He is half hidden by the trees, but I see his naked body in the moonlight. He holds his hands up in surrender.

"Don't be scared, Lacy."

Lacy? Why would he think I'm Lacy?

I shouldn't wait around to find out. I should run back to my room. But I don't.

Too many things are running through my mind. Human things. I can't hold the phase. My skin grows cold as I return to human form. Jase's eyes bulge from their sockets.

"Holy shit."

CHAPTER TWENTY:

JUST A DREAM

I stand before him, naked, and wonder why I don't feel embarrassed. It seems like the most natural thing in the world.

"How come I didn't know? I thought I was supposed to have some sixth sense." He steps closer and his eyes drift over my naked body.

I keep my eyes above his waistline.

"Maybe it has something to do with being part human."

He's part human.

"How did you phase?" I step closer to him in amazement. Half-breeds don't phase.

"Why did you call me Lacy?"

"Today was Lacy's eighteenth birthday. It doesn't always happen. I came out here just to make sure she wasn't wandering the woods alone."

"That isn't how it works. You only phase under the harvest moon." I don't know why I'm telling him this. He's a half-breed. He shouldn't be phasing at all.

"I didn't phase under the harvest moon. I phased in July one day after my eighteenth birthday."

"How old are you?" I ask as the full moon shines down on us.

"I'll be twenty this summer." Jase's eyes finally find mine. He steps closer and takes my hand. "You're the most beautiful thing I've ever seen, in both forms."

An energy courses through us when we touch. I can't control the burning in my stomach, my chest. My entire body is on fire. The feeling is so intense; I couldn't stop it even if I wanted to.

My hands are in his hair; his lips press into mine. We lose ourselves and fall to the ground. The twigs and dirt aren't as forgiving when you're in human form.

"Let's go back to my room." I suggest as I pull a pine cone from a place that pine cones shouldn't be.

Jase stands and helps me to my feet.

"I thought you'd never ask," he says with a smile.

He is quite possibly the sexiest creature I've ever encountered. At least that's the thought running through my mind right now.

"I'll race you." His blue-gray eyes light up.

"You're on." I phase and take off running. I fly around trees and jump over logs with ease. I even circle back and come up from behind, just to pass him again. He howls and jumps for me. We tumble end over end, over each other until we reach the road. I race back up the mountain, and he follows.

By the time we return to my room, we're spent. That's the longest time I've ever stayed in wolf form.

I shower quickly and leave the water on for Jase. I wrap myself in a towel and open the door.

"Your turn." I step into the bedroom and find him fast asleep.

His left arm is above his head, gripping the pillow. I don't think I've ever seen anyone look so peaceful. Nothing about Jase makes sense. I run my finger along the scar above his left eyebrow. There is no question that he is human. Martha said his father is a pureblood. Maybe that has something to do with him being able to phase. Are there more half-breeds like Jase?

Lowell Dukes will kill them all.

That must be what Martha meant by my being here is putting him in danger. I won't let anyone know his secret. Tomorrow I will leave and never see him again.

I turn off the shower and climb into bed beside Jase. I curl up at his side and pull the covers over us. I try not to think about Dillan or Cassie, or my pack. I just want to live in this moment. I want to steal some of his peace, even just for a night.

I drift to sleep and imagine another life, a life where I'm just a girl who is in love with a boy. I have no family duty; I have no pack to look after. I can just be me, but who is standing beside me? I see Drake and Leah, watching me, judging me. I see Cassie with her baby. We are standing in front of camp. I'm on the outside of the gate, while they are on the inside. Dillan straddles the line, looking confused. *Come with me, Dillan.* I reach for his hand, and even though he's close, I can't touch him. He's slipping out of my reach. *Dillan, come with me.* The gates are closing. Dillan steps back, inside the camp, and leaves me on the other side, alone.

"No!" I sit up in a strange room.

Dillan—no—Jase, Jase stirs beside me.

"Are you ok?" He sits up and turns on the light.

"I had a bad dream." This is the first nightmare I've ever had.

Jase pulls me into his arms and caresses my shoulder.

"You're ok, Kali." He still doesn't know my name. He turns off the light, and we lie in silence for a few minutes. "Was it about me?"

"No, of course not." I pet his smooth chest. "I have a lot going on at home."

I wonder if Cassie is lying in Dillan's arms right now. If they're talking about what color their baby's eyes will be. Pain shoots through my chest. I don't want to think about them. I want to live this fantasy a little longer.

"Yeah, so where is home? Are you Shasta?" Jase asks.

"I'm Sierra." I feel the air drain from Jase's lungs. "My mother was a Shasta, is Shasta. She is an Orrin. Do you know her family?"

"No, but that isn't saying much. I don't socialize with the pack. Not since I was a kid."

I'm an idiot. Half-breeds aren't accepted because they don't phase. Only Jase did. I sit up and rest my head in my hand. "Can I ask you a question?"

"Ask away."

"You didn't have to wait until the harvest moon to phase?"

"No, we phase after our eighteenth birthday."

"So, no Lunam, no harvest moon. You just phase."

He runs his finger down the side of my face. "Pretty sweet, huh?"

He has no idea how powerful that makes him. Our entire belief system is based on our ability to phase and that only happens under the harvest moon. If a half-breed can phase regardless of Lunam, that would make them the most powerful being in our pack.

"Are there others are like you?"

"Yes, but there are a lot more that don't phase. We don't know why it happens to some and not others."

"That's why you were in the woods tonight, in case Lacy phased."

"Yes, it's scary the first time it happens. Most of us don't even realize we can until we're running naked on all fours through the street." Jase looks at the ceiling and sighs.

It must be awful not knowing who or what you are. "Did you know you would phase?"

Jase nods. "Yes. When I was eight, one of the Shasta pack leaders tracked me down. He told me the pack was evolving and that I had a destiny to fulfill. He said he was planning to change things and that I would be accepted into the pack once I phased."

I recall the conversation between my mother and Conall. He must have been trying to allow half-breeds to attend Altum Lunam to make them official alphas. Ones that could lead the Shasta pack.

"I don't want anything to do with the pack. I was going to run away," Jase continues. "But I just couldn't do it. I didn't want to leave Lucky or Lacy, or Joe and Martha. Really it was Delilah that kept me here. I couldn't leave her to be taken by those animals."

"How does the pack even know about Delilah?"

"The pack leader keeps records of births, then shows up on your eighteenth birthday to see if you will phase." Jase sort of laughs. "On my eighteenth birthday, I sent Lucky in my place. He was only seventeen at the time. When he didn't phase, they took me off their list."

"What would've happened if you did go and phased?"

"Then I would have been obligated to go to Lunam. Not your Lunam," he clarifies. "Shasta has their own fucked-up version. Anyone can go. It's basically just an excuse for old alphas to prey on young girls. For guys like me, they expect us to match with a girl, but we don't have to stay together. It's just a hook-up to get her pregnant." He says the girls are other half-breeds, betas, or even low alphas. "If I have a child with someone from the pack, Shasta will consider it a full-fledged alpha."

This must be what my mother and Conall were discussing. This is why the blood test is so crucial now. Will it even matter once they find out half-breeds can phase? "Do you realize what this means?"

Jase shrugs like he doesn't really care. I know he does, he has to. He's still part wolf. It has to mean something to him.

"The one thing that keeps half-breeds out of Lunam, out of the pack, is your inability to phase. But you do. This means you are the future of our kind. The purebloods, like me, are getting too close in relation. We have one or two more Lunams at most before the bloodlines are too close to match. If we include your kind, or even just open up to the idea that we no longer have to limit who we love, we can create a new pack. One of diversity and acceptance, yet still powerful." I sit up and move closer to Jase. "You are the beginning of an entirely new breed."

"Whoa, wait a minute." Jase sits up. "I don't want to be the start of anything. I just want to be me." He smiles and pulls me close. "Me with supernatural abilities."

I have so many questions, but I doubt Jase has the answers. Cassie will. This is her fucked-up pack, her heartless father. I reach for the Shasta paw dangling around my neck and pull the chain until it snaps off. I don't want any part of Shasta. I keep the necklace clasped in my palm. It was a gift from my mother, something I thought I would pass on to my daughter one day. Now it's a symbol of evil. I toss the necklace on the nightstand and turn back to Jase.

He looks at it then turns his eyes back to me. "I won't be controlled by anyone, nobody should be." His jaw tightens.

I feel his body temperature rise. I kiss his shoulder and his heart rate slows down. He squeezes me to him.

"You're not going to rat me out, are you?" Jase sounds like he is only half joking. "You don't believe in all the pack bullshit, right?"

"No, I wasn't raised in my pack." I don't want to say anymore. I don't want to tell him I went to Lunam. He might hate me if he knew. I would hate me. "Your secret is safe with me."

Jase tangles his hand in my hair and kisses me. My chest swells with emotion. Usually it's the burn, the itch that drives my desire. But with Jase, it's something different, something new. Jase rolls on top of me and my legs part, inviting him in. I'm about to lose myself in pleasure when a cloud shifts and the full moon shines through a crack in the window curtains.

Jase pulls himself back. "Stop."

I kiss his neck and nibble his earlobe. "Do you really want me to stop?"

"No, yes, no." He can't make up his mind. Jase's mouth crashes into mine, and I gladly take him in. His tongue slides against mine and I moan. Then he pulls away again.

"No, we have to stop." He moves from between my legs and lies beside me.

"Is everything ok?" I pull the sheet over my naked body, feeling totally rejected.

"Yes, it's amazing. You are amazing." He kisses my hand. "But you know what time of year this is?" He gestures to the full moon. I'm surprised he knows about the season and the moons. "Martha warned me about all of that." He waves his hand around my head. "Believe me, the conversation was as bad as it sounds."

I laugh and sit up, letting the sheet fall away. "I can't get pregnant by you," I say. "Once you go through Lunam, you can only get pregnant by an alpha." I feel my cheeks flush.

Jase looks wounded. "Oh." He seems to be processing what I said, like he was told something different. "I always thought...I don't know, I thought I was an alpha."

"If your father was a pureblood you would be an alpha. But your mother's human blood makes you just a half-breed."

Jase still looks upset, like he's been lied to his whole life.

"This is a good thing." I stroke his chest. He grabs my fingers and brings them to his lips.

"Well, in that case." He flings the sheet off the bed and pounces on me.

Making love to Jase is a whole new experience. His kiss, his touch, and the way we fit together—it's like he was made for me. I anticipate his desires and he reads my mind. I don't want to leave. I want to stay in his arms forever. That is a fantasy I know will never come true.

Dillan, Lowell, hell, even Layla would kill him if they ever found out.

When the first hint of dawn creeps in the window, I know my fairytale has come to an end. I dress quietly; I don't want to wake him. I can't stand the idea of saying goodbye. I'm afraid I won't be able to leave. I look back one more time, and I can't do it. I can't walk out on him like this. I take the notepad from the nightstand and write him a note.

See you next lifetime.
Love, Kalysia

He at least deserves to know my name. And the love part, well, it just feels right.

The parking lot is peppered with empty red cups and beer bottles. I make it to the truck and start the engine. It roars to life, and I hope it doesn't wake anyone. I put the truck in reverse and look down at the clock. It's barely five a.m. I pull out of the parking lot and edge onto the road, when I see Lucky's iPod sitting on the seat.

I leave the truck running and hurry to Joe's door. I'm trying to shove it through the mail slot, when the door opens. Joe stands before me with a cup of coffee in his hand.

"And here I thought you were going to leave without saying goodbye."

"Uh, yeah." I look at room three to make sure the door hasn't opened.

"Are you returning your key?" Joe looks at my hand.

"Oh, no, um, this is Lucky's iPod. He left it in the truck." I hand him the iPod. "I gotta go." I motion to the truck idling in the driveway. White smoke billows out in the cold morning air. "Thanks for the room and everything. It was nice to meet you. Tell Martha I said bye."

I jog back to the truck; the icy morning air burns my throat.

"Hey Kal, hold on," Joe's voice echoes through the parking lot. I pray he doesn't wake Jase. "The key to the room?"

Oh, shit. "Um. Jase is still using it."

Joe breaks into a grin and waves me off.

I stop at a gas station and fill up on the edge of town. I need to put as much distance as possible between me and Quincy. I look in my rearview mirror every few minutes, expecting to see his headlights flashing behind me. The road remains empty. I make it back to the fork where he rescued me and my heart sinks. It's over. Whatever that amazing feeling was, it's gone forever. The closer I get to home, the more Jase and his family feel like a dream. I know what I've just done is wrong. So wrong. I was selfish and reckless; two traits I've fought hard to avoid my entire life. Considering why I left camp and what I'm going home to, makes my actions over the last twelve hours seem justified.

When I'm two miles out, I radio camp. Rusty's anxious voice calls back. The gate is open when I pull up. Rusty is bundled up, but I see the smile on his face. I pull inside and stop to let him in.

As soon as he closes the door, his smile fades. "What did you do?"

I shrug. "What are you talking about?" I drive up the road to the parking lot, biting the inside of my cheek. "I got a flat tire. I stayed at a motel in Quincy."

"Where the hell is Quincy?"

"They closed highway eighty-nine, so the tow truck driver had to take me north. I called Layla," I huff. "She knew where I was." Thanks to her sneaky GPS.

I start to pull into the line of trucks in the lot, but Rusty tells me to keep going.

"No, this truck smells like...you smell...just go to my cabin."

I pretend not to know what Rusty is talking about, even though I smell traces of Jase's scent in my hair and on my skin. He smells like sweet jasmine and mint, not as earthy as the Sierras. I wonder if it's a Shasta thing or just a Jase thing. The thought of him causes an unexpected grin.

"Oh Kalysia." Rusty puts his head in his hands. "What's his name?"

I bite my lip and straighten up. "I don't know what you're talking about?" I clear my throat.

"You can deny it all you want. Hell, I'm the king of denial, but you reek of sex." Rusty laughs as I stop in front of his cabin.

I pretend to be offended as I watch him jump out and run to his door. My jaw falls open when I see Carrick walk out.

CHAPTER TWENTY-ONE:

DAMAGE CONTROL

Rusty paces on his porch while I gawk at Carrick. "I, I mean, how... You have a daughter?" I finally choke out.

"Actually, I was married." Carrick kicks at the snow and stares at his hands. "She was my best friend and she knew about me."

He is quick to explain that he never deceived her. "We saw an opportunity to help each other. She wanted a child and I needed a diversion. My father suspected I was different, and he wasn't the kind of man that accepted different."

Rusty places his hand on Carrick's shoulder; it's a simple gesture, like a friend comforting a friend. "We've seen how they treat males like us. It isn't like we can just be ourselves. Taking a female partner is the best way to hide."

"Deann was a sweet girl. She accepted me for who I was and never judged me. I loved her." Carrick looks at Rusty and shrugs. "In a different way." My brother breaks into a smile and socks Carrick in the arm.

"You're not hiding, Rusty." I look at him in admiration. "Aren't you worried?"

Rusty walks down the steps and hugs me. "I don't have to worry here, not with you and Dillan. You two are the future. Once you set the tone, the others will follow. By the time Taylor reaches Lunam, who you love won't matter."

Carrick walks down the steps and hugs me, too. He looks around to make sure nobody is nearby, and then kisses Rusty. I guess he's still not completely convinced the others will let go of their ways just because Dillan and I are accepting.

A pain stabs at my heart. If we leave, what will happen to them? All the horrible things Carrick has seen could happen again.

Especially, if the packs merge. With everything I've learned about Shasta, there is no way they will accept my brother and Carrick's lifestyle.

"Whoa." Carrick steps back. "Where have you been?" His eyes narrow at me, and I can't help but smile. After all they've shared with me, the least I can do is share my secret.

I tell them how I met Jase and about his family. I leave out the fact that he phases.

Carrick and Rusty smile nervously and exchange worried looks.

"Sweetie, you know what will happen to him if anyone ever finds out." Rusty takes my shoulders and looks me in the eye. "You have to forget about him."

I shake loose and walk away. "I know." I feel tears building. "I know Dillan will kill him. I know I'll be shamed and maybe even outcast." I think of Dillan taking Cassie as his partner. "But, I don't want to." I wipe a tear from my face. "I don't want to pretend it didn't happen. Why should I be ashamed when Dillan doesn't have to be?"

Carrick throws his hands in the air and walks away. Rusty sighs and watches him pace in front of the truck.

"Carrick, roll the windows down. Better yet, get the pine tree." Carrick opens the door and waves at the air, shaking his head in disapproval. Rusty turns to me. "Is that what this is about? Dillan and Cassie?" Rusty rubs my back.

"I don't know, maybe." I would have never been on that run if they weren't together. I know I sort of condoned it, but now I don't know if I can live with the aftermath. My time with Jase makes it easier to deal with.

Carrick reappears from Rusty's cabin holding a small green air freshener in one hand and his walkie in the other.

"That was Drake. He's checking to see if she's back." He points the walkie at me as he crosses over to the truck. He hoists himself inside and puts the air freshener on the dash. "That should kill the smell. But what about her?"

"You need to phase." Rusty walks me to the woods near his cabin and tells me phasing is the only way to clear the scent.

"Trust me, we know. Carrick has seen you phase, so I know you can do it."

Carrick shrugs and says, "Your cabin is right in front of the tower."

Great. I bet they get a nice show.

"Leave your clothes. I'll take them to the laundry with mine. Then I'll go to your cabin and run you a bath." Rusty pushes me into the trees and runs back to the truck.

I take off my boots and undress. I take a huge whiff of my Howlin' Ale t-shirt and log Jase's scent to memory. Rusty and Carrick will have erased him completely when I return. I close my eyes and let the tears flow freely as I phase.

I run around the perimeter fence until I reach the tower. As much as I want to go for a real run, into the woods, I know time is not on my side. I watch Rusty leave my cabin. If I listen close and focus, I can hear the bathtub running. I realize Rusty never seemed worried that Dillan would be home.

I feel a growl in my throat at the thought of him soaking up as much time with Cassie as he can. Murderous thoughts flip through my brain. I stalk through the snow and focus my hearing on the cabin with no backdoor. I hear them breathing, sleeping. I can crash through the window and tear out their throats before they even open an eye.

I pick up my speed and something crashes into me. I roll into a bush and recover quickly. I spring to my feet and growl. The eyes staring back at me are a mirror of my own. Standing a few yards away is a larger, darker wolf – Rusty.

Carrick peeks from behind him. They must have been watching me. Rusty bows, submissively, and edges towards me. He whines and nudges my snout with his nose. I lick him in return. Carrick trots towards the gate and motions for us to join him. I follow Carrick and Rusty to the hole in the fence. We slip through and run up the hill. Rusty and Carrick prance over each other playfully; they look like two pups. When we reach the top of the hill, Carrick plops down and Rusty rests his head on his back. I sit and look out at the lake. It's so still and peaceful.

Layla taught me to swim in the pool at Harrah's when I was seven. She said I wouldn't need the skill very often, but it was something everyone needed to learn. Dillan promised to show me the ocean, but all of that seems like a fantasy now. Just a game we play to make the reality bearable. I don't even know if I'll be here when summer comes. I don't know anything anymore.

I hear Carrick start to growl, then Rusty follows. By the time I catch the scent, they are in front of me, protecting me. I see them emerge a few hundred yards away; there are five of them. Even though they are small, mangy creatures, these coyotes have been living in the woods all their lives. They are survivors, hunters, fighters. Unlike us.

I break down the hill for the fence, and Carrick and Rusty flank me. They are fast, as fast as I am. The coyotes follow suit, but maintain a safe distance. It's like they're corralling us back to our side of the fence. I skid under the chain links and crash into a garbage can. Its contents spill into the dirty snow. Carrick and Rusty come crashing through almost simultaneously, they phase back to human before they stop. Their naked bodies skid across the snow.

Carrick jumps up and pushes the garbage container against the fence to block the hole. Rusty pulls a pair of pants from one of the trash bins and slides them on. Carrick runs over and does the same. They have stashed boots and jackets in the bin as well. I stand on all fours and watch them dress. Rusty turns to me and yells, "Go home!"

I sprint to my cabin. I leap onto the back porch and land on two feet. *That was fucking awesome.* I'm getting better and better. My hand is on the knob to the back door when I hear the front door open. I hop off the porch and hide underneath.

It's Dillan. I smell his sagey scent mingled with Cassie's. Cassie's scent is similar to Jase's, except she has more of a minty odor. It makes me gag.

The back door opens and Dillan steps out. I'm right beneath him, under the stairs. He pulls his shirt off, then his jeans. He plucks both socks off, and then steps out of his boxers. Is he going to phase? My heart races in anticipation. I wonder if he's been phasing all this time and I never noticed. Suddenly, he stops and goes back inside.

"Kalysia?" He crosses back through the kitchen. "Are you home?"

He must have smelled me, sensed me. I hear him fumble with the dresser drawers, and then I hear his footsteps on the front porch. If he walks around back, he will see me crouching naked under the stairs. I should phase and run. I close my eyes and listen to his footsteps fading in the snow. Then I hear Drake. He calls out to Dillan and tells him I'm back. He says Ray spotted my truck in the lot. Dillan's pace quickens like he's running out to greet me. I hope that pine tree works.

I bolt up the back stairs and step over Dillan's discarded clothes. My feet leave muddy prints through the kitchen and hallway, but I could care less. Rusty must have turned off the water before he intercepted me at Cassie's. I dive into the bathtub, and water splashes all over the floor. I submerge my body in the large jetted tub and scream.

CHAPTER TWENTY-TWO:

LAYLA

I stay in the bath until the water turns cold. I sort of hoped Dillan would come back and find me. Not that I want to sleep with him, but seeing me naked might defer his anger. Dillan finding out Tripp didn't go on the run is inevitable. Rusty thought it was best for him to break the news; this way, Dillan wouldn't feel like he was duped by his closest allies. Rusty is loyal to Dillan, but he is my brother, so him following my command wouldn't be completely out of the ordinary.

I stand at the entrance to our bedroom, wrapped in a towel. The bed hasn't been touched since I left. Dillan has spent every moment I was gone with Cassie.

Dillan will never feel the same sting of jealousy that I will live with for the rest of my life. There is nothing to gain by telling Dillan about my night with Jase. The information is a dangerous weapon that will devastate Dillan and probably get Jase killed. It's something I will guard with my life. The only people that know are Rusty and Carrick, and I know they won't tell. Their lives are built around secrecy; they hold a lot of value in privacy.

I let the towel drop to the floor and open the dresser. No use waiting around for Dillan. I'm sure he's had his fill with Cassie. I pull on my underwear, and I hear the front door open and close. *Dillan.*

I run to the living room and find Elle, Gavin's mom, standing just inside the door with a laundry bag.

"Oh my gosh!" She covers her eyes with her free hand. "I didn't know anyone was here."

I look at my bare breasts and duck back into the bedroom. "Sorry!"

I put on a bra and throw a clean Howlin' Ale t-shirt on with a pair of sweatpants. I return to the living room with the towel I just used and hand it to Elle.

"Here you go."

She shoves the towel in the laundry bag marked with our cabin name.

"Thank you." She takes a step around me. "Do you mind?" She holds up the bag. "I'll just take a quick lap and be out of your hair in a minute."

I'm never here when they come and straighten up or get laundry. I've always taken care of these things myself. I didn't want anyone cleaning our cabin or doing my laundry, but Dillan says everyone needs a job in order to contribute to the camp. Not everyone is an engineer. I'm defiantly not, yet I don't have to clean other people's dirty clothes. The only thing that separates me and Elle is our DNA.

"How's Gavin?" I call to her.

"Uh, he's great." She sounds surprised that I know her son's name. "Thanks for asking."

I wonder if Elle likes cleaning cabins for a living. What is her life like knowing she will never rise higher than this? She reappears in the living room with a large smile on her face.

"I think that's it." Elle draws the string on the bag.

I look around awkwardly, like she may have missed a stray sock, then I remember Dillan's clothes on the back porch.

"Oh, um, Dillan left some things on the back porch."

Elle grins and says, "Yeah, I know. I ran into him on my way over."

"You saw him? Was he coming here?" I move away from the door and stand in the hall, behind Elle, as if she can protect me.

She looks towards the door, like the big bad wolf is about to burst into the room.

"He was walking towards...um, he was going the other direction..." Elle looks at her feet and fidgets with the string on the bag.

"Oh, ok. Well thanks for stopping by." I walk Elle to the door.

"Have a nice day, Kalysia," she says and closes the door behind her.

I grab my walkie from the holder next to the front door. "Rusty, come in."

I call him three times before he finally answers. "Hey sis, Dillan seemed to take it pretty calm, especially after I told him that you called Layla from the road to let her know you were ok. How'd it go on your end?"

"I haven't seen him." I picture him running to Cassie this morning, hoping to get one last quickie. Asshole.

"Oh."

I don't care about Dillan right now. He can wait. I want to talk to Layla about what I can and can't do. If running this pack is my job, then I should be able to have final say on job distribution. Lowell and Adel only spent two years in the pack before moving out on their own. Who decides when you leave? Can I choose to move people out earlier?

"Rusty, can you take me to the brew house? I need to use the phone." I release the talk button and wait for him to reply. I look at the empty hook beside the door and remember I don't have a jacket. Rusty took my clothes to expel all traces of Jase.

"Rusty, I'll meet you at the laundry. I need to pick up a coat, over."

I pull one of Dillan's beanies on and wrap a scarf around my neck. The sun is out, but the air is icy, as usual. I'm a few feet from my cabin when Rusty calls back.

"Kal, yer ma...*click*...On her wa—" *Static.*

"Rusty, I didn't catch that. Say again?" I hold the walkie to my ear and wait. Then I see her. She's dressed in a white snow parka and white pants, with gray snow boots. Sun glints off her dark glasses, and her hair is hidden under a scarf, but I would recognize her anywhere.

I wait for her on the porch with a big fake smile. Layla gives me a quick hug then heads inside.

"Oh my." She pulls her glasses off and unravels her scarf. "I forgot how thin the air is up here." She grips her chest. I lean against the back of the sofa and wait for her to take off her coat and settle in.

"What are you doing here, Mom?" I cross my hands over my chest. "Are you checking up on me?"

"Course not. I just thought I ought to see your new place." She looks around, unimpressed, even though the room is exquisite. "It's cozy."

"Yeah right," I huff. "So, what do you consider the apartment in Pahrump?"

Layla's eyes meet mine. "Functional," she says sternly. "Pahrump was a temporary arrangement; it was never meant to be a home."

I throw my arms in the air and walk towards the hallway. "It was only my entire childhood, Mother." I spin around and bite my lip. I don't want to tear up in front of her. "It wouldn't have killed you, or me, to warm it up a bit. You know how embarrassing it was bringing friends over and not having one baby picture of me on the wall?" I meet her eyes. "They thought you kidnapped me or something."

Layla laughs a little too hard at my joke, and I wonder if there is some truth to it.

"I happen to *love* this place." I wave my arms around. "I've never felt more at home." I pause and clear my throat as I think of me and Dillan. This is our home. "I've never been happier."

Layla narrows her eyes at me. "You sure about that?"

I want to throw myself in my mother's arms and cry. Instead I stand tall and say, "Yes."

"So, have you seen Dillan today?" I can tell from her tone that she already knows the answer, so I don't bother responding.

"I'm surprised you're here actually. I thought I would beat you home after partying all night." Layla sits on the sofa. "Do you have any coffee?"

My jaw drops. She knows. She knows about Jase. I don't know how, but I can tell by the smug way she's watching me.

"We don't keep food in the cabins. If you want coffee, you have to go to the lodge."

"What good is a kitchen if you don't have food?"

I think about our first council meeting, which feels like a lifetime ago.

"Not all the cabins have kitchens. I didn't think it was right for a privileged few to keep camp food for themselves."

Layla looks impressed. "So who has access to the food?" She looks genuinely interested.

"The council has keys." I reach around the kitchen door to the hook where the keys are. I hold them up for Layla to see. I explain the log and signing out food. "It keeps us all accountable."

Layla nods with a sly smile on her face. "And what if someone abuses the rules and takes food for themselves. Are they punished?"

"No, geez. It's just an honor system."

What does she want me to do, tie them to a tree and starve them out?

"If only council members have keys, and they aren't punished for taking extra food, then why bother? I mean, the betas are still only getting what you allow them."

Layla makes a huge point. I never looked at it like that.

"Except I left a spare key under a mat at the cabin, so the others can have access anytime they want." Checkmate.

Layla nods in consideration. I can't tell if she thinks it's brilliant or utterly pointless.

"Look, you didn't come here to talk about food distribution," I say to her. "So, what is really going on?"

Layla admits that she was worried after our call last night. "I know the family you were with. The Parkers have ties to the Shasta pack that go back for generations. They're like a halfway house for half-breeds."

I think about the only tie I care about.

"Did you meet any of them? Martha said it was her niece's birthday." She raises an eyebrow to me. We both know the importance of the milestone, but it doesn't mean anything to half-breeds since they don't phase. Except some do.

Layla sees the acknowledgment on my face. "Kalysia, did you see something?" She stands and comes towards me. I spin around and go into the kitchen so she doesn't see the lie on my face. "Honey, you can tell me." She turns on her sweet voice. "I've heard rumors; I know Shastas are keeping something from the rest of the pack. It's something to do with the half-breeds who mate with purebloods."

She knows, which means Lowell and Monte must know. They are her only source of information. I can't tell her I saw Jase phase. I don't know what they will do to him if they find out. Lowell hates half-breeds; he thinks they are a threat. He will kill Jase.

"Kalysia, listen to me." Layla grabs my arm. "If you saw someone phase, you have to tell me. I need to report it. I just want..."

"It wasn't Lacy," I blurt out. Fuck. I shouldn't have said that, but I don't want them harassing Lacy. She's so sweet and shy. She isn't a threat to anyone.

Layla's grip tightens. "What did you see? I need to know." Her words bounce off the walls of the kitchen. "Who was it?"

"I don't know. I didn't see them in human form." I focus on the cabinet behind Layla's head. It's the only way I can keep a steady face while I lie to her.

"I phased and I saw someone in the woods." An image of Jase's naked body glistening in the moonlight pops into my head. It takes amazing self-control not to sigh. "I never saw who it was, I just know it was a male."

I think about Dillan so my face doesn't give anything away. I wonder where he is. If he knows Layla is here. "Does Dillan know you're here?"

"Of course. Any alpha that comes to camp has to report to the leader, even me." Layla smirks. She considers the story I've just told her and seems to relax. Her eyes search mine for any sign of a lie. I think I've pulled it off. "So, how did you know the wolf you saw was a male?"

Damn. Nothing gets past my mother.

"Um, I don't know. I just knew, I guess." I shrug and turn towards the sink. I pull a clean glass from the cabinet and fill it with water. I drink the whole glass and fill it again. When I turn back to Layla, her eyes are wild with anger.

"Who is he?" Her words come in slow individual sentences. She steps closer to me, like a cobra about to strike, or in my case, a crazy angry she-wolf.

I don't answer, not with words. My eyes give me away as an unsuspecting tear rolls down my cheek.

"Oh Kalysia, you didn't?" She places her hands on my shoulders and I flinch. Layla looks wounded by my fear and takes me in her arms. "It's ok, we can work through this. I just need to know everything."

I shake my head in her arms. "I can't tell you. Dillan and Lowell will kill him," I sob.

"I'll take care of it, don't worry. You can trust me." Layla fills a glass of water for herself and takes a drink. "Ugh. Do you at least have bottled water?"

I reach under the cabinet and pull out a bottle of wine. "These are the only bottles I have." I crack a wry smile and hand the bottle to Layla.

After gulping down two glasses of wine, I tell Layla everything. I tell her about Gallup Saloon, the snow storm, and how I got on the wrong freeway. I explain how Jase just showed up as if it was destiny, my destiny. I don't realize I'm twisting the story to sound as if Jase and I were meant to be together until I'm done and I see the way Layla reacts.

"Kalysia, you know you can't have a life with this boy."

I roll my eyes and sip my wine. "Then why do I feel so connected to him?"

Layla pats my hand as if I'm a child. "This could be your way of dealing with Dillan and Cassie." I pull my hand away from her and wrap it around my wine glass. "And, he is a half-breed." She chokes on the words.

"So." I sit up boldly. "Just because pureblood blood pumps through my heart, doesn't mean I can't love someone like Jase." *What am I saying?*

Layla looks like I just slapped her across the face. It takes her a full minute to gain her composure. "You don't love him," she says through gritted teeth.

"You don't know that." *I don't even know.* "I don't even know if I love Dillan."

Layla's shoulders relax a bit. "That's perfectly normal." She reaches for my hand, and I pull away. "It's ok to be confused, especially this early on. But you will grow to love him, in your own way."

"The same way you loved Monte?" My words sting her. "You don't understand what love is. You didn't love Monte and you didn't love Miles. I doubt you even love me."

I feel dizzy from the outburst and realize it's the alcohol.

Layla stands and walks to the fireplace. Neither of us speaks for a while.

I take my glass to the kitchen and dump it in the sink. I had no right to say that to her. I don't know what she feels or the things she lived with. I barely know who Layla is.

"I only want what's best for you, Kalysia," she says softly from the doorway. "Maybe part of me wanted to live through you. I wanted to make sure you made all the right choices, but I never thought about whether they would be *your* choices. I never stopped to ask if you wanted any of this." She bites her lower lip and swallows back tears. "Nobody ever asked me what I wanted. It was assumed, and I hated it. I think that may be why I matched with Monte. I wanted to make my own decision. I never realized the effect my choices had on other people, my family—my pack." Layla crosses the room and takes my hands. "Our lives are not our own, I wish it were different, but it isn't. We have a duty. We have others to take care of."

"This pack doesn't need me," I start to say. Then I think of Rusty and Carrick. I think of how safe they feel here because of me and Dillan.

"They do need you. The alphas in my branch took all the food for themselves and left scraps for the betas. I couldn't do anything about it because I was a cross-over. No longer Shasta, not really a Sierra." Layla gains her composure and steps towards me. "That's why I left. I refused to let them brainwash you into thinking you weren't as strong, as powerful, as worthy as the others because you are part Shasta. It killed me to leave your father, to leave my family."

I know now why she never shared her stories. I would have never gone to Lunam.

"I'm sorry your match didn't turn out any better than mine. But this is the life you have chosen, Kalysia. You must see it through, and you must produce an heir." I open my mouth to protest, but Layla won't let me. "Our only hope to change the way the pack is run, is to gain power. Having a child will give you power. They will be forced to pay your stipend and when the time comes, you will have a spot on the council. We have to have as many people like you, like Monte, on the council as possible. You, Leah, Drake, Dillan, even Rusty—you are the future."

The thought of being with Dillan makes my stomach hurt. It isn't that I'm not attracted to him; he's beautiful, but he's tainted now.

"Isn't it too late?"

"You still have time." She takes my hand and pulls me into her arms. "You care for Dillan. If you didn't, you wouldn't be here. You wouldn't have let him mate with Cassie to appease Lowell. Deep down I think you want to give him a child, you're just scared."

She's right. She's always right. There is more to it. I'm selfish. I want to do all the childish things Dillan and I planned. I want to zip-line in Cancun and make love in the ruins. I want to kiss him at the top of the Eiffel Tower and eat pizza until we puke in Naples. I want to do all of those things before we have a child. I want to live my own life, something my mother never had a chance to do.

"The Sierras need purebloods more than ever. If the packs merge now, Monte will lose control and things will get bad. Very bad."

If Shasta takes control with their screwed-up values and backward thinking, who knows what the future holds for Rusty. What kind of world will Taylor grow up in? Will she be homeschooled and live in a trailer park like Cassie?

"If we can prove their lines are tainted, then the Shastas lose all credibility. Dillan and Cassie's baby won't matter because her bloodline will be in question. She didn't match for a reason; we just have to prove she is not pure." Layla looks desperate. I wonder if her concern is about the future of the pack, or if she is just worried about Monte. Seeing them in Napa, they looked happy and in love.

"Right now only Shasta can prove their half-breed phase. Sierras turn a blind eye or are just too damn stubborn to accept we have evolved. I spoke to the elder council about the possibility of phasing half-breeds, and they looked at me like I was crazy. They won't even consider it."

I need to tell her about the deal Conall made with Lowell. She needs to know what they're up against. Now that we know half-breed Shastas phase, this changes everything. It makes the merge even more likely to fall in Shasta's favor.

My radio buzzes on the counter and my heart jumps in my throat. Rusty's voice echoes into the kitchen. "Kalysia, pick up." He sounds hurried.

Layla goes to the sink for water and fills a glass.

"Go Rusty."

"Hey, is Layla still with you?" He clicks off and I look at my mom. She looks at me curiously.

"Yeah, why?"

"Looks like we're about to have a family reunion." He clicks off and then back on again. "Monte just pulled in."

CHAPTER TWENTY-THREE:

AKWARD

"Did you tell him you were coming here?" I scramble to hide the wine bottle and place our glasses in the sink.

"Well, sort of." Layla bites her cheek, and I realize how alike we are. "I left him a note."

Oh my God, we are alike. I break into a huge smile. "I love you, Mom."

We run into the living room. I sit on the sofa while Layla stands, awaiting Monte's arrival. I don't know why I feel so nervous. He doesn't know anything. Yet, my heart is pounding as if Dillan is going to walk in the door.

"What should I say?" I run my hands through my thick hair.

Layla sits beside me and takes my hand. "Don't worry, I'll handle him. I'll make sure he doesn't know about, uh, what's the boy's name?"

"Jase." I hope telling her isn't a mistake. He went to great lengths to keep his identity a secret.

"His mother is a half-breed and his father is a pureblood Shasta, right?" Layla seems to be logging all the details in her head. We won't be able to discuss him once Monte arrives.

"Yes. His aunt Martha told me his mother was a half-breed Shasta and his father was a..." I can't remember if she said Shasta. "She said his father was a pureblood, I assumed she meant Shasta."

Layla nods in agreement. "It has to be; no true Sierra would mix with a half-breed Shasta. And he was a tow-truck driver?" She grips her chest at the thought of her daughter with a grease monkey.

"He actually owned the shop where he fixed my car." I recall the sign on the building, Jase's Tow and Repair Service.

"How old is this boy?" Layla looks at me disapprovingly.

"He's only nineteen; he'll be twenty this summer."

"How can he afford a business at his age?"

"His aunt and uncle probably help him."

"The Parker's own a rundown motel. There's no way they can carry two businesses." Layla stands and looks out the front window. "He's coming."

The blood drains from my face, until I realize she means Monte and not Dillan.

Layla opens the door before Monte knocks. "Darling, what are you doing here?" She pulls him to her for a kiss. "I told you not to worry. It's just girl stuff." She winks at me, and I flash a nervous smile. "How was the drive?"

I love watching my mom in action. I wonder if I will be like her one day.

"The drive was horrible." He kisses Layla again. "Kalysia, you look healthy."

Is that the best he can do?

"Thank you, Monte." I remain on the sofa while Layla shows Monte around the cabin. I suspect she is telling him a lie about why she is here. I'm sure it's something to do with me and Dillan. When he returns from the extensive tour of the bathroom, he is blushing.

"I'm glad to hear you are, uh, feeling better." Monte gives me a tight-lipped grin and offers me a hug. I stand and hug him.

"So, how do I get to the brew house? I might as well take a look while I'm here."

"Oh, um..." I retrieve my radio from the kitchen. "Here, call Rusty and he can pick you up." I hand him the walkie. "Have you seen Leah?"

"No, I uh, haven't had a chance." Monte fiddles with the knob on the walkie.

"Well, her cabin is right next door. You can say hi before you head to the brew house."

Monte finally reaches Rusty and asks him to pick him up. "Hurry," he adds and then hands me the walkie. "Yeah, I don't know if I'll have time to see Lisa, er, uh, Leah. I'm on a tight schedule."

Layla decides it's best for her and Monte to wait outside after she sees my reaction. He doesn't even know her name! I doubt he even knew mine before Lunam. I know Leah's birth was for the pack, not because he wanted her. Will Dillan be just as cold as Monte is with his child? I run to the bathroom and puke. It's mostly wine and water with a few undistinguishable chunks. I flush it down and wash my face.

How could I have assumed Dillan and Cassie's baby was just a business transaction? What kind of monster would I be if I asked Dillan to abandon his child for me?

I sip water from my hand and spit it at my reflection. "Idiot."

I hear the door open and close. Layla must have forgotten something. I pat my face dry and wipe off the mirror. I listen to the footsteps crossing the living room towards the hall. Those aren't Layla's boots. I smell her before I see her.

"I saw Layla and Monte leave with Rusty." Cassie looks tired from staying up all night with my boyfriend.

"What do you want?" I growl. Murderous fury builds in my chest as I step towards her. The image of her and Dillan sleeping beside each other burns in my head. Images in the room start to turn fuzzy; I feel like I'm about to phase.

"I just want to talk to you, to explain before the others try..." She steps back into the living room. "It isn't what you think." She holds her hands in front of her, as if her weak ass could stop me if I attacked. I'm stronger, smarter, and deadlier than she will ever be.

"Kalysia, please." Her back is pressed flat to the front door. I press my forehead to hers and I smell him. I smell him on her face, her hair, even her breath smells of his.

"Phase," I hiss. Cassie's eyes are a mix of fear and bewilderment. "Phase." The word roars from my chest. I step back to allow her room to turn.

"Here? Now?" Cassie's eyes are wet with tears yet to fall. Her weakness fuels my rage.

"Outside." I point towards the back door, and she cautiously moves past me. Once we are on the back porch, I tell her to strip.

"You want me to take off my clothes?" She wraps her arms around her body. I nod, and she squeezes herself tighter. I step towards her, and she begins to undress. She unzips her fleece jacket and then takes off her shirt. She isn't wearing a bra. Next she unzips her pants and pulls her underwear off. "Kalysia, please. Don't make me do this."

Seeing her weakness breaks me a little. The insecure way she holds herself, the smell of fear emanating from her skin.

"You have to." My tone softens. "It's the only way to remove *his* scent." I look at the tower and wonder if Carrick is watching.

If he is, he will call Rusty.

"Just phase now, hurry." I gather her clothes in my arms. "I'll meet you at your place."

Cassie slowly descends the stairs; her arms are wrapped around her body. When her feet make contact with the icy dirt, she shrieks. She lifts her foot and examines the mud, making a noise of disgust.

"Just phase already!" I yell down to her. She takes another couple of steps and focuses on the woods. Her phase is sloppy. Her body twists and she lands on her side with a yelp. Her paws slip from under her and she looks up at me like a scared puppy.

"Go home," I command, and she takes off towards her cabin.

My arms are filled with Cassie's discarded clothes. I don't see the sled lying in the middle of the path until I'm on the ground.

"Ouch!" I yank the sled from under my back and sit up.

"Are you ok?" Leah is suddenly by my side. She offers me her hand.

"I'm fine." I dust myself off and kick the sled.

"I'll make sure someone is punished for this." She tosses the sled into a bush.

"No, Leah, geez. It was an accident." I gather Cassie's clothes from the ground.

"Do you need help with that?" Leah gestures to the muddy clothes in my arms, but I can tell she doesn't want to touch them. Leah was raised as the daughter of an alpha. She's used to being waited on by betas.

"I got it." I wait for her to move on. When she doesn't, I ask her if she needs anything else.

"I was just, uh, wondering if you spoke to our father." She looks nervously at the ground.

"I did."

"Do you know why he's here? Is everything ok?" She looks up at me.

"He's here because of me."

Leah's face turns red. "Oh." I feel the bitterness in her tone.

I feel bad about Monte not knowing her name. I wonder if she knows how unimportant she is to him now that I'm back. "He's not really here for me, he came because of Layla. She's here for me. She wanted to make sure I got back safely." I roll my eyes for a dramatic effect. "He's at the brew house. Why don't you ride up there with Drake and say hi?"

Leah shrugs. "I don't know, he's probably busy. I don't want to bother him."

"He's your father. You have every right to disturb him." I nudge her with my elbow in a sisterly fashion.

I don't truly believe what I'm saying. How much right do we have as Monte's children? I know I can call Layla anytime night or day and she will pick up. She would drop everything for me. She would drive two hundred miles at the drop of a hat to make sure I'm ok. Will Dillan do that for his child? Will I let him? Do I have a right to decide?

"Honestly, I'm scared of him." Leah says this with a laugh. "I mean, shit, I've only spoken to him a handful of times in my life. The longest conversation we ever had was when he told me about you going to Lunam."

I never thought to ask when my brother and sister found out I existed. I thought everyone knew about Layla. "You didn't know you had a sister?"

"I didn't. Rusty knew, I think. He didn't seem surprised to hear your name, just shocked that you showed up for Lunam."

"What did Monte tell you about me?"

Leah shrugged and shoved her hands in her coat pockets. "He said he had another daughter, a pureblood daughter, and that there wouldn't be as much pressure on me to make a good match. He actually pointed you out and said, 'She's the prettiest girl here.' So, yeah, it sort of stung."

"I'm sorry." I readjust the clothes in my arms. "I guess Monte can be a bit of a douche."

Leah giggles. "Yeah, I guess. But you are nothing like I thought you'd be."

"Is that a good thing or a bad thing?"

"Definitely good."

Leah's walkie interrupts our sisterly bonding, and she takes off for the kitchen.

As soon as she rounds the corner to the lodge, I hurry to Cassie's. I creep in slowly and call her name. She doesn't answer. I look at her unmade bed; the sheets have been stripped. The smell of pine mingles with her scent and Dillan's. Rusty must have instructed the beta that cleans her cabin to use the pine. *Thanks, Rusty.*

I hear a rustling at the door before Cassie's naked body stumbles inside.

"What took you so long?" She shivers and runs to the bathroom.

"Leah stopped me." I place Cassie's dirty clothes on the floor near the door and close it.

I stay while Cassie showers. I don't know why; I'm hiding I guess. Cassie's is the last place Dillan would look for me. Or maybe I want to see if Dillan shows up.

Cassie jumps when she opens the bathroom door and sees me sitting at her small dining table. She doesn't speak; she crosses the room to a mini-fridge and pulls out a bottle of water. She places it on the table in front of me and then takes one out for herself. We drink the water in silence.

I don't know how much time passes, but the sun is high in the sky, and some of the older kids are running past the cabin, towards the field to play kickball. I feel my stomach rumble. I haven't had a real meal since the pulled pork sandwich at Gallup.

Joe and Martha shoved plates of food in my hands, but they were replaced by red solo cups from Delilah.

"Are you hungry?" I stand and walk to the garbage can with my empty water bottle. Her trash can has the little step on the bottom that flips the lid open. I step on it and toss the bottle inside. It shuts just as quickly as it opens, but not before I see the gold and brown box inside. I place the toes of my boots on the lever again. The lid pops open. I reach down and pull out the empty box of chocolates.

"I'm sorry, Kalysia. I didn't ask for them. He just brought them over."

I imagine him feeding her chocolates in bed and I want to snap her neck.

"We talked about stuff during the drive here, the day I moved in. I mentioned I liked chocolate, and he brought them to cheer me up. He knew how much I missed my family."

I believe her. At the end of the day, Dillan is a sweet guy. The chocolates could have been an innocent gift. He signed them out himself. He wasn't hiding anything.

"Ok." I exhale and walk to the door. "Are you going to the lodge for lunch?" I realize how awkward it will be if she does show up, and I hope she says no.

"I don't think so. I'll stop by later and pick something up or grab a snack from Hopi."

"That's probably best." I open the door and leave without saying goodbye.

CHAPTER TWENTY-FOUR

INEVITABLE

I'm surprised to find Monte and Layla in the lodge eating lunch when I arrive. Leah is all smiles as she serves Monte a helping of her chili. Monte tells me the brew house looks great and that Lowell reported good numbers so far.

"If things keep going this well, you'll be able to leave sooner than expected. I mean, after you have a child." Layla kicks Monte under the table and he yelps.

"What?"

"Will you be heading back soon?" I push my untouched bowl away and take a sip from my beer. Monte insisted we all join him for a taste. He said we have to know our product inside and out.

"As soon as Rusty gets back with a keg for the road, we'll be on our way." Monte pats his stomach. "Leah, this was just delicious." Leah jumps up from her seat and clears his bowl.

"It's nothing." She waves off the compliment, but she's beaming with pride.

"I'm a horrible cook," I tell the table. "Isn't that right, Mom?"

Layla hates when I put myself down. It's very un-alpha of me, but I nod my head toward Leah so she understands the self-deprecating remark.

"Oh yeah, Kalysia's the worst. She almost burned down our apartment trying to make microwave popcorn. The smell didn't go away for a week." Layla winks at me then compliments Leah on her cooking skills.

As lunch winds down, Monte invites Drake and some of the other men to have a drink with him at the bar they set up on New Year's Eve. It's still fully stocked and used pretty often. Dillan doesn't mind if the guys unwind with a drink, as long as it's in moderation.

My eyes are glued to the door. If you told me a week ago that the thought of seeing Dillan would instill this kind of fear, I wouldn't believe it. But fear is exactly what I feel. I'm afraid to see him, like he will see through me. Or maybe it's because I'm afraid that I'll see him differently. Either way, we've both changed.

The lodge is filled with quiet conversation. Pete and Elle are in the corner, coaxing Gavin to eat. His face is covered in chili. Elle sees me watching and waves. I remember what I wanted to call Layla about today.

"Mom," I say. Layla turns her attention away from the males and looks at me. "I was wondering if I could rotate responsibilities. You know, spread the work around so the betas aren't always stuck doing the same jobs."

"Absolutely." She smiles in approval and sips her wine, then remembers who she's dealing with. "You mean just the betas, right?"

"Um, no." I brace for her wrath. "I mean for everyone. It isn't fair that the alphas get to choose their jobs, while the betas are stuck with the laundry and cleaning."

Layla breaks into a huge smile. "See, this is why I took you away. You don't see things the way the others do. I think it's a great idea, but it will be a hard sell to the alphas, especially your half-sister." She gestures to Leah, who is hanging on Drake's arm. "She's been raised in pack life; she won't like the change. She'll think you are punishing her and the others. They will see it as a power trip."

243

Layla makes sense, but I know I can talk Leah and the others into it.

"I can make them see things my way." I say with confidence.

The door opens, and a cold breeze chills my back. I'm afraid to turn around. I watch Layla's face. When she has no reaction; I know it isn't Dillan. A few minutes later, I feel a tug on my pants.

"Taylor!" I scoop her into my arms. She's warm and cuddly and smells like maple syrup. Taylor claps her hands when I set her in my lap.

"Taylor, this is my mom." I take her hand and wave at Layla. If I didn't know my mother, I would think seeing Taylor in my lap choked her up, but it must be the spice in the chili. Layla clears her throat and says hello to Taylor.

Taylor claps again and then looks up at me.

"Mumm," she dribbles. My eyes dart to Layla's.

"Did she just call you mom?" We say at the same time to each other. Before either of us recover from the shock, Carrick arrives.

"Come on, princess. I'll get you some mum-mum." Carrick smiles at Layla and takes Taylor from my lap.

Layla and I exchange a smile. "I thought she was talking to you." I point at Layla.

She shakes her head and says, "No, sweetie, she was talking to you." Layla pats my hand. "You're a natural." I feel my heart tug a bit at the thought of giving Layla not just an heir to her family line, but also a grandchild.

"You ready to hit the road?" Monte caresses Layla's back.

"You're drunk." She stands with her hand held out. Monte places the keys to his Mercedes in her palm. I love their dynamic.

"Who will drive your car?" I ask.

Layla waves it off. "Next time someone heads our way; they can bring it down."

Layla winks at me and whispers, "Until then, I guess I'll have to get a new car."

Layla is always two steps ahead. I hug Mom, then Monte. He tells me to call him Dad, and a tear forms in the corner of my eye. I've never called anyone Dad. My mom and *dad* are about to walk out when Leah yells from the kitchen.

"Wait! Let me pack up some chili to go!"

Layla gives me a wide-eyed look, but calls to Leah and tells her she would love to take some home. *Who is this person?* The Layla I know was never this sweet. Monte's pleasing personality must be rubbing off on her. Layla drags Monte to the kitchen to retrieve their doggie bag and to say goodbye to his other daughter.

"Mum mum mum," Taylor cries from her high chair in the corner. I wave and she claps her hands. Carrick turns to see who is making his daughter smile.

"We have a thing," I explain. Carrick looks thrilled to know I care about Taylor.

"Don't we, Taylor!" Taylor claps again and reaches out for me with chili-stained hands.

Carrick turns around to say something then stops. I hear the door open and close behind me. His scent is still mashed with hers. I wonder how long it will last. I walk away, my back to him. I pluck a napkin from the buffet and take it to Carrick. He mouths thank you and wipes his daughter's face.

"Kalysia," Dillan calls my name and the lodge goes silent, except for Monte, who is laughing as he returns from the kitchen with Layla and Leah.

I don't want to turn around, but I have to. No use avoiding the inevitable. Seeing him here, in public, may be the buffer we need. Neither one of us wants to make a scene in front of my parents. When I turn around, my eyes find his instantly. I can't read his expression. It's part anger, part guilt, part love. Or maybe that's how I'm feeling. Then I see her, standing timidly behind him. The air in my lungs deflates.

How can I stand here as if nothing is wrong? My eyes turn to daggers as a low rumble builds in my throat. The next thing I know Taylor is in my arms. Her chubby hands find my face. I can't help but laugh.

Dillan remains frigid at the door with all eyes on him. Monte looks from me to Dillan. Then he looks at Layla, who is trying to maintain a level of calm.

"Looks like the honeymoon is over," he bellows as they walk out. He slaps Dillan on the back when he passes him and says, "Take care of my girl." Dillan's jaw tightens. He doesn't reply.

"Come on, Monte." Layla pushes him out the door.

Dillan and Cassie quietly get their lunch. Cassie takes her bowl back to her cabin, while Dillan sits at the center table, his table.

The room has turned cold since he arrived, but this is his pack. He won't be ignored. It was probably his idea for Cassie to come get lunch. She will be the mother of his child if all goes according to plan; it's only normal for him to make sure she's properly fed.

I wonder if she told him I made her phase. I don't care. That's between me and Cassie. Just like what happened over the last two days is their business.

The reaction of the pack shocks me. I thought the males would see Dillan taking Cassie as a good thing. It's a trickle-down effect, what's good enough for the pack leader is good enough for the pack. That doesn't seem to be the case. The pack is on my side. Although their allegiance feels good, I know it's wrong for them to shun Dillan. I tell Carrick to join him while I finish feeding Taylor. He doesn't argue. Soon other males sit at Dillan's table.

I'm new at this feeding thing, and Taylor's face and clothes can prove it. I hold the bowl too close to Taylor, and she knocks it to the floor. Elle runs over to clean it up, but I wave her away.

"I got it." I look up and see Dillan watching me clean the floor. He continues to watch as I clean Taylor's face and hands. When Carrick is called to the tower, I keep Taylor, promising to take her to Mara when she gets tired.

Eventually everyone returns to work. Leah and Clio clear the lunch dishes and disappear into the kitchen to prep for dinner. Before I know it, it's only me and Dillan in the dining room. Taylor is sleeping in my arms when Dillan sits beside me. He puts his arm over the back of the couch. I look over Taylor's head, at him. She's the buffer we need—a warm, soft, loveable little buffer.

I feel Dillan's fingers in my hair and close my eyes. My heart flutters, but not like before. There is something else there, something that makes me want to vomit.

"You look so beautiful with her," he says quietly. "I didn't know you helped in the nursery."

"I don't, I mean, not usually. I just helped out during..." I don't finish. He knows what I mean.

"It suits you." He places his hand on my shoulder and I shudder. The reaction surprises us both. Dillan removes his arm from the couch and leans forward with his head in his hands. "I don't know if you want me to touch you or leave you alone."

I don't know either. I clear the lump in my throat and stand up. Taylor twitches in my arms. I lean my cheek on her sweaty head and I look at Dillan.

"Do you *want* to touch me?"

His face is a tangled mess of emotion. I want to care about his feelings, but I can't. He smells like her. It's faint; I can tell he showered. Probably at the brew house where they have a small apartment set up for overnight shifts.

"Of course I want to touch you. I love you. That hasn't changed." But something has. I can tell by the way he lets the sentence hang there, unfinished.

I take Taylor to the nursery then head to my cabin. I walk slowly. It's the first time since we met at Lunam that the thought of being alone with Dillan makes me nervous. In fact, I wish I could just avoid him altogether.

My parents' arrival this morning couldn't have been more perfect. Their visit gave us the excuse we needed to avoid the awkward conversation that is about to take place.

What am I going to say?

What will he say?

I love him, *that* hasn't changed, but so much has. Even if he doesn't know about Jase, my night with him, the connection we had, it changed me. I will never see Jase again, but he will always have a small place in my heart.

I find Dillan standing in front of the unlit fireplace. He turns when I close the door; his eyes are glossy, his hands hidden in the pockets of his cargo pants. Whatever he's about to say is something he's thought about, agonized over. It's something I don't want to hear. He's still looking for the courage to speak when I approach him. He takes my hands in his and kisses my forehead. I close my eyes and concentrate on his lips touching my skin. There is a spark, a tingle. I know that after it's all said and done, I love Dillan. I don't want this to end. I don't need an apology. I just need to forget. Forget Jase. Forget Cassie. I want to rewind back to when it was just me and Dillan.

I look into his pained eyes and place my finger to his lips to prevent him from speaking. My heart beats like a jackhammer as I walk him to our bed.

CHAPTER TWENTY-FIVE:

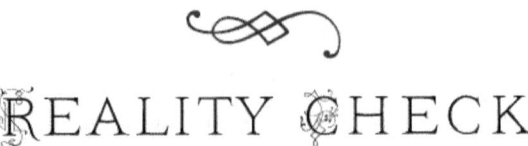

REALITY CHECK

"Pete, you are my hero!" I tell him as I watch the MSN home screen scroll through today's top headlines.

"All the cabins have Wi-Fi now?"

"Yes." Pete smiles proudly. "I made sure Mara was up and running first so the kids could start on their school work, just like you requested."

I decided that I want the betas with school age children to have the option to leave. Mara said she is certified to homeschool, but I want these kids to have every option available to them. Getting them up to speed on their schoolwork is a top priority. I already sent requests to the council to have some of the families relocated to cities so the kids can attend a real school.

Layla is helping to find jobs for them within Howlin' Ale that won't require them to live at camp. Monte is looking at space to open a restaurant and brewery along the San Francisco bay. Once it opens we can start moving people out to live and work in San Francisco.

After Pete leaves, I log into my old email address. My inbox has over a thousand emails, too many to weed through and find any worth keeping, so I delete them all. Layla never allowed me on social media, so other than email, there isn't really anything else for me to look up online. Except, maybe.

I get up and close the office door. My heart is in my throat when I return to my chair. It slides sideways, and I crash into the wall. I hold my breath as I type his address in the search bar. I'm looking up his business website; there's no harm in that. It isn't like I'm going to talk to him. It isn't like I'm going to sneak him chocolates or something.

I hear the birds outside my window trying to out-sing each other and the screaming children in the playground nearby. The weather is getting warmer. It's still cold, but a sunny cold. I'm pretty sure everyone is where they should be; no chance of Dillan showing up here unannounced.

Suddenly, the front of his shop is staring back at me. It's a photo taken from the street; the sign above the garage and the entrance to the office are centered on the screen. I click through each page, scanning, searching. When I click the About Us page I find what I'm looking for. His blue-gray eyes smile from under a baseball hat. He's laughing at something, probably Lucky. I stare into his eyes, and I feel his hands on me. I smell him. I close my eyes and see him smiling beside me in bed.

The door to the office creaks and I slam the laptop closed. My eyes dart to the door and find Cassie.

"Sorry, I didn't mean to interrupt." She is always apologizing. Everyone is so cold when she's around. Dillan didn't ask me to be nicer; he didn't have to.

I'm really not catty by nature. Not like Leah and the other females. Even the betas refused to wait on her. I finally had to ask Elle to take over her cabin. She gave me a little resistance until I told her it would be a personal favor to me.

"What is it?" I lean protectively over the laptop.

Cassie shifts her weight from one foot to another as she fidgets with the water bottle in her hand. She places her hand softly to her belly then makes a sour face.

"Are you ok? You look like you're about to puke." I don't realize what I've said until I see the sorrowful expression on her face. I don't outright ask her and she doesn't confirm, she doesn't need to.

This was the whole point, the reason I allowed Dillan to sleep with Cassie, so she could give Lowell an heir, so I wouldn't have to. I should be happy. I should be ecstatic. This means I'm free to leave. *We* are free to leave, as long as Lowell keeps his word.

Dillan and I haven't spoken about the time I was away. We went to bed that afternoon and stayed in our cabin for two days. We never spoke about Cassie or the Truckee run. We played our "what if" game, made love, and slept. Our list of places to visit when we leave has grown to two pages.

I pull a post-it note from the pad on the desk and fold it in half, then in half again, until it's too small to fold in on itself. I remember the sex-education class from school as I hold up the tiny square and realize this is the size of Cassie's baby.

"I wanted you to be the first to know." She unscrews her water bottle and takes a small sip. "And I want you to know how grateful I am."

I make a disgusted sound in my throat that stops Cassie from speaking. It makes me ill to hear her thank me for letting Dillan get her pregnant. I didn't anticipate feeling this emotional.

"Just stop..." I close my eyes and put my head in my hands. When I look up again, she's gone.

I open the laptop and close the window to Jase's website. I'm about to click off my email when I see a new message come in. It's from Layla.

Kalysia,

Welcome back to the real world! I hope you and Dillan have found a happy medium. I understand why you did what you did. I might have done the same if I were in your shoes. But I don't regret any of the choices I made. I want you to have all the opportunities available to you. I'm working to make sure that happens. I've been doing some research on that thing we discussed. The question you had about the Shasta pack and their lineage. I found some stuff on phasing that I thought you may find interesting. Once I know more, have more concrete information—you'll be the first to know. In the meantime, do what makes you happy. You're the alpha female, don't forget that!

> *Love always,*
> *Mom*

I know she's talking about Jase, so I delete the email, then empty my trash. I don't know if anyone is monitoring our computers or can hack into them. I wouldn't put it past Sid. I wonder what Layla meant about concrete evidence? It must have something to do with why Jase can phase.

Conall knows they phase; it's the reason why he has been trying to legitimize the half-breeds in his pack. I just wonder why he doesn't tell Monte and Lowell? Unless Shasta has been trying to build their numbers all these years so they can overthrow Sierra. Now that Lowell is on Conall's side, it's just a matter of time until they get rid of Monte.

I spend the rest of the afternoon modifying the work schedule. It's just a temporary reassignment to allow the betas a break. Once the females confirm they're pregnant, the whining and complaining will ensue. This is the only week I have to try this out. I'm just finishing when I see Dillan walking towards the office. I close the blinds and turn back to the spreadsheet on my screen. I take a deep breath when I hear his heavy footsteps on the stairs.

"Kalysia," Dillan calls out as his head appears around the door. His eyes are narrow, angry. His reaction to Cassie's baby news isn't what I thought it would be. I don't know what I thought. He paces in front of Leah's desk like a, well, like an irate wolf.

I close the laptop.

"It's ok," I start, but Dillan's cold glare silences me. There is nothing I can say to console him. Being with Cassie was my idea, my fault, just as much as it was Lowell's.

Dillan places his hands on top of my desk and leans in towards me. I think for a moment he might kiss me, but his steely eyes tell me otherwise.

"What's ok?" he hisses.

My mouth falls open, but I don't dare speak.

"You have nothing else to say?" His words are harsh, harsher than they should be, especially towards me. He crosses his arms in front of his chest and stands before me, a wall of muscle. This has nothing to do with Cassie. This is something else, someone else. I feel my heart in my throat. Was he monitoring my web searches?

"Let me explain..." I stand up, not liking the weak position I'm in with him standing above me.

He steps away from my desk, glaring at me. His arrogant stature is starting to piss me off. He has no right to treat me like this, no matter how guilty I am. I'm still a pureblood, and I deserve the respect of one.

I kick my chair out from behind me and it crashes into the wall. I cross my arms in front me and we stare each other down; I won't dare be the first to speak. I need to know how much he knows before I say a word. If he was monitoring my email from Layla, he'd know something was up, but she never mentions Jase or Quincy.

I hear Leah ringing the annoying bell that Drake hung for her. The lodge is right next door; everyone will be headed to dinner.

"Do you really want to do this here?" I think our cabin is a better venue for the fight that is about to happen. I really don't want any of the others to overhear. The pack will see my night with

Jase as a betrayal, even though Dillan was here, doing the same thing with Cassie.

"It doesn't matter." Dillan walks back to the door and closes it. "They already know."

The blood drains from my face. "Who knows?" I'm ruined.

"Drake. He took the call from Gallup." Dillan leans against Leah's desk.

"Gallup? What about Gallup?"

"You must have made a pretty good impression, because they doubled their order, but insisted you make the delivery."

I sigh in relief and fall into my chair.

"Drake spoke to Bud from Gallup Saloon."

I can't help but laugh a little at Dillan's overreaction. If he saw Bud, he wouldn't be jealous.

"Bud is a married man." I open my laptop and wait for it to load.

"So? Humans don't give a shit about their wedding vows," Dillan spits back.

I open a web browser and search for Gallup Saloon, praying to find a pic of Bud and Sissy. "He's also old enough to be my grandfather."

I see Dillan's resolve falter slightly.

"Men shouldn't be calling for you."

The possessive, jealous boyfriend thing does not work for me. I find Bud's picture on the front page of his website and spin the laptop around.

"This is Bud." I point to the round, balding, short man in the photo.

Dillan leans onto my desk and peers at the screen. His face softens. "Oh."

I turn the laptop around and click off the page. I deleted my internet search of Jase's shop, but you never know.

"I think you owe me an apology." I feel like an asshole for demanding Dillan to say he's sorry. I did do something unforgivable when I was on the Truckee run, he just doesn't know about it.

"I'm sorry." He backs away and shoves his hands in his pockets.

I should let it go, but it doesn't feel right. If I were innocent, I wouldn't let him get away with this type of behavior. "What was that all about?"

"I don't like men calling here for you. I don't care how old or short they are." He cracks a smile. "Come here." He reaches his hand to me. I walk around my desk into his arms. "It drives me mad to think of another man wanting you."

I feel the same way, but I let it happen. I let him be with another woman.

"I would never hurt you like that." I mean the words; they aren't a lie. I would never hurt him by telling him or even worse, seeing Jase again. He will be blissfully ignorant for the rest of his life, while I will always have a reminder of his time with Cassie.

"Let's get dinner. I'm starved." Dillan releases me, and I grab my coat from the hook on the wall. I flick off the light and walk out behind him.

I see Carrick carrying Taylor into the lodge and I realize Dillan must not know about Cassie yet. Dillan reaches for my hand and brings it to his lips. We've been so happy these past two weeks, but all of that comes to an end the moment he knows she is carrying his child. I want one more evening where he is mine and I am his. I want to share one more meal with Dillan while I'm the most important thing in his life.

We say the baby won't mean anything, but I'm not sure anymore. Even if it doesn't mean anything to Dillan, it might mean something to me.

Leah and Patsy have made the most of our current food run. The lodge smells of fried chicken and biscuits. I see Tripp and Rusty with mounds of mashed potatoes on their plates—it looks like they are having one of their eating contests. Carrick is trying to balance his plate with Taylor in his arms. She is gripping an ear of corn while her father attempts to pour gravy on his potatoes.

"Let me help you." Dillan reaches out to Carrick, but instead of taking the plate, he takes Taylor. Taylor looks curiously at Dillan with her big blue-gray eyes, Sierra eyes, and a frown forms on her mouth.

"No, no, no," I soothe her. "Dillan is a nice guy. He's my friend." I kiss Dillan on the cheek, and Taylor laughs. She leans in with her corn and butter-covered tongue and gives Dillan a fat baby kiss on the cheek.

"Uhhh, thanks Taylor." Dillan tries hard to sound enthused by her show of affection. He bounces and she cracks up. Dillan's face is filled with joy.

For the first time since all of this started, I see that Dillan may want to be a father. I consider telling him Cassie is pregnant, he's fulfilled his duty. Only this isn't just some duty, some chore like doing the dishes. I will tell him after dinner, for sure. He needs to know; he deserves to know. Dillan and I finally take our seats at the center table. Leah, Drake, Clio, and Tripp are halfway through their meal when we sit down. Drake looks at Dillan with a strained expression. He's dying to know about Gallup.

"I heard you spoke to Bud." I scoop a spoonful of mashed potatoes into my mouth. Drake raises an eyebrow to my question. Maybe he's surprised at how casual I'm being. He's the one that made a big deal out of nothing.

"He's a sweet old guy; his wife is an amazing cook. I'll bring back a bottle of their famous barbecue sauce for you on my next run."

Dillan chokes beside me. "What do you mean your next run?" He sips his water bottle and looks across the table at Drake, who looks just as shocked.

"I figured I would make the next run." I look at Leah; her eyes are fixed on her plate. "I mean, I thought since he requested me—"

"I don't think so," Dillan scoffs.

"Yeah, I mean, we have the manpower now," Drake adds.

I toss my fork onto my plate and potatoes fling across the table, nearly hitting Tripp's beer.

I recall Layla's email, her words in my head. I will do what makes me happy. "He is a customer that doubled his order because of me. He won't order from us again if I don't make the delivery."

"You've done enough." Dillan bites into his corn as if the conversation is over.

I push my plate away and excuse myself. Dillan doesn't even bother to look up when I leave. Clio is the only one that says goodnight.

I hear the tinkling of my cell phone as soon as I open the cabin door. I run to the nightstand where the phone has sat useless for weeks. I guess cell service has been restored along with Wi-Fi. My phone is buzzing with missed messages and texts.

Most of them are from Layla when she was trying to track me down. I delete them all. Then I see one from an unknown number.

HI!!!! It's Delilah. Just wanted to remind u bout my bday party on the 14th. Joe and Martha didn't go for the Elks, so it's at the lodge, but it's gonna be WAY better than Lacy's. Hope you can make it.

How did she get my number? I check my call log and I find a five-three-zero area code. That sneaky runt called herself from my phone to get the number. I smile despite the devious trick.

I can't be mad at Delilah, she's just a kid. That's not really true though. She will be eighteen. By pack standards, she is old enough to find a partner and have a child. It seems ludicrous. Thankfully, she is not in a pack. She's just a normal girl with her whole life ahead of her.

I wish I could go to her party. I'd love to tell her not to grow up too fast and to enjoy her freedom. I consider texting her back, but I know she will see it as an invite to chat, and I can't explain to Dillan how I know her. I delete her text and put my phone on silent.

Thinking of Delilah makes me think of Jase. I lie on the bed and imagine a world where I could visit Delilah and go to her birthday party. A world where I lived with Jase in his little trailer, and I went to school while he worked at his garage. And Jase didn't demand things from me. He didn't try to run me or power trip on me. Jase would love me for me, Kalysia. He doesn't care about my bloodline or who my parents are. He doesn't care about pack rules or duties. Jase is free to live his life the way he wants. I want to live in that world.

Dillan shakes me awake around midnight. I'm not sure what time he returned to the cabin, but he's already dressed for bed. I kick my shoes onto the floor and pull off my jeans. I don't bother to wash up or even brush my teeth. I just crawl under the covers and will myself back into my dream.

CHAPTER TWENTY-SIX:

FULL MOON ENVY

I ask Cassie not to tell Dillan she thinks she's pregnant. Not until we know for sure. Once we confirm she is knocked up, Dillan and I can start making plans to leave. No use getting worked up for nothing. The first full moon after mating season is the only way you can really confirm you're pregnant. The female attempts to phase under the full moon. If she can't, she's pregnant. Another full moon that will determine my future.

Even though most of the females claim to know either due to morning sickness or fatigue, Layla said those are just phantom symptoms. When I call to tell her that Cassie thinks she is pregnant, she scoffs into the receiver.

"I'm not surprised," Layla says. "She's willing it to be true. Having this baby is her only hope."

It's mine too, but I can't tell her that. I don't mention that I might be leaving. I'm not even sure Dillan and I will be together in nine months. We've been strained. That's the word I used to describe our relationship to Layla. She said it's normal in the first year. At least Layla isn't telling me things will work out, that we will live happily ever after. She's still holding out hope that I'm pregnant even though chances are very slim. Dillan and I were only together the first and last day of the season, so I'm not worried.

"I heard through the grapevine that Conall planned to match her with a half-breed. I can't believe he would throw his entire legacy into the fire and end his pure bloodline just to please his bratty daughter. A female nobody even wants."

She is wrong. Somebody did want her. Dillan still visits Cassie every few days. He doesn't stay long, but the fact that he stops by makes my insides boil.

You've never really been in love until you've plotted somebody's murder.

I would never act on my instincts, but just thinking about it makes me feel better.

I've entrusted a few of the beta females and my brother to keep me informed of the comings and goings around Cassie's cabin. Elle is especially helpful; she was the one who told me about the gold and brown box Dillan carried out of Hopi the other day. She wasn't able to see where he was going since she was on duty in the nursery and couldn't leave. I don't need a spy to tell me where Dillan took the chocolates.

The loud buzzer from the washer goes off, and I clamp my free hand over my ear.

"I have to go, Mom."

"Ok, call me anytime, sweetie." Layla ends our conversations with the same line: "You're the alpha, do what makes you happy." The words seem to apply to my life a bit more each time she says them.

Elle and the other betas love the job rotation. Leah and the alphas, not so much.

I gather the last of the towels and shove them in the industrial-size dryer. I put myself on the shittiest work detail, just to prove a point. If I do it, the others have no excuse when it's their turn. Leah did ask if she would have to do anything strenuous after the full moon. I told her that beta females have been doing laundry for centuries while pregnant, and since we are stronger by nature, it shouldn't kill us.

"Kalysia," Clio calls from the door. "Are you still in here?"

"Back here," I yell and start folding a pile of sheets. Clio's face is a mash of fear and sickness. If anyone is pregnant, it's her. She's pale and hasn't eaten in two days. She can barely keep liquids down.

"You look like crap," I tell her. "Why don't you get some rest before dinner? Mara can get things started without you." I toss a stack of sheets into the transport bin.

"I'm fine." She puts her hand on the bin to stop it from rolling as I lay the sheets on top of the clean towels. "Dillan's looking for you."

"Oh, ok." I push the laundry cart to the side and step towards the door.

Clio grabs my arm and stops me. Her eyes dart from the dryer humming behind me to the floor and back.

"Is something wrong?"

"He didn't look happy."

Dillan isn't at the cabin, so I take a quick shower. I hear someone shuffling around the kitchen when I turn off the water. I sense its Dillan without having to confirm. I walk from the bathroom to our bedroom in a towel. There was a time when I would have called to him, or he would have joined me in the shower. Two months ago, he would have thrown me on the bed and said, "One day you'll be waiting in here for me, naked." Now we don't even speak to each other unless absolutely necessary. He spends all of his time at the brew house. The fact that he's still training Ray to brew, leads me to believe he still plans to leave.

I let the towel drop to the floor and slam the dresser drawer, frustrated that my partner, the supposed love of my life, doesn't even bother to sneak a peek at my naked body. He doesn't want me anymore. Maybe there's somebody else he wants to see naked, someone he's already seen. Did they shower together? Did he toss her on her sofa bed and make her promise to wait for him one day?

I dress quickly, angrily pulling on my clothes. Dillan finally comes in when I'm putting on my socks. He must know how long it takes me to dress; he timed his entrance perfectly. Asshole.

He leans against the door frame, filling every inch. He watches me yank socks onto my feet. I feel words hanging in the air, and I wait for him to give them a voice.

"What?" I finally say. "Do you want something?" My question confuses him. He looks to the bed and quickly back to me. It's been nine days since we made love. It's the longest I've gone without sex since we met.

There were a couple of mornings I thought he would pull me to him, take me under the covers, but he got up and went for a run instead. I wonder if he went to Cassie's. I would have smelled it on him, unless...unless Cassie told him phasing cleanses you of any foreign scents. Bitch.

I step towards him to leave, and he steps back. Seeing him move away from me hurts. He's careful not to touch me when I pass him. Part of me wants to fling my arms around his neck and kiss him. But I won't do it. I won't make the first move; he has to. He is the one who is supposed to be showing me he loves me. Instead he treats me like a disease. He won't touch me or even look at me.

I go to the kitchen and fill a glass with water. I'm not thirsty, it just gives me something to do.

"Kalysia." His voice is low, steady. "We need to talk."

My heart is in my throat; I push it down with a gulp of water. I nod my head to acknowledge him. I turn and sit at the small kitchen table without meeting his eyes. He sits opposite me and places his radio on the table.

The leaky faucet drips into the stainless steel sink, one, two, fourteen times before Dillan speaks. "I don't want to fight." He clears his throat.

Generally, when you start a conversation like this, a fight is inevitable. I don't respond. I'm not promising anything.

"I want to know the truth about why you didn't want to have a baby with me." His eyes flit to mine when he says the word baby. "Just tell me," he says, desperate for an answer I don't have.

I don't know why I was so against it a month ago. I guess the idea of being a parent seemed outrageous, especially at our age. But the more I hear the others talk about it and the more time I spend with Taylor, I don't know. I get it. I wasn't raised in a pack, I never even held a baby until Taylor. The other females grew up with dozens of children in various stages of infancy. They knew the joys and perils of parenthood by the time they were ten years old.

I see now that being a mother isn't something to be afraid of. I can do it. I know I can. And I'm sorry. Sorry to Dillan and to my parents, but mostly I'm sorry for my future child. My baby won't be an Altum alpha. Cassie's child will be the leader, not mine. I just hope the world these kids create is better than the one we have now.

I look at my lonely hands resting on the table. It's been so long since Dillan took my hand in his and kissed my knuckles. "I don't know."

Dillan sits up in his chair; he looks me square in the eye and says, "Liar."

I watch his jaw tighten and release. He's fuming. Why didn't I see this before?

I stand and my chair falls backward onto the floor. "You're the fucking liar!" I pick up my water glass, and the next thing I know, it's shattering against the wall behind Dillan's head. He scrambles to his feet.

"Are you out of your mind?" He reaches for his radio and snatches it from the table as he backs towards the door. "You almost hit me!"

I shrug carelessly as my heart rages out of control. It's a volcano about to erupt and destroy itself. The fissure that cracked the morning I saw Dillan at Cassie's cabin and spread the night I spent with Jase. Now it's destroyed. My heart will never be the same. I swallow the lump of jealousy in my throat. I won't feel bad about Jase. I'll never see him again.

Unlike Cassie. Dillan is probably sneaking off with her every day. That's why he won't have sex with me. I whirl around and lean on the sink. I'm hyperventilating. I can't stop the images of Dillan and Cassie in bed, showering, eating chocolates. "You're still fucking her, aren't you?"

I hear Dillan suck in a breath when he hears what I'm accusing him of. I spin around and face him. He changes his stance, his right foot forward, like he's ready for a fight. He shakes his head with a sad expression on his face. One of pity more than shame.

"LIAR!" My body shakes with anger. I want to phase and rip his throat out, the same way I did the morning I came back from Quincy and found out he was still in her bed. A low growl builds in my chest. I want to kill him and her.

"I'm not sleeping with Cassie." Dillan's tone is softer, soothing. He knows I'll kill him. "I swear, Kalysia, on us. I haven't slept with her since..." His voice trails off when he sees the murderous look in my eyes. "Please calm down. I don't want to hurt you."

"You don't want to hurt me?" I'm seething now. I grind my teeth to keep from screaming.

"You. Hurt me. Every day." I choke out each word. Tears roll freely down my cheeks. Dillan slumps into the doorway and bows his head.

"Every time I see her I think of you kissing her, holding her, the way you *used* to hold me. When you touch me, I wonder if it's her you think of, if it's her you really want." I fall to my knees. My heart is burned beyond repair. We are beyond repair.

Dillan tosses the chair from between us and kneels in front of me. I lean forward and rest my head on his thighs. He rubs my back and makes soothing noises. I sit up. We are face to face on the floor. His eyes are wet with tears.

"You aren't even going to deny it?" I bite my lip, and another wave of tears falls.

Dillan takes my head in his hands and holds my face close to his.

"Of course I deny it. I love you, Kalysia. You. Not her." His breath is warm on my face. "But we started something here and we have to see it through." I know he means the baby, the heir to his line.

"But you can't leave now, can you?"

Dillan's eyes flicker to my mouth. He pinches his eyes closed, to trap his tears inside.

"I won't ask you to leave. I can't take you away from your child," I sob. I want to pull away, but he holds my head in his hands, searching my eyes for an answer I don't have.

Suddenly, Dillan's lips are on mine, his tongue in my mouth. I barely have time to suck in a breath before he is back again. I run my hands through his hair and down his back. I pull the collar of his jacket and try to take it off, but he stops me.

"Kalysia," he breathes my name. "Just tell me, I need to hear it from you."

I pull back, and he drops his hands from my face. We are breathless and wanting, yet here we sit with doubt looming between us. What does he expect me to say? What does he think? I watch the love in his eyes fade to suspicion.

"Did someone say something to you?" I ask. He shakes the look from his face, but it's too late.

"What did Cassie tell you?" I knock his hands off of my legs and stand.

Dillan remains on his knees.

"She told me you might not be able to have children." He pulls one foot from underneath him and rests on one knee, the way men do when they are about to propose.

I gasp when he takes my hand. I don't know if it's the fact that Cassie has betrayed me, or because it looks like Dillan is going to ask me to marry him.

"I'll love you no matter what, Kalysia. I just need you to tell me yourself." He puts my hand to his lips. "It makes sense now— you allowing me to be with Cassie. You didn't want to deny me the chance to be a father."

I shake my head so hard that my ponytail whips my cheeks. I never wanted him to be a father. I just wanted him to leave, with me. I can't let him think I'm so selfless. This can't be why he loves me.

"No." I pull my hand away and motion for him to stand. "What Cassie told you isn't true."

He scoffs as if Cassie is incapable of a lie. "So, you didn't take the pill?"

"Yes, I took the pill. But the pill doesn't make you sterile. It's just a stupid Shasta myth."

Dillan watches me closely for any signs of a lie. It angers me that he would doubt me, not her.

"Why would she even tell you that?" I feel the wall between us being hoisted back into place when Dillan begins to protect her.

"She was trying to comfort me." He pauses and clears his throat. Bad choice of words. "I was upset and a little buzzed from too much wine. I was going on and on about why you would offer Cassie to me. I understood why Lowell wanted me to be with her, but I couldn't make sense of why you would go along with it. I would kill before I let another man touch you."

Which is why he will never know about Jase. I want to remind him about the deal with Lowell, about him being outcast if he didn't create an heir, anything to change the subject. He won't let me speak.

"You know I don't care about my father. I would've left without a dime and spent my life with you."

Would have left. My heart can't take anymore. "You don't have to worry about that now." I lean on the sink and put on the bitterest face I can muster. "You can stay here and live happily ever after with Cassie, eating chocolates." It's easier to have him hate me than know he won't leave with me.

"What are you saying?" Dillan steps towards me. "I love you, Kalysia." I roll my eyes in response. "You don't believe me because I gave Cassie a box of candy?"

It's not just the candy. Once she confirms she's pregnant, he will dote on her, care for her. It's in his nature. I just shrug. I don't want to come between him and his child. I bite the inside of my cheek to keep from crying. I fucked up. I should be the one having his baby, not her. Tomorrow they will become a family, and I will be alone.

"It isn't just the candy. It's you and her. Something has changed between you two, something that I didn't anticipate. You care about her. You will care about your baby. I don't fit into the scenario anymore, so I'm withdrawing myself from the equation."

"What are you saying?" Dillan leans in the doorway like he might fall over.

I swallow hard and try to keep an even face. "It's over."

CHAPTER TWENTY-SEVEN

JUST DANCE

I don't ask Dillan for permission to go on the Truckee run. I don't need to. I'm not his and he isn't mine. Rusty and Carrick volunteered for the run and didn't seem to mind that I was crashing their weekend.

Carrick told Dillan he is going to visit some family in South Lake Tahoe, really he and my brother plan to spend the weekend together so we take two vehicles. Rusty is driving my truck, while Carrick follows behind in the larger delivery van.

All the sales have doubled, tripled in some cases, since the first order. The beer is a huge success. Lowell must be in heaven.

Today he'll learn he's going to be the grandfather of a future pack leader, making his role, and Dillan's, all the more powerful.

If I wasn't a complete idiot, my child would be the one with all the power, giving Monte and Layla the control they need to stand against Lowell. But I failed them and myself.

"You've been quiet all day." Rusty turns down the stereo. I see him watching me from the corner of my eye.

"Watch the road, please." I gesture to the two-lane highway in front of us. "I'm fine." I bite my tongue every time I say that these days. "You're killing me slowly with this." I hold up the Taylor Swift CD case.

Rusty just laughs like I'm joking.

"Well, I was thinking, maybe you want to stay the night in South Lake Tahoe with me and Carrick."

The plan was for Rusty and me to take the delivery truck back to camp and let Carrick have the Ford for his trip to Tahoe. At least, that's what they told the others. Rusty planned all along to spend this weekend, Valentine's Day weekend, with Carrick. Me coming along blew their plan.

"Come on, sis. You don't want to be around for all that full moon bullshit anyway."

I shrug. I don't know what I want anymore. I've shut down.

We pull into the parking lot of the Gallup Saloon, our last stop. Bud and Sissy treat us to an early dinner of barbecue chicken and baked sweet potatoes. Bud says our fancy beer is selling like free water in hell. He even added a special pairing to his menu featuring Howlin' Ale.

"Your fancy brew and my barbecue sauce are a match made in heaven. My customers can't get enough." Bud gives us a case of Willis' West Coast Barbecue Sauce to take back this time.

Rusty and Carrick love Bud and think Gallup is a hoot. They even join in a couple of line dances before we leave. The women in the place fall all over my brother and his boyfriend. I have to pull them off the dance floor and tell them we have to get going.

The sun is setting when we walk outside. Bud gestures to the clear sky.

"Hellava lot better than the shit storm you drove through last time you were here."

When he says that, my mind goes instantly to Jase.

I'm so close.

Rusty starts the delivery truck and waits for Carrick to pull out first. I can see the longing in his eyes. I pick up the two-way radio and call to Carrick.

"Change of plans, pull over." I can hardly believe what I'm about to say, but I'm too close. He's too close.

"I'll take the Ford, you two take the delivery truck, and we'll meet in Meyers tomorrow at noon. I'll call camp and tell them we're going to stay in Tahoe together. That way, you don't have to lie."

Rusty just nods. He knows why Dillan won't fight me. We look at the dash; it is ten past five. The full moon was at 4:56pm. He knows he's going to be a father. He's probably off celebrating with Cassie, bathing her in chocolates.

"He loves you, you know that." Rusty pats my hand, sensing my despair.

"That isn't the issue." I leave it at that. "Come on, get out. Carrick's waiting." I push my brother's shoulder.

Rusty grabs his phone from the ashtray and his duffle from behind the seat. "You can come if you want. We can get drunk in the casino and stuff ourselves at the buffet." His smile falters when I shake my head. "I don't know if I should leave you alone. Where are you going to go for the night?"

I feel my face flush. Rusty recognizes the clandestine look.

"Kalysia....no!" He closes the door as if someone will hear us. "You can't go back to Quincy."

"I'm not going there to see him. I'm going to his sister's birthday party." I hold up my phone and wiggle it in my hand. "She invited me."

"Please don't do anything you'll regret." Rusty hugs me.

My life has been an endless stream of regret lately. "I'm not making any promises." I pull back and push him out the door. "Now go."

I watch the delivery truck turn out of Gallup's parking lot and then pull my cell phone from my pocket. Dillan has a cell phone, but he never carries it, not when he has the walkie. Plus, the cell service is still blotchy at camp. He said he was pulling the night shift at the brew house. For all I know, he's been with Cassie since the moment I left.

He was out of the cabin before dawn. There's nothing left to say anyway. We're over. When Cassie's baby is born, I will leave. With or without Dillan.

I don't recognize the voice that answers the brew house phone.

"It's Sid. Who's this?" I hear him chewing the toothpick he always has hanging from his lips.

I tell him it's me and asks where Dillan is.

"I assume he's at dinner." Sid knows where Dillan is at all times.

"Tell him I'm going to Tahoe with Rusty and Carrick. We'll be back tomorrow around lunch." I end the call quick, before he can ask any more questions.

The drive to Quincy is much quicker without the snow storm. I make it to Main Street Lodge around seven. The parking lot is packed. There are lights strung around a makeshift dance floor in the center of the parking lot. I can't help but think of Lunam. I pull over and park behind a line of trucks.

I thought showing up like this would be a great surprise for Delilah. She did invite me. But I never replied. She may be mad about that. I also gave Jase my real name, and it wouldn't be hard for him to find out who I am. What if he doesn't want to see me? I grip the steering wheel and watch Delilah's guests arrive carrying pink boxes with big bows. I don't even have a present.

I look around the cab of the truck, looking for something an eighteen-year-old would like, but all I have is beer.

"Holy shit!" someone yells, and I look up to find Lucky standing in front of the truck with a huge grin.

"Get your ass out of that truck and give me a hug!"

I smile in spite of myself. Lucky has that effect on people. Before I know what's happening, Lucky's hand is yanking me out of the cab and into his arms.

"Couldn't stay away, huh?"

"I didn't want to disappoint Delilah." I keep up the façade.

Lucky grins and says, "Sure you didn't."

He walks me to the entrance of the hotel, but rather than go straight into the party, he guides me to Joe and Martha's apartment. Joe has a large smile for me. We exchange pleasantries until Martha walks in. We all see the surprise on her face, even though she recovers quickly and offers me a hug.

"Does Jase know you're coming?" Martha pretends the question is light and meaningless. She walks into the kitchen to check a boiling pot, so I can't gauge the reaction on her face when I tell her it's a surprise.

I look at Joe and Lucky—even they seem nervous.

"It was a last-minute decision. I was on my delivery route to Truckee and remembered Delilah's birthday."

Martha peeks her head around the wall to glare at me.

"Delilah texted me, she told me I should come." I hold my phone up, as if I have the proof.

Martha sighs and shakes her head. She mumbles something about Delilah being childish. I'm starting to think this really was a bad idea. Jase must hate me. I should leave now before he sees me, before he can reject me too.

I'm working up the courage to tell Joe and Lucky that I'm going to leave when Joe claps his hands together. "So, you got any of that swill left?"

I hold up my keys and Lucky snatches them from my hand.

"I'm on it!" He runs out of the apartment. I watch him pass by the front window. He stops to talk to a couple of boys his age, and they follow him out to the street.

Joe and I head outside; he is staying close, as if he's protecting me from something yet to happen. "I don't see him," Joe murmurs almost to himself. I'm not going to pretend I don't know who he's talking about.

I hear a shrill from deep in the crowd. People part and Delilah emerges. She's in a frilly bright yellow dress made of tulle. It's strapless, with an empire waist and an audacious bow just under her breast. Her hair is curled, and she's wearing a tiara. A tiara. With her ridiculously high heels, she is almost as tall as me.

"Kali!" she squeals. "I knew you'd come." She gives the stink eye to Joe.

"I didn't want to miss your party." I feel like an ass for lying. Everyone knows why I'm here. "Everything looks amazing." I squeeze her hands.

"I know, right!" She pulls me into the party. Delilah is whining about the music or lack thereof when I get my first glimpse of him.

He hasn't seen me, and nobody has told him I'm here. I can tell by the lazy way he moves through the crowd. He looks relaxed. Once he hears about me, all of that will change. He might even be angry enough to ask me to leave. I'm glad I have these few moments to observe him like this, before shit gets bad.

Delilah asks me to join her for a quick touch-up, and I follow her. My heart pumps a little faster when I see that Delilah is in room three. She closes the door behind and spins around.

"I know who you are and I don't care," she says quickly and checks the window. She must have seen Jase too. "I've never seen Jase as happy as he was the night he met you. Even after you left the way you did."

I recall the note I left on the table. I owed him a goodbye at least.

I sit on the bed and run my hand over the comforter. "My life is complicated," I start to tell her who I am, but Delilah waves her hand in the air like she's heard it all before.

"Yeah, pack life, I get it. But you have a connection with Jase, don't you?" She kneels in front of me. "He told me that night—that you were the one, Kalysia."

My heart is in my throat. I want to tell Delilah she's right, but I don't know anymore. When I'm with Dillan, I think he's the one. When I'm with Jase, there is no denying that I want him.

"What are you doing here?" I look up and find Jase standing in the doorway. "Are you trying to get me killed?"

My heart falls to the floor. He hates me.

Delilah is on her feet, face to face with her brother. "She cares about you, Jase."

She looks back to me, encouraging me to speak up, but I'm frozen.

"She wouldn't be here otherwise." I'm grateful to Delilah. She's saying the things I can't say.

"I'll leave you two alone to talk." She raises an eyebrow at me and socks Jase in the arm. "Be nice." She closes the door and cuts us off from the rest of the world.

Jase stands near the door, while I sit on the bed. He looks at me like he's waiting for me to start. I'm tired of waiting for someone else to make the first move. I'm tired of being let down. I stand, because what I'm about to say seems more appropriate standing. Jase looks amused by the determination on my face.

"Look, I know I didn't handle things very well when we first met. I should've told you who I was. That I wasn't available. Things have changed now, and I came here to apologize."

Jase leans on the windowsill and crosses his arms with a smug look on his face. I keep going anyway.

"Delilah is right; I do feel a connection to you. That's part of the reason I signed the note with my real name."

"You mean this note." Jase places two fingers into the pocket of his work shirt and pulls out a small folded piece of paper. It's crumpled and dirty, as if it's been read hundreds of times.

Seeing the tiny sheet of paper in his fingers sends my heart into hyper drive.

"You saved my note?"

Jase smiles and tucks it safely away without saying a word. He doesn't have to. The fact that he kept the note is everything. I know what I want to say.

"I never believed in destiny or fate, not really. Even when I was standing under the canopy at Lunam, I never believed that a magical force was going to draw me to my soul mate." Jase sits up a bit straighter. "I was raised like you, out of the pack. I didn't know my father either."

Jase raises an eyebrow when I tell him this.

"There was this huge deal about me pairing with a pureblood, and when I did, I thought maybe it was fate or destiny. I don't know, but I bought into it. All of it." I cross the room and stand in front of Jase. His scent is mixed with car oil and exhaust.

"Then I met you, and everything they told me made sense. I felt the pull of the moon, the string that seemed to tether us together. It was strong, unbreakable. If you had gone to Lunam, if you were allowed to go. I know we would've matched." Jase stands and moves towards me. "It wasn't right for me to deceive you," I say as he reaches for my hand. "Please don't hate me." My eyes fill with tears. "I didn't know how to make sense of what I was feeling. I didn't know if I was being selfish or selfless by being with you. I still don't know."

Jase places two fingers on my lips.

"You don't have to say anything else." He holds me in his arms while the party rages outside. Two, maybe three songs play before we break apart. "What do you want to do?" he asks.

I haven't given any thought to what all of this means, why I'm really here. Am I running? Did I just leave Dillan for Jase?

"I don't want to go back. I can't stay here. I have no idea where I belong. When I'm with you, it feels right. But I can't just leave, people depend on me."

"Kalysia." Jase interrupts. "I just need to know one thing." He raises my hand above my head and twirls me around. "Do you want to dance?"

"Dance? You're asking me to dance?"

Jase shrugs with a crooked smile. "Did you think I wanted something else?" I fall into his arms, laughing. "Or we can make use of that bed." He grips my waist and pulls me against him.

"Tonight that bed belongs to your sister." I remind him.

"Then let's dance."

CHAPTER TWENTY-EIGHT:

REVELATIONS

I love the way my head fits in the crook of Jase's neck and the lazy way he smiles at me, as if me being in his arms is the most natural thing in the world, and not something so wrong it will crush another man's soul.

The song ends, and Jase leaves me to get a drink. Everything about him is so relaxed, unhurried. He hands me a cup of Howlin' Ale and sits in the chair beside me. The music stops, and Delilah begins opening her gifts in the center of the dance floor. She steals glances at me and Jase in between gifts. I take a sip from my cup and smile at her.

"She's afraid you're going to disappear and leave me heartbroken, again." Jase grins behind his red plastic cup, pausing for a second to let the words sink in before taking a drink.

I look at him with an apology on my face. I hate that I caused him any kind of pain, and the fact that I'm here can cause even more. Dillan and I may be over, but that doesn't mean shit to the pack, or to Lowell. Going to Lunam made me part of the Sierra pack. It isn't something I can just walk away from. I need support from the council. My parents. Even permission from Dillan, to release me after Cassie has his child. I will fight until my dying breath for my freedom.

"I didn't mean to upset you, I was joking." Jase strokes my back.

I love the way he can sense my mood. I lean into his touch, and he slides his arm around my shoulders. "I don't want to cause you any trouble, with the pack I mean."

Jase shakes his head arrogantly. "I'm not worried." His eyes sparkle under the twinkling lights.

"What you said earlier, about me getting you killed..." I try to tell him the threat is real, but he won't let me finish.

"I was joking, Kalysia. I'm not a threat to them because they think I'm just another half-breed that doesn't phase. As long as it stays that way, I have nothing to fear."

He places his cup on the ground and pulls my chair in between his legs. The chair scrapes against the blacktop. Without the music on, it echoes through the party. Heads turn in our direction, including Delilah's. Seeing us together is her favorite gift of all. She smiles and yells for the DJ to turn the music back on.

"I don't believe in any of their myths about matching or soulmates. You wouldn't either if you've seen the things I've seen," he says. I won't ask him to elaborate. I don't want to know the horrible things that happen to half-breeds.

"The only thing I have to worry about is a jealous boyfriend, and I've dealt with my fair share of those." Jase smiles and tilts his head to the side with a cocky grin. Even though he's trying to pretend he's got game, I know he's just messing me.

"How do you explain us? Our connection is not a human one; it's so much more than that. It feels like Lunam. Something strong and absolute." I'm lightheaded at the thought of falling in love with Jase.

The grin slips from Jase's lips and he leans towards me. "Why do we have to label what we feel?" Jase looks at the ground. "Can't we just enjoy this moment?"

"This moment? Like this is all we will have?" My chest constricts when I see the look on Jase's face. "Are you saying you don't feel our connection?" Was Delilah lying? Did he really tell her I was the one?

Jase's grin turns humorous.

"What's so funny?" My cheeks flush when he doesn't answer. Maybe I was wrong, and what I feel is nothing more than lust. I was wrong with Dillan. I convinced myself I loved him, that I could love him for the rest of my life, until I met Jase.

I pull my hands free and stand up. My chair falls backward; the way it did in the kitchen yesterday when I was breaking up with Dillan. The thought of him with Cassie or me with Jase becomes too overwhelming.

I need air. More air than this space offers. I need to run.

"Where are you going?" Jase yells as I bolt for the woods. "Kalysia!"

My name bounces off the trees as the world blurs in front of me. My skin grows warm like I'm about to phase. I haven't phased in weeks, not since the morning I returned from Quincy and phased with Rusty and Carrick.

My breathing turns shallow and my heart patters out of control. Something's wrong. I fall to my hands and knees and grip my stomach. I heave and vomit into the dry leaves. Jase runs up behind me, and I yell for him to stop.

"Don't come closer!" I wipe my mouth with the sleeve of my jacket and sit back on my knees. The trees swirl above me; I see the full moon peer through the bare branches. Its light pierces me, and the world turns dark.

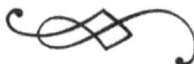

I hear Delilah's voice nearby. She's whispering to someone. I open my eyes and find her and Martha standing in the middle of Jase's trailer.

"Kalysia." Delilah rushes to the bed. "Can you sit up?"

She helps me sit and then hands me a bottle of water. I take a small sip. When it goes down easily, I drink the entire bottle. I must be dehydrated; the beer didn't help.

"I'm ok." I swing my feet onto the floor and notice I'm not wearing shoes. The trailer floor is freezing. Delilah makes a big deal about me standing. "I'm fine, really. I think I had too much to drink."

"You had two beers," Delilah says. "You had ten times as much at Lacy's party."

Delilah releases my arm and moves towards the sink, where Martha is standing. They look at each other like they know something I don't.

I find my shoes and sit on the bed to put them on. "I don't know what the big deal is." I stand up and flatten my hair. "I just got dizzy."

Martha looks stressed, like what she's about to say is going to be bad. I had a feeling she resented my coming back; maybe she's choosing this moment to let me have it.

"Jase and I were talking." I recall our conversation and how I've been a fool this entire time. "I was just overwhelmed."

"This might seem intrusive, but did you and Jase sleep together the last time you were here?"

"Martha!" Delilah looks at her aunt as if she's lost her mind.

"It's a valid question."

I'm so humiliated. Martha must think I'm a slut. I am. If there is a special hell for people like me, I want to go there now.

"I'm not trying to judge you," Martha says softly. "The last time you visited us, it was during a certain time of year." I look at Martha and realize what she's getting at.

It can't be that. I shake my head no. "I'm a pureblood."

"And Jase is a half-breed," Delilah adds.

"Where is Jase?" I don't want him to hear our conversation.

"I sent him to the store for ginger ale." Martha shrugs. "It was the one thing we didn't have."

"This can't be happening to me. This isn't my destiny. I have another plan." I look at Martha and Delilah with tears in my eyes.

Martha sits beside me and puts her arm around my shoulders. "It looks like the world has its own plan, because I'm certain that you are pregnant."

Martha and Delilah leave when Jase's Bronco pulls to a stop outside. I can't hear the words they exchange but Jase looks really nervous when he walks inside the trailer.

"Martha said you need this," he hands me a bottle of ginger ale then backs away like I'm contagious.

I put the soda on the table and clear my throat. I should tell him I'm pregnant, but I can't. I'm so embarrassed by my behavior. One minute I'm declaring my loyalty to Dillan, the next minute I'm rolling around naked with Jase. There is something seriously wrong with me. Aside from the fact that I'm pregnant.

"Are you ok?" Jase finally asks.

I shrug and stare at my feet.

"Do you want me to go?" He moves towards the door and I look up.

"Do you want to go?" I ask, because he looks like he's about to puke.

"Maybe I should get Martha; she'll probably be more help than I will. I get freaked out around sick people." He shivers and pushes his door open to leave.

He has no idea I'm pregnant, he's freaking out because he thinks I'm sick. When Dillan thought I was ill, he covered me with a blanket and brought me a glass of water. Does that matter? Does that make Dillan a better person? A better partner?

"I don't want you to go, but if you feel like you need to…" I fold my hands over my chest.

"Alright, cool. I'll just be outside or hanging with Lucky. Call me when you feel better." He hands me a business card. "That's my cell." He points to the phone number in bold. "I'll come back if you need something." Jase bolts out the door and I sit in his trailer stunned.

What the hell just happened?

How did I not see that Jase is a selfish asshole? Maybe because I don't really know him. I've spent less than fifteen hours in his presence. Each time I see Jase, I'm running away from Dillan. I run to Jase like he's my savior. When all I am to him is a booty-call. I don't know if he lied to Delilah about his feelings or if she just lied to me. I feel vomit creep up the throat. I open the ginger ale and take a drink, as I place my hand over my belly. Martha is right, the world has another plan for me. Maybe this is a sign that I belong with Dillan. Jase was just a fling. He doesn't have to mean more than that.

I leave the trailer with Jase's card sitting on the table. I don't need it.

I walk back to the party and find Jase is sitting on the tailgate of a truck with a bottle of beer in his hand. He's laughing with a group of guys, it's like I'm not even here.

"Kal, you feelin' better?" Joe calls from the doorway to his apartment.

"Yeah, I think I'm going to head home before it gets too late." I turn back and scan the crowd. "Have you seen Delilah? I want to tell her I'm leaving." *For good.*

"She's inside with Martha, they're huddled up in the back bedroom plotting God knows what." Joe moves to the side to let me in the door.

I'm walking through the apartment towards the back bedroom when I spot a familiar logo on a business card pinned to a cork board on the wall. It's a Sierra-Duke business card. I look closer and see the name foiled stamped in the center of the card. Othello Weston.

It can't be the same Othello Dillan told me about. He said he was fired.

I pull the card from the board and hold it in my hand. Dillan is going to be elated when I tell him Othello still works for his father. Wait a second. I can't tell him I found Othello, he'll ask where I got the card.

"Kalysia." I look up and see Martha watching me. "Are you feeling better?"

"Where did you get this?" I hand her the business card.

"A man came by a week or so ago. He was asking about Jase, he said Sierra-Duke was looking to partner with local businesses. He wanted to list Jase's repair shop to their vendor list as a local repair shop for their trucks. It's a great opportunity for him."

Martha places the card back on the wall then walks towards the kitchen and checks something cooking in the oven.

That might be true, but it's too much of a coincidence. I take the card from the board and place it in my pocket.

"Martha, I have to go. Please tell Delilah that I'm sorry I didn't say goodbye."

Martha walks out of the kitchen and meets me at the front door.

"It's best for everyone if I leave. You know why," I say.

Martha takes my hands and gives them a squeeze. "I know. Your life isn't your own anymore. You have a child to think of." She pulls me into her arms. "Don't you worry about us. We can take care of ourselves, have been for years."

She is referring to the years of conflict with the Shasta pack. Keeping the unwanted half-breeds safe and cared for. Martha is strong and I have no doubt she can take care of herself.

But they have no idea what is in store if the Sierras get involved. "Tell Jase." I search for the words to finish that sentence but they don't come.

"Jase has a lot of growing up to do," Martha says. "I don't think he was ready for someone like you. Someone that made him feel." I look out the window and watch him sit with his friends like he doesn't have a care in the world. He doesn't. I'm not his to care for. "He'll be just fine," Martha says with her angelic smile.

I get in the truck and drive. This time, my eyes are glued to the road in front of me. For the first time in my life, I know exactly where I'm going. I've made such a mess of things. I don't even know if Dillan will take me back. I have to work out all the thoughts swirling in my head. I need someone that will help me make sense of it all.

I need my mom.

CHAPTER TWENTY-NINE:

ONLY MOM CAN HELP

I pull over in Marysville to get gas and call Layla. She doesn't ask why I'm calling in the middle of the night; she just gives me a few instructions and tells me to drive safe.

According to the clock on the dash, it's just past one in the morning when I park in front of Layla and Monte's home in San Francisco. The house is an old Victorian in the fancy Nob Hill neighborhood of San Francisco. The porch light flickers on when I near the gate. Monte opens the door, wearing an honest-to-God smoking jacket with a cigar burning in his left hand.

"Hi, Mont...I mean, uh Dad." Feels strange calling an actual person Dad.

"Hey sweetie." He pulls me in for a one-armed hug, careful to hold his cigar away from me. "Your mom is waiting for you in the library, top of the stairs to the right." He points to the staircase behind him. "Can I get you something to drink? Have you eaten? We have some left-over pot roast." Monte's doting is sweet, but I need to get this over with.

"No, I'm fine." I start up the staircase. "Thank you though." I disappear up the stairs while Monte remains on the bottom floor.

I find Layla standing in the middle of the room. She's wearing a pair of black yoga pants and her favorite teal workout jacket. I half expected her to be in a lavish nightie, but she's still the same old Layla.

I pause at the door, unsure what to say. After the argument I mounted for not having a baby, I feel stupid, careless. Layla's eyes fill with tears and she holds her hand out to me. The gesture causes the floodgates to open, and I fall into her arms.

"Everything will be fine." She strokes my head and sits me on a small sofa. She's always been there for me. Sacrificed for me.

I hear the door open and look up to see Monte set a glass of water on a small side table. Layla says thank you, her face is glowing as she looks at him. I was wrong all these years, they love each other, always have. My tears finally slow, and I sit up as Monte closes the door to give us privacy.

"Have you finished?" Layla hands me a box of tissue.

I pull a sheet from the top of the box and dab my nose. "For now."

"What's going on? Why did you leave camp?"

I inhale deeply to steady my breathing. I have to tell Layla everything.

"I wasn't at camp. I was in Quincy." I brace for her reaction. She just nods and waits for me to continue. "I didn't want to be in camp for the full moon." She nods again, without the contempt in her eyes.

I tell her I went on the Truckee run with Rusty and leave out the part about him spending the night with Carrick. I also skip the part about getting a text from Delilah and knowing it was her birthday. The how and why I was in Quincy aren't important.

"You went to *him*." All empathy has been drained from her face. I hate her tone, but I won't deny my reasons for being there.

"Well, what happened? Did Dillan find out?"

I shake my head. I can't say it. Once I tell her it's real, there is no turning back. I will have to return to camp.

I stand up and retrieve the water from the desk.

"Kalysia, honey, please tell me what is going on. Did Dillan call you? Did he tell you Cassie is pregnant? Is that why you're here?" She stands and looks out the window, into the fogless sky.

"You knew this was going to happen. You planned it for Christ's sake. I can't for the life of me figure out why."

I gulp down the water and stare at her back. I can't believe I was going to betray her by running away. Now she is going to lose everything to Lowell and Conall. If I tell her everything now, she might be able to do something about it.

"I was going to leave the pack. With Dillan."

Layla sucks in a breath and spins around. "You were going to what!"

"Don't worry." I set the glass down harder than necessary on the wooden desk.

"I'm not leaving now." I cross my arms like a sullen teenager, not a soon-to-be mother. "Dillan would never leave his child."

"Goddamn right he wouldn't. I can't believe you even entertained the idea. Dillan can't leave the pack. Lowell would never allow it." Layla paces between me and the window.

"Dillan was going to leave, with Lowell's permission. As long as he had a child..."

"And you decided to offer up Cassie as a surrogate to give Lowell his heir so you and Dillan could ride off into the sunset?" Layla is yelling now. "How could you be so ignorant?"

My heart races and my skin grows warm. I know I won't phase, but I don't want to get sick either. I return to the sofa and sit down. I close my eyes and take a deep breath.

"I don't understand what is going on with you, Kalysia. You orchestrated all of this, and now that it's come to fruition, you can't handle it. I thought you were stronger, smarter..."

Her words hurt.

"I'm sorry to say this, but you made your bed..."

"Stop!" I yell, and Layla's face turns white. I've never yelled at my mother, but I can't take it anymore. "We didn't look at the baby as being anything more than a business transaction. I know it's stupid and childish, but I didn't know back then. I didn't realize the connection." I choke up at the thought of Taylor's chubby hands on my face. "I never even held a baby until I went to camp. I thought it would be easy to walk away." I cry into my hands. Layla joins me on the sofa and rubs my back. "After I saw the connection Dillan had with Cassie, I knew things would never be the same. I knew he wouldn't leave. So, I decided to leave." I look up and find Layla is crying. "I'm sorry, Mom." I throw my arms around her.

"Oh, Kalysia." She squeezes me tight. "All I've ever wanted was for you to be happy. Bringing you to Lunam, setting you up with Dillan, it was only to ensure your place in the pack, so you would have power. I thought you'd embrace it once you figured it all out." Layla plucks a tissue from the box and blows her nose. "If you want to leave, I understand."

I'm confused by what Layla is saying. I pull away and stand up. "What do you mean, set me up with Dillan?"

Fear creeps into my mother's eyes.

"You said you set me up with Dillan?"

I don't give a shit about being used as a pawn in her game with Lowell and Monte. I do care about her messing with my fate.

"I didn't mean set up." Layla stands and paces the room. "I might have spoken to Lowell and Monte. I wanted to make sure you had an equal."

I remember the way Dillan looked at me across the dance floor that night, and the way Leah assumed we would match. Dillan said he was thinking about leaving, until he saw me.

"It wasn't fate at all. Dillan chose me because his father told him to."

"No," she says adamantly. "Dillan loves you, everyone can see that. I know he does. Even Adel thinks so."

I shake my head in rebuttal. "I'm not talking about Dillan. I mean me."

Layla stops pacing and focuses on what I'm saying.

"I thought my connection with Dillan was real, unbreakable. Then I met Jase and I felt the same way. I was wrong about both of them."

I think about Dillan's eyes when I told him it was over. I remember Jase laughing at the party like I didn't exist. I'm the only person I can count on. I don't need a man to define my happiness.

"None of that matters now." I wipe my face with my sleeve, remembering why I'm here.

"You're right." Layla points at me. "Monte and I have discussed the possibility of you leaving camp if something like this happened. You don't have to go back; you can stay here with us. He will call Lowell in the morning and declare that Dillan has taken another for his partner." I literally choke when I hear what she is planning. "Lowell thinks he's pulled a fast one on us to gain control, but he forgets the clause in rule seventy-five. If you do not conceive a child with your partner and he takes another, then he voids his partnership with you." Layla is almost smiling as she tells me this. "That means you can leave and find another partner." She crosses the room and takes my hands. "I think you have, right?"

She searches my eyes for any hint of hope. She can't mean, no it can't be. "You mean, Jase?"

"Yes. We did some digging." She flits to the desk and pulls out some papers. They look like birth records. "The Dunsmuir pack is a cesspool of half-breeds. I doubt Conall is even a pureblood. I know his daughter isn't." She shows me the Dunsmuir pack family tree. "Cassie's mother, Stacy, was a second generation half-breed. Making Cassie a third generation. The pure blood overpowers the human blood, giving them the ability to phase."

I look through the names on the sheet; my eyes suddenly stop when I see his. I point to Jase's name. There is no father listed beside it. "Why is Jase on this list?"

"Shasta keeps a record of all the births connected to their pack. I think they've known about the half-breeds phasing for years." Layla looks at the page over my shoulder and points to a black dot beside Jase's birthday. "For some reason they believe Jase didn't phase." She looks at me suspiciously. "But you've seen him turn."

"Yes." I don't tell her why they think Jase didn't phase. I don't want to involve anyone else in this situation. I read the rest of the list until I find her name.

Delilah is listed near the bottom. I realize the names are in order by birthday. No black dot appears by her yet. "Is there another list somewhere?" I don't see Lacy's name on the sheet.

"This is just the Shasta list. Sierras don't keep track; they didn't think the half-breeds mattered." Layla returns to pacing. "They've lost years of records. There is no way we will ever find them all. That doesn't matter now. We need to focus on who fathered Jase. If my research is correct, it has to be a pureblood. It looks like only half-breeds with links to purebloods phase."

Layla is babbling about who the candidates for Jase's father could be, when there is a soft knock on the door.

"I don't want to interrupt, but the truck is in the neighbor's driveway." Monte's head appears in the doorway; he avoids eye contact with either of us.

"Sorry." I walk to the door and hand him my keys.

"Everything's, uh, working out?" he asks.

"Yes, darling, everything's is working out just fine." Layla blows him a kiss and he leaves. When the door closes, she continues talking about Jase.

"Another thing we learned about these half-breeds is that they phase on their eighteenth birthday, regardless of the moon."

My mother confirms what I already know about them being more powerful than even an Altum alpha, because they don't have to wait until the harvest moon to phase.

"That means any child you have with this Jase character will be eligible to lead regardless of when you conceive." She picks up a new stack of papers and shuffles through them. "We just have to convince the elder council that this is the future of our kind."

I can't believe my mother is even contemplating me being with Jase. I can't have her fighting to allow me to leave Dillan for Jase, when Jase doesn't even want me.

"Mom, I have to tell you something that will change all of this." I point to the papers on the desk.

"Are you ok? You look pale." Layla puts down the papers and gives me her full attention.

"I can't be with Jase." I take a deep breath. "I have to go back to camp, back to Dillan."

"Honey, why? I just told you he violated his partnership with you by only conceiving with Cassie. You can leave and be with Jase."

Why does the idea of me and a half-breed appeal to her all of a sudden? Even if Jase's father is a pureblood, he's still tainted, by her own admission. "Why do you want me with Jase so badly?"

Layla looks shocked. She starts to backtrack a little. "I don't want you *with* him. I want you to be happy."

I raise an eyebrow at my fibbing mother. I know her too well. "What's going on? I thought being with a half-breed would muddy our bloodline."

"That's what we thought, but it turns out Conall is right, the line does purify itself. This is how the Dunsmuir Shastas have kept their numbers so high. They figured out how to make an alpha with humans."

All the Shasta alphas are real; they have the numbers to take over the pack. My hands are shaking, then my legs. My body convulses. I double over, ready to vomit all over a very expensive-looking throw rug.

"Kalysia!" Layla kneels beside me on the floor. She yells for Monte, and he arrives in half a second.

Monte asks if I'm hurt, sick, thirsty. Layla screams at him to do something, but there is nothing he can do. He can't fix me. Nobody can. Layla and Monte help me to the sofa and lay me down. I feel stupid having them dote on me, but then again, they are my parents. Caring for me is their job. A job Monte was robbed of because Layla selfishly stole me away. I won't do that to my child. He or she will grow up with the love of two parents.

"Do you need a doctor, honey?" Monte asks as leans over Layla, who remains by my side.

I finally find my voice. "Not yet." I look at Layla's worried eyes. "Not for at least nine months." Realization seeps into Layla's face. I can't believe I'm about to say these two words. Something I didn't think I would say for a long time. My mother smiles. She knows without having to hear it. I need to hear it. I need to say it. "I'm pregnant."

CHAPTER THIRTY:

GAME PLAN

When Monte leaves to get champagne, I drop the bomb on Layla.

"I thought it was Dillan's, until you said Jase is a pureblood alpha," I whisper. "I thought for sure it was Dillan's. I think it's Dillan's."

Layla paces in front of me, biting her thumbnail. She only does that when she's plotting. "Why do you think it's Dillan's and not Jase's?"

"Because Dillan is a pureblood." I shrug. "And, we had sex the morning of the full moon. I wasn't with Jase until the third night."

Layla doesn't stop pacing. "Was that the only time you were with Dillan?"

I tell her we were together near the end of the season. She says the odds are in Dillan's favor. "We don't even know if Jase can be the father. Just because he phases, doesn't mean he can father a child with a pureblood." I can tell by the look on her face that she doesn't believe her statement. "When you go back to camp, tell Dillan you were here with me. Tell him I figured out you were pregnant. If I'm right about his feelings, this riff between you will disappear." She strokes my hair.

"What about Jase?" I think about the look of horror on his face when he thought I was sick. He'd probably faint if he knew I was pregnant and there was a chance he was the father.

"If the baby is Jase's, we'll cross that bridge when we get to it."

Does she even realize she's dealing with real people with real feelings? Not to mention a baby. My baby. She looks at the dread on my face and her eyes soften; she's out of game mode.

"You're strong and independent, just the way I knew you would be. Despite the pickle we're in now, I know you are going to be an amazing mother. That is all this baby will need." She kisses my forehead and a tear falls onto my cheek. "I love you so much."

"I love you, too, Mom."

I go to bed feeling like I've royally screwed up. I don't care how much praise Layla throws at me. I know what I've done is going to hurt a lot of people.

I wake in the morning to the smell of bacon. The guest bedroom, which Layla says she will convert to a nursery for the baby, is decked out with a plush queen bed and antique dressing table. It's the kind of room I dreamt about having my entire life.

I sit on a tiny cushioned stool to put on my shoes and admire the small pieces of art on the walls. They are a collection of miniature frames. When I look closer, I realize they are pictures of me. They've been converted to black and white. I remember Layla had a camera; she would take photos of me when I was little. She must have been sending them to Monte all these years.

When I finally locate the kitchen tucked into the back of the house, I find Rusty sitting at the breakfast bar drinking coffee.

"What are you doing here?"

"Hey, sis." Rusty spins around on his stool and opens his arms.

I give him a hug then ask where Carrick is.

"Well, when Dad called last night and told me you were on your way here, I knew something was up. So, we went back to camp. I dropped off Carrick and the truck, then I drove down in the Mercedes." Rusty hops off his stool and walks around the counter to pour me a cup of coffee. He seems to know his way around this kitchen.

"Hey Layla, your bacon's burnin'!" He flips on the fan above the stove.

"Does Monte know about, your um, life choice?" I leave the question hanging in the air.

"Of course. I told him when I was sixteen. We were driving back from the DMV after I got my license. He said I was free to do as I pleased and that he loved me no matter what." Rusty places the mug on the counter with a bowl of sugar.

"What about breeding and bloodlines and all that." I can't believe Rusty was let off the hook that easily.

"My mother wasn't a pureblood. My kid would have been alpha, but not with the same power you or Leah have. My bad genes worked to my advantage." He smiles.

Layla comes running in from the back porch holding an arm-full of tomatoes. She drops them in the stainless steel sink and tends to the bacon. "Rusty, rinse those for me, please."

Rusty clicks his heels and salutes my mom. "Yessir!"

She whips him with the towel slung over her shoulder and removes the bacon from the pan. I can tell they've spent time together by the comfortable way they move around each other. I wonder how often Rusty has visited since Lunam? He never mentioned it before.

We eat breakfast on the sun porch, only there is no sun. I devour six strips of bacon and two slices of toast. The idea of eggs and tomatoes makes my stomach turn. Layla teases me about morning sickness and Rusty almost chokes.

"You're pregnant?" He walks around the table and hugs me. "Congratulations, sis."

I thank him and then Layla tells him not to mention anything to the pack.

"This is Kalysia's news to tell." She ruffles Rusty's hair and kisses his cheek.

"I wouldn't dare tell a soul." Rusty raises an eyebrow at me. "I just want to be there when she tells him." He doesn't think this is going to be happy news either. "Who needs TV when you have my sister?" Rusty folds a piece of bacon in his mouth as Monte walks in and slaps the back of his head.

He's right, I'm a walking soap opera. That polygamist love triangle thing I was trying to avoid just got real.

After breakfast Monte suggests we leave early to avoid traffic. Layla packs a nice care package for the road. She includes a couple of boxes of Leah's favorite cookies and some fancy cheese Monte says she likes.

He knows more about her than I thought. He obviously had a relationship with Rusty, and he has my pictures hung in his spare room. Monte did care about us, he still does. He is going to start a war with Lowell and Conall, for me.

"Monte is going to drive to Quincy tomorrow to meet with Jase." Layla says he wants to make sure Jase doesn't try anything cavalier and storm the camp looking for me.

I assure her he won't. He probably doesn't even know I left.

"Monte will be discreet," Layla adds. "We don't want Lowell to start sniffing around up there." Layla's remark reminds me of the card I found.

"I think he's already been there." I pull out Othello's card and hand it to her. Monte looks over her shoulder and makes a disturbed face.

"If that guy is poking around, then Lowell already knows something," Monte points at the card.

"Do you know him?" I ask Monte.

"Yes, he's one of Lowell's men." He clears his throat. "He does special assignments for the Duke family."

I wonder if Dillan's time with Othello was also just a special assignment. Dillan thought he really cared for him. He spent last year worried that he got Othello fired and he's been working for Lowell this whole time. I tell my parents what Martha told me about Othello wanting to add Jase to their vendor list. Monte says it's possible. They do recruit local businesses to do work for them. It's how they create goodwill with the public.

"There's one more thing, Martha knows I'm pregnant." I brace for Layla's wrath. She looks at Monte and he nods like he has it covered. "And there's one more person, Delilah."

"Oh yes, the sister," Layla says sarcastically. "Do you know if she phased?"

"I don't know." I saw her name on the list, Shasta knows about her. I wonder when they will show up to find out if she has phased. If she will be forced to attend Lunam.

"Do you know about the Lunam ceremony that Shasta holds?"

The color drains from Layla's face. "Yes, a little."

I can tell she's lying, but something that looks like pain creeps across her face. "I thought all of that ended."

"It hasn't," I tell her. "But if the packs do merge and I am in power, it will end."

Layla smiles and kisses my cheek. "That is one fight I know we can win."

CHAPTER THIRTY-ONE:

COMING CLEAN

Carrick is waiting for us at the gate. Once we're inside, he closes it and hops into the truck beside me. He puts his arm around my back and pats Rusty on the shoulder. He smiles at me and kisses the top of my head. I feel so safe, so loved in the truck with Carrick and my brother. I can't imagine leaving the pack and leaving them behind. It isn't just Rusty and Carrick. It's Leah and Clio, and even Taylor. They are my family as much as Layla and Monte.

I've been alone most of life. I don't want to be anymore. I know exactly what I want. And it is nothing like I thought.

Rusty parks in the lot and we get out.

"Where is he?" Rusty asks Carrick. We all know who *he* is.

"He was in the lodge about thirty minutes ago getting dinner." Carrick and Rusty stand side by side, watching me.

"I can walk over there with you. I need to get Taylor for the night."

I shake my head. "No, I'm going to go to my cabin."

Rusty takes my hand to walk me home, but I pull away. "You go with Carrick. I'll be ok." I know he wants to see Taylor, too.

Once I'm out of sight, dread washes over me like a wet blanket. My steps are slow and heavy, like I'm walking in a thick layer of snow, but the ground is covered in dead mushy leaves now. The only thing slowing my pace is me. I should want to see Dillan. Telling him I'm pregnant should be the happiest moment of my life. Him learning he is going to be a father should have been saved for me, not Cassie. I can't blame her for this, for any of this. This is all my fault.

As I pass Leah's cabin, I see a shadow move past the window. A second later the door opens and my sister comes barreling towards me.

"You're back!" She throws her arms around me and kisses my cheek. "Are you ok? How do you feel?"

I step out of her arms, confused.

"Layla called, she told me your news." Leah grabs me for another bear hug. "I literally screamed. I'm so happy for you. For both of us." She pulls back with teary eyes and a huge grin.

"You're pregnant?" She nods and tears up. "Congratulations." I give her a quick hug. I don't have time to be mad at Layla for blabbing to Leah. I know she did it for my benefit, to make sure someone is watching out for me. I don't think Leah had time to tell anyone else, but I have to ask.

"Of course not!" She pulls her jacket closed when a cold gust blows through the camp. "I've been in my cabin resting most of the day. I haven't seen anyone. Not that I would tell. It's your news, not mine."

Or Layla's.

I look down the row of cabins at Cassie's. "Have you seen her?" Leah follows my gaze and shakes her head. "Have you seen Dillan?"

"Like I said, I've been inside all day. Clio and Patsy stopped by earlier. I haven't seen anyone else." I can tell Leah is uncomfortable with our conversation. I never thought I was the type of person to employ spies, but that's what I'm asking my family to do.

"How are they, Clio and Patsy?"

The smile on Leah's face tells me they are also pregnant. That means all the alphas will produce an heir. This is good news for the Sierras. Shasta may have ten times the alphas, but a hundred half-breed alphas do not outrank a pureblood. That is one thing Monte and Layla were adamant about.

I tell Leah I'll see her later. I walk the last few steps to my cabin and sniff the air. I pick up only traces of Dillan's scent, which means he isn't home. I head inside, strip off my clothes, and take a shower to wash away any lingering traces of Quincy.

The weight of what I was going to do finally catches up to me. I was going to leave Dillan for Jase. I let the hot water run over my face to mask my tears. What was I thinking? I have a duty to my family, to my pack, and most importantly, to myself to do the right thing. I see that now. I'm going to make sure from here on out that I make the right choices. For me and my baby.

My hands are wrinkled and my skin is raw from the scalding hot water by the time I step out of the shower. I grab a towel from the rack and run it over my skin. I stop at my flat stomach. I look into the steamy mirror and imagine myself fat and pregnant.

A small sad smile creeps onto my face. I'm going to have a chubby dark-haired baby of my own to bounce on my knee and feed Leah's chili. The thought fills me with a warmth and joy like no other. I'm so stupid for thinking motherhood was a death sentence, for thinking Dillan and I couldn't see the world if we were parents. Having a baby wouldn't have hurt us, it would have made us stronger, made us a family.

I run my hand over my stomach. How can I just pretend there is no chance Jase fathered this child? Layla is right, we have to focus on the facts, otherwise doubt will eat me alive. Still, it feels wrong to tell Dillan I'm pregnant knowing there is a chance he isn't the father. Just like it isn't right to keep this from Jase. How am I going to get through the next nine months carrying this secret?

"Kalysia?" Dillan's voice echoes into the bathroom.

I'm not ready to face him, but I can't run away. I have a duty, not to my mother or Monte, not to my pack or Dillan. I have a duty to myself and to my baby to stay. I have to do what's right for her or him. If that means swallowing my pride and my honor, then I will. I drop the towel to the floor and open the door.

"I'm in here."

Dillan appears in the doorway two seconds later. I smell the musty air from outside on his skin. He looks at my naked body, and a low soft moan escapes his lips.

"Come here." I take his hand and wrap it around my waist.

He moves in close and takes me in his arms. "I missed you so much." He kisses my neck through my wet hair. "I'm so sorry."

He takes my face in his hands and kisses my lips. I try to get lost in it, but I can't, not with Jase on my mind.

Dillan pulls back. "I want you to hear it from me. Cassie is pregnant, you know what this means." He searches my eyes for a glimmer of hope. "Everything we talked about is still on. We are leaving this place and never looking back."

I put my hands over his and peel them from my face. "Dillan, wait..." I try to stop him, to tell him I'm pregnant, but he keeps going.

"I was confused about a lot of things, but I had time to think while you were gone. I realized that I don't care about my father or the pack. I don't care about anything or anyone but you."

He is beaming as if his words are good news. Three days ago, they would have been.

"Finding Othello, showing you the ocean. Me surfing and you going to college. That is what I'm focusing on. Just me and you." He kisses me hard and deep. When he pulls away, I'm breathless.

It isn't just us, not anymore. Even if I wasn't pregnant, he is going be a father.

"You can't leave..." I start to argue.

"Yes, we can and we will. This camp, this pack, is tearing us apart, and the last thing I want to do is lose you. I made a lot of mistakes. I didn't say the things I wanted to say or do the things I should have done. I can make it right. I know I can. I can make us right. Kalysia, you are the only sure thing in my life. You were the reason I went to Lunam. Not for my father or my duty to the pack." He places my hand over his heart. "This wasn't whole until I met you."

He doesn't know how capable I am of ripping his heart out and breaking it. I've done something so terrible. So unforgivable. I played with the lives of others for my own gain. Cassie and her baby, even Jase.

"And Cassie and the baby?" I pull back and look in his eyes. "Leaving them isn't the right thing." I choke back tears. "You care about her."

Dillan seems to have thought about this. He's ready with an answer.

"We can see the baby whenever we want. We can Skype and Facetime." He thinks it will be enough, but he won't be here to kiss her goodnight or watch her take her fist steps. He doesn't know it yet, but it will kill him to walk away.

"And Cassie?"

"It isn't what you think. I couldn't be the robot you wanted me to be. I couldn't show up, have sex with her, and leave. So, yeah I gave her candy and I was nice to her because I'm a nice guy." He takes my face in his hands again and stares into my eyes. "I care about her, but I love you, Kalysia." He kisses me softly on the lips. "You are the one I will spend the rest of my life loving."

A steaming hot tear rolls down my cheek. I have to tell him, now. I just hope he's as happy to hear I'm pregnant as he was when Cassie told him. Cassie's baby meant freedom for Dillan, but my baby will be a responsibility and an obligation.

"Say something." Dillan smiles nervously and gives me space to speak.

I wipe a tear away and look for my discarded towel. I feel so exposed. Dillan pulls a clean towel from the cabinet and wraps it around my naked body. He pulls me into his arms and stares into my eyes. This is where I belong. Not with Jase. Not in a desert town with Layla. I belong here, with Dillan.

"I'm pregnant."

It takes a moment for Dillan to register the two most relevant words a woman can tell a man. It pains me to know I wasn't the first person to say them to him.

"You're pregnant?" His eyes widen. "*You* are pregnant?"

I nod, unable to speak through the tears stuck in my throat.

Dillan crushes me to his chest, and I feel him take a deep breath. He holds me like this for a long time. Thoughts race through my mind, good and bad. I need to see his face. I pull back and wriggle my arms free from the towel. It falls to the floor on top of the other one. Dillan pulls me closer and kisses me before I have a chance to see his eyes. I put my hand on his face and feel the tears on his cheeks. He's crying.

"Are you ok?" It seems like a silly thing to say, but I've never seen a man cry before.

"Yes. I'm more than ok." He takes me in his arms again and lifts me in the air. He carries me to the bed and lays me down gently. He pulls his shirt off and kneels beside the bed, surveying my naked body. "You are so perfect, so beautiful."

"Yeah, well I won't be for long." He lays his ear on my belly and I rub my hand through his hair. He's happy. I'm happy. We are going to be a family.

I hope.

ACKNOWLEDGMENTS

This book, or any of my books, wouldn't exist without Murphy Rae. I hope people judge my books by your beautiful covers. Thank you times a thousand!

A special thanks to Holly for helping me make sense of this story. You got it, even when I didn't.

My family, my pack, without them I'd be a totally normal and upstanding citizen. Thank you for keeping it crazy and always fun.

To Ali & Crysta for believing in magic.

To Achilles for only making me get up seventy-eight times to let you in and out of the house while I was writing.

Tas, thank you for letting me be right.

To all the kids in my life – you guys are the only reason I get up in the morning, literally.

And to gin, you get all the blame and most of the glory.

ABOUT THE AUTHOR

Nicole Loufas lives in Northern California. She loves books, music festivals, and bloody mary's. She prefers gin to wine, and hates the smell of fried fish. She writes poetry in her spare time and books the rest of the time.

Other books by Nicole:
Thizz, A Love Story
Illusion of Ecstasy, 2nd dose in the Thizz
The Excursion

Stalking is in encouraged.
Online, I mean. Real-life stalking is illegal…or true love.

www. nicoleloufas.com
Facebook.com/NicoleLoufasAuthor
Twitter: @NicoleLoufas
Instagram: @nicoleloufas
Goodreads: Nicole Loufas

Join my Facebook Group
Nicole's Book Rehab

Don't forget to leave a review!